The Sisters at the Last House Before the Sea

BOOKS BY LIZ EELES

LIZ EELES

The Sisters at the Last House Before the Sea

bookouture

Published by Bookouture in 2023

An imprint of Storyfire Ltd.
Carmelite House
50 Victoria Embankment
London EC4Y 0DZ

www.bookouture.com

ISBN: 978-1-83790-547-8
eBook ISBN: 978-1-83790-546-1

For little Elsie, with love

PROLOGUE

Jessie glanced at the framed photograph sitting on her polished walnut bureau. Two teenaged girls beamed back at her, their heads bent together and their arms around each other's shoulders. They'd been close back then, and it broke Jessie's heart to see them now – little more than strangers, linked only by blood and obligation. She'd tried so hard to bring them back together but her efforts had failed.

Jessie brushed a strand of white hair from her forehead and picked up her fountain pen. She let the cold metal of its barrel rest on her bottom lip for a moment while she chose her words carefully. Then she painstakingly wrote out her final riddle, narrowing her pale blue eyes as she concentrated: *Don't get in a spin, girls, though mistakes can cost you dear. This one brings good fortune and, I hope, will make you cheer.*

How long would it take Caitlin and Isla to solve the mystery? Jessie wondered, patting blotting paper onto her words so they wouldn't smudge.

She was sure they would work it out before too long – Isla, in particular, who was a crossword addict, just like her, and would enjoy the challenge. But she hoped it would take the girls long enough that they would spend time in each other's company and remember how close they had once been. Before Caitlin had left Heaven's Cove and everything had changed.

Jessie looked out of the window, at the green shoots in her garden and the shimmering sea beyond. She would see this spring, but she was old and unwell, and she doubted that she would see another. How she would miss beautiful Heaven's Cove, and her darling girls who had brought her so much joy, along with some heartache.

With a sigh, she carefully placed the riddle inside the envelope that had arrived in the village more than one hundred years earlier. Isla had sacrificed so much for her, and she so wanted to make things right. Even if that meant making things right from beyond the grave.

1

CAITLIN

Everything here was grey: the sea, the sky, the faces of villagers passing by. Caitlin sighed, the drab surroundings perfectly matching her mood.

She shifted on the sea wall where she'd been sitting for the last five minutes. The chilled stone was turning her thighs to ice, but it was either brave the cold and all-pervading grey, or endure the tense atmosphere inside Rose Cottage. Neither of which were terribly appealing.

Cold salt water splashed onto her jeans as waves rippled against the wall, but she couldn't be bothered to move. She couldn't be bothered to do much these days, not since she'd ended up back in Heaven's Cove.

She thought she'd got away from this tiny village on the Devon coast fifteen years ago. She thought she'd escaped. But now she was back and every cobbled street she walked, every corner she turned, was bringing up painful memories.

Caitlin sighed again as she thought of her grandmother, Jessie, whose death only three weeks ago still felt raw. Of course, she was sad that Jessie was gone, but her sorrow was laced with shards of guilt.

She shook her head, trying not to think of all the times she'd made excuses to avoid visiting her grandmother. So many pathetic excuses. Caitlin gazed across the grey expanse of water, wishing with all her heart that she'd made more of an effort. But regrets were pointless when it was too late to make amends.

The sad thing was she hadn't been avoiding Jessie at all. Not really. She'd mostly been keeping away from her own sister, Isla, and with good reason. Isla had said very little since Caitlin had arrived two days ago with Maisie, but her mournful blue eyes said more than words: *You lied to me. You lied and you left*.

It was quite unbearable, and, if you added in Maisie's furious adolescent glares, life was pretty rubbish right now. And that didn't even take into account Stuart's betrayal. How had Caitlin not realised the scale of her husband's problems until it was too late?

'Eek! Well, isn't that just perfect!' she hissed as a larger wave washed up her legs. Here she was, with her life imploding, and now she had wet trousers into the bargain.

Caitlin got to her feet, wincing at the squelching coming from her ankle boots. She'd have to stuff them with newspaper and hope the salt water didn't discolour the leather. They'd cost a fortune and she couldn't afford to replace them for the time being. Maybe not ever, thanks to Stuart.

She set off walking, back to the house that was home to her and her stepdaughter Maisie for the time being. The home that her twenty-year-old self had been so eager to leave. She'd been different back then: naive and sporting a terrible mono-brow, drowning in responsibility and filled with dreams.

That's why she'd loved university and the freedom it gave her. And that was why she'd been so reluctant to come back. And her new life had gone well, mostly – until Stuart's behaviour had brought everything crashing down.

Caitlin had reached the house and she stood, with her

hands on her hips, staring at the building that might prove to be the answer to her prayers.

The house in front of her was very unlike her modern home in Hammersmith, West London, which had floor-to-ceiling windows, a state-of-the-art heat pump and a verdant roof garden. Her grandmother's home, on the edge of Heaven's Cove, was Victorian and made of red brick. It was called Rose Cottage, though Caitlin thought the name both twee and inaccurate – the building was too large to be a cottage, and Caitlin had never seen a single rose in the flower beds that led to the front door. In spring and summer, the garden was festooned with geraniums, lupins, lavender and phlox. Though now, as November slid towards December, the earth was barren and dark, with no flowers to add any cheer.

But it was a handsome house, Caitlin had to admit. The building was perfectly proportioned, with a large bay window at the front, and the original door with its stained glass in blues and greens. A wooden balcony wrapped around the upper floor. Not that anyone could step onto it and enjoy the sea view, not unless they wanted to risk plunging through the rotting wood and landing in the garden below.

Whoever bought the house would need to carry out a good number of repairs but that would be their problem. All Caitlin needed was the money from the sale so that she and Maisie could go back to London and get on with their lives. Rather than being suffocated by guilt and regret in this tiny village where modernity came to die.

Caitlin stood for a moment longer, with her hand on the garden gate, psyching herself up to go inside. The house felt strange without Jessie bustling round or sitting in her favourite chair, doing the *Times* crossword.

Sometimes, Caitlin almost believed she could feel Jessie's presence, hovering in the ether, though that was ridiculous. It was far more likely she was being spooked by Isla, who had a habit of appearing out of the shadows, with a pained expression, like a Victorian wraith. She was grieving for their grandmother, but then so was Caitlin – though she didn't feel she was allowed to because of the apparently unforgivable way she'd behaved…

Caitlin shut down that train of thought immediately and walked briskly through the garden towards the front door. She needed to get things moving, otherwise she would end up spending the whole winter in Heaven's Cove and she wasn't sure she could stand it when storms rolled in off the sea.

She could remember lying in her bedroom at the back of the house, feeling the building shake as the wind roared. She'd held on tight to her boyfriend and wondered if the house could withstand such a battering.

Caitlin blinked, trying to erase the memory. That was the trouble with coming back here after all this time – memories were rekindled, like spectres rising from the grave. Memories that did nothing but make her feel unsettled and lost.

She needed to leave Heaven's Cove sharpish, for her own sake and also for Maisie, who would lose her mind if they were stuck here for much longer. Never an easy fifteen-year-old, she was furious about being dragged to Devon and was ready to explode.

Caitlin turned her key in the lock and stepped into the hallway. At least the will was being read tomorrow. Then this house could be sold, and all of the inconvenient memories it held would disappear.

2

ISLA

Isla stepped back behind the bedroom curtain and watched Caitlin standing at the garden gate. She didn't seem keen to come inside. But then nothing changed. She'd never been keen on coming back to Heaven's Cove since she'd left the village fifteen years ago. A fact that had broken their grandmother's heart, though she'd tried to hide it.

'Caitlin's had a lot to cope with from a young age and she's just trying to find her way,' her grandmother had said, glancing up from the crosswords and riddles that had kept her brain active, right until the end. 'I know that she loves you and me, and I know that she'll come back to us one day.'

Isla fought back tears at the thought of her generous grandmother who had taken in her and Caitlin after their mother had died. She'd kept them together and had given them a home – but now that home would be sold because that was what Caitlin wanted. Even though she had quite enough money already. It wasn't fair but, as Isla had learned in her relatively short life, fairness often didn't come into it.

Isla had visited Caitlin in London a few times over the years. But the obvious differences in their lives simply widened the gulf between them, and Isla was always glad to return to the familiarity and security of Heaven's Cove. She felt safe here.

She hadn't been to her sister's latest home at all, but she'd seen enough photos of it on Instagram to feel as if she'd had a tour of the place. It was roomy, uncluttered and bright, with a top-end kitchen, designer cushions artfully placed, and huge brass lamps that must have cost a fortune. Everything was for show, along with Caitlin herself, it seemed, who posted the occasional tasteful selfie, at a charity committee meeting or coffee morning. She acted like a fifty-year-old trophy wife when she'd only hit thirty-five a few months ago.

Isla jumped when the front door slammed. So Caitlin had decided to come indoors at last.

'Who the hell's that?' grumbled Paul, who'd followed her into the bedroom.

'It's Caitlin.'

'Huh. No wonder her stepdaughter's so noisy too.' He glanced at Isla's open wardrobe. 'Hey, I thought you'd got rid of this,' he said, pulling out one of the only dresses Isla owned. 'You said that the neckline was too low.'

'Did I?' Isla took it from her boyfriend, sure it was him who'd made that observation, and placed it back on the hanging rail. The beautiful, eye-catching dress, made of midnight-blue silk, had once belonged to her mother and she could never get rid of it. That would break her heart. But perhaps Paul had a point. She ran her finger along the square neckline that was edged in silver thread. She'd felt good in this dress at last year's Christmas party in the village hall, but maybe it was too much for someone like her.

She carefully pushed the dress back amongst her jeans and sweatshirts and quietly closed the wardrobe door. 'I'd better go and see how Caitlin is getting on.'

'I guess so. Honestly, she's very high maintenance. You'll be pleased to see the back of her,' said Paul, pulling her into an embrace, his beard tickling her forehead.

She breathed in his familiar scent of coal-tar soap and mint toothpaste and rested her head against his chest. She supposed she would be pleased to say goodbye to her sister, even though her emotions felt jumbled at the moment.

She sighed and stepped away from him. 'She'll be gone soon enough. Are you really going into the office today? It's a Sunday.'

'Afraid so.' Paul pushed up the sleeve of his shirt and squinted at his watch. 'I have a few things to catch up on, but one of the benefits of owning the business is that I can work when I want to and there's no one to harangue me about it – except you, of course.' A frown crossed his face and was gone. 'Anyway, Fizz, my new receptionist, will hold the fort if I claw some time back later this week and bunk off early. Did I tell you that she fancies me something rotten?'

'You have mentioned it,' said Isla, wishing that he wouldn't and wondering why any grown woman would choose to go by the name of Fizz.

'Let's go to the pub later.'

'I'm not sure. I might treat myself to a bath and have a quiet evening in,' said Isla, who was finding it hard to shake the lethargy that had settled over her since her grandmother's death.

'Oh. That's a shame.' Paul's face fell, but then he breathed in and smiled brightly. 'I'll come over later then.'

'You really don't have to. I'll be fine on my own,' said Isla, who'd been quite looking forward to some peace. The house had been so noisy since Caitlin and Maisie had arrived.

'I know I don't have to.' He laughed. 'But you're better with me around, aren't you, sweetheart. You need me to look after you.' Paul leaned forward and kissed her on the nose. 'So, I'll come round straight after work and we can eat together. I'll bring steak.'

'OK, great,' said Isla, with as much enthusiasm as she could manage.

She followed Paul out of her bedroom and down the stairs, bracing herself to face Caitlin and strike up a conversation. She should make an effort, for their grandmother's sake, to get to know this sister who felt like a stranger.

'Did you have a wander and get some fresh air?' she asked, walking into the hall and frowning. Caitlin's feet had left damp footprints on the hall tiles and the denim of her jeans was darker below the knee. 'Has it been raining?'

'No, though it looks as if it might.' Caitlin nodded at Paul as he went out of the front door, before slipping off her boots and her olive-green leather jacket. She followed Isla's gaze and glanced down at her shins. 'My jeans got wet when I was sitting on the sea wall at the quay.'

'Ah.' Isla suppressed a smile. Tourists sitting on the sea wall were often surprised by a rogue wave that swamped their legs. The locals knew better than to sit there on a day like today, when the wind was whipping at the water as the tide came in. Caitlin had known better, too, when she lived in Heaven's Cove, but she'd seemingly forgotten since. 'Would you like to borrow some different trousers?'

'No, thanks,' Caitlin shot back, sounding less than happy for her exercised buttocks to be enfolded in a pair of Isla's tracksuit bottoms. In any case, Isla's clothes mostly came from supermarkets, and she felt sure her sister wouldn't be seen dead, these days, in anything so downmarket. But she'd offered at least, and Jessie would have approved.

Isla's mind spooled back to happier times, when the two sisters had talked about clothes, and boys, and the future. They'd had great fun on shopping expeditions to Exeter, and had been close back then, before everything went pear-shaped.

'Where's Maisie?' asked Caitlin, cutting into her thoughts. She smoothed down her caramel-coloured hair.

'In her bedroom, I think,' said Isla, trying to remember what Caitlin's real hair colour was. 'She's been there all morning. Do you think she's all right?'

Caitlin shrugged. 'She spends most of her life in her bedroom at home so I imagine she's fine. Just sulking.'

Sulking about being dragged to Heaven's Cove, thought Isla, picking up a pile of Jessie's Sudoku puzzle books that were still on the hall table. She opened a drawer and slipped the books inside. They were too painful a reminder of her vibrant, loving grandmother whose absence was so keenly felt.

'Maisie spent most of her time in her bedroom when she stayed with us at Easter too,' said Isla, trying not to wince at the thought of those three weeks when the house had been filled with the sound of doors banging and loud music.

She'd done her best for her niece, even securing her temporary work in the local ice cream parlour so she could earn a bit of money over the holiday. But Maisie clearly hadn't wanted to visit her stepmother's sister and aged grandmother. And she obviously wasn't happy with her repeat visit right now.

Isla had never got to the bottom of why Caitlin had decided that Maisie should spend Easter with them. And she wasn't quite sure why Caitlin was still hanging around now the funeral was over.

But surely the will reading tomorrow would bring an end to their visit. They would go haring back to their posh London house and leave Isla here to sell up and move out.

Isla didn't want to think about having to pack everything up at Rose Cottage and clear out Jessie's things. Lots would have to go because she would have nowhere to store them. And without this house, she would have to move out of Heaven's Cove.

It was ironic, really, she mused. She'd been keen to move

out of the village once and yet now, when forced to leave it behind, she was aching to stay.

But staying wasn't an option. Though there would be a sizable sum from half of the house, it wouldn't be enough to buy a decent flat in the village. Not when they went for ridiculous money and rarely came onto the market anyway, because they were all rented out to holidaymakers.

Isla sighed and caught a flash of irritation in Caitlin's eyes, as if she wasn't allowed to be sad or to grieve the grandmother she missed so much.

'Why don't I light the fire in the sitting room and you can dry out in there?' she said, trying her best to be cordial.

Caitlin gave a genuine smile at that. 'Thanks. That's a good idea.'

She followed Isla into the cosy room and watched as her sister got the fire going. Then she sat in front of the flames, stretching her wet legs towards them.

Isla wandered to the window and looked out across Heaven's Cove, with its whitewashed cottages that led down the hill to the quay. Gulls were swooping over thatched roofs and soaring into the leaden grey sky. Paul had said she should move in with him at Cutter's Path, a small town a few miles inland. But she was unsure about that, and he'd seemed annoyed by her hesitation. He didn't fully grasp how safe she felt in this village with its close-knit community, and how she loved being so close to the sea that changed shade by the hour.

But she had to accept that life moved on and things changed. Her relationship with Caitlin being a case in point.

Twenty years ago, when the sisters had first arrived at Rose Cottage, still bewildered by the death of their mother, they'd been inseparable. Caitlin was the older by four years, and had been a source of protection and comfort for Isla.

She glanced at her sister, who was stretching her hands towards the crackling fire. Once upon a time, they were so close you could hardly have passed a piece of paper between them. Whereas now they were separated by a chasm of difference and resentment. They had become different people leading very different lives.

Isla bit her lip to stop the tears that were so close to the surface these days and started making for the door. She would go and do something practical – maybe start packing up her bedroom, ready for the inevitable move from this house that she loved.

3

MAISIE

The last place Maisie wanted to be – the actual last place in the whole wide world – was where she was right now: sitting in a solicitor's cramped office, wedged between her stepmother, who was bristling with suppressed emotion, and Isla, who looked ready to blub at the slightest provocation.

It was hard to believe the two of them were sisters, even though they looked alike in some ways. Isla had almond-shaped eyes and thick hair – like Caitlin – and she would look good too, if she made the slightest bit of effort. She had long, dark eyelashes to die for, but wore a succession of dreary clothes and pulled her hair into an unflattering ponytail.

Maisie pouted her lips and dipped her head, like the beautiful women she followed on Instagram. It was easy to look good if you tried, but Isla seemed to have given up the ghost.

She'd looked better when Maisie had visited at Easter and Maisie supposed that losing the old lady had dragged her down a bit since then. But even so, a woman should have standards, when it came to looks... and boyfriends.

There was nothing inherently wrong with Paul, who wasn't grotesque or anything. But he had a stupid goatee beard, and his shirts were too tight, and he could be bossy at times. Overall, Maisie felt that Isla could do better.

She breathed in deeply, her mind flitting back to that awful Easter visit to Heaven's Cove seven months ago. She'd only been shipped off to Devon because Caitlin and her dad were having problems and they'd wanted her out of the way. So while people at school were going skiing in Italy or lying on Spanish beaches, Maisie had been mooching around this poky little village and trying not to get frostbite at the local cove.

When she'd complained about it, Caitlin had said they couldn't afford to go abroad as a family. But that was a lie because they had plenty of money. The real reason was she'd wanted shot of Maisie. That was why she'd sent her to see her 'aunt' for the school holidays – even though Isla wasn't her real aunt, just as Caitlin wasn't her real mother.

Maisie frowned, and then opened her eyes wide to eradicate any wrinkles on her forehead.

'Are you all right?' Caitlin asked, giving her a close look.

Maisie found her concern irritating because it was all for show. Caitlin, while not the evil stepmother of fairy tales, didn't care about her. Not really. She'd ditch her for good, given the chance. Just as her father appeared to have done. He'd gone abroad, for work apparently, and she hadn't heard from him for days. She could text him, of course, but this was a test, of sorts – a test to see how long he would go before checking that she was still alive. As things currently stood, quite a long time, it seemed.

To her horror, Maisie felt the prickle of tears and she blinked furiously. Crying would make her look as sad a sap as Isla, and it would ruin her eye-liner. Plus, everyone would think she was crying about the old lady, when she'd hardly known her at all. Jessie had been kind to her and Maisie was sorry that she'd died. She did feel quite sad about it, actually, but she couldn't cry when Caitlin and Isla were currently dry-eyed.

At least her momentary loss of control hadn't been noticed. Though Maisie began to wonder if that truly was the case when Isla put her hand on her knee and squeezed. *Great!* she thought, giving a long, loud sniff. Now boring Isla, with her big sad eyes and hangdog expression, was feeling sorry for *her*.

She fidgeted, which had the desired effect of prompting Isla to remove her hand, and pulled her phone from her pocket. A host of new WhatsApp messages had arrived and Maisie scanned through them, before wishing she hadn't. Now she didn't know whether to reply, in a jokey 'what am I like?' kind of way, or pretend she'd never seen them – though Madison and her friends would be able to check who'd opened them, wouldn't they? It was a lose-lose situation, as far as she could see.

'Here she is,' said Caitlin, breaking into her thoughts, and Maisie turned off her phone, grateful to be spared making any decisions for the time being.

A stern-looking woman in a grey dress that was covered with frills came into the room. She was too old for what she was wearing, really, but Maisie had to admit she almost carried it off. Her honey-blonde hair was swept into a bun at the back of her neck and her nails were a deep pink, with lips painted to match. A pair of horn-rimmed glasses hung from a gilt chain around her neck.

The woman – the solicitor, apparently, whose name was Frances or Frankie or something similar, Maisie wasn't properly listening – proceeded to express her condolences and to read out some boring legal stuff about Jessie's will.

Then, she got down to dishing out the old lady's belongings, which was sad, thought Maisie. It struck her that worldly possessions counted for nothing when you were dead, and she felt a flush of satisfaction as she realised that was quite an adult observation. Though having lots of possessions was very important while you were still alive, she decided.

Maisie pictured her large bedroom in London, decorated just as she liked it, and scowled. She didn't get why she couldn't have stayed at home, rather than being dragged to this tedious place full of boring people. Or she could have gone abroad with her dad – even though she knew something about him that she'd rather not. She glanced at Caitlin, wondering if her stepmother knew his secret too. Perhaps that was what they'd been fighting about. She sighed, wondering why people got more stupid as they got older.

'Maisie?' The solicitor had turned to look at her.

Maisie jumped, feeling awkward when everyone in the room stared at her. 'Yeah?'

'This part of the will mentions you.' Frances or Frankie smiled and read from the paper in front of her. 'To my great-granddaughter Maisie, I leave the contents of the small jewellery box in the bottom drawer of my dressing table.'

Maisie blinked again, feeling an almost overwhelming urge to cry. The old lady had left her something in her will. That was surprising enough, but it was the fact that she'd referred to her as her great-granddaughter that made the breath catch in Maisie's throat. That was pretty decent of her, seeing as Maisie had made very little effort to speak to her at Easter. She hadn't been rude, but she hadn't exactly been kind either. Maisie swallowed hard, wishing she'd given Jessie more of her time. She would have, if she'd known that she was about to die.

'That was very kind of Gran, wasn't it,' murmured Caitlin and Isla nodded in agreement as the solicitor carried on reading and distributing various items, from her collection of puzzle books (to Isla) to her cashmere jumpers (to Caitlin).

'And the house...' The solicitor stopped reading and narrowed her eyes at the little group in front of her. 'Jessie has left her house to both of you, Isla and Caitlin.'

Maisie noticed Caitlin's shoulders slump with relief, presumably at the prospect of a big pay-out.

'But there is one condition attached,' said the solicitor, hardly pausing for breath. 'Jessie stipulates that Isla be allowed to live in the house for as long as she desires, with no sale taking place until she wishes to move out.'

Wow. Maisie glanced at Caitlin, whose jaw had dropped. That clearly wasn't expected.

'I'm sorry?' Her stepmother leaned forward, smiling politely. 'Would you mind repeating that?'

When the solicitor duly did, Caitlin leaned back in her chair again and folded her arms. She pursed her lips while Isla stared at her with an unreadable expression on her face – Maisie couldn't work out if it was surprise, concern, or triumph.

'O-K,' said Caitlin slowly. 'Well, that's a bit of a curveball but I guess it won't make any difference in the great scheme of things.' She glanced at Isla, who'd got her face under control and was looking back to normal. 'Did you know anything about this?'

Isla shook her head. 'No, but you can count on Gran to do something unexpected.' She swallowed loudly. 'I miss her.'

'I know. Me too,' said Caitlin, giving Isla's back a pat.

For a split second, Maisie thought she was about to give Isla a hug, which would be mega-awkward, seeing as they didn't seem to like each other much.

But then the solicitor said: 'There's something else. Your grandmother left you both this letter.' She handed a small, tattered envelope to Isla, which, Maisie noticed, reading upside down, was addressed to a Miss Edith Anstey at Rose Cottage. 'There's a letter inside, to a member of your family, that she found recently in her mother's possessions. She wanted you both to have it.'

'Do you know why?' sniffed Isla, taking the envelope and turning it over in her hands.

'She had her reasons,' said the solicitor, being unnecessarily enigmatic, in Maisie's opinion.

'Reasons that you're aware of?' asked Caitlin, raising an eyebrow.

'Reasons that Jessie insisted were kept quiet until you'd both worked things out,' said the solicitor, even more enigmatically. She was starting to get on Maisie's nerves. 'Anyway, read it when you get home. That's probably best,' she urged, as Isla pushed her fingers into the envelope, which had already been cut open at the top. 'There's nothing inside that affects the rest of the will. It's a last... request, if you like, from your grandmother.'

Isla hesitated but tucked the envelope into the open handbag at her feet.

And that was that. The solicitor rose to signal that the will reading was over, and Maisie stood up, feeling relieved. No one had dissolved into tears, no one had kicked off about the old lady's final wishes, and she and Caitlin were one step closer to being back in London.

Everyone was quiet on the journey back to the house, as they drove along narrow lanes lined by sodden hedgerows, and through hamlets of houses that were so old they looked ready to fall down. As they drove into Heaven's Cove, the grey sea looked freezing, and Maisie was glad to get back to Rose Cottage, which was warm at least.

She stomped upstairs while Caitlin and Isla put the kettle on. They did nothing but drink tea these days, or make excruciatingly polite conversation when they'd probably rather tear each other's hair out.

Maisie stopped on the landing and took a deep breath before pushing open Jessie's bedroom door. She'd never been in here before and was expecting floral wallpaper and clutter – china ornaments, old postcards, lace doilies. But the room was painted a restful cream and had only a single bed, a small wardrobe, a clutter-free chest of drawers and a dressing table.

When Maisie stepped into the room, she noticed there was a faint smell of talcum powder and lavender in here: an old lady smell which made her feel equally comforted and sad.

Tiptoeing across the worn carpet, she went to the dressing table that sat next to the window. There were two photographs on top, in simple, silver frames, and she picked up the one of two girls about her age. It was Caitlin and Isla – Caitlin with long, brown hair, and Isla, her fairer hair pulled into her trademark ponytail.

They both looked different – younger, obviously, but also less worn down by life. Getting older was the pits, Maisie decided, putting the photo down and peering at the second black and white picture. This was of a young man in a dark suit, staring into the camera with the hint of a smile on his lips. Beside him stood a young woman, her arm hooked through his and her head resting against his shoulder. It was Jessie, Maisie realised with a start, taking in the shape of the woman's nose and her direct gaze. She'd never thought of Caitlin's grandmother once being young like her.

It was probably best not to think about it or the realisation would properly hit her that one day she would get old and die, just like Jessie. Maisie shook her head and pulled open the bottom drawer of the dressing table. It felt as if she was snooping, but Jessie had told her where to find whatever she'd left for her.

Maisie began to push her fingers through the scarves and thick woollen socks in the drawer, until her fingers closed around something hard. It was a small white box.

Maisie sat on the bed, opened it and winced when a plastic ballerina popped up and began to turn while the box played a plinky-plonk tune. There was a piece of paper inside the box which said in spidery writing: *For Maisie*.

Beneath it sat a large diamanté brooch, a gold cross and chain, and a small piece of wood. Maisie picked up the wood, which fitted into the palm of her hand, and inspected it closely. It was lighter than she'd expected and was pale like the driftwood she'd seen washed up on Heaven's Cove beach.

Lines and grooves were carved into its surface, and she suddenly realised that someone had carved an angel. The angel's wings were unfurled in flight and there was a smile on its face. The carving was rough, but it had been done with care. It had been done with love, Maisie thought, before placing the figure back into the box, feeling foolish. Done with love, indeed. She knew nothing about this peculiar angel that Jessie had left her so there was no point in making up stories about it.

Maisie closed the lid of the box, desperate to stop its tinny tune that seemed to be on repeat, and sat for a while, wondering why Jessie had left her these objects. There was nothing else in the box: no note of explanation. It was a real puzzle, which felt appropriate seeing as the old lady had always seemed to have a half-completed crossword in her hand.

'Thanks, anyway,' said Maisie out loud, brushing the top of the box with her fingertips. 'Thanks...' She hesitated because saying this felt very strange and so very sad. But it felt right, somehow, to say it, here and now. She swallowed. 'Thank you very much, Great-Gran.' She shivered, feeling as if she was being watched, even though the room was empty.

4

ISLA

Isla noticed her hand was shaking as she poured the tea. It was the emotion of the afternoon, she decided. The finality of it all as their grandmother's possessions, including this house, were distributed.

She put the teapot down and clasped her hands together to stop them from trembling. Paul had suggested she cancel this evening's yoga class and spend time with him instead, but she was glad now that she'd stood her ground. The class would do her good – moving her body and getting into the flow would make her feel better and might stop her brain from pinging about all over the place.

It was funny how life turned out, she mused, going back to pouring the tea from Jessie's favourite teapot. Once upon a time, she'd seen herself living a very different life from the one she had now. She'd harboured dreams of being a film director or a travel writer, exploring the world. But instead, she'd ended up as her grandmother's carer in a tiny village that she was now too nervous to leave – even, it seemed, to move in with her boyfriend.

And now she had to make a stand with Caitlin and she

was nervous about that too. But it had to be done. Losing Gran had made her braver, in a way, even though it felt as if a layer of her skin had been scraped off. She no longer had Jessie to look out for her, so she would have to look out for herself. Though there was always Paul, of course, who looked after her so carefully.

Isla carried the tea into the sitting room where Caitlin sat, her ankles crossed, staring out of the window. Isla followed her gaze, across the garden and over cottage roofs to the shimmering sea in the distance. There had just been a hail storm and the garden was scattered with spheres of ice.

Isla put down the tray and wiped a hand down her dress. Caitlin was chic, as ever, in a navy jumpsuit and chunky cream cardigan which looked as if it cost a bomb. Isla had put on a simple dress made of brown jersey for the will reading, and was very aware that it was inexpensive and dated. She looked like a local yokel whereas Caitlin looked like a fashionable visitor from the big city. Which, in fact, summed up the two of them very accurately.

Isla sighed and sat down in the comfy armchair that had once been Jessie's favourite.

Caitlin glanced across at her. 'That was very kind of Gran to leave a few bits and bobs to Maisie.'

'I thought so too, but I'm not surprised. Gran really liked Maisie, even though...' Isla stopped speaking because she didn't want to bring up how difficult it had been at Easter. 'What I mean is, she was fond of Maisie because of her link to you and she wanted her to feel a part of the family.'

'Mmm.' When Caitlin swallowed, Isla wondered if her sister was about to cry. But she gave her head a shake instead and said: 'What's in that letter, then? The one she left for you and me? Trust Gran to add a touch of mystery to the proceedings.'

Isla had completely forgotten about it in the emotion of the afternoon. She put down her tea, pulled her handbag towards her, across the carpet, and found the mysterious letter inside.

The envelope was obviously old. It had a red and blue stamp on its right hand corner and an address written in thick black strokes: *Miss Edith Anstey, Rose Cottage, Steeple Hill, Heaven's Cove, Devonshire, England.*

Edith had the same surname as their grandmother, before Jessie had married Arthur – the love of her life who'd died when Isla and Caitlin were small children. Caitlin remembered him but Isla had been too young to lay down memories of the man who was smiling at them now from a photograph on the windowsill.

'What does it say?' urged Caitlin, pulling her cardigan tightly around her as if she was cold.

Isla pulled out a folded sheet of paper and opened it. She admired the rounded, dark strokes of a fountain pen: the same thick strokes as in the address.

'So?' urged Caitlin impatiently. 'What's in this mysterious letter?'

Isla cleared her throat and read it out loud:

March 20th 1919

My dearest Edith,

My plans are made at last! I arrive into Southampton on RMS Sylvestria on April 18th and will travel immediately to join you in Heaven's Cove. Our return passage is booked for midday, exactly one week following, and we are due to dock in New York late in the evening of May 2nd. From there, you, I and my grandmother will travel on to our new life in Florida.

I will not write more now because there is much to be organised. But know that my heart is full at the thought of seeing you again, my beloved girl. I cannot wait to bring you

*home and make you my wife. I am counting the days until we
are together again, and I remain forever yours,*

William

Isla stopped reading, feeling choked with emotion. She was
a big softie when it came to romance. She re-read the words
penned by William, who had crossed the Atlantic one hundred
years ago to make the woman he loved his wife. What had
happened to them? she wondered. Were their lives together
happy ever after?

Her thoughts were interrupted by Caitlin, who'd come to
stand nearby and was craning over her shoulder at the letter.

'Who the hell was Edith?' she asked.

'I have no idea but I imagine we're related to her in some
way. What are you doing?'

'I'm looking Edith Anstey up on the internet,' said Caitlin,
jabbing at her phone screen. She scrolled through the information that came up and shook her head. 'Nope. Nothing comes
up immediately that might relate to her. What's William's
surname?'

'I don't know. He's just signed it "William", though...' Isla
picked up the envelope, turned it over and smiled. 'He's put his
return address on the back. It says William Columbus,
1 32 W 1 25th Street, New York.'

Caitlin did another quick search on her phone and puffed
air through her lips. 'Nope. That's a dead end too.' She peered
at her screen. 'Looks like he lived in Harlem. Harlem's a fascinating place. I read that it takes its name from a city in the
Netherlands.'

'Whatever,' said Isla, riled by Caitlin's propensity to be
easily distracted. 'But is it definitely a dead end?'

Caitlin puffed out her cheeks. 'Who knows? But I can't see

anything about a William Columbus. He'd have died a long time ago.'

'I guess so,' said Isla, feeling disappointed by the lack of instant information and desperately wanting to know more about Edith's move to America.

She suddenly had a mental image of New York, one hundred years ago, with the Roaring Twenties about to begin: the sounds and smells; the buzz and excitement of the big city. And she had a flash of yearning for how her own life might have been, if things had been different.

'So that's it, is it?' Caitlin reached over her shoulder, took the letter and scanned through it. 'It's all very sweet – a heart-felt letter to someone who's probably distantly related to us. But why did Gran leave it to us in her will? We'd have come across it when we were clearing out the house.'

'I expect we would, but we might not have given it enough attention. Not if we didn't know it was special in some way.'

'But in what way is it special?' Caitlin shook the piece of paper, as if she was hoping the answers would fall from it. 'At the end of the day, it's just an old love letter from a man who's coming to collect his fiancée so they can start their new life together. With his grandmother in tow, which isn't the most romantic of prospects.'

Isla shrugged and, on a hunch, turned the envelope upside down. A piece of paper dropped out and fluttered to the carpet. When she picked it up, Jessie's familiar spidery handwriting made Isla's stomach flip.

'It's from Gran,' she said, her throat tight. 'It says: *Don't get in a spin, girls, though mistakes can cost you dear. This one brings good fortune and, I hope, will make you cheer.*'

'You what?' Caitlin raised one of her perfectly plucked eyebrows.

'It's a riddle,' said Isla, bittersweet emotion rushing through her. 'A riddle from Gran.'

'It certainly is, but why is she leaving us a riddle in her will? It's a bit ghoulish, don't you think?' Caitlin shivered. 'One last riddle from beyond the grave.'

'I don't know. It's just very Gran. She was obsessed with her puzzles and quizzes.'

'I know that,' said Caitlin sharply, which was a bit rich seeing as she'd hardly known Jessie at all since leaving Heaven's Cove. Jessie had gone to stay with Caitlin in London several times over the years. But, though Jessie never said as much outright, Isla got the impression that Caitlin was often prickly and distant, so the visits weren't terribly relaxing.

Caitlin picked up the letter and went through it again, her lips silently moving as she read the words. She looked up from the paper. 'So what do *you* think it means?'

'I have absolutely no idea. All I know is that Gran is telling us that solving the riddle would bring us good fortune.'

'Good fortune as in luck or money?'

'Who knows? But we have to find out. It's a final message from Gran.'

It would also give them something to focus on, thought Isla. Something that wasn't directly tied up with death and grief and change.

But Caitlin wrinkled her nose. 'We're going to be too busy sorting out this house and getting it on the market to faff about solving riddles, I'm afraid.'

Here it was. Isla took a deep breath and said what she'd been wanting to say ever since the will was read. 'I don't want to put the house on the market.'

Caitlin stared at her. Isla remembered that stare from years gone by. 'I know it's hard, Isla, and we don't have to put it on the market right this minute. We can spend a week or so sorting out Gran's stuff first and tidying the place up. But the sooner Rose Cottage goes on the market, the sooner it'll be sold. And it should sell quickly. Houses like this don't come up that often in the village. It's mostly wall-to-wall tiny cottages.'

'I expect this place would sell almost immediately. The house next to the lifeboat station went within hours of being put up for sale. A couple from London bought it.'

'A holiday home, no doubt,' murmured Caitlin. Her eyes lit up. 'Actually, that's not a bad idea. We could list the house with a few London estate agents too – the ones that focus on seaside boltholes for rich city types.'

'No, that's not what I mean.' Isla took another deep breath. 'What I'm saying is, I don't want to sell this house at all. I didn't think I had a choice in the matter, but then Gran made it clear in her will that I did.' Isla's stomach was churning because Caitlin was staring at her again, with her mouth open. But this had to be said so she ploughed on. 'I'm sorry if it's inconvenient, Caitlin, but this is my home, and I want it to remain my home.'

Caitlin frowned. 'What? For ever?'

'No, not necessarily for ever, but for the time being at least.'

'But... it's too big for you,' said Caitlin, her forehead creased. 'It was always too big for you and Gran and it'll still be too big, even if Paul moves in.'

Isla was taken aback by that comment. She hadn't thought about Paul moving in, now that she could stay in the house. Would he expect it? It made sense and she supposed it would be the next step forward in their commitment to each other.

'Earth to Isla!' said Caitlin. 'I said the house is too big for you.'

'OK.' Isla gave her head a shake to get her thoughts in order. 'If that's the case, I can take in a lodger or two and split the rental income with you. So you don't miss out.'

She was thinking out loud and, as the words came out of her mouth, realised that Paul probably wouldn't be keen on her idea. But Caitlin seemed even less enamoured at the prospect.

'No, you don't understand.' Caitlin had started pacing the

room. 'I don't want bits and bobs of rental income every month. I need half the proceeds of this house.'

Isla shook her head, at a loss to understand why Caitlin was so obsessed with money. She had a lovely house in London and seemed very well off.

'Look,' she said, determined to be conciliatory because she couldn't face a row today. 'I'm sure Gran said I could stay in the house for a while because she knew you don't need the money immediately. You'll get it some time, just not right now. That's OK, isn't it? Surely you can wait for your half of this house?'

Caitlin opened her mouth, as if she was about to speak, but then snapped it shut and walked to the window. She looked out across the village and down to the sea.

After a few moments, she said quietly, her back still to Isla: 'I realise that you've lived here for years, Isla, and you've become very attached to the village. But you can buy somewhere else local with your half of the proceeds from Rose Cottage.'

Isla rolled her eyes because Caitlin really didn't have a clue about Heaven's Cove these days. 'I doubt I'd be able to afford anything decent. Have you seen what cottages in the village go for, especially with Londoners pushing up the prices? And there's a dearth of accommodation for sale anyway because so many local homes have been turned into rental properties, to accommodate tourists.'

'There must be some way round it,' said Caitlin, swinging round from the window to face her.

'There is. I stay here for the time being and we see what pans out.'

'What pans out?' Caitlin shook her head, a pink flush rising across her cheeks. 'Honestly, Isla, it's selfish of you not to sell Rose Cottage.'

Isla deliberately breathed out slowly so her voice would be

level when she replied: 'I'm sorry you feel that way, but I don't think I have the monopoly on being selfish.'

Caitlin narrowed her eyes at that but said nothing, because what could she say? She knew what she'd done. Though Isla felt sure Caitlin didn't fully appreciate the impact of her actions on Isla's life over the years.

Caitlin leaned back against the stone windowsill. 'I'd just like the money now,' she said.

'Why?'

'Because... because...' She sighed, looking weary behind her make-up. 'I just thought we'd sell the house.'

'And we will, one day. I agree the house is bigger than I need and maybe I'll feel like moving out before too long. But right now, I need the stability and familiarity of Rose Cottage, and I can't face moving so quickly after losing Gran. She must have known that, which is why she made sure in her will that I could stay.'

To Isla's alarm, Caitlin looked as if she might really cry this time. 'You don't understand everything that's—' she began. But she stopped and shook her head when Maisie walked into the room, a small jewellery box under her arm, and threw herself onto the sofa.

'What's going on?' she asked.

'Nothing,' said Caitlin breezily, her face now expressionless.

'Huh. If you say so.'

Maisie obviously didn't believe her stepmother, and Isla felt sorry for the girl, remembering how hard it was to be a teenager. She lived a pretty cushy life, by the sound of it, but she was still fifteen, with all the associated hormonal and emotional upheaval that entailed.

Caitlin was just fifteen when she and Isla first moved to Heaven's Cove, following the death of their mother. And Isla, though Caitlin had delayed going to university for two years, was still only sixteen when her sister had moved to London and left her behind.

'So, Maisie, is that what Gran left you in her will?' asked Caitlin, her tone flat.

'Yeah. I found it in her dressing table, like that solicitor woman said.'

Maisie sniffed and opened the lid of the box she was carrying. A plastic ballerina turned to a tuneless rendition of 'Edelweiss' as Maisie began to lay out her treasures on the coffee table. Isla recognised the gold cross and chain that her grandmother would sometimes wear, and the brooch that adorned her coat on special occasions. The last time she'd worn it had been to the Halloween festivities in the village. That had only been four weeks ago but, to Isla, it felt like an age.

'She left me this too,' said Maisie, 'though it's a bit odd.'

Maisie laid a small piece of driftwood on the table and Isla's breath caught in her throat when she recognised it.

'It's Gran's guardian angel.' She picked up the lightweight wood and ran a finger across the etched grooves.

'Her what?'

'She called it her guardian angel and reckoned it was her lucky charm.'

'Random!' Maisie frowned and began to fiddle with the stud in her nose that Isla had at first mistaken for adolescent acne. 'So where's it from?'

'I have no idea. Gran never said. I wish I'd asked her but...' Isla stopped, unable to say the words... *but it's too late now*.

Maisie twisted her mouth, looking far younger than her heavy make-up suggested. 'So why did she want me to have it?'

'Gran, your great-gran, would slip it in her pocket some-times. She told me once that it was her protector, so maybe she wanted it to protect you too.'

The muscles in Maisie's jaw tightened, as if she was trying

to control her emotions, but then the blank look was back. 'Sweet. That was nice of her.'

'She liked you,' said Isla.

'I liked her too,' Maisie mumbled.

She glanced at her stepmother, who murmured, 'She was a very special woman,' while looking as if her mind was somewhere else entirely.

Isla heard the front door open and close and a deep voice rang out. 'Is anyone about? Isla, where are you?'

'I didn't realise that Paul had a key,' said Caitlin.

Isla felt a flash of irritation when her sister and Maisie exchanged a look. Gran might be gone, but this was still her home and she could give a front door key to whomever she chose.

'We're in here,' Isla called out.

The door opened and Paul came into the room. He walked straight to her and planted a kiss on her lips. 'How are you, sweetheart? How did the will reading go?'

'Fine. It was fine but sad.'

'Of course it was,' he said, draping his arm around her shoulders, 'especially for someone like you who's so fragile and sensitive.' Isla winced inside as Caitlin and Maisie exchanged another glance. 'So what's happening about this house?'

'Nothing for the moment,' Isla told him, deliberately not catching Caitlin's eye. 'Gran left this place to both Caitlin and me, but she made arrangements for me to stay in the house for as long as I'd like.'

'That's excellent news!' When Paul leaned down and kissed her on the lips again, his beard tickled her chin. 'I mean, where else would you rather be?'

'Anywhere,' Maisie murmured, but Paul either didn't hear or pretended not to.

'What's that?' he asked, nodding at William's letter, which Isla was still holding.

'I'll tell you later.' She pushed it back into its envelope and into her handbag. Then she linked her arm through Paul's. 'Why don't we head for the kitchen and I'll see if there's any tea left in the pot?'

'I'd rather have a fresh cup,' Paul grumbled as she almost pulled him from the room.

The tea in the pot was still hot and perfectly fine, but Isla threw it away and brewed Paul a fresh cup. He was quite the connoisseur when it came to tea and poked fun at Isla, who preferred good, strong 'builder's tea' to the more perfumed taste of lapsang souchong.

'I'm sorry, sweetheart,' he said, putting down his cup and sweeping her into a tight bear hug. 'It must have been very upsetting, listening to the will being read. It was good of Jessie to let you stay in this house, rather than have to sell it.'

'Mmm.' Isla nodded against his chest. 'I don't think Caitlin is very happy about it.'

'Surprise, surprise!' said Paul, his voice harsh. 'Caitlin is out for herself and what she can get. That's obvious enough.'

Isla pulled away, feeling uncomfortable that Paul was being rude about her sister when she might step into the kitchen at any moment. And though she'd had similar thoughts about Caitlin just a few minutes earlier, Paul's criticism of her sibling made her feel defensive.

'Caitlin hasn't had it easy,' she told him. 'She took care of our mum for years and looked out for me when I was a child. She kept me safe when Mum died.'

'And then, I don't mean to be harsh, but she abandoned you. Anyway.' He pulled her close again. 'Let's not talk about your sister. You don't have to worry about a thing because I'm here, now, to look after you, and I've booked us a table at Barney's at seven thirty to help you relax.'

Isla pushed herself away from him. 'Seven thirty tonight?'

'That's right. It wasn't easy getting such a last-minute booking, but I sweet-talked the woman who answered the phone. Made it clear that we're valued and loyal customers who deserve a table. Blah, blah, blah... It worked a treat.'

'I'm going to yoga this evening. I thought you knew that.'

Paul shrugged. 'You did mention it but a meal out with me will do you more good, don't you think?' He smiled and brushed her cheek with his finger. 'Anyway, you can go to yoga any time.'

'But I wanted to go tonight,' said Isla, suddenly feeling rebellious. 'We'd agreed.'

'I don't think *I* agreed.' Paul pulled his phone from his pocket. 'Right,' he said, his tone clipped. 'If you don't want to eat out with me this evening, I'd better cancel the booking. No doubt, someone else will want the table that I went to so much trouble to get.'

He found the number in his contacts and Isla heard the tinny buzz of a phone ringing at the restaurant that overlooked the village's castle ruins.

'No,' she said quickly, grabbing the phone from him and pressing *end call*. She was being over-emotional and ungrateful. 'It was really kind of you to go to the trouble of getting us a table.'

'I just thought it might cheer you up, sweetheart.' Paul brushed a strand of hair from her forehead. 'That's all. I love you and always want to do what's best for you.'

'I know you do,' said Isla, feeling guilty for throwing his good deed back in his face. 'And you're right. I can go to yoga next week instead. It's just been a long and emotional day, that's all.'

'Which is all the more reason to let me take care of you.'

He folded her into his arms again and Isla relaxed against him. She felt safe here, and protected from the world. She was just being silly because yoga could wait.

5

CAITLIN

The huge, sliding doors of the garage were open wide and a cold wind was whipping through the building. A yellow Mini was hoisted high on a hydraulic lift and the young mechanic studying one of its wheels smiled at Caitlin when she walked in.

'You all right?'

'Yes, thanks.' Caitlin pulled her leather jacket more tightly around her. It was freezing in here. 'I'm looking for the manager.'

'You'll find him over there.'

The man wiped his hands down his thighs and tilted his head towards a black Volkswagen which was raised slightly above the ground. A pair of legs were poking out from underneath, covered in oily overalls.

Caitlin walked to the legs and said: 'Excuse me.' She raised her voice as a drill sounded from beneath the vehicle. 'Could I have a quick word please?' The noise was vibrating through her head and making her wince. She waited a moment but the drilling went on. 'Excuse me,' she tried, more loudly this time but the drilling continued. 'Can I have a word?' she yelled, just as the drilling stopped. Her voice echoed around the garage and everyone looked at her.

She cleared her throat, feeling her cheeks grow hot, as the man slowly pushed himself out from under the car. He sat up and ran a grubby hand through his fair hair. 'Did you want me?'

'I did. I... I...' Caitlin's words faltered when she realised that the man she was looking at was someone she knew. Even with his face covered in grime, she'd know those piercing blue eyes anywhere. 'It's my car,' she managed, feeling totally thrown.

'It usually is, when people come in here,' said Sean, getting to his feet and wiping his hands on a filthy rag hanging from his waist. 'Where is it?'

'Outside. I parked it in the lane,' said Caitlin, her heart hammering. This was horribly awkward.

Sean tilted his head slightly and sniffed. 'We'd best go and see it then and you can explain the problem.'

She followed him out of the garage, feeling confused. He didn't appear to have recognised her, though that was probably good, all things considered.

She'd changed, of course, over the last fifteen years. Her hair was a different colour, for a start – a rich caramel now rather than the boring brown it used to be – and it was shorter and cut into a chic bob. She was also far better dressed, having swapped jeans and sweatshirts – Isla's perpetual uniform – for tailored shirts and trousers. And she wore far more make-up.

But her overwhelming relief that Sean had forgotten her, and any awkwardness could be avoided, was tinged with a shard of something else... disappointment, maybe, that she'd been so unmemorable back then?

'Is this it?' Sean stopped and gestured towards the racing-green Jaguar she'd parked next to the oak tree. When she nodded, he wandered around the vehicle, his hands on his hips. 'What's wrong with it?'

'It keeps spluttering when I'm driving, as if it's about to cut out.'

'Does it ever stall completely?'

'No, but I don't want it to die when I'm in the middle of nowhere. There's obviously something wrong, so I thought it might be prudent to get it seen to.'

Sean stared at her for a moment. 'Yep. Makes sense. We can check it over and see what her problem is.' He ran his hand gently across the bonnet. 'She's a beauty.'

'Presumably you're OK with fixing this... type of car?'

When the corner of his mouth lifted, Caitlin felt her stomach lurch. She recognised that expression of suppressed amusement.

'Posh cars, you mean?' he said. 'Yeah, I think we can manage that.'

'It's second-hand, obviously. Well, more like fourth-hand by the time I got it,' Caitlin blustered, hating herself for feeling the need to justify having a 'posh car' at all. 'Um, how long do you think it'll take to fix, and do you have any idea of the cost?'

Caitlin's stomach turned again at the thought of a large bill but she couldn't risk the car breaking down on her way back to London. Being towed to a garage would cost a fortune.

Sean rubbed his eyebrows as if he had a headache. 'That depends on what we find. But if you leave your mobile number with Jen in the taxi office next door, someone will give you a ring.'

'OK,' said Caitlin, doing some mental calculations. If she could persuade Isla to put Rose Cottage on the market after all – and if she had a reliable, working car by then – she might be able to leave Heaven's Cove in a day or two. Isla had seemed calmer this morning after yesterday's will reading and might be open to persuasion. Though she'd been talking too much about the bizarre riddle they'd been bequeathed for Caitlin to broach the subject of the house over breakfast.

'When do you *think* the car might be ready?' she asked.

'A couple of days? If it's nothing too serious, you should be able to collect it on Thursday.'

'Can you let me know how much it'll cost before you go ahead with any repairs?'

Sean eyed her coolly. 'Of course. Like I said, Jen will give you a call.'

'OK, that's fine. Thank you,' she said, pushing the car keys into his hand. If all went to plan, she could be out of Devon by the weekend.

Caitlin had turned and started walking towards the taxi office when she caught Sean's muttered aside: 'That's if you ever *do* come back for it.'

Her step faltered but she kept on walking. So Sean had recognised her, after all. It was hardly likely, really, that he would completely forget the woman who'd promised to come back for *him*, but never had.

Sean had been her first real boyfriend, her first real crush and she'd believed herself to be madly in love with him at the time. But she wasn't. That was what she'd told herself when she hit the bright lights of London and her life in Heaven's Cove began to fade away. It was simply adolescent infatuation and the ache she felt to see Sean, to laugh with him and kiss him, was simply an illusion.

Her new life, alone in busy London, had frightened her to death at first. But the fear of being dragged back to Heaven's Cove was worse. It wasn't the village itself she feared, or the people in it. The village was a peaceful haven from the chaos of her earlier life, and she loved Isla and Jessie with all of her heart.

But what made her throat tighten with panic was the prospect of stepping back into the life she'd once had. She'd been a carer for her mum for years – sometimes she felt that she'd hardly had a childhood at all. Then, after her mum's death, she'd cared for Isla, who was so young and sad and lost.

There had been a brief respite when Jessie, their maternal grandmother, had taken them in – their father, who'd done a runner years before, was never going to step up to the plate. And Caitlin had enjoyed a few years of simply being a teenager, with no particular responsibilities, other than looking out for her younger sister. The peace of mind and freedom had been unfamiliar and wonderful.

But things had changed just before Caitlin went to university, when Jessie's health began to go downhill. At first her slide into poor health was gradual – a condition diagnosed here, a mobility restriction there – but Caitlin could see it accelerating.

In the end, Jessie had lived a lot longer than Caitlin had feared she would. But back then, fifteen years ago, the writing was still on the wall: Jessie was getting older, and her health was failing, just as her mother's had done. History was repeating itself and Caitlin couldn't bear to go back to suffocating responsibility, not when a brighter life was beckoning.

So she'd left Heaven's Cove, with promises to return as soon as university was finished, in order that Isla could have her own adventure. But she'd quickly realised that she could never return full-time. It was selfish, she knew it. But the thought of being trapped in the village for years as a carer once more made her physically shake. There was something wrong with her – maybe a therapist would pin it on childhood trauma – but she didn't want to explore the past. And she didn't want to go back to Heaven's Cove.

So she'd made a new life for herself: she'd finished university, got a job, married Stuart, kept her distance from Jessie and Isla, and she'd shut out Sean.

Occasionally, she'd wondered what had happened to that handsome, earnest boy, after his increasingly desperate calls and emails to her at university had petered out. He was never mentioned by Isla or Jessie, and she'd never asked, because not knowing was better than remembering her bad behaviour.

Caitlin sighed and pushed open the door to the taxi office. A young woman, with short black hair, looked up from her phone and gave her a friendly smile.

'Are you Jen?'

'That's me. Are you after a taxi?'

'No, thanks. I've just come from the garage. I was told to leave my details with you, so I can be contacted about my car.'

'Sure.' Jen reached into her desk drawer and took out a bright pink notebook. 'What car is it?'

'The green Jaguar over there,' said Caitlin, pointing out of the window.

Jen glanced up briefly, revising her initial opinion of the woman who'd just walked into her office. Caitlin saw it all the time. Driving a Jaguar gave you gravitas, which was why Stuart had insisted on buying it for her in the first place. Caitlin would have chosen something else, something less *look how well I'm doing!* But it was a lovely car to drive and she'd be glad to have it back.

'Can you give me your contact details, then, and I'll pass them on to the hubby.'

'The hubby?' asked Caitlin distractedly, searching her phone for her own number, which she could never remember.

'Sean,' said Jen. 'He owns the garage. Oh, hold on a moment.' She picked up the phone on her desk that had just started ringing. 'Hello? I'm with a customer, Evie. Can I call you back in a minute?'

Caitlin studied the woman in front of her while she brought the phone call to a close. So, *Jen* had happened to Sean. She was striking, with her elfin haircut and pretty face, and she gave off kind vibes. The two of them probably lived an idyllic life in a whitewashed cottage, with a couple of adorable children running around. Sean had had a lucky escape when she'd dumped him so callously all those years ago.

'Do you have your number?' said Jen, looking at her

strangely. It probably wasn't the first time she'd asked.

Caitlin dragged herself away from her thoughts and read her number out from her mobile.

'Great!' Jen closed her notebook and pushed it back into the drawer. 'Sean or one of the other guys will be in touch once they've had a look at your Jag. Are you new round here?'

'Not really. I lived in the village a few years ago, with my grandmother, but she's just died so I came back to help sort things out.'

'Oh, you must be Jessie's granddaughter.'

'That's right. I am.'

Jen's eyes filled with sympathy. 'I was really sorry to hear that your gran had died. I only knew her to say hello but she seemed like a lovely lady.'

'She was.'

'So...' Jen's face clouded with confusion. 'What's your connection to Isla? Are you cousins?'

'No, I'm her sister.'

'Really?' Jen's eyes opened wide. 'I didn't realise she had a sister. Though I don't really know Isla, either, to be fair. We're on nodding terms when we bump into each other around the village, that's all.' She paused. 'Anyway, like I say, I'm very sorry about your gran. You must have been close if you lived with her.'

'Mmm.'

All of a sudden, Caitlin needed to escape from Sean's wife and her sympathy. She garbled something about needing to get back to Rose Cottage and fled, walking quickly past the garage, without looking in to see if Sean was there. She walked on and on until she reached the very edge of the village and then the beach that gave Heaven's Cove its name.

Aptly named in the summer, today the cove was empty and far from heavenly. A cold wind was whipping sand into the air and Caitlin could taste salt on her lips. It was high tide and white waves were curling and crashing nearby. The cave at the corner of the cove, where Isla had played as a child, was surrounded by water. It was unreachable, just as Caitlin had been for the last fifteen years. Sean had simply been the first casualty of her new life.

Caitlin stopped and closed her eyes, surprised by the rush of regret that engulfed her. Seeing Sean, and then Jen, had thrown her completely. But she was being ridiculous because what Sean and Jen had could never have been her life.

Who settled down with their first ever boyfriend? And if she had, she'd never have stayed in London after university and met Stuart and Maisie. And, while she now had reason to regret meeting Stuart, she'd never regret her time in the city. Her life there had been mostly vibrant and interesting. And all she truly regretted, when she allowed herself to think about it, was the hurt that her decision to stay had left in its wake.

But people moved on. Sean was now with Jen, Isla had Paul, whom Caitlin didn't much like, but her sister's love life was none of her business, and Jessie was gone for good. Stuart was... Caitlin didn't even want to think about her husband. And then there was Maisie. What on earth was she going to do about Maisie?

For Maisie's sake, if not her own, she had to persuade Isla to sell up and move out. Her sister would be perfectly happy in a flat, and if she couldn't afford to buy in Heaven's Cove and had to live somewhere nearby, that wouldn't be the end of the world, would it?

You're a terrible sister, said the little voice in her head that sounded very much like her mother's. *I'm so disappointed in you, Cait. So very disappointed.*

Caitlin gulped down the tears that were threatening to fall and stepped onto the cold sand. Everything would be better once she'd returned to London and left Heaven's Cove and its painful memories behind.

6

ISLA

Isla opened her laptop at the kitchen table and began to check work emails. She was officially on leave from her part-time job at Callowfield Library, but she craved familiarity this morning and trawling through – she double-checked and sighed – one hundred and thirteen emails might do the trick.

Familiarity felt grounding when her life was in such upheaval, with her grandmother gone and Caitlin and Maisie showing no signs of leaving. Was her sister staying on in the hope of twisting her arm about selling Rose Cottage? Isla hoped not, as she deleted another email that she'd been cc'd into for no apparent reason. She'd made her decision about Gran's house and she intended to stick to it. Malleable Isla who thought her sister walked on water had disappeared a long time ago and it was time to stick up for herself. That's what Paul had said before he'd left for work this morning, and she felt that way too – most of the time.

It was sad, but she and Caitlin now lived totally separate lives. That was highlighted by her sister going out over an hour ago with no word about where she was going. Wherever it was, she'd taken her car and still wasn't back.

And though her other current housemate, Maisie, was at home, she might as well not be because she was still in bed. Isla checked her watch. It was only quarter past eleven and Maisie rarely showed her face before midday.

Isla went back to her many emails and was mindlessly scrolling through them when a thought hit her out of the blue, about her mysterious ancestor Edith and the riddle her grandmother had left behind.

'Of course!' she said out loud to the empty kitchen.

She obviously wasn't thinking straight these days because the answer to who Edith might be was literally staring her in the face.

Isla crossed the kitchen and went through the open door into the hall where a bookcase sat against the wall, near the stairs. Standing on tiptoe, she reached up and pulled a book from the top shelf, bringing with it a shower of dust that danced in the air.

The black book felt heavy in her hands, its leather binding cracked and battered.

'What's that?' asked Maisie, who'd appeared at the top of the stairs, her long, dark hair tousled and her skin pale. She yawned and pulled down the sweatshirt she was wearing on top of her pyjamas.

'You're up early.'

'I know, right? Some people outside were making lots of noise which is, like, totally inconsiderate,' answered Maisie, not picking up on her aunt's sarcasm. She glanced at what Isla was carrying. 'What's that, then?'

'It's the family Bible.'

Maisie absent-mindedly scratched her stomach. 'The what now?'

'It's a very old Bible that Gran had. It's been in her family for a long time and I think...' Isla opened the front cover and smiled. 'Yes, I was right. There's a family tree drawn inside.'

'Who did that? Your gran?'

Isla shook her head. 'No, it's much older than that but it's been added to over the years, as people got married and new babies arrived. I was hoping it might tell me who Edith was.'

'And who's Edith?'

'She's the woman mentioned in the letter that Gran left me and your—' Isla hesitated. Did Maisie refer to Caitlin as Mum? Probably not because she did have a mother somewhere. 'To Caitlin,' she said, deciding to play it safe.

Maisie trailed down the stairs, her fingers brushing the wooden bannister. 'Are you trying to work out that puzzle thing? I can't remember what it said.'

'Don't get in a spin, girls, though mistakes can cost you dear. This one brings good fortune and, I hope, will make you cheer.'

Maisie's lip curled in amusement, as if Isla was the saddest woman she'd ever met for knowing the riddle off by heart. She sniffed. 'It's all daft, though, isn't it?'

'I don't think so, not if Gran composed the riddle specifically for us.'

'Yeah, but what's all that "good fortune" about? Working out what Jessie was going on about won't lead you to a pot of gold or anything.'

'Probably not,' Isla agreed. 'But I don't care about finding money. No, I really don't,' she repeated when Maisie raised an eyebrow. 'I love solving riddles and puzzles, just like Gran did, and if she left me and Caitlin the old letter and this riddle, then it must mean something. And aren't you fascinated to know more about Edith and William and their love story? Anyway...' Isla continued quickly as Maisie opened her mouth, no doubt to proclaim that she wasn't in the slightest bit interested in a couple now long dead. 'Let's have a look and see if the family Bible can shed any light on the mystery.'

She led the way back to the kitchen, placed the Bible down with a thump on the table and peered at the family tree etched inside. She and Caitlin were at the end of the tree, with their mother, Rebecca, above them and Jessie, Rebecca's mother, above her.

Isla gently ran her finger over her mother's name: *Rebecca Jane Gillard, born 12th Feb 1963*. The date of her death, forty years later, was not noted. A vivid picture of her mother swam into Isla's mind. She was smiling at her, wearing the blue silk dress, edged with silver thread, that she'd always loved.

'You all right?' asked Maisie, giving Isla some serious side eye. 'You look like you're gonna pass out.'

'I'm fine,' said Isla briskly, although she could hardly breathe. It was twenty years since her mother had died yet she could still be floored by grief. She sat down at the table and tried to gather her thoughts by focusing on the here and now and the font of family knowledge in front of her.

A man named Archibald Anstey, born in 1872, was at the head of the tree that had been inked onto the page over the years, and Isla quickly worked out that he was her great-great-grandfather. His name seemed familiar. She drummed her fingers on the table, trying to remember why, until it came to her: Archibald, mentioned once or twice by her gran, was the person who had originally built Rose Cottage.

He had also helped to build a family. Isla ran her eye over the branches that spread from Archibald's name – brothers, sisters, children... all people, like her mum, who had once lived and breathed and loved and laughed, and who were now gone.

'So is Edith in the tree thing?' asked Maisie, pulling a box of cornflakes from the cupboard.

Isla scanned down the names and smiled. 'Yes, here she is. Edith Anstey, born on the seventeenth of January 1898. It looks like she was Frederick's sister.'

'Like I'm supposed to know who Frederick is,' said Maisie grumpily, pouring cornflakes into a bowl and sploshing milk on top.

'Sorry. Frederick is Gran's dad, so my great-grandfather. He was born two years before his sister.' Isla leaned back in her chair, pleased with her detective work. 'So that means the Edith whom William was madly in love with was my and Caitlin's great-great-aunt. I don't remember Gran ever mentioning her.'

'Probably never met her if she'd very sensibly escaped from this place and gone to America,' muttered Maisie.

Isla ignored her and studied the list of ancestors laid out before her. Edith didn't have children, if this family tree was correct. Or perhaps she'd lost contact with her Heaven's Cove relatives after moving across the Atlantic and they didn't know much about her family over there.

Isla frowned. It was good to know who Edith was, but that knowledge didn't bring her any closer to solving her grandmother's final riddle. She would have to go online again and try to track Edith down in America – or, rather, track down any descendants because both Edith and her husband, William, would definitely be deceased by now.

Isla clicked off her work emails, which could wait, and began to search online for anyone who might be related to her great-great-aunt. She'd only just learned of Edith's existence, yet she felt bizarrely proud to be related to a woman who, unlike her, had shown the courage to set sail and see the world.

Even if she and Caitlin were never able to solve Jessie's riddle, at least she now knew about her adventurous relative. Isla gave a wry smile, wondering if Edith's courage might rub off on her one day.

'It's good to kind of meet you, Edith,' she muttered under her breath. 'Thanks, Gran, for introducing us.'

Maisie harrumphed in the corner, obviously concerned that Isla was now talking to herself, but Isla continued scrolling, searching for her long-gone relative who was once the love of William Columbus's life.

7

MAISIE

Isla was still wasting time searching for a ghost. She'd had her head stuck in her computer for the last ten minutes, clicking on this website and that, looking for elusive Edith. Yet she was no closer to solving that stupid riddle if the furrow between her eyes was anything to go by.

If she kept frowning like that, thought Maisie, dropping her bowl into the dishwasher, she'd end up with horrific wrinkles.

The clink of crockery prompted Isla to look up from her laptop. She gave Maisie a smile. 'So, what are you up to today? Do you have any plans?'

What kind of daft question was that? The options round here weren't exactly epic. It was either huddle at the beach in the freezing cold or wander past endless sad little cottages. Her school kept sending work for her to do, but she didn't intend to spend much time on it.

'Dunno,' grunted Maisie. 'Thought I might go back to bed for a bit.'

'Really?' Isla frowned so hard it must surely be destroying what little elasticity her skin had left. She should be more careful, now she was over thirty.

'Yeah, really. Why?'

'I was thinking I might walk down to the church in a bit, St Augustine's by the Mini Mart. And you could come with me, if you like, to get some fresh air.'

Maisie would not like, but she recognised that Isla was trying to be kind so she rewarded her with a half-smile. 'Thanks, but churches aren't really my thing.'

'I'm not planning on going inside, but seeing the names of my great-grandparents in the family Bible has reminded me that Gran used to tend their grave in the churchyard. I might wander down to have a look at it.'

That had to be the most boring invitation Maisie had ever received but she managed another smile. 'Thanks, but I think I'll give that a miss.'

'OK.'

Isla went back to doom-scrolling about dead people while Maisie escaped upstairs to throw herself back into bed, and to wonder where her stepmother was. Caitlin was being very mysterious at the moment. She was all 'everything's fine' and 'there's no need to worry', which usually meant 'It's all gone to hell so start panicking!' Not that anyone would ever tell her the truth.

Maisie drummed her heels against the crocheted bedspread and stared at the ceiling. What she really wanted to know was when she and Caitlin were going home to London, and when her dad would be back from his work conference. If that was where he really was.

Maisie squeezed her eyes tightly shut, wishing for the hundredth time that she didn't know what she knew. If only her train hadn't been delayed that day, giving her time to kill around Waterloo Station. If only she hadn't decided to wander over Waterloo Bridge, she'd have been none the wiser. There was a lot to be said for never going for a walk unless it was absolutely necessary.

But she had gone for a walk, and now she knew. And if Caitlin didn't that was her look-out. Maisie wasn't about to lob a grenade into what appeared to be an already dodgy relationship.

She opened her eyes when a seagull began pecking at her window, and thought back to when she was a child and her mum and dad had split up. Her mum had sunk into depression as the marriage had failed, whereas Caitlin had been over-the-top jolly recently, which was particularly irritating. But perhaps it meant she was totally oblivious to what Maisie knew and this marriage would last.

If it didn't, Maisie reasoned, she was fifteen and totally able to cope with another divorce. She would go back to their house in Hammersmith and live with her dad and her life would go on pretty much as normal.

Hopefully, she'd still see Caitlin sometimes. A rush of anxiety made Maisie's stomach burn. Caitlin was annoying but she'd treated Maisie pretty well since first appearing on the scene six years ago, and Maisie might... She took a deep breath and admitted it to herself. Yes, she *would* miss her stepmother. A little bit. Actually, she didn't like to think of not seeing Caitlin every day.

She blinked, annoyed with herself for feeling as if she might cry. Because the truth of the matter was that Caitlin had no right bringing her to this place, which was just dire in winter, and making her live with Isla, who looked so sad all the time, was plain mean. And that wasn't even taking Paul into account. Quite what Isla saw in him, Maisie couldn't imagine. She'd decided back at Easter that he was totally wet and boring, and this latest visit hadn't changed her view that he was a drip. Yet at the same time he bossed Isla about quite a lot.

A little man from a little village on a power trip, Maisie decided, giving a loud, theatrical sigh, even though it was point-less when there was no one around to hear it.

The sooner she and Caitlin went home, the better. It wasn't as if they needed stupid money from this house. Her dad was well off, so much so that Caitlin didn't need to work. She'd given up her job when they moved house and hadn't found another one yet.

Maisie didn't need a Saturday job either and hadn't been too chuffed when, at Easter, Isla had announced she'd found her holiday work – as if she was doing her a big favour or something. In the end, working at the ice cream parlour in the village hadn't been too bad. It had passed the time, and she'd been allowed to eat the merchandise.

She'd still been glad to get back to London and back to school – until, that is, she'd carried out that stupid practical joke a few days ago which had resulted in her immediate suspension. Maisie shivered, remembering the Head's face after she'd been summoned to her office. Maisie was expecting her to be angry, but what she hadn't anticipated was her disappointment.

Maisie, it seemed, was a disappointment to the Head and to the whole school – but then she was to Caitlin, too, who, let's face it, had been saddled with her. Caitlin had been presented with a passive stepdaughter at first: a young girl who missed her real mother, who was living and working in Canada. But now Caitlin was landed with older Maisie, who was stroppy, complicated, and horribly sad – although she hid her sadness well, mostly by kicking off and being lippy when she felt threatened.

A lot of things made Maisie feel threatened: snarky comments from the girls at school; Caitlin and her dad being in a strop with each other; teachers who expected her to do well when, in fact, she found schoolwork horribly hard. And then there was Heaven's Cove, which was too sickly sweet to be anything other than terrifying. There had to be a serial killer sheltering in one of the whitewashed cottages with their twee thatched roofs. Or a mugger hiding along one of the lanes that criss-crossed the village.

Nowhere could be this perfect, Maisie decided, kicking her magazine off the bed so it dropped onto the floor with a thud. She definitely did not want to be here – but the problem was she didn't really want to go back to school either. The teachers there knew what she'd done. And though Madison in her class had let her join the WhatsApp group for her select band of friends – what Maisie had wanted for ages – their comments about other people, including Maisie, were not always kind.

It was all very complicated. Life was complicated, she thought, staring at the tree outside her window, that was dancing in a sea breeze. The locals laughingly called it a breeze. She called it a freezing cold gale that swirled through the cracks in this old house and moaned like a ghost.

Dark clouds were gathering outside, filtering out what little winter daylight there was, and her bedroom was gloomy and full of shadows. Maisie shivered and turned on her bedside light before closing her eyes and trying to sleep. She'd only just got up, but there was nothing else to do around here.

8

ISLA

The churchyard was peaceful this afternoon. Tourists were few and far between as winter drew in, and an icy wind was keeping the locals indoors. It was just as well that Maisie had opted to go back to bed, thought Isla, closing her gloved hands around the piping hot coffee she'd just bought from Gathergill's Mini Mart. She'd only have moaned about the weather and complained that she was terminally bored.

Isla took a sip of her warming drink and placed it carefully on the wall that encircled the church. Then she pulled a trowel from the tote bag she was carrying, knelt on the cold ground and began to tidy the grave of Jessie's parents, Frederick and Mary.

Jessie used to come here regularly, to make sure the grave was shipshape and, when she became more immobile, the local residents' association took over its upkeep. The association offered because its members were already tending several of the graves, on behalf of older residents who were no longer up to the task.

But Isla felt guilty as she pulled a weed from the damp earth. She should have said that she would look after the Anstey family grave, and she would definitely do so from now on. Her grandmother would be pleased, even though she hadn't been one for lasting memorials.

Jessie had preferred to be cremated and scattered to the four winds from the clifftop, just as her beloved husband, Arthur, had been almost thirty years ago.

'I don't need a slab of stone with my name on it,' she'd said. 'All I want is to be remembered fondly by you and your sister. That'll do for me.'

Isla swallowed back tears. She would always remember her grandmother with great affection, and she hoped that Caitlin would, too, in spite of being so distant these last few years.

She pulled her hat further down over her ears as a blast of cold air swept across the graveyard, and thought about the mysterious letter that their grandmother had left them. No wonder Great-Great-Aunt Edith had set off for warmer climes with her love, William, even though she must have missed this little village and her family. It was hard but she'd had the courage to strike out and make a new life for herself, thousands of miles away.

Ten minutes later, once the grave was tidied and gravestone cleaned, Isla pulled a small potted poinsettia from her tote bag and placed it beneath the etched names of Frederick and Mary. Its red leaves provided a splash of colour and brought some cheer to the churchyard.

Isla stood up, stretched her legs and smiled, imagining Jessie at her shoulder. It felt as if she was honouring her grandmother by doing a task that the old lady had once done herself. She glanced up at ancient St Augustine's Church, remembering Jessie's funeral service there that was so well attended. And she thought back to Caitlin's tears that day which must prove, surely, that she, too, had loved their grandmother. Though Isla couldn't shake the feeling that some of Caitlin's weeping had been guilt for not coming back to see her family while she could.

A familiar stab of anger struck Isla and she tried to smother it. Jessie had been distressed by the sisters' estrangement and would hate to think that her death had made it worse. Just as she would never have wanted the stipulation in her will to stoke resentment between the young women. But that's what it had done. Allowing Isla to stay on in the house for as long as she wished had been a kind and generous gesture, but Caitlin seemed determined to get her out.

A tendril of guilt wrapped around Isla's heart. Was she wrong to insist on staying at Rose Cottage? Paul seemed delighted about it and was already talking endlessly about moving in. He had plans for how the house could be improved. Isla felt a flicker of... something. An emotion that flared and disappeared so quickly, she couldn't put a name to it.

She stooped to adjust the potted plant slightly, before straightening up. It was fine for her to stay on in the house, she told herself firmly. Caitlin, who didn't need the money, would soon be heading back to her posh home, anyway. Then, life in Heaven's Cove could get back to normal – as normal as it could be without Gran.

Isla sighed and shook her legs, which had begun to cramp in the cold. When stamping her feet didn't help, she began to walk briskly round the churchyard, to get her circulation going.

Behind the red-stone church was a patch of ground which held a number of battered gravestones. Many of them were standing at an angle, as if they might fall at any moment. This edge of the churchyard faced east and was blasted by storms, blowing in off the sea, that sloughed away the names of the dead.

But the residents' association had been busy here, too, Isla noticed. The grass had been cut right back and the stones looked scrubbed clean. It made names on the more sheltered stones easier to read again, now they were cleared of moss and dirt – people from the past were being revealed after being lost for generations.

Isla wandered among them, the cramp in her legs beginning to ease. There were lots of local surnames amongst the stones and she became caught up in the stories that were hinted at by the information still legible: Emma Blackmore, who died at the age of twenty-nine in 1901 and was buried with an infant; John Crump, a sea captain, who was pre-deceased in 1857 by his 'beloved wife', Agnes; Ernest Hallett, who was only twelve when he passed away in 1906. So many lives filled with joys and sorrows. So many stories that were lost for ever.

Isla could feel her mood dipping as she walked among the dead. It was all too soon after losing her darling gran. She turned, determined to head for home, and glanced at a grave-stone tucked away at the back of the churchyard. The surname had caught her eye.

She made her way across the uneven grass, towards the stone that sat beneath the branches of a yew tree, and her jaw dropped.

'Well,' she said out loud, to no one in particular. 'That's unexpected.'

9

CAITLIN

Being too nervous to ring your own husband was ridiculous. Caitlin shoved her mobile phone into her pocket and, after a moment's hesitation, pulled it out again. Yes, it was ridiculous but that was how she felt. And she needed to get over it, seeing as they were united in matrimony, and that wasn't going to change.

Before she could talk herself out of it, she rang Stuart's number and leaned against one of the boulders that edged the back of the beach. A cold wind was whipping around her, and she buried her chin into her scarf that worked perfectly well in London but seemed wholly inadequate in Heaven's Cove.

After a few rings, the phone was picked up and a deep voice she recognised said, 'Caitlin? Is that you?'

Who else would be ringing on this number? Caitlin briefly closed her eyes and took a deep breath. 'Yes, it's me. How are you?'

'I'm doing OK, I suppose,' said Stuart in the slightly sulky voice she sometimes recognised in Maisie. 'It's far too hot here, though.'

'Lucky you,' mumbled Caitlin, her lips going numb in the

mist that had started rolling in off the sea. 'How's the conference going? Are you finding it useful?'

'Yeah, it's not bad.'

'The scenery must be amazing.'

'Yeah, that's not bad either, though it's very touristy around
here.'

'But it's still Gran Canaria. In the sunshine.'

'True, but don't forget that I'm working, Cait. I'm not here
on holiday. I'm here for work, and we've been really busy.'

'We?'

'Me and Chiara. I told you she was coming too.'

'Did you?'

Caitlin couldn't remember Stuart mentioning that the
young trainee in his office was going to the conference with him,
but she'd been so thrown by his latest bombshell that she hadn't
taken much in at all.

'I did. So, is Maisie all right?'

'She's... just Maisie. You know what she's like. She's bored,
though she doesn't appear to be missing school, unfortunately.
You could always give her a ring, for a chat. You haven't called
her for a while... Or me,' Caitlin added quietly.

Stuart ignored her aside. 'I was going to call Maisie but I'm
not sure what you've told her about, you know...'

'About you gambling away our house?'

There was a sharp intake of breath, from three and a half
thousand miles away.

'Keep your voice down, Cait. Where are you? Can anyone
hear you?'

Caitlin looked across the deserted beach, to the surging
waves which were fading in the thickening mist.

'No one can hear me. I'm deliberately standing on my own
in the freezing cold so I won't be overheard. So tell me, what's
happening about the house, Stuart?'

'It's all in hand and you don't need to worry.'

'That's all very well you saying that, but of course I'm worried if we're about to be homeless. Where are we going to live? Rents in London are sky high. And what effect will losing our home have on Maisie? She's already suspended from school for that stupid practical joke.'

'Which is why I don't want you to tell her. Not yet, she might never need to know because I've got plans in hand to get us out of this mess.'

Caitlin sighed quietly. 'That doesn't fill me with confidence because it was your plans that got us into this mess in the first place.'

'And this is why I haven't called you for a few days.' Stuart sounded mortally aggrieved. 'You're being very judgemental about something that's not my fault.'

Caitlin answered in as calm a voice as she could muster. 'I'm not being judgemental. I understand that gambling can become addictive, and that's why I found some potential help and support for you. Have you called any of those numbers that I gave you?'

'Not yet. I've been so busy with this conference, and calling from over here isn't a great idea. But I will as soon as I get back. I promise.'

'You've had the numbers for a while.'

'And, like I said, I'll call once I get back home.' If they still had a home for him to get back to, thought Caitlin, but she bit her lip and said nothing. 'And I'm going to speak to my boss about a pay rise and to the bank about a loan, so I'm sure we won't lose our house. I was just being over-dramatic when I told you that. Honestly, Cait, you just need to trust me for a little bit longer. Can you do that, sweetheart? I love you.'

Did he? Caitlin wondered. He'd been distant and grumpy for ages. So much so, she'd begun to think they might be happier apart. But then she'd discovered his gambling habit and he'd got upset and said he was sorry, and she'd known that she could never leave him. Not when he was vulnerable and in need of support. She'd abandoned people who needed her before, and she couldn't bear to do it again. Stuart had lied to her about the amount of money he'd lost. That was distressing. But it was also a symptom of his addiction so she would have to put up with it and stay.

'Can you at least let me know what's going on, please?' she asked. 'I'm on tenterhooks, wondering what's happening and whether our house is safe or not.'

'I will, but you need to chill out, Cait. You're being a bit doom and gloom about all of this when it hasn't even happened yet and probably never will. Something always comes up.'

Until it doesn't, thought Caitlin. She immediately castigated herself for being pessimistic. Stuart's overly optimistic view on life might be unrealistic, but it did help to lessen his anxiety. Whereas every day recently she'd woken up with her insides churning and a question running on a loop through her mind: What happens when we lose our home? *When*, she noticed. Rather than *if*.

Caitlin tried to relax because the cold was making her so tense, the muscles in her neck were starting to ache.

'OK,' she told the man she'd married in Hammersmith and Fulham Register Office five years earlier. They'd both been optimistic then and filled with hope for the future. 'I'll stop catastrophising and you do what you can, but please be realistic, and keep me informed.'

'I will. I've already said.' He sniffed. 'What happened about your grandmother's house, by the way? When do we get the money for that?'

We? Caitlin hesitated. 'I'm not sure. There's been a slight hold-up.'

'But you'll get the cash soon?'

'I expect so,' said Caitlin, her mind whirling. She didn't trust Stuart with their money any more, and if she *could* persuade Isla to sell Rose Cottage, she would have to make sure that Stuart couldn't get his hands on the proceeds. She was applying for work at the moment and would have to do the same with her wages, too.

A woman's voice sounded in the background, far away in sunny Gran Canaria.

'Sorry, Cait, I'm needed and have got to go. We can't afford for me to lose my job right now. Speak soon.'

Caitlin kept the phone to her ear for several seconds after Stuart had ended the call. She suddenly felt so exhausted, so wrung out, she could hardly move. Or maybe it was hypothermia setting in as tendrils of mist wrapped around her and the world beyond began to dim. Even the squawking of seagulls looming at her out of the fog sounded muffled.

With an effort, she pushed herself away from the damp boulder and shoved her phone back into her pocket. The waves were getting closer and the air smelled of salt and seaweed.

A sudden flash of déjà vu dragged Caitlin back through the years. She'd been here before, on a misty day like this, when the world shrank to arm's length and everything beyond might as well not exist. Only, on that day, she hadn't been alone. Sean had been by her side, with his arm around her shoulders, and his breath warming her ear as he whispered how much he loved her. He'd trusted her and she'd let him down.

Caitlin shook her head, trying to dislodge the memory. He was married to Jen now, presumably happily, whereas she was married to Stuart... She stopped the thought before the word 'unhappily' was fully formed. She was staying with Stuart and that was that.

'I've been thinking,' Paul said, idly rubbing his hand up and down the back of Isla's neck as he re-read the love letter from William to Edith. When Isla shifted on the sofa, he stopped stroking her neck but kept his hand on her shoulder.

'What were you thinking?' she asked, distracted now from trying to make sense of Jessie's accounts. Her gran had always been fiercely independent when it came to paying bills and wouldn't let Isla get involved.

'I was thinking about this letter,' he said, giving it a shake. Isla glanced at William's words in Paul's hands, wishing that she'd put the letter away when she got back from the graveyard. She'd left it on the kitchen table and he'd spotted it straight-away. 'It's all a bit strange, isn't it? I mean, who cares about these people after all this time, even if Edith *was* your great-great-aunt? And that riddle doesn't make any sense at all.'

'Riddles don't, at first. That's the point,' said Isla, closing her gran's accounts book. 'Riddles are meant to be challenging and I think that's why Gran left it for me and Caitlin. She wanted to challenge us.'

'Why?'

'I don't know but hopefully it'll all become clearer when we work out why the letter is important.'

'So, you're going to waste your time on it, are you?' He stuffed the letter, none too gently, back into its envelope.

'I don't see it as wasting time.'

'Well, I do, when there are so many other things that we could be focusing on.'

The riddle was a last link to Jessie, and felt like a way of holding onto the grandmother she'd lost. But Isla wasn't sure that Paul would understand so she held her tongue.

'Perhaps your gran was just having a joke,' Paul continued. 'I mean, the bloke who wrote this letter must be long dead. And he lived in America, for goodness' sake.'

Paul said 'America' as if it was another planet. Which it might as well have been to him. He hated flying. He hated travelling, full stop, and took great pride in telling people that he hadn't been farther than Swansea, 150 miles away, in five years. 'Why do I need to go anywhere else?' he'd say. 'This part of beautiful Devon has everything and everyone I could possibly need.'

Once upon a time, Isla would have found that constricting. But her world had shrunk over the years, as she'd cared for Jessie, and now she felt much the same in Heaven's Cove – in familiar surroundings which felt so safe.

'I don't think Gran would have left the riddle unless it meant something,' she said, tucking the accounts book down the side of the sofa, 'and, actually, I've found out something about—'

She stopped speaking when she heard the front door open and close. It was Caitlin, who'd driven off hours ago, not saying where she was going. It obviously wasn't Maisie because Maisie always slammed the door – however many times Caitlin asked her not to – as if she wanted to bring the whole house down.

It had been the same at Easter, when Maisie had been dropped on them with very little warning – just so Caitlin and

Stuart could go off on some exotic jaunt, no doubt. Maisie hadn't been thrilled about it, and neither had Isla. Initially she'd welcomed the chance to get to know Maisie better... until she'd got to know Maisie better.

Jessie, bless her, had said she enjoyed having a youngster in the house again and had done her best to get on with the stroppy teenager. They'd almost been friends by the time Maisie left – which was proved by the fact that she'd bequeathed Maisie her carved angel protector.

Tears sprang into Isla's eyes at the thought of her grand-mother's generosity. She missed her so much.

The door swung open and Caitlin came in and dropped into a chair, with a loud 'oof'.

'I can't believe how steep the hill up to this house is. And it's a death-trap when it's so icy. It never seemed so steep when we first moved in.'

'That was a long time ago,' said Isla. 'And you were prob-ably wearing flat shoes back then.' She nodded at Caitlin's high-heeled leather boots. 'You need sensible walking boots around here, especially at this time of year.'

Caitlin shuddered at the prospect. She seemed like a totally different person these days and Isla missed the sister she'd once had. They'd lost their mother twenty years ago and their grand-mother four weeks ago. But they'd lost each other the day that Caitlin had left her behind and moved to London.

'Why are you walking anyway?' asked Isla, pushing herself away from Paul. 'I heard you drive away in your car.'

'I dropped it off at the garage, the one around the back of the pub. It's been playing up a bit and I want to nip any prob-lems in the bud. I don't want to break down halfway back to London.' She paused and studied her nails, painted a perfect pink, like her perfect life. 'I didn't realise that Sean owned the business.'

'Yeah, he bought it from Derek Falkirk when he retired, a

few years ago,' chipped in Paul, who always perked up when it came to business dealings. 'I heard he was running a garage over Heaven's Brook way before that. It's a tidy little business, I imagine. Why? Are you friends?'

'We were. More acquaintances, really,' murmured Caitlin, staring out of the window at the white sky.

Isla glanced at her sister. She remembered a heartbroken Sean knocking on their door after Caitlin had left, asking when she was coming back. Isla had said 'soon' because that's what she'd believed back then. Before the timings between Caitlin's visits got longer, until they hardly happened at all. 'Anyway, he's done all right for himself,' said Caitlin briskly, taking off her leather jacket, which was totally impractical in such cold weather. She glanced up at Paul, who'd reached across Isla to grab Jessie's accounts book and was studying the figures. 'No work today, then, Paul?'

'One of the joys of being my own boss is that I can take time off whenever I want.'

'What is it that you do again?'

'I run a logistics company that arranges transportation and warehousing for select clients. I help them move their products from A to B and find storage facilities when their output requires it. Isn't that right, Isla?'

'Mmm,' answered Isla, who tried really hard to take an interest in Paul's work, even though it sounded dead boring when he was wanging on about it.

'And I've been working very hard today already.' Paul gave a brief laugh. 'I can assure you that I'm not skiving.'

'I never thought you were,' said Caitlin mildly. 'I was simply surprised to see you here in the early afternoon. That's all.'

'I'll be here a lot more when I move in.'

Isla shifted uncomfortably on the sofa. Paul sounded defensive, and Caitlin's face had fallen.

'I didn't realise you were planning on moving in,' she said, one eyebrow lifting.

'We didn't co-habit when Jessie was alive, out of respect. She was a game old bird but, you know, people still have old-fashioned ideas. But now she's gone...' He spread out his arms. 'This is a big house, and I need to move in to look after Isla.'

'I'm sure my sister is perfectly capable of looking after herself,' said Caitlin with a smile that didn't reach her eyes.

'You'd think but she does daft things all the time. Don't you, sweetheart? For a start, she's horribly accident prone and would burn this place down without me following round behind her, turning off gas hobs. Fortunately, I'm not a clumsy or forgetful person myself or it would be carnage around here!' He laughed and patted Isla's knee. 'Anyway, what else are you up to today, darling?'

'Nothing in particular,' said Isla, ignoring Paul's comments because the awkwardness between him and Caitlin was putting her teeth on edge. 'Sorting out Gran's things, mostly, and trying to get my head round her finances.'

'I've told you, I can do all of that. You don't need to worry about anything because you've got me. And like I say, you certainly don't need to worry about an old letter and riddle.'

Caitlin gave Paul one of her straight stares. 'Could you give me the letter, please.'

Paul, huffing slightly, picked up the envelope and handed it over. 'I hope you're not fuelling Isla's obsession with this. It's not good for her.'

'It's hardly an obsession,' Isla murmured, but Paul simply clasped her hand and gave it a squeeze.

Caitlin pulled out the letter and read it through. Then, she tipped the riddle out of the envelope and read that as well. 'It is intriguing, I must admit. Have you got anywhere with finding out anything more?'

'I've discovered that Edith was our great-great-aunt.'

'Really?' A spark of interest flared in Caitlin's hazel eyes. 'How did you discover that?'

'I looked in Gran's family Bible and there was a family tree.'

'Sweet.' Caitlin smiled at Isla. 'That was a smart move. I hadn't thought of the family Bible. I didn't know that Gran still had it.'

'It's not the kind of thing she'd ever get rid of.'

'No, I guess not. It has great sentimental value and, anyway, Gran was a bit of a hoarder on the quiet.'

'Not so much on the quiet. She insisted on her bedroom being restfully uncluttered, but that certainly wasn't her approach in the rest of the house!'

Caitlin glanced around the sitting room, crammed with ornaments and books that Jessie could never bear to part with. Then she grinned at Isla and, just for a moment, it was like the old days. When it was the two sisters against the world and nothing could come between them.

'We'll need to hire a skip to get rid of everything,' said Paul, and Caitlin's grin faded.

'So,' she said briskly. 'Did you find out anything online about Great-Great-Aunt Edith's life in America? Did she have kids and grandkids? Maybe we could contact them to see if they can shed any light on Gran's mysterious riddle.'

'I don't know about contacting people that you come across online.' Paul looped his arm around Isla's shoulders. 'I think you should always check with me first, before you contact anyone, sweetheart. You never know what people are like, and they'll be American, after all.'

Isla sighed quietly and avoided catching Caitlin's eye. She loved Paul but he sometimes came across like a hick from the sticks. Though she felt annoyed with herself for being embarrassed by him. It was pretty ironic her feeling that way when she was hardly adventurous herself.

She had been, once upon a time, back when she'd had a

head full of dreams. But those dreams had faded and now she was happy being here in Heaven's Cove, with Paul, she told herself. Even if he wouldn't pass muster with her sister, who was giving him a very straight look.

Isla glared back at her, daring her to say anything. She had no right. Not after what she'd done.

11

CAITLIN

Caitlin had tried very hard to like Paul. He was Isla's partner of almost eighteen months, and that was that. She had no moral right to be dictatorial about her sister's choices or, quite honestly, to have any opinion at all. She'd given up that right many years ago, when she'd upped and left. But Paul certainly wasn't making it easy to step back and keep her mouth shut.

He'd been charming enough, at first – all good manners and generous bonhomie. But the cracks were starting to show. He obviously found having two permanent house guests rather trying, and the way he treated Isla was bothersome. On the surface, he was devoted to her sister, and Isla seemed happy enough being part of a couple. But there was a vibe going on with him, an undercurrent that made Caitlin uneasy. Maisie didn't like him at all, though she didn't really like anybody so that wasn't a great indicator of Paul's character.

Isla was glaring at her, so Caitlin forced herself to smile.

'Don't worry, Paul. If we do contact anyone online, I'll make sure that we keep safe,' she told him sweetly.

He smiled back. 'Thank you, Cait. I appreciate that.'

Caitlin swallowed because no one called her Cait except for

people she loved – her mother and husband, Jessie, Isla and, once upon a time, Sean. But she let it go, worried that commenting on it would sound petty and unfriendly. And she didn't want to fall out with Isla over anything else. Their relationship was already on shaky ground.

Paul was speaking to Isla now, his face very close to hers. 'I'd really rather, though, that you just let things lie with this letter and riddle. There's no good to come from chasing strangers on the internet.'

For a moment, Caitlin thought Isla might cave, but she pulled her shoulders back and smiled. 'I know you're only looking out for me, Paul, but it'll be fine.'

Paul breathed out slowly, a frown on his face. 'It sounds as if you've made up your mind.'

'I have, but you honestly don't need to worry.' Isla leaned against Paul but he got to his feet.

'Anyway, I've got work to do, so I'd better be going.' He leaned down to kiss Isla, who tilted her chin towards him, but he swerved her mouth and landed a chaste kiss on her cheek. He straightened up. 'See you again soon, Cait.'

'Yeah. See you,' said Caitlin as Paul left the room.

Neither of the sisters spoke when they heard the front door close, and the silence lengthened as Paul's footsteps sounded along the garden path outside and faded into the distance.

'What does he mean when he says that you're accident prone and do daft things?' asked Caitlin, able to keep her mouth shut no longer.

'Did he say that?' asked Isla, idly picking at a cuticle. 'I suppose I do leave the hob on occasionally by mistake and I've broken a few glasses while washing up... Oh, I've locked myself out of the house twice this year as well.'

'We've all done that. Maisie never takes her key with her when she goes out. Ever.'

Isla shrugged. 'Paul cares about me and worries about me. That's all.'

'And that's great. It's just...' Caitlin hesitated but she had to ask. 'Is everything all right between the two of you?'

'Of course,' said Isla, bristling as Caitlin knew she would at her sister poking her nose into her life. 'How are things going with you and Stuart?' she shot back.

Now was the perfect time to tell her the truth, and Caitlin was tempted. But how could she admit that the choices she'd made – choices with consequences for both Isla and their grandmother – had ultimately backfired on her?

'Fine,' she said, sitting back in her chair.

'Only you've hardly mentioned him since you arrived.'

Isla always was canny when it came to wheedling the truth out of Caitlin, but not this time.

'He's away at a work conference in Gran Canaria and is probably spending a lot of time on the golf course nearby. He's been in touch. Anyway, what about this riddle, then?' Isla's mouth tightened at the change of subject but she picked up Jessie's riddle. 'Can you read it again?'

'Don't get in a spin, girls, though mistakes can cost you dear. This one brings good fortune and, I hope, will make you cheer,' said Isla, gently brushing her fingers across their grandmother's spidery writing.

'What did Gran mean by "good fortune"? I don't see how the letter can be worth any money, unless...' She bit her lip.

'Unless what?'

'Unless Great-Great-Aunt Edith... oh, what a mouthful! I vote that we drop the extra "great".' She began again, 'Unless Great-Aunt Edith made her fortune in the States and we're inheritors. Or perhaps this American man she married was absolutely loaded and the letter is giving us a clue about how we can lay claim to some of it.'

Isla sighed and pulled her feet up beneath her on the sofa.

'Why are you so fixated on money? You're the last person I
know who needs it.'

Her sister obviously thought she was a dreadful money-
grabber. Caitlin's heart sank at this latest black mark against her.

'Anyway,' Isla continued, 'Edith didn't go to America in the
end. Or if she did, she came back.'

Caitlin frowned. 'How on earth do you know that? You said
you'd had no luck on the internet.'

'I didn't. I can't find any mention online. But I actually
found *her* today. Great-Aunt Edith, in Heaven's Cove
graveyard.'

For a split second, Caitlin thought Isla meant she'd bumped
into Great-Aunt Edith near the church. She shook her head to
banish the ridiculous notion. 'You found her grave, you mean?'

Isla narrowed her eyes. 'What else would I mean? It's
behind the church, near the wall and quite hidden away. It's
with a few tumbledown stones which look as if they've recently
been cleaned by volunteers from the residents' association. Her
stone said she died in 1922, at the age of twenty-four.'

'That's so young.'

'I know, right?'

'Perhaps she and William were over here, visiting family at
the time.'

'No, that's the strange thing. Her surname wasn't Columbus. It was still Anstey.'

'Are you sure it's the same woman?'

'The birthdate was the same: born on the seventeenth of
January 1898. So it must be her.'

Caitlin sat up straighter in her chair. 'That is very odd, then.
I wonder what happened between her and William? He
sounded devoted to her in the letter but perhaps Edith wasn't as
enamoured.'

'Who knows, but the epitaph on the gravestone was strange.
It was hard to read because it was so weathered by a hundred

years of Devon storms, but it looked like: *Beloved daughter and aunt, who died of a broken heart.*'

'A broken heart?' Caitlin frowned. 'Was she broken-hearted about William? Thinking about it, she must have cared a great deal about him or she'd never have kept his letter. So I wonder why she didn't go with him back to America?'

'Perhaps she lost her nerve,' said Isla quietly.

'Perhaps, and maybe that decision haunted her. But how could a broken heart kill Edith?'

'Maybe that William guy murdered her,' said Maisie, who'd just barged into the room and caught the end of the conversation.

'Really?' Caitlin raised an eyebrow. 'Why would William kill Edith?'

'Why does *anyone* kill *anyone*?' muttered Maisie darkly. 'He could have been upset that she came to her senses and decided not to get married, so he used strychnine to get his revenge. I've been reading about the Lambeth Poisoner, who killed his victims with it in the eighteen hundreds.'

Isla did a double-take at the teenager, probably disturbed that she was reading up about historic murders. But Caitlin, who knew her stepdaughter's penchant for the grisly, was unfazed.

'Do shush, Maisie,' she said, before turning back to Isla. 'So it looks as if Edith didn't go to America. Or maybe she did, the marriage didn't happen, and she was brought home after she passed away.'

'It's intriguing, don't you think?' said Isla.

Caitlin sighed and sat back in her chair. 'You're so much like Gran. Always keen to solve something.'

'But don't you think this riddle is fascinating? And it means even more because Gran wanted us to solve it. Together.'

'Maybe you two should set up the Heaven's Cove Detectives Agency,' muttered Maisie, shifting from foot to foot.

Caitlin shot Maisie a look. 'OK. So what do we do about it? How do we find out what happened to Edith?'

'I guess we get hold of her death certificate, if we can,' said Isla, 'and try to find out what was happening in Heaven's Cove around then? The village cultural centre might be worth a visit.'

'And I can help,' said Maisie. 'What?' She raised her palms to the ceiling when both sisters stared at her. 'There's nothing else to do around here, and the sooner you solve that stupid riddle, the sooner we can get back to London. Right, Caitlin?'

Caitlin nodded, even though solving the riddle wasn't the real reason for their longer than expected stay in Heaven's Cove. She was still hoping to persuade Isla to sell Rose Cottage because the cash from that sale would solve one very big problem in her life.

But, she had to admit, her interest was piqued by what Isla had discovered about their long-lost relative. What on earth had caused her romance with William to implode and meant she was buried in Heaven's Cove after dying of a broken heart?

Caitlin couldn't help but feel a kinship with Edith because her heart was also hurting. Stuart had let her down badly but she had no choice other than to stand by him. She glanced at Isla, who was still studying their grandmother's riddle, and felt a rush of sorrow at the loss of closeness between them. She'd abandoned her sister, and she couldn't do the same again to someone she cared about, so she would support her husband, however much she felt trapped.

12

ISLA

The next morning, Isla clicked onto Skype and sat waiting for Eleanor Columbus to accept her call, halfway across the world. It was embarrassing how quickly Maisie had managed to track down one of William's descendants, after she had failed miserably.

'That's 'cos old people don't know what they're doing online,' Maisie had muttered, handing over details of the people she'd found in the New York area who were named Columbus. Isla had winced at the comment – though twice the teenager's age, she was hardly in her dotage. However, Maisie had come up with the goods so she'd simply thanked her and let it go.

Caitlin had contacted Eleanor, who was the only person whose email address was online, and Eleanor had replied almost immediately, confirming that her family did, indeed, have a link to William, and suggesting that she and Caitlin should speak.

So a call had been arranged, and Isla had insisted on making it. She wasn't sure, now, why she'd been adamant that it should be her who spoke to this American stranger. Perhaps it was because Caitlin had said Paul wouldn't like it, as if Isla couldn't

make up her own mind. Not that she'd told Paul what was going
on. He definitely wouldn't approve, and there was no point in
getting him riled up about nothing.

Isla sighed and glanced round to make sure that Caitlin had
disappeared into the kitchen. She'd turned down her offer of
support, fearing that both of them on the call might be overwhelming for Eleanor. But, annoyingly, she was feeling nervous
as she waited for her call to go through.

Perhaps it was exhaustion, rather than anxiety, that was
making her head ache and her leg twitch up and down. She
hadn't been sleeping well since Jessie's death and, even before
her gran died, she'd not been a good sleeper. She was always
listening out for Jessie's call, in case she needed help to get to
the bathroom.

What she would give now for her sleep to be interrupted by
her lovely grandmother. Isla was lost in thought when a smiling
woman with short blonde hair suddenly appeared on her
screen.

'Hey! Is that you, Caitlin?'

The woman's voice was warm and her brown eyes twinkled.

'No, I'm Isla, Caitlin's sister. Hello. Thanks so much for
speaking to me, Mrs Columbus.'

The woman laughed. 'Nell, please. And I'm delighted you
got in touch. I've begun researching my family tree for my children, and I'm so happy to discover this link to the UK. Thank
you so much for sending over a photo of the letter from William.
It's utterly charming.'

All Isla knew about American accents had been gleaned
from TV series, but Nell, she decided, came from the Deep
South. Maybe from Savannah or New Orleans, both places that
Isla had once longed to visit. She'd been fascinated as a child by
the swamplands and traditions of the sultry South.

'Did you say the letter belonged to your grandmother?'
asked Nell.

'It was in my grandmother's belongings, after she passed away. Edith, the woman William wrote to, was my gran's aunt, so my great-great-aunt.'

The smile on Nell's face faded. 'I was very sorry to hear about your grandmother's passing. I'm so sorry for your loss. How are you doing?'

It was such an unexpected question, Isla dug her nails into her palm so she wouldn't cry. She swallowed. 'I'm doing all right, thank you for asking.'

Nell's face crumpled into sympathy. 'Losing someone you love is hard. My husband, Jackson, passed away last year and it takes time to...' She stopped mid-sentence.

'That must be hard for you and your family,' said Isla, her nerves starting to subside. She and Nell might be strangers, but they had one major thing in common – overwhelming grief.

Nell pursed her lips and breathed out slowly. 'It is very difficult, but that's why I'm so caught up in this genealogy business. I've been researching my husband's family tree, which has made me feel closer to him, you know?'

Isla nodded because she did know. 'That's why I want to find out more about this letter that my gran left behind.'

'You're not ready to let her go yet?' When Isla shook her head, too choked up to speak, Nell reached a hand towards the screen, as if she was sending sparks of empathy across the Atlantic. 'Then, let's see what we can find out about William and Edith. I'd love to know, for me, and for my children, who share a little of William's DNA. Both of my children are grown up now. My daughter's married, with children of her own. She lives not too far away in Chautauqua County.' Chautauqua... Isla let the word rattle around her brain. It sounded so exotic compared to the names of Devon villages. 'My son lives and works in New York City, but he's travelling right now. Anyway, what can I tell you about William Columbus?'

'We know nothing about him, so anything you can tell us will be much appreciated.'

'Sure.' Nell cleared her throat. 'He came up briefly in my research, as my husband's second cousin once removed, but he's a shadowy figure. Jackson's mother had heard a little about him in stories told at Columbus family gatherings. Apparently, he was brought up in New York by his grandmother.'

'Who's mentioned in the letter.'

Nell nodded. 'She is indeed, but I'm afraid the news about William is terribly sad because he died of what sounds like an asthma attack. He had damaged lungs, apparently.'

'Do you know exactly when he died?'

'I do, and that's why reading his letter to Edith was so poignant. He died not very long after writing it, in the winter of 1919. Jackson's mom heard that the cold weather in New York was what carried him off. It did for his grandmother shortly afterwards, too.'

Isla felt her jaw drop. 'That's incredibly sad. According to the letter, they and Edith were all going to move to Florida. Perhaps that was for his health.'

'Very possibly. East Coast winters can be brutal for people with respiratory problems.' Nell shook her head. 'But what about Edith? Your sister said in her email, confirming our online call, that this lady is buried near you and it seems that she and William never married?'

'That seems to be the case. She still had the surname Anstey when she died.'

'When was that?'

'Just a few years later than William, in 1922.'

'No! That's tragic. They were both so young. Much younger than my children.'

'What I can't work out—' Isla began her sentence again. 'One of the *many* things I can't work out, is how he and Edith met in the first place?'

'I'm not entirely sure about that. Trans-Atlantic travel wasn't so popular back then and, unlike my son who's in Europe right now, I doubt that William or his grandmother had the funds to spend time abroad. I'm doing some research to see if he served in World War One and I'm going through old family photos in case he shows up. Do you think Edith maybe did travel back with him to the States in 1919 and their relationship broke up over here?'

'Perhaps, though I've no proof that she did go back with him. Caitlin has been trying to find the passenger list for the *Sylvestria* but no luck so far.'

'What about birth and death certificates?'

'We're trying to track those down too.'

Nell sat back in her chair. 'Well, I wish you luck. Their love story has been lost in the mists of time, which is terribly romantic in its own way. I'm not sure what else I know that can help you, Isla, but—' She stopped and frowned. 'I've just had an idea, actually. I'd like to find out more about William's story, and Edith's as well. She was obviously very special to him and I'd love to know more about where William came to in the UK, all those years ago.'

She sucked her bottom lip between her teeth. 'Tell me if this sounds crazy but, as I say, my son's in Europe. He's been travelling around the south for a few weeks and will be arriving in London early tomorrow, before he heads home for the holidays a few days later. I was wondering, maybe he could call in on you folks, to have a chat about the old days and take some photos of the area for me?'

'Oh.' Isla hesitated. She didn't feel up to entertaining strangers at the moment. 'We're a bit at sixes and sevens here—'

'He wouldn't presume to stay with you,' said Nell. 'He could find his own accommodation. But please don't worry about it. You have far too much to do at the moment, I'm sure, with your grandmother's passing. It was just a thought.'

Isla bit her lip, weighing up the suggestion. Nell was obviously still grieving the loss of her husband and found focusing on his family tree comforting. Perhaps her son's visit to Heaven's Cove would be a distraction for her that would do her good. And maybe she'd find out something else about William that her son could pass on when he came to the village.

Isla made up her mind. 'Do you know what?' she said quickly, before she could change it. 'That would be fine, if your son's happy to visit Heaven's Cove. Can you pass on my email details to him and get him to contact me? What's his name?'

'It's Benjamin – Ben.' Nell's face broke into a wide smile. 'That's wonderful, Isla, thank you. I'm sure Ben would love to walk in the footsteps of his ancestors. I'll get him to mail you. And maybe we can keep in touch too?'

'That would be wonderful. And I wish you the best of luck with your genealogy research.'

'You too.' Nell leaned in closer to the screen. 'And I am *so* sorry for your loss.'

'Thank you. Likewise. Take care.'

Isla clicked off the call and rested her chin on the heels of her hands. Nell seemed like a lovely woman, and she'd learned more about William during their chat – though not enough to solve the riddle and bring her and Caitlin the 'good fortune' their grandmother had promised.

But she was already regretting her impulsive decision to welcome Nell's son to Heaven's Cove. Having Caitlin around was trying enough, with her barbs about Isla not selling Rose Cottage, and Maisie could be challenging. Then there was the huge hole that Jessie's absence had left in her life, and Paul taking umbrage when she dared to communicate with people who didn't actually live in Devon. Isla sighed because he wouldn't be at all happy about Nell's son showing up.

Oh, well. She closed her eyes and tried to relax her tight shoulders. It was done now, so she would show willing and email a list of local guesthouses to Nell, including Driftwood House that sat high on the cliff above the village.

Staying there would give Ben a great view of Heaven's Cove, which was a wonderful place to visit. Isla looked out of the window, at the rain lashing down and the grey clouds sitting on top of the village. Well, maybe it wasn't quite so wonderful in winter. But hopefully Ben's visit would be a fleeting one.

13

CAITLIN

The Smugglers Haunt was a welcome haven from the icy wind that was whipping round Heaven's Cove. Caitlin took off her cashmere scarf – a present from Stuart when their marriage had been on less shaky ground – and tucked it into her jacket pocket.

'Grab a seat by the fire, Isla, and I'll get the drinks in. Martini and lemonade, is it?'

'I haven't drunk Martini since I was sixteen, swigging from a bottle with my friends on the quayside.'

'OK. What would you prefer?'

'White wine, please.'

'Any particular type?'

'Something decent. Not the house white because even Fred admits it's got a vinegary aftertaste. I've no idea why he doesn't change it.'

Isla nodded at Fred, the man who'd been landlord here for ever. He had less hair and more stomach than the last time Caitlin had seen him.

'All right. You grab us a seat and I won't be a minute.'

It was just like old times, thought Caitlin, hanging her

jacket on the coat stand and making her way to the bar. The place smelled the same – a heady aroma of alcohol fumes and smoke from the fire. The pub hadn't changed in centuries: the wooden counter of the bar, the whitewashed walls laden with horse brasses, the low ceiling and wide stone window ledges. But there were a few modern touches including the gleaming optics behind the bar that was festooned with fairy lights, and a neon sign declaring CHRISTMAS PARTY. GET YOUR TICKETS HERE.

Christmas! It was approaching fast but Caitlin had never felt less festive in her life. Where would she and Maisie be when the 25th of December hit – in their comfortable house in London, or in some rental dive, God knows where? Would she even be able to afford a decent Christmas present for her step-daughter?

Caitlin, realising that her life was out of her control, felt a gnawing rush of anxiety. What happened next depended on either Stuart getting his act together and saving their home, or on Isla selling the only home she'd known for the last twenty years.

'All right, Caitlin?'

A voice sounded across the pub, from a woman Caitlin vaguely recognised from her teenage days. She gave her a smile and a wave, unable to recall her name, even though she'd never forget the hours spent in here – mostly drinking lemonade or Coke because it was impossible to wangle an alcoholic drink when everyone in the village knew you were underage.

She'd made up for it on her eighteenth birthday, of course, with plenty of alcohol, and she could well recall how ill she'd been afterwards. Sean had held back her hair while she was sick over the harbour wall.

Caitlin shook her head to wipe away any thoughts of Sean, who hadn't been around when she'd collected her car that afternoon. There was a note stuck to the dashboard, in handwriting she recognised as his.

Fixed and ready to drive back to your London life.

Was she being over-sensitive or was that a dig? If so, though it might be warranted, it was ridiculous to bear a grudge after so many years. True, she hadn't treated Sean very well. But the two of them had been very young and what was he expecting? That they'd get married and live happily ever after? Caitlin sighed because her union with Stuart was living proof that this was not a realistic notion.

'Well, look who it is! Welcome back to Heaven's Cove,' said Fred, pushing a pint across the bar, towards the customer he was serving. 'Back because of your gran, are you? We were all very sorry to hear that she's gone.'

'Absolutely,' said the customer next to her, who was already sipping at his pint, froth coating his upper lip.

'Thank you. We both miss her.'

'How's Isla doing?' Fred asked after Caitlin had ordered her drinks. 'She's been a saint, that girl, looking after Jessie as she got more frail and unwell.'

'She's sad, obviously, but I think she's OK.'

'Hmm.' Fred gave her a straight stare. 'Are you here for long?' he asked, taking the twenty-pound note Caitlin proffered and counting out the change into her palm.

'I'm not sure. Hopefully not.'

That came out rather more bluntly than she'd intended, and Fred scowled as he dropped a final pound coin into her hand. It was obvious what he thought of her. What had he heard about her over the years? she wondered. Were her no-shows in Heaven's Cove the talk of the village? *'Jessie took those girls in and only one has stuck around to look after her.'* Or was she so insignificant around here, no one really cared about her at all?

Caitlin picked up her drinks and made her way over to Isla, who'd chosen a table almost on top of the fire. She pulled her jumper over her head and sat down, far enough from the fire not to be roasted by it.

'He's not here yet then?'

'I don't think so. I can't see anyone new.' Isla checked her watch. 'He hasn't let me know that anything's changed since I emailed suggesting we meet here at seven.'

'Has he got a car?'

'I think so. He was planning on hiring one at Heathrow.'

'And did he say where he's staying?'

'No, but I suggested Driftwood House.'

Caitlin frowned. 'That road to the top of the cliff, if you can even call it a road, isn't great at this time of year.'

Isla shrugged. 'He's been travelling across Europe for a few weeks. I'm sure he can manage a steep incline and a few potholes. And the view from up there is magnificent. I want him to see Heaven's Cove at its finest.'

Caitlin ignored the urge to ask why and said, instead: 'Let me see the first email he sent again.'

Isla handed over her phone and Caitlin re-read it.

Isla – my mom's insisting I should pay Heaven's Cove a visit and speak to you while I'm there. I arrive in London tomorrow, Thursday morning. Would that evening be acceptable to meet?

Ben Columbus

He didn't sound overjoyed to be paying Heaven's Cove a visit, and while Caitlin sympathised, she was also irritated by his abrupt tone. She had better things to be doing than talking to some random American in a village pub.

But there were two good reasons for being in The Smugglers Haunt tonight: one, Paul had insisted on coming along with Isla, until Caitlin had stepped in as chaperone. Quite what he thought Ben was going to do to her sister in the middle of The Smugglers Haunt was a mystery. He seemed to have taken against Ben simply because he was American.

And two – though it was a long shot – maybe there was something to Jessie's riddle, after all. Perhaps there was some financial 'good fortune' attached to solving the mystery of William and Edith's wedding that never was. If so, Caitlin could certainly do with the money. Her faith in Stuart putting things right was beginning to waver.

'What's the matter?' asked Isla, frowning as she leaned across the table.

'What do you mean? Nothing. I'm fine.' Caitlin rearranged her features into their usual bland expression that gave nothing away. She wasn't about to start chipping away at the façade of her perfect life in the middle of The Smugglers Haunt. 'I can't believe Fred's putting the Christmas decs up already,' she said as a distraction, nodding at the garlanded tree in the corner. 'It's not even December yet.'

'It will be soon though, and on Sunday it'll be Gran's birthday. Her ninetieth, if she'd made it that far. You were invited.'

Isla's lips pursed while Caitlin wondered if she would have come back for her grandmother's ninetieth celebration. She'd have sent flowers and a generous gift, that's for sure. But would she have made the effort to actually turn up? Tears prickled her eyes. 'We should celebrate such a special birthday anyway,' she said. 'We can celebrate having Gran in our lives and all that she did for us.'

Isla swallowed. 'Actually, that's a lovely idea.' She looked up at Caitlin from under her long eyelashes. 'If you're still around, that is.'

'I'll make sure I am,' Caitlin assured her. Maisie wouldn't

like it, but this was one last thing she could do for her grandmother.

Isla narrowed her eyes, as if she didn't know whether to believe her sister or not. Then, her gaze shifted over Caitlin's shoulder.

'I think he's here,' she hissed as Caitlin felt a draught on the back of her neck. When she turned, a big bear of a man in blue jeans and a charcoal-grey jacket was standing in the doorway. He pushed both hands through his thick, dark hair, which was damp from the drizzle outside, and, when Caitlin caught his eye, he made his way across the crowded pub towards them.

'Which one of you is Isla?' he asked on reaching them.

'That's me. Hello.' Isla stretched her hand across the table for Ben to shake it. 'And this is my sister, Caitlin.'

Ben's hand was wet with rain and Caitlin noticed Isla surreptitiously rubbing her fingers along the thigh of her jeans, beneath the table.

'So you're Ben.' Caitlin nodded at the chair opposite her. 'Would you like to take a seat?'

'Sure, might as well.'

He took off his jacket and draped it on the back of the chair before sitting down. 'Well. Here we are.' He breathed out slowly. 'It's a pleasure to meet you both.'

Caitlin, used to her husband's half-truths, recognised a lie when she heard one. She smiled sweetly. 'You too.'

'It was good of you to break into your travels to come to Heaven's Cove,' said Isla.

Caitlin's phone suddenly began to ring and she fumbled for it in her pocket, as people at the bar turned to look at her. It was Stuart, and he might have news.

'Please excuse me but I have to take this,' said Caitlin, ignoring Isla's wide-eyed stare. Her sister would have to deal with this reluctant visitor on her own. Paul would have a fit, but what he didn't know wouldn't upset him.

'Hey,' said Caitlin, after answering the call. 'Hold on a minute.' Pushing her way through the throng at the bar, she made her way to a corner of the pub which was quieter. 'What's going on, Stuart? You haven't been answering my calls or replying to my texts.'

'I've been busy, Cait. I know you think this work conference is a jolly because it's in Gran Canaria, but it's exhausting, actually.'

'So you haven't managed to get to the beach or golf course then?'

He paused. 'I have, but not for long. Anyway, where are you?'

'I'm still in Heaven's Cove.'

'With Maisie?'

'Of course with Maisie.' Did he think she'd abandoned his daughter on the side of the road somewhere? 'It might be nice if you texted her some time. She's been asking after you and I didn't know what to say.'

'Have you told her what's going on?'

'No, because I wanted to give you a chance to put things right first. Like you said, she might never need to know what you've done.' When Stuart fell silent, Caitlin prompted: 'So *does* she need to know?'

A long sigh echoed down the line and Caitlin's heart sank.

'I'm not sure how to tell you this.'

'You've definitely lost the house,' said Caitlin dully. 'Our home is gone.'

'It wasn't my fault, Cait.'

'Then whose fault is it?' Caitlin blinked furiously, determined not to cry. She'd tried so hard to balance her anger and feeling of betrayal with understanding that Stuart might need help. But he'd promised so much and here they were, losing everything.

'I made a few bad calls. That's all. I'm the victim here. Fate has conspired against me.'

'*You* conspired against you, Stuart. It's you who lost the money through your irresponsible gambling, and it's you who's left your daughter without a roof over her head.'

'These people I owe money to, they're not to be messed with,' said Stuart, the hint of a whine in his voice. 'I'd get out of it if I could but I can't so the house will have to be sold right away, and that's that.'

'To pay off the debts that you've built up.'

'There's no need to rub it in. I know it's difficult and I appreciate you standing by me.'

'You appreciate it?' Caitlin was beginning to feel shaky. 'I've been as understanding and supportive as I can be over the last few months, since I found out what was going on. But you've lied to me over and over again. You told me you were getting help, which was a lie. You promised me you weren't gambling any more, which was also a lie. What else are you lying to me about?'

'Nothing. I've lost the house. I know that's bad—'

'Bad?' A sob caught in Caitlin's throat.

'Don't guilt-trip me, Cait.' Stuart's tone had changed from contrite to belligerent. 'I'll get the money back.'

'How? More gambling?'

'No, of course not.'

'How then?'

'I'll find a way.'

Caitlin rubbed a hand across her forehead which was beginning to ache. 'Will you at least get yourself some help?'

'Come on, Cait, I don't need any help from do-gooding professionals offering counselling. Losing the house is just the jolt I needed to get my life back on track. So it's good, in a way, if you look at it from a different perspective.'

Caitlin closed her eyes and breathed out slowly.

'Is there anything else you need to tell me? Because now's the time. I really can't take any more surprises.'

'There's nothing else I've kept from you, I swear. Are you coming back?'

'How can I, after all of the lies you've told me?'

'I lied about the money because I thought I could stop what was happening. And I know I've messed up big time. But I'm all right now. Our life can go back to the way it was.' He sniffed. 'Eventually.'

Caitlin shook her head. Her husband was still in denial and she didn't know how she felt about him any more.

'I've got to go, Stuart.' She couldn't continue this conversation. It was too painful.

'I'm sorry,' were Stuart's final words before she ended the call.

Caitlin shoved the phone into her pocket, her mind spooling back to when she and Stuart had first met. He was a businessman – nine years older than her – and had seemed immensely debonair and self-assured to a lacking in confidence twenty-nine-year-old. So self-sufficient and cool – the kind of man who would never need looking after. The kind of man who might look after her instead.

And they'd been happy at first, as they became a ready-made family – the two of them and Maisie, who'd been just nine years old when Caitlin had come into her life. Becoming a surrogate mother in one fell swoop had been a shock because it had reminded Caitlin of the responsibility she'd felt for Isla from a young age. She didn't think she'd be able to cope with looking after another child, but she had and she'd grown to care deeply about Maisie, even if the stroppy teenager would never believe that.

So what should she do now? Her marriage with Stuart was battered and bruised, but how could she leave him when he was in the grip of a gambling addiction? What kind of a woman would that make her? The answer came back loud and clear: the kind of woman who left her sister and grandmother behind, and hardly ever visited.

Caitlin leaned against the stone wall of the pub, her legs feeling like jelly. Her life was a complete mess and she had no one to turn to for help, support and sympathy. She'd lost her true friends over the years, as her life had changed, and she'd burned her bridges with her family. Isla, with good reason, thought she was a money-grabber who couldn't be trusted. And Jessie, the generous grandmother who had taken them in when no one else had wanted them, was gone for ever.

An image of Jessie wishing her goodnight and kissing her on both cheeks swam into Caitlin's mind and the sudden rush of grief she experienced felt like a punch to the stomach.

She leaned forward, trying to catch her breath. She hadn't had a panic attack in years, not since her first months at university. But she recognised the familiar feeling of pins and needles as black spots began to dance before her eyes. She was going to collapse right here in the pub. She was going to die.

'Breathe, Cait!' A hand was on her shoulder and a deep voice sounded in her ear. 'Deep breaths. In for four and out for six. In, two, three, four, and out, two, three, four, five, six.'

Caitlin felt as if a heavy weight was crushing her chest but she focused on the calm voice and tried to breathe more deeply as the counting continued, low and steady. And gradually the panic began to ease and the weight began to lift. She began to feel safer.

'Sorry,' she managed at last, pulling air into her lungs. 'Sorry. So sorry.'

'It's all right. Just keep breathing, slow and steady.'

Caitlin looked up into Sean's piercing blue eyes. His hand was still resting on her shoulder.

'Sorry.' All she could do was apologise.

'Do you need a drink? Water or something?'

Caitlin shook her head, her breathing starting to return to normal. The dizziness that had made her head swim was also easing.

'I'm starting to feel better.' She gulped in more air and made an effort to pull herself together. 'What are you doing here?'

Sean let go of her shoulder. 'I was over there, having a drink with some workmates, when I saw you taking a phone call.'

'Did you hear any of it?' asked Caitlin, glancing at the corner where a small group was sitting watching her, the crazy woman having a panic attack.

'Not really. But I could see you were upset. Who was on the phone?'

'My husband.' Caitlin glanced again at Sean's colleagues. She recognised a couple of men from the garage. And Jen. Sean was out having a drink with his wife and didn't need to be dealing with an old girlfriend who was still being a pain, several years on. 'I got in a spin about nothing,' she said, standing up straight. 'But it's all sorted now and I'm sorry for causing such a fuss.'

'It's all right,' said Sean mildly, searching her face with his eyes. 'Are you sure you're all right?'

'Absolutely.' Caitlin tried to sound bright and brisk. 'I think I'm still grieving for my grandmother and I over-reacted to something. But I'm fine now. Honestly. So, thanks very much but I'd better be going. Maisie needs me.'

She turned and strode quickly past the bar until she reached the door. Isla would kill her but she couldn't stay. Not now.

Caitlin grabbed her jacket from the coat stand and paused, her hand on the door latch, until she caught Isla's attention. Her sister was listening to Ben, seemingly calm and attentive, but her body language – all folded arms and crossed legs – told another story. She was nervous and waiting for Caitlin to come back. But that couldn't happen.

'I have to go,' Caitlin mouthed. 'Sorry.'

Isla, still listening to her American visitor, widened her eyes and shook her head, but Caitlin couldn't stay. 'I'm really sorry,' she said, before pushing open the door and rushing outside. She gulped in deep breaths of cold, damp air as she moved quickly through the dark streets of Heaven's Cove towards Rose Cottage.

She'd abandoned Isla again, and she felt wretched about it, but she'd had to get away. She'd had to get away from the memories that threatened to overwhelm her. She stopped at the quayside for a moment and took deep breaths, watching the grey sea swell against the wall and retreat. The never-ending push and pull was soothing and, after a few minutes, the panic she was feeling began to subside.

She turned and started walking again for home. She felt different – as if the wall she'd built around her had been torn away and now everything could hurt her. She picked up her pace and hurried on because all she craved was the comfort of Rose Cottage where, long ago, before she'd messed everything up, she'd been loved and safe.

14

ISLA

Isla could hardly believe her eyes. Caitlin was leaving – her hopeless, unsupportive sister was ditching her. Again.

Isla shook her head, trying not to make her gesture too obvious to Ben, but it did no good. Caitlin simply mouthed 'I'm really sorry', as if that made everything all right, and stepped out of the pub door, into the rain.

'Is everything OK?' asked Ben, his soft drawl competing with the crackle of the fire nearby. The two of them had been making excruciating small talk for the last five minutes, waiting for Caitlin to come back.

'Yes, everything's fine,' said Isla, her voice too high. 'So how long was your flight delayed in all?'

'Three hours. I told you.' Ben sat back in his chair and gave Isla a straight look. His thick hair had dried into spikes where he'd pushed his fingers through his fringe. 'Look, let's get on with this. Is your sister coming back?'

'Um... I don't think so. She had to go.'

'Really?' He glanced over his shoulder, as if Isla was kidding him. 'Well, if we're not waiting for her, I need a drink. What would you like?'

'I'm so sorry. I should have got you one,' said Isla, feeling flustered and starting to get to her feet. But Ben had beaten her to it and was already standing in front of her. When Isla looked up, she felt her neck crick into a painful spasm because she was so tense.

'Don't worry about it,' he said languidly as Isla rubbed her neck muscles. 'Another white wine, is it?'

He nodded at Isla's glass, which she'd drained, hardly tasting the wine at all as she made awkward conversation with a stranger and willed her sister to come back.

'Yes, thanks. Though, actually...' Isla hesitated. White wine was Paul's drink of choice and he took a dim view of drinking anything else. But he wasn't here and she could have whatever she wanted. 'Actually,' she said, feeling rebellious, 'I'll have a Martini and lemonade, if you don't mind.'

'Why on earth would I mind?' asked Ben, raising an eyebrow. 'With any luck, I won't be long.'

Isla watched him as he made his way to the bar. It was obvious that he wasn't from around these parts. His glowing tan stood out amongst pasty-faced villagers and the weather-beaten faces of those who manned fishing boats. He was wearing blue jeans, a long-sleeved burgundy T-shirt and tan hiking boots. He seemed exotic, somehow – well-travelled and worldly wise, albeit a bit grumpy.

He chatted to Fred at the bar and glanced round at Isla a couple of times. What was Fred telling him? she wondered. Did Fred think the two of them were here on a date? Would he say anything about it to Paul? Paul would go bananas if he knew the two of them were here on their own, though Isla wasn't sure why.

He worried about her too much, and, actually, it felt rather nice to be sitting alone in the pub while Ben got her a Martini. She never came to The Smugglers Haunt on her own these days, not since she and Paul had become an item eighteen months earlier.

Isla switched her gaze from the bar to the fire crackling behind her and watched the orange flames leaping up high. Paul loved her, even though she drove him mad sometimes with her forgetfulness. He could be a tad overwhelming at times, but, all in all, she was a very fortunate woman, she decided.

'There you go, one Martini and lemonade.' Ben put the drink down in front of her, slid back into his seat and placed his beer on the table. 'Thought I'd treat myself to a pint of Old Peculier. The landlord recommended it.' He took a sip and licked his upper lip. 'Nice. Anyway, let's cut to the chase, shall we, Isla? I was hoping to be riding the London Eye round about now but I was told by my mom that you wanted to see me?'

'Well, not exactly... I mean, I didn't...'

Isla stopped speaking and took a deep breath. Ben didn't look overjoyed to be sitting in a rainy corner of Devon, rather than marvelling at the bright lights of the capital laid out before him.

'When did you actually arrive in Heaven's Cove?' she asked, hoping to ease into the conversation about why his plans had been upended.

'An hour ago. I was expecting to arrive mid-afternoon at the latest, only I hadn't factored in the traffic jams I'd encounter on the way. I can't believe how much traffic you have on such a tiny island.'

He frowned at Isla, as if the state of Britain's roads were entirely down to her.

She gave a deliberately warm smile back. 'The roads down here can get busy in summer, but in winter it's not usually so bad. Are you staying at Driftwood House?'

Ben nodded. 'It seems like a nice place.'

'It does have a lovely view.'

'I wouldn't know. The clouds are so low, I can hardly see my hand in front of my face. And the road up to the house is shocking. It didn't do my rental car any good whatsoever.'

Isla sighed quietly, wishing that Nell had never suggested to her son that he journey to Heaven's Cove. The sooner they discussed his ancestor, William, and he beat a hasty retreat back to London, the better.

'So what exactly did your mum tell you about me?' she asked, taking a sip of Martini and relishing its familiar, sweet taste.

'She said you were researching an ancestor of yours who had some dealings with one of my ancestors, a guy named William who was a distant cousin of mine. My mom is very into family research right now and wanted me to see what this place is like for myself. My feet standing in the same spot where William once stood... that kind of thing. Only I don't think she realised that Heaven's Cove isn't right next door to London.'

'Your mom... I mean, mum... was really nice when I spoke to her. She was intrigued by William's story, like me, and she suggested that you might want to...'

Isla stopped speaking because it was abundantly clear that Ben didn't want to. He regarded her with his grey eyes, the colour of a winter sea. 'Yeah, well, I'm here now so why don't you show me this letter. Mom said you had a letter from William?'

'I do.' Isla searched in her handbag for the envelope. 'It was left to me by my grandmother who died recently.'

'Oh.' Ben puffed air into his cheeks. 'I didn't realise you'd suffered a bereavement. I'm sorry for your loss. My father—' He stopped speaking and bit his lip.

'Your mum told me that your dad had passed away, last year.'

Ben swallowed, distress flitting across his face. 'Mom's taken it hard, and she's become caught up with finding out more about Dad's family. A little obsessed, really.'

'Perhaps delving into your dad's family tree is her way of still feeling anchored to him. She probably feels there's a huge hole in her life now that link to such a significant person has been severed.' Isla had felt the same way since Jessie had died – adrift with no anchor in the sea of life. Buffeted by the waves, with no sense of direction.

'Maybe you're right.' Ben tilted his head and caught her eye until she looked away. 'Anyway...' He ran his hand across the faint stubble on his chin. 'Where's this letter I've been told about?'

'Oh yes.' Isla pulled it from her bag, took the precious piece of paper from its envelope and passed it to Ben, who read through it quietly. Then he folded the letter and passed it back.

'So William was sweet on Edith, who apparently changed her mind about marrying him. Do you know why she didn't travel to the States with him?'

'We're not one hundred per cent sure yet that she didn't. Caitlin is checking out trans-Atlantic passenger lists.'

'But Mom said she's buried here and she wasn't married.'

The way he said it was so matter-of-fact, it rankled with Isla. This was a woman's life he was talking about so disinter-estedly.

'That appears to be the case. Perhaps when your cousin arrived, Edith realised he wasn't such a great catch after all.' Ben leaned back in his chair and folded his arms. 'Or maybe she didn't want to leave Heaven's Cove behind.'

Ben looked out of the window, at the rain drops running down the glass and the tendrils of mist curling around the pub. 'That can't be the reason, surely.'

'Who knows? Anyway, I imagine it was very sad for William, and for Edith, too. She died a few years later and her gravestone says she died of a broken heart.'

'That sounds very dramatic but this was back in the early

twentieth century, right? Before the discovery of antibiotics. So Edith just as likely died of a bacterial infection.'

'The last of the great romantics, are you?'

When Isla raised an eyebrow, Ben actually smiled, his first smile since arriving in the pub. 'I can be romantic when I want to be – when the occasion calls for it. What about you?'

Isla blinked, not sure how the conversation had taken such a personal turn so quickly.

'I'm in a long-term relationship. Well, long-ish. Eighteen months. With Paul. He runs his own business, doing logistics.' Was it *doing* logistics? That didn't sound right. And what if Ben asked what exactly he did at work? Though Paul had talked about it at length, she was still none the wiser. Isla winced and ploughed on. 'He would have come tonight only Caitlin said she'd come with me instead, but then she... um...'

Ben grimaced. 'Then she took one look at me and decided against it?'

'I'm sure Caitlin had her reasons and that wasn't one of them,' said Isla with a smile, even though mentioning her sister had reminded her that she'd quite like to kill her for leaving her alone with this prickly stranger.

Ben drained the last of his pint and licked froth from his upper lip. 'So what happens now, with the Edith-William mystery? I don't suppose we'll ever know the truth of what happened when William arrived in this very dank, very cold little village.'

Dank? 'We're getting hold of Edith's death certificate, which might at least tell us why she died,' replied Isla, ignoring Ben's withering description of the place she called home. When a silence stretched between them, Isla added: 'Are you heading for London tomorrow?'

'That's the plan. Back to the bright lights before my flight home early on Sunday.'

'Right.' Isla hesitated a moment, wondering if she'd be crazy to propose the idea that had just popped into her head. She pictured Nell's friendly, helpful face and made up her mind. 'Only, it's supposed to be sunny here tomorrow and I could show you round the village, so you could get some photos for your mum.'

She didn't want this irritating American to go home with a bad impression of Heaven's Cove. It seemed important, for some reason, that he see the village in its full glory.

'Um...' Ben seemed non-plussed by her suggestion.

'I could meet you at Driftwood House at ten tomorrow and give you a guided tour of the local sights.'

Isla felt hot all of a sudden. What if Ben thought she was doing this as some sort of come-on because she fancied him? He was nice enough looking, with his broad shoulders and dark hair that shone chestnut under the lights, but his good looks were countered by his unfortunate personality. She thought he was being unnecessarily abrupt. After all, it hadn't been her idea that he journey to Heaven's Cove and he should have said no to his mother if he was that upset about the whole idea.

'A guided tour?' Ben stared at her.

'Yeah, but I'm sure you have to get back to London before—'

'OK.'

Isla stopped speaking. 'OK, what?'

'OK, why not have a look around this place, now I'm here. And I have no urge to spend two days in a row stuck in a traffic jam going nowhere.' He got to his feet. 'Ten o'clock it is then, Isla. I'm heading off 'cos I'm beat, but it was good to meet you.'

Was he being sarcastic? Did Americans even *do* sarcasm like the Brits? Isla decided to treat his comment as sincere, so she smiled at him and said: 'Likewise. I look forward to seeing you tomorrow.'

She wasn't looking forward to it at all. She should never have suggested it. But the deed was done and she'd make the best of tomorrow's tour... and hope Paul wouldn't kick off about it.

'Oh, Gran,' Isla murmured as Ben walked away, her face flushed from the flames crackling behind her. 'What on earth have you started with your mysterious letter and riddle?'

But there was nothing else for it. She would show Ben around Heaven's Cove tomorrow so he could get some photos for his mother, and then she would very happily wave him goodbye.

15

ISLA

'Come on in, quick,' said Rosie, ushering Isla through the front door of Driftwood House and closing it behind her. 'It's absolutely freezing out there today.'

'Thanks,' said Isla, her cheeks burning after walking so swiftly up the steep cliff path. 'I'm here to meet Ben, the American bloke you've got staying.'

'Is he expecting you?'

'We agreed to meet here at ten.' Isla glanced at her watch. She was a few minutes early but she'd got the impression last night that Ben wouldn't take well to being kept waiting. 'I said I'd show him around the village.'

'You'll both freeze, but that's nice.'

When Rosie gave a smile that made her russet-brown eyes twinkle, Isla was reminded again how much she liked this woman who'd run Driftwood guesthouse since returning to the village from her life in Spain. And how touched she'd been by her kindness after Jessie had died.

She remembered the knock on the front door, while she'd been waiting for Caitlin to arrive. Still numb with shock, she'd pulled the door open to find Rosie, carrying a large casserole dish.

'I heard about Jessie and I'm so sorry,' she'd said, pushing the dish towards Isla. 'There's nothing I can say to make you feel better right now, but you need to eat. You won't feel like it. I didn't, after my mum died. I almost wasted away. But being weak from hunger just makes everything worse, believe me. And there's no need to return the dish. Look after yourself, and I'm around if you'd ever like some company.'

With that, she'd turned on her heel and left, which Isla had appreciated. Other villagers had descended over the ensuing days and stayed far too long, needing cups of tea and biscuits, and lots of sympathy as if it was their grandmother who'd just passed away.

'How are things going at Rose Cottage?' Rosie asked, with a sympathetic tilt of her head.

'Oh, you know. It's strange without Gran but we're getting used to her not being around.'

'It takes time.' A frown crossed Rosie's face and then was gone. 'I heard on the village grapevine that you have your sister staying from London.'

'That's right, and my niece.'

'That must be comforting for you.'

'Mmm,' said Isla, feeling her jaw tighten.

She was still smarting from Caitlin abandoning her in the pub last night and her sister's muttered apology and explanation at breakfast this morning – something about not feeling well – hadn't helped. There was obviously something going on that Isla didn't know about, and she felt hurt that Caitlin wasn't willing to confide in her. Hurt, but not surprised.

Rosie smiled. 'Anyway, I expect they'll be heading back home quite soon.'

'I expect so,' said Isla, though she had no idea when they were leaving.

Maisie was champing at the bit to go but Caitlin seemed more reluctant all of a sudden. That was possibly because she had a growing interest in Edith and William's story. But Isla couldn't shake the feeling that there was money involved in her sister's decision to stick around. Caitlin either thought she could persuade her to sell Rose Cottage, which wasn't going to happen. Or she was holding out for the 'good fortune' mentioned in their grandmother's riddle – which wouldn't be anything financial, Isla was sure.

'Can I get you a cup of tea while you're waiting?' asked Rosie. 'Or a hot chocolate, to warm you up? You're going to need it out there.'

'That's really kind of you but I expect Ben will be ready any minute.'

'He's an interesting man, don't you think? And well-travelled. He was telling me about his trip to India last year, which sounded amazing.'

Had he been to India? Isla had always wanted to explore the backwaters of Kerala and bathe in the Arabian Sea. She could almost feel the heat of the sun on her skin and smell frankincense and sandalwood.

'Have you ever been to India?' she asked Rosie.

'No, afraid not, but Liam and I are still owed a proper honeymoon, so who knows, maybe some day?'

Rosie smiled and twirled the shiny gold ring on her fourth finger.

She and local farmer Liam had been married for a few months now and had thrown a fabulous post-wedding party in a marquee up here on the cliff. It was one of the last events that Jessie had been to before her death and Isla had happy memories of her grandmother having fun with people who'd been friends for years. It had been an excellent final hurrah, before her sudden decline.

Isla swallowed and tried to focus on the grandfather clock in the corner of the hall, which was ticking loudly.

Rosie, always empathetic, gave Isla's arm a comforting pat. 'How about I give Ben a call? Just in case he's forgotten—' She glanced at the top of the wide staircase that led up from the tiled hallway. 'No need because here he is now.'

Ben had just appeared on the landing in his donkey jacket, with a navy-blue scarf wrapped around his neck.

'Hi there, Isla. You're here already,' he said, walking downstairs. 'Are you sure you still want to show me around?'

Isla wasn't sure at all, not after Paul had gone into a sulk and deemed it another of her Bad Ideas. But she smiled and told him, 'I'm happy with it if you are.'

Ben didn't look particularly happy but he nodded. 'Might as well, seeing as the fog's lifted this morning.' He gave Rosie a smile. 'Thanks again for an awesome breakfast. I could get used to a Full English.'

Rosie beamed. 'You're very welcome. Maybe you can have one tomorrow, too, if you have time before you head for London?'

He nodded. 'I'm here until a quarter after nine so that would be wonderful, thank you.'

Rosie stood aside to let Ben walk past and raised her eyebrows at Isla as he opened the door and stepped outside. Was she implying that Isla was fortunate to be spending the day with a big, burly American, or was she wishing her luck? Isla bid Rosie goodbye and followed Ben out into the chilly air.

He'd already walked off and went straight to the edge of the cliff, where he stood looking out to sea, his hands on his hips.

'Wow,' he said when Isla joined him. 'I gotta admit that's quite a view.'

'Is it the first time you've seen it?'

'The first time I've seen it properly. It was shrouded in mist yesterday and my room is at the back of Driftwood House so I'm looking over to... some moor in the distance, rather than the ocean.'

'Dartmoor.'

'Dart what?'

'The moor is called Dartmoor and it's a shame you're not staying longer in the area because it's well worth a visit. Acres of grassland, topped by ancient tors.'

'And tors are what, exactly?'

'Raised outcrops of granite.' Isla shrugged. 'They look better than they sound. They're awesome, actually.'

Was awesome a particularly American word? Isla wondered. Would Ben think she was taking the mick? She glanced at him but he was still looking out over the water, which, today, was a translucent blue. Surging waves were crashing into the base of the cliffs and shooting pearly plumes into the air.

'Mom would like this,' said Ben quietly, pulling out his phone to take a few photos. 'Dad too.'

Photos captured, he put his phone back into his jeans pocket and pulled a beanie hat from his jacket. 'OK. What other gems have you got to show me in Heaven's Cove?' When he shoved the hat onto his head, curls of dark hair peeped out.

'Well, I thought we'd start with the castle,' said Isla, banging her gloved hands together to help keep them warm.

Ben laughed, his teeth bright against the cornflower-blue sky. 'There's a real life castle here?'

'Yes, but only the ruins of one, obviously.'

'Obviously.' Ben shook his head. 'So when does this castle date from?'

'There's an information board you can read when we get there but I know the oldest part, the keep, was built in the thirteenth century.'

'So it's eight hundred years old?' Ben whistled through his

teeth. 'You certainly know how to do history over here.' He peered at Heaven's Cove far below them – a tumble of white-washed cottages hugging the coast, with the squat tower of St Augustine's Church at its centre.

'This whole freaking place is like a museum,' said Ben, shielding his eyes against the bright sun. 'Where I live, buildings just a few centuries old are thought to be ancient.'

'In that case, St Augustine's Church, which dates back to the tenth century, is going to blow your mind.'

Isla had been apprehensive about the tour and kicking herself for suggesting it in the first place. But actually, once the initial meet-up was over, and the tour proper began, the awkwardness she felt with Ben began to fade. This was helped immeasurably by Ben being less of an arse than he'd been the day before.

This morning, after a night's sleep, he seemed less obviously irritated about being in Heaven's Cove in the first place. And he appeared genuinely interested in the village's 'best bits' that Isla showed him: the castle ruins; the quayside where bright fishing boats bobbed on the water; the narrow streets crammed with cottages and gift shops; the wooded headland stretching out into the sea, and the cliff that towered over the village, on top of which stood Driftwood House.

He was particularly interested in St Augustine's and he took photos of Edith's gravestone to show his mum, even though he said it was ghoulish. In fact, he took so many pictures of the village, Isla began to worry he'd run out of space on his phone.

After two hours, and dozens of photos, the chill wind was beginning to bite through Isla's thick gloves, and she suggested they head to The Heavenly Tea Shop to thaw out.

'Just so long as I don't have to drink tea,' Ben insisted. 'I don't know how you all get through so much of the stuff. I'm a coffee man myself, the stronger the better.'

'Drinking tea isn't obligatory in Devon,' Isla assured him, leading the way to the bustling café, which was strung with bunting and fairy lights.

It was busier than usual inside but Isla managed to bag a table near the door. The plate-glass window was misted with condensation and Isla noticed, with a start, the shopping bags on the floor. Many of them sported Christmas logos, and two people were decorating a fir tree in a corner.

'You OK?' Ben asked, wrapping his hands around the steaming mug of coffee that had just arrived for him.

'Yeah, fine.' Isla pushed a spoon into the cream on top of her hot chocolate but didn't eat it. She didn't fancy it any more.

'Are you sure you're all right?' Ben leaned across the table towards her. 'You look a bit off.'

Isla carefully placed the laden spoon on her saucer. 'It's nothing, really. I just saw all the festive bags in here, and the tree over there, and it made me think about Christmas without my gran.'

Ben nodded. 'Yeah, I expect it'll be tough. I know my mom's dreading the holidays without Dad around. Me, too, really, even though he's been gone a while now. Dad was always the life and soul of the party and it's too quiet without him.' He gazed into the distance for a moment before asking, 'Will your sister be around for Christmas?'

'Caitlin?' Isla gave a wry smile. 'I doubt it. She and Maisie, her stepdaughter, will be leaving Heaven's Cove soon and they won't be back.'

'Will they visit on New Year's?'

'No, they won't be back at all,' said Isla, who felt sure she wouldn't see Caitlin for dust once she realised there was no chance of Rose Cottage being sold.

Ben winced. 'I see. So, I guess you'll be in the house on your own for the holidays.'

'Yeah, but it won't be so bad.' She smiled. 'Paul will be there, of course, though he doesn't really approve of Christmas.'

'He doesn't really approve of Christmas?' repeated Ben. He took a sip of his coffee and wrinkled his nose. 'That's... surprising.'

'Well, it's not Christmas per se that he doesn't approve of. It's the commercialism that goes with it, so we won't be buying each other gifts.'

'That's a shame.'

'Not really. I know what he means,' said Isla loyally, even though the thought of a gift-free Christmas made her feel sad. She'd suggested they stick to a small budget or even make each other something – she wasn't sure what – but her suggestions had been dismissed. Paul didn't approve of St Valentine's Day either, which he claimed was 'a cynical ploy to make money through playing on the emotions'. Isla knew what he meant, but she'd still have liked a card on the 14th of February.

'You don't need flowers to know how much I adore you,' Paul had told her. 'You're mine, Isla.' And she'd nodded in agreement, even though a bunch of roses would have been nice, all the same.

Ben reached into the pocket of his jeans for his phone, which had just beeped with a notification.

'It's an email from Mom,' he said. 'She says she hopes I'm enjoying seeing Heaven's Cove... oh, she's found out that William served over here in World War One. She's been digging through Dad's old family photos and has found this.'

He passed his phone over for Isla to look at the picture his mother had sent. A handsome young man in a drab military jacket stared back at her. He wasn't smiling but there was still a sparkle in his eyes. The message from Nell underneath said: *writing on back says 'William, France 1918'. I reckon it's him!*

'What do you think?' asked Ben, leaning across the table.

Isla handed the phone back. 'That's amazing to actually see the man who wrote the letter. And if he was serving in France, maybe that's how he met Edith.'

'Perhaps he came to England on leave.'

Isla sucked her bottom lip between her teeth, as she often did when she was thinking. Though she was trying to break the habit because it appeared to irritate Paul.

'But why would he have come to Heaven's Cove? It's not exactly on the way to anywhere.'

'Tell me about it.' Ben raised an eyebrow. 'I'll do some googling to see if I can find out more about Americans serving in France during the war.'

Isla suppressed a smile because Ben was becoming interested in William and Edith's romance in spite of himself. 'Can you send me that photo so I can show it to Caitlin?'

'Sure.' He forwarded the email and pushed his phone back into his pocket.

'So, what will you do at Christmas?' Isla asked, feeling more relaxed in Ben's company now and wanting to hear more about his life and travels.

'I'll go and visit my mom and see my sister and her family and I'll eat too much and drink too much and then it'll be back to work. We don't have... Boxing Day, do you call it? I'll probably be straight back into the office on December twenty-sixth.'

'I don't know what job you do.'

'I work in real estate, helping people find suitable sites for building projects. And yeah, it's as boring as it sounds. That's why I took a few weeks off to go travelling.'

'Weren't you nervous travelling on your own?'

Ben shook his head. 'Not at all. I met some really great people and saw some amazing places.' He took a sip of his Americano. 'Don't tell my mom but I'd love to give up my job some day and go travelling for a few months. I'd like to spend time in Asia and Australia.'

Isla closed her eyes. She'd always longed to see the Taj Mahal and the Great Wall of China, Mount Fuji, and the sacred red stone of Uluru. She could picture them all. But they were so far away, so out of reach, when her life was here in Heaven's Cove.

'Do you work or were you a full-time carer for your grand-mother before she passed?' asked Ben.

Isla opened her eyes. A small child was crying nearby and there was a hum of conversation around them. 'I was working full-time for a local mental health charity, but I needed a part-time job when Gran got more immobile and in need of care, so I switched to working at the library in Callowfield, which is about ten miles away.'

'And what about Caitlin?'

'She's between jobs. She used to work for a firm of solicitors in London, as office manager. But I think she left a while ago, when she and her husband moved house and it was too far for her to commute.'

'You don't sound too sure.'

'Caitlin and I aren't close,' said Isla briskly. 'Not any more. Anyway, please tell me about India; Rosie told me that you've been there.'

'It's an amazing, vibrant country. It's one of the favourite places I've visited, along with Peru. That was pretty special too.'

'Did you go to Machu Picchu?'

When Ben nodded, Isla sighed. 'I'd love to trek the Inca Trail and climb up to Machu Picchu. It's on my bucket list. But Paul doesn't much like going abroad.'

'That's a shame 'cos it's well worth a visit.'

Isla sat back, listening intently while Ben talked about his ascent to the fifteenth-century Lost City of the Incas. He

described it so well, she could imagine she was there, with the
sun on her face and the ancient citadel spread out before her.

She suddenly became aware of someone standing close
beside her and looked up.

'Isla! I didn't expect to see you in here.' Paul was standing
there, a take-out coffee in his hand. 'I just nipped out from work
to grab a drink, and here you are.'

Isla frowned. There were far closer cafés to Paul's office,
and he rarely drank takeaway coffee. Was he spying on her? She
batted the thought away because she was being paranoid. How
on earth would Paul know that she was here? It had to be a coincidence.

When Paul smiled at Ben and asked: 'Who's this, then?' Isla
cringed inside. Paul knew exactly who he was. She'd told him
this morning what she was doing, but she went through with the
charade anyway.

'This is Ben, the American visitor I was telling you about
who's here to find out more about his family history. Ben, this is
Paul, who—'

'I'm Isla's boyfriend,' interrupted Paul, thrusting out his
hand for Ben to shake. 'It's wonderful to meet you.'

'Yeah, you too.' Ben shook the proffered hand. 'Isla's
showing me around Heaven's Cove before I head back to
London. She's been very kind.'

'I bet. Isla's always kind. Too kind sometimes, which lays
her open to being taken advantage of. Isn't that right,
sweetheart?'

He laughed and Isla laughed too, because she felt she
should. But Ben's smile had frozen on his face.

'I'd hate to take up too much of Isla's time.'

'You're not,' Isla assured him, feeling awkward. 'Paul didn't
mean that. He was just talking generally and...' She tailed off,
not sure what else to say.

'How long are you in beautiful Devon, Ben?' Paul asked,

still towering above Isla.

'Just until tomorrow, and then I head back to the States the day after.'

'That's good to know.' Paul glanced down at Isla's mug. 'What on earth are you drinking, sweetheart? I thought we were on a health kick and that doesn't look terribly healthy to me.'

'It's just a hot chocolate to warm me up. It's freezing out there.' Isla shifted in her seat. She remembered Paul talking about eating more healthily but she didn't remember saying that she would join him.

'We don't want you getting chunky, do we?' Paul laughed again and gave Isla's shoulder a squeeze. 'What is it they say? A minute on the lips, a lifetime on the hips?'

'Something like that.' Isla gave a wan smile and glanced around her. Some young mums at the next table had stopped talking and were staring.

'Anyway.' Paul sniffed. 'I'd better be getting back to work. My business won't run itself, more's the pity. It was lovely to meet you, Ben, and I wish you safe travels.'

'You, too.' Ben picked up his coffee and took a large gulp.

'I'll see you later then, sweetheart.' Paul leaned down, put his palm on the back of Isla's head and pulled her towards him. Then he kissed her hard on the mouth for longer than felt seemly in the middle of The Heavenly Tea Shop, released her and swept out of the café.

Isla watched him go, feeling agitated. She'd been enjoying listening to Ben's tales of his travels. But she couldn't help feeling as if she'd been doing something wrong.

Ben looked at Isla as the mums on the next table giggled and went back to their babies and coffees.

'So that's Paul,' he said, after a while. 'Does he always talk to you like that?'

'Like what?'

'Like...' Ben flapped his hand at the door through which Paul had just left. 'That!'

Isla knew Americans had a reputation for being upfront but she felt offended by Ben's question – and slightly ashamed that she'd let Paul embarrass her, without any comeback. But it wasn't any of Ben's business when he hardly knew her or Paul, and he'd be heading off tomorrow anyway and she'd never see him again.

'Paul's fine,' she said quietly, so the mums nearby wouldn't hear. 'He can be a little over-protective at times but that's because he's always looking out for me. He has my best interests at heart.'

'If you say so.'

'I do say so.'

When there was a frosty silence between them, Ben drained his coffee cup and nodded at Isla's mug. 'Are you going to drink that hot chocolate?'

Isla pushed it away from her. 'I don't think so. It's a bit sickly for me.'

'Right. Well, let me get the check. I'm paying.' He waved away Isla's protestations. 'It's the least I can do after you've shown me round. And then I'd better let you get on with your day. I'm sure you have lots you'd rather be doing.'

Isla nodded mutely, although listening to tales of Peru was far more fun than trying to avoid Caitlin, who was still in her bad books, and Maisie, whose teenager quips could be trying.

After paying, Isla and Ben stood in the narrow street, outside the café. Ben pulled up the collar of his jacket against the icy wind blowing in off the sea.

'Well, thanks again,' he said in his gravelly New York accent.

'You're welcome, and I hope your mum will like the photos of Heaven's Cove.'

'I'm sure she will. And good luck with finding out more about Edith who died from a broken heart.'

Isla nodded, not sure if Ben was being facetious.

She watched as he walked off, taking long, loping strides on the cobbles. So that was that. Her eyes widened when he suddenly turned and marched back towards her.

'If you want to trek the Inca Trail to Machu Picchu, you should,' he said. 'With or without your boyfriend.'

And with that, he turned and marched off again.

16

MAISIE

Maisie opened one eye and snuggled further under the duvet. Something was different this morning. The air was cold, but it was always freezing in this house. She tried to focus her drowsy brain and work out what had changed. It was quieter than usual, she decided. The stupid seagulls that woke her most mornings with their raucous screeching seemed muted. But there was something else... and then it hit her. The light was different.

She pulled herself up to sitting, dragging the duvet with her. The light coming through the thin curtains was normally a dull grey. But today it was brighter, lighter. And there was no traffic noise. The house was close to the edge of the village and there was usually a distant hum from the cars navigating Heaven's Cove's narrow streets. But not today.

Getting out of bed, Maisie padded to the window, pulled back the curtains and gasped.

Overnight, Heaven's Cove had been covered in a thick blanket of snow. The thatches of the cottages going in steps down the hill from Rose Cottage were coated in white and the sea in the distance was pale, like spilled milk.

Maisie's heart leaped, in spite of her best efforts to remain unexcited at all times. There was something about snow that was joyful and London didn't often get much. When the city did, the covering was quickly blemished with footprints, and snow that edged the roads swiftly turned to blackened slush. But the snow here was untrodden, unslushed, and utterly beautiful.

She quickly pulled on jeans and a jumper and checked her phone, as she always did first thing. More WhatsApp messages awaited her and she opened them gingerly, desperate to see what Madison and her friends had to say and dreading it at the same time.

There were several messages about Eden, the fittest boy in their year group, who apparently wanted to kiss Madison. She'd posted a meme of a kitten puking but probably would end up making out with him and then telling them all about it. Maisie liked Eden herself but he'd never taken any interest in her.

Maisie suddenly caught sight of her name and her stomach lurched. It was a message from Carly, Madison's right hand woman.

Hey Maisie, when are you back at school? You're not hiding are ya? Your face when Welby got slimed! You looked well scared. More than usual. We laugh about it A LOT!

It was followed by several laughing emojis, to hammer home the point, and Madison had added her own brief message below: *LOL*

Maisie gulped and sat down on her bed. She rarely commented in the group but life at school would be unbearable if she couldn't put her practical joke behind her. Summoning up her courage, she composed a reply:

*Ha. Not hiding. Have been dragged by awful stepmum to the
end of the world (Devon) but will be back soon. Probably best
to let Welby thing die down if that's OK. Don't need any more
hassle after being suspended.*

Maisie pressed the 'send' arrow and bit her lip, wondering
if she should have kept quiet. Her eyes fell on Jessie's carved
driftwood angel on her bedside table and she picked it up to
run her thumb along the cuts and grooves. There was something strangely comforting about this rough figure with its
wings unfurled. Isla reckoned it had been Jessie's protector
over the years, so perhaps it would do the same for her?
Though that was highly unlikely, Maisie pushed the angel into
the pocket of her jeans anyway before making her way
downstairs.

'Why are you putting your jacket on? Where are you
going?' asked Caitlin, appearing in the hall in her silk dressing
gown. Quite how her stepmother didn't turn to ice in this house,
with its antiquated heating system, was a mystery.

'Nowhere,' Maisie replied sullenly. 'Thought I'd go out for a
walk.'

'A walk?'

Caitlin raised an eyebrow, which was annoying, even
though Maisie hardly ever went for a walk in London. What
was the point? If she wanted to get somewhere, there were
always Tube trains, or buses, or Ubers, or lifts from Caitlin
or Dad.

And the last time she'd ventured out for a walk, across
Waterloo Bridge, it had ended in disaster when she'd spotted
something she so wished she hadn't.

'*Why* are you going for a walk?' asked Caitlin.

'Just for something to do, if that's all right with you?'

She was being unnecessarily snarky and she didn't blame
Caitlin when she gazed at her coolly.

'It's absolutely fine with me, but you'll need more on your feet than trainers.'

Maisie looked down and twisted her mouth. Caitlin was right, for once. She'd have sopping feet in minutes.

'Have you seen the snow!' Isla declared, appearing at the top of the stairs. Which was a ridiculous comment because of course they'd seen the snow. It was hard to miss it when everywhere outside was smothered in the stuff.

Isla hurried down the stairs, her shiny, fair-brown hair swishing around her shoulders. Maisie coveted that hair, which was so much thicker than her own.

Isla hurried to the front door and opened it, sending a draught of frigid air through the house.

'Really? Close it, quick!' moaned Caitlin.

Isla slammed the door shut and frowned. 'Ben will never get back to London today, which means he'll miss his plane first thing tomorrow.'

'Which probably won't be taking off anyway, in this weather,' said Caitlin.

Maisie ignored an urge to say 'Duh!' and made do with rolling her eyes instead.

But Isla fished in her pocket for her phone and jabbed at the screen. 'Nope. They don't have snow in London so the airports are still operating normally, which means he'll miss his flight and blame me for encouraging him to stay on for an extra day.'

Caitlin shrugged. 'Will he though? I'm sure he can re-book his flight, and it's not your fault it snowed overnight. They didn't forecast a dump of snow like this, as far as I'm aware.'

To Maisie's surprise, Isla gave Caitlin a withering look. She didn't think her sort-of aunt, who always looked as if butter wouldn't melt, had it in her. It was a real 'get out of my face' glare. But there was something going on between them, something more than the usual sisterly spat that rumbled on tediously. It had started after their visit to the pub two days ago but, of course, no one had told Maisie what was going on. It was probably linked to that stupid letter and riddle that they talked about endlessly.

'I certainly hadn't heard of snow,' Isla agreed, sounding tetchy. She frowned. 'I am worried about Ben though.'

Isla was far more concerned about the American's travel arrangements than Maisie thought she should be. Though she could imagine him being miffed if he couldn't get out of the village. Heaven knows, she was keen to leave. Though she'd made peace with the idea that she'd be here a little longer, until Caitlin sorted out the sale of this stupid house.

'Where are you going?' asked Isla suddenly, staring at Maisie's jacket.

'Out for a walk.'

And there it was again. A slight lifting of the eyebrow, as if Maisie was completely immobile.

'I said she can't go out in those trainers,' Caitlin butted in.

Isla wrinkled her nose. 'Definitely not. You can borrow Gran's snow boots, if you like.'

Maisie did not like. Wearing an old lady's boots was bad enough. But a dead old lady's footwear was beyond the pale. Yet she had to admit that the boots did look warm when Isla hauled them out from the under-stairs cupboard.

'You've got small feet, like Gran,' she said, placing them next to Maisie. 'Why don't you give them a try?'

'My trainers will be fine,' Maisie insisted.

'Give it a go, then,' said Caitlin, pulling open the door again and letting in a blast of frigid air.

Maisie strode to the door and glanced outside. Caitlin was right but there was no way she was going to back down with both her stepmother and Isla watching her. So she stepped outside and winced as her feet sank into the snow. It had to be at least six inches deep. Snow tumbled around her trainers and began to soak through her socks at the ankle.

'So, how's that working out for you?' asked Caitlin, being ultra-annoying as usual. 'Come on, Maisie,' she urged in a more conciliatory tone. 'Gran's boots will be far more comfortable, don't you think?'

Maisie stepped back into the hallway and closed the door with a bang. Then, she pulled off her trainers, leaving discarded snow to melt on the hall floor, and gritted her teeth as she pushed her damp socks into Jessie's boots.

They looked horrendous. People at school would take the mick mercilessly if they ever saw her in them. But, Maisie had to admit, the fur lining was cosy and warm, they came up way past her ankles, and the fit wasn't too bad.

'There you go.' Isla smiled. 'Gran would be glad that her boots are still being used. I remember her standing in them in this hallway last winter.'

That really didn't help, but Maisie tried not to grimace, when Isla fished in her pocket for a tissue. Honestly, even talking about her departed grandmother's shoes set her off.

Maisie felt a sudden pang of sadness for Isla, because she knew what it was like to miss people – she hardly ever saw her mum since she'd moved to Canada for work – but she pushed it down quickly. She didn't want to start liking Isla, because she wouldn't be here for long.

'Right.' Maisie opened the door again and braced herself as the chill wind hit her. 'See you later.'

'Be back soon,' shouted Caitlin. She said something else but Maisie didn't hear because she'd already slammed the door shut.

She stood still in the garden and pulled in a deep breath of icy air that hurt when it hit her lungs. It was amazing how a coating of ice crystals could transform the world. Heaven's Cove, usually a boring picture postcard village that felt divorced from reality, had turned into a winter wonderland. It looked like a scene from *Frozen* – a film she loved though she'd never admit it.

Maisie glanced up at the sky, which was blanketed in grey-white cloud, and frowned. It looked as if there was more bad weather to come. Perhaps they'd be snowed in for weeks. She shuddered and started trudging down the hill towards the centre of the village, her cosy boots leaving deep footprints.

A surprising number of people were out and about, although it was fairly early. She glanced at her watch. It was nine o'clock but that was definitely earlier than Maisie was usually out and about on a non-school day. Children ran past her, screaming with delight and throwing snowballs at their friends. And Maisie stopped for a while by the quay, watching small fishing boats going in and out of the harbour. The pale sea looked so cold, even watching it ripple and swell made her shiver.

She was walking along what villagers laughingly referred to as 'the High Street' – they'd obviously never been to rammed Hammersmith – when her jeans came out of her dead old lady boots.

Maisie stopped to tuck them back in and was bending over when she heard a shout.

'Hey, you there. Could you give me a hand? Quick!'

Maisie looked up in surprise. 'Are you talking to me?'

A teenaged girl, in a thick coat, tragic woolly hat and mittens, nodded. 'I'm about to drop this.' She tilted her head towards the wooden crate she was carrying. 'Help!'

When the crate began to wobble, Maisie moved forwards and grabbed hold of it before everything went flying. The crate was heavier than she'd expected but, between the two of them, they managed to haul it into the back of a pick-up truck that was parked nearby.

'Thanks. I almost dropped the lot.' The girl sniffed and

rubbed a mitten across her cheeks that were red with cold. 'Are you here to do a run?'

'A run?' Maisie screwed up her nose. The prospect of her going for a jog in perfect running weather was unlikely... but in snow? Dream on!

'Great, everyone's here,' said a slim man with greying hair as he walked past her. He had bright green eyes that reminded Maisie of a cat, and he was carrying another crate that he pushed into the back of the truck. Following him was a woman in a Barbie- pink ski jacket.

They got into the vehicle and left the door open for the girl. 'Are you going to get in, then?' she asked Maisie.

'Um, why would I?'

Realisation dawned in the girl's pale eyes and she laughed. 'Sorry. I assumed you were here to help.'

'Help with what, exactly?'

'We're taking provisions to some of the outlying houses which are cut off by the bad weather, and checking up on people. We're due more heavy snow later so they might be without food for days.' She glanced up at the leaden sky. 'Anyway, I'd better go, before it does start snowing again. Thanks for helping me with the crate.'

She was almost fully inside the truck when Maisie called after her, 'Stop! Wait a minute.' When the girl looked round, half in and half out of her seat, Maisie asked: 'Do you need more help, then?'

The girl smiled. 'I guess so. The more hands the better.'

Maisie hesitated a split second before saying: 'OK. Count me in.'

'Great.' The girl swung her second leg into the truck and slid across the seat so there was room for Maisie to climb in beside her. Was this a good idea? Maisie got in quickly before she could change her mind, slammed the door shut and the truck pulled away.

As the vehicle drove slowly through the snowy streets, Maisie stared out of the steamed-up window and wondered what on earth had possessed her. She was being driven out of Heaven's Cove, to who knows where, with people she'd only met two minutes earlier. It was ridiculous, and unwise, and unsettling... and strangely exhilarating. She felt fired up with an excitement she hadn't experienced in a long time. And the fact that Caitlin would be horrified by her actions was a bonus.

'Are you both OK there, in the back?' said the man in the passenger seat as the truck slid across a narrow lane, trying to gain traction on the slippery road.

Maisie nodded, hoping that the woman driving knew what she was doing. It was all very well going off and having an adventure, but she'd rather not end up in a ditch.

The woman was called Freya, Maisie quickly ascertained, and the man was Ryan. They didn't look like kidnappers or perverts, Maisie reassured herself, feeling extra-nervous as the truck rounded a corner – rather more quickly than she thought prudent – and Heaven's Cove disappeared in the rear-view mirror. She had a sudden urge to leap out and run back to Caitlin, which was ridiculous for three reasons – one, jumping from a moving truck wasn't to be recommended; two, she'd probably die of hypothermia in her dead woman boots before she got back to Rose Cottage; and three, Caitlin was no doubt enjoying the peace while she was out and wouldn't be overly delighted to see her.

'What's your name?' The girl squeezed into the back seat next to her was talking to her.

'Maisie. Um... what about you?'

'I'm Bethany. You can call me Beth, if you like. Most people do.'

Most people, as if she knew lots of people and had loads of friends. Maisie didn't have many friends, partly because she didn't fit in with the in-crowd – though things were looking up now Madison had accepted her into her WhatsApp group. But also, she suspected, because potential 'nice' friends were warned off by their parents: *Don't get too involved with that Maisie girl. She often seems to be in trouble.*

She didn't mean to get into trouble so much. And being in trouble wasn't always pleasant, in spite of the insouciant 'I don't give a monkey's' air she'd carefully cultivated. But she could be spontaneous and do things without thinking them through, which seemed to annoy the hell out of the people around her.

Maisie shifted in her seat, feeling uncomfortable. Here she was, in a stranger's car, heading away from people she knew. That was the height of spontaneity, and Caitlin would not be impressed.

'Have you just moved to Heaven's Cove?' Beth asked, wincing when the truck slid across the road.

'No, I'm visiting. I'm from London.'

Maisie waited for Beth to look suitably impressed that she was sharing a vehicle with a streetwise teenager who lived at the centre of... everything. But she simply nodded and said, 'Cool.'

Cool? No one Maisie knew said 'cool' any more.

'Do you like living in London?' Beth asked.

Maisie went to say that of course she liked it – she loved it. But the words wouldn't come. She looked out of the window at the beautiful snowy landscape – trees and fields stretching into the distance on the right and, to the left, the occasional glimpse of sea, a flash of brightness under the white-grey sky. It was very different from the skyscrapers and litter and constant noise.

'It's all right,' she mumbled.

'What's your school like?' asked Beth, who seemed full of questions.

'All right,' mumbled Maisie again. 'Actually, I'm suspended at the moment.'

Beth's eyes opened wide. 'Why?'

'I played a practical joke on a teacher.'

Maisie remembered the door to the classroom opening, the tub of slime she'd balanced on top tipping and thick, yellow gloop sliding down Miss Welby's hair. The girls in the class whom Maisie was trying to impress had laughed and clapped but all Maisie could focus on was Miss Welby's face: her shock and upset. Miss Welby was a pain and she picked on Maisie constantly, but still... Maisie had wished with all her heart that she could rewind time and never carry out such a stupid joke, which suddenly hadn't seemed funny at all.

Maisie swallowed, desperate to ward off any more questions from Beth. 'Anyway, why are you out here doing all of this, delivering food parcels?'

'We belong to the Heaven's Cove Residents' Association and, as part of that, we look out for local people who need help. Belinda, who heads the association... have you met her?'

'I don't think so.'

Beth spoke quietly. 'You'd know if you *had* met her. She's dead bossy. Like a headmistress. And nosy. But, fair play, she gets things done. Anyway, she rang round this morning to see who could get involved in Operation Whiteout.'

When Maisie wrinkled her nose, Beth laughed. 'Belinda's name for it – she enjoys a touch of drama. Anyway, there's no school 'cos it's Saturday so my sister and I said we'd help. She's already gone out on a different food run. My mum's a GP at the local surgery so she's gone in to work.'

'Cool,' said Maisie without thinking. She winced because she was sounding more local by the minute.

'Did you say your name is Maisie?' the woman driving called over her shoulder, turning slightly to glance towards the back seats.

'That's right,' said Maisie, wishing that the woman – Freya – would concentrate fully on the road ahead. The man's hand was on her thigh, which, Maisie couldn't decide, was either because the two of them were an item or because he was terrified by the prospect of skidding to his death.

'It's very kind of you to lend us a hand.'

'That's all right. There's nothing else to do round here.'

Maisie worried that might sound a little too curmudgeonly when she was with strangers, but Ryan laughed. 'You're right there. My daughter, Chloe, is always complaining about it. That's why Freya and I have joined the village residents' association and we're setting up some local activities for young people.'

Maisie sniffed. They probably had a Sunday School, a reading club, and a learn to love maths group in mind.

'Yeah,' said Freya beside him, wincing as the truck hit a pothole. 'We're planning an alcohol-free night club once a fortnight, white-water rafting in the summer, a fashion design course, and trips to the cinema.'

Maisie sniffed again because that didn't sound bad at all. It would certainly liven up the place.

'It's a shame you won't be around for that,' said Beth beside her.

'Mmm,' said Maisie. 'We've got all that kind of stuff in London already.'

Which was kind of true, apart from the white-water rafting, though Maisie never seemed to take advantage of any of it. She spent most of her time stuck in her bedroom, with her nose pressed up against the screen of her phone. Was she horribly boring? Maisie wondered. Was she wasting her life?

Her introspection was interrupted by Freya declaring: 'We're here! First stop,' as the truck slid to a halt outside an isolated cottage surrounded by woodland. 'Let's check on Mrs Bolton, make sure she's warm and has enough food and then we can move on to the next person.'

'How many people are on the list?' asked Beth.

'Six,' said Ryan cheerfully. 'I doubt we'll be back in Heaven's Cove before lunchtime.'

Lunchtime? Maisie supposed she ought to let Caitlin know where she was, not that she expected her stepmother to care. She patted her jeans pocket and realised she'd left her phone at home.

'Is everything all right?' asked Beth.

'Yeah. I just realised I didn't bring my phone.'

'Did you need to ring someone? You can use mine, if you like.'

Maisie shook her head. The only mobile number, other than her own, that she could remember was her father's, and it would be a fat lot of good letting him know where she was. 'Thanks, but it's OK.'

Beth nodded and got out of the car, her feet sinking into the thick snow. She was wearing tragic clothes – a boring navy coat, and a green woollen scarf that looked as if it had been knitted by her gran. But she was kind, Maisie decided. And she could hardly pass judgement anyway, in her old lady footwear.

Maisie sighed and stepped out of the truck into a Narnia landscape that was so beautiful it took her breath away. A curl of smoke drifted from the chimney of the whitewashed cottage, and the trees surrounding it were laden down with snow. A salt-laced breeze was moving through the branches and puffs of powder were floating down to earth. London, and her past life, seemed a very long way away.

'Are you sure you don't need to make a call?' asked Beth behind her. 'Do you need to let someone know where you are?'

Maisie shook her head without turning round, unable to drag her eyes from the fairy tale scene in front of her. 'No, thanks. Everything's fine, and if I'm not around for a while, no one will care.'

17

CAITLIN

Caitlin stared out of the window. Everything was white, which, she supposed, made a pleasant change from grey. Though it wasn't just Heaven's Cove that seemed drab these days. London, too, had lost its allure. And the longer she was away from the city, the less she looked forward to returning to it. The buzz and excitement she'd first felt on arriving in London as a naive twenty-year-old had waned over the years. And here, in the peace of Heaven's Cove, it seemed to be fading even further.

Caitlin sighed and focused on the sight before her. The sun had just peeped out from behind a thick bank of cloud and the garden, blanketed in glinting snow, seemed scattered with diamonds. Beyond it, the sea shimmered winter-white. It was a breathtaking scene – but Caitlin had too much on her mind to appreciate it fully.

She glanced at her watch again and felt a crease appear between her eyebrows when she frowned. 'She should be back by now. Maisie hates the cold.'

Isla stopped pacing, the phone glued to her ear. 'She's probably enjoying stomping through the snow. She's fifteen years old, Cait, so I'm sure you don't need to worry.'

Her words were clipped because she hadn't yet forgiven
Caitlin for abandoning her in the pub. Caitlin understood why.
She fully appreciated why Isla might take a dim view of her
sister disappearing and leaving her to cope alone... again. But
Isla didn't know what Stuart had told her in his phone call –
that their home was definitely gone, collateral damage from his
gambling. Isla didn't know what Stuart was really like.

Caitlin rubbed her eyes. The problem was, Isla didn't know
what Maisie was like, either. Of course, she knew that Maisie
could be grumpy and sullen, but she didn't realise what bad
choices the teenager sometimes made. In that respect, Maisie
was very like her father. Caitlin's mind drifted again to the
phone call she'd taken from Stuart in the pub, and her panic
attack when, humiliatingly, Sean had come to her aid.

'Oh, hi, Rosie,' said Isla into the phone, her face lighting up.
'Is Ben there, please? Could I speak to him?'

She listened for a moment, gnawing at the inside of her
cheek. 'Oh, right. I thought he might not be too happy about it.'
She listened again. 'Has he? OK. Do you have his mobile
number? I've only got his email address... Oh, never mind.
Could you ask him to give me a quick call, then, when he gets
back?' She listened again and smiled. 'Absolutely. This snowfall
seems to have taken a lot of people by surprise... Yes, I will. You
stay warm, too.'

Isla ended the call and dropped her phone onto the coffee
table. 'Well, that's just great!' she said, giving a dramatic sigh.

'Are you still worrying about Ben?' asked Caitlin, still
staring out of the window in the hope that Maisie would
appear, trudging up the lane. 'He's a grown-up and will manage
in this weather.'

'I'm sure he will but, like I said, I'm concerned that he'll
miss his flight.'

'That's a shame but I'm sure he can re-book, and it's not
your fault.'

'It feels like it is because I encouraged him to stay in Heaven's Cove an extra day. And who knows how long this snow will last? He could be trapped here for ages.'

'I expect it'll thaw soon.' Caitlin paused. 'Maybe you could do a sun dance though, just in case?'

As a small child, Isla had insisted on doing sun dances when the weather was pants. And her faith in their efficacy had lasted for some time, even when persisting torrential rain had indicated otherwise.

Caitlin wasn't sure that her sister would remember but Isla's mouth twisted up in one corner, as if she was trying not to grin. 'I can't believe that I ever thought my dancing would bring out the sun.'

'You were a very imaginative child, and it did work, in a way.'

'In what possible way did my sun dances work?' exclaimed Isla, staring at Caitlin as if she'd gone barmy.

'Your dancing made Mum smile, and that brought out the sun.'

Was that too cheesy? Caitlin swallowed, wishing she hadn't said anything, even though it was true. Their mum was often unwell. Her life was hard for years. But Isla's uninhibited gyrations to appeal to the sun god had always put a smile on her face.

Isla stared at the floor for a moment and then lifted her face towards Caitlin. 'I can picture Mum so clearly in her beautiful blue dress, blowing me a kiss from across the room. I still really miss her, you know, even though it's twenty years since she left us. Is that daft?'

'No.' Caitlin gave her sister a sad smile. 'I miss her too, but Mum didn't leave us. That makes it sound as if she had a choice when she didn't have any choice at all. She fought her illness as much as she could because she wanted to stay with us. She really tried.'

'I know.' Isla gazed past Caitlin, at the view beyond the window. 'I think that maybe losing Gran has brought it all back a bit. I've been thinking a lot about Mum over the last few days.'

'That's not surprising, is it.'

When Isla shook her head, her thick hair tumbled around her shoulders and she looked so young, Caitlin wanted to give her a hug. But Isla wrapped her arms around her middle, like a defensive wall that Caitlin should not breach.

'I found out some stuff about Edith,' said Caitlin after a few moments, wanting to break the painful silence that was stretching between them.

'When?'

'Yesterday, but you were busy showing Ben around and...' Caitlin's sentence petered out. The truth was she'd still felt guilty for abandoning Isla in the pub, and her attempts to apologise had been rebuffed so she'd kept out of her way. 'Anyway, shall I tell you what I've discovered?' She gave Isla a small smile. 'It's really interesting. Promise.'

Isla puffed out her cheeks. 'Go on, then, and it better had be interesting.'

'I eventually managed to track down some passenger lists online for the *Sylvestria*. I can't find William's journey to England, but I found his return trip, and he made it on his own. There's no Edith Anstey listed.'

'So Edith never left Heaven's Cove at all?'

'That's what it looks like. But there's more.' Caitlin walked to her handbag that she'd slung onto the sofa and pulled out a piece of paper. 'This is Edith's death certificate, which I ordered and fast-tracked. It arrived in the post yesterday afternoon.'

'Why didn't you show me this yesterday?'

''Cos you were being a bit... you know.'

Isla's cheeks flushed pink. 'Yeah, well, you know why.'

'I do and I'm sorry. Really sorry.'

Isla narrowed her eyes and pushed out her lower lip. Then,

she shrugged. 'Whatever.' And just like that, they were friends again. Sort of. 'Hand it over,' she demanded, grabbing the certificate and scanning through it. 'Oh, my goodness!'

'Yes, exactly. Have you got to Edith's cause of death?'

Isla nodded. 'I wasn't expecting that. So, let me see… it says she died on the fourteenth of February 1922. The location of death is Higher Black Tor on Dartmoor and the cause of death is given as…' She squinted at the paper in her hand. 'Am I reading this correctly? I think it says that Edith died of exposure to cold.'

'The handwriting isn't very clear but that's what it looks like to me too.'

'So poor Great-Aunt Edith froze to death in the middle of February in the wilds of Dartmoor?'

'It looks like it.'

'That's so sad! Poor old Edith.'

'Poor *young* Edith. She was only twenty-four. So what went wrong for her? She had the chance of such a glittering life – marriage to a man who clearly adored her and an exciting new life in America. Maybe she didn't love William back, though Edith's gravestone says she died of a broken heart, which implies that wasn't the case. And now we know that she actually died on St Valentine's Day, presumably alone, in the middle of nowhere. What on earth went on one hundred years ago?'

'I don't know, but it sounds as if you're getting invested in unravelling Edith's story and Gran's riddle.'

Caitlin sniffed. 'Maybe. Though, as Maisie would say, there's nothing else to do around here.' She gave a wry smile because that was only true if you didn't take into account the amazing walks available locally, or the cafés and shops, or the beach. 'I guess I am a little curious about the whole thing.'

At first, she'd found the letter interesting, up to a point, and the riddle endearing, as a last hurrah from their grandmother.

But the more she'd found out about Edith and William, the more she wanted to know what had really gone on in this house, back in 1919.

'Did I send you the photo of William?' asked Isla.

'No. Does Ben have a photo of him?'

'His mum sent him one yesterday during our village tour. I thought I'd forwarded it on to you.'

Isla knew she hadn't – her sheepish expression gave her away. But she'd been miffed with her sister at the time so Caitlin let it go.

'You must have forgotten. Can I see it now?'

Isla found the photo on her phone and passed it over. William was staring out at Caitlin from the screen – a handsome, dark-haired young man in what looked like a military jacket. Seeing his face made him seem far more 'real', and realising he might have once stood in this very same room gave her the shivers.

'Someone's written "William France 1918" on the other side of the picture,' said Isla, taking her phone back. 'Perhaps he spent time in England while he was over here, fighting, and that's how he first met Edith.'

'In Heaven's Cove? That seems unlikely.'

'That's what I thought, but who knows?'

There was still so much about William and Edith that they didn't know, and Caitlin's interest was definitely piqued. Even Maisie seemed curious about them at times.

Maisie! Caitlin glanced again at her watch. She really should be back by now.

'I'm going to have to go and look for her,' she told Isla, doing up the buttons on her cosy Fair Isle cardigan.

'Are you really worried about Maisie? She seems the kind of girl who can look after herself.'

'Sadly, not always.' Caitlin remembered some of the times she'd had to bail Maisie out: there was the time she flooded a friend's bathroom by forgetting to turn off the tap, when she'd shoplifted as a dare, and more recently, the time she was excluded from school for playing a ridiculous and cruel practical joke on a teacher. 'Maisie makes out that she's grown up,' she explained, 'but she can be very unpredictable, and a bit of a pain at times, to be honest.'

She immediately felt guilty for criticising Maisie. But Caitlin often felt more like her handler these days than her stepmother. And how on earth would the teenager react to news that her home was being sold off to settle her father's debts?

She pursed her lips to stop them from wobbling, and noticed Isla giving her a straight stare before she asked, 'Are you going out in those shoes?'

'They'll probably be all right.' Caitlin looked down at her fashionable leather boots whose smooth leather soles might as well be made of glass in this weather. She was behaving like Maisie whose brief foray outdoors in trainers had ended in disaster. 'Well.' She grimaced. 'Maybe not.'

Isla gave a wry smile. 'You never were particularly equipped for the countryside, were you, Cait?'

Caitlin wasn't sure whether she should take offence at the comment, but Isla was right. She'd found it harder to move to Heaven's Cove twenty years ago than Isla had. Isla had taken to the great outdoors and the peace of the village almost immediately, but it had taken Caitlin longer to feel settled in this quiet, alien environment. She had relaxed, eventually, when she'd begun to trust that Jessie wasn't about to get fed up with them and turf them out.

'You can borrow my wellies,' said Isla, going into the hall, and rummaging in the under-stairs cupboard before brandishing a pair of white boots decorated with garish yellow sunflowers. 'I'm going out too, so I'll keep an eye out for Maisie, and please give me a call when you find her.' She gingerly placed a hand on Caitlin's arm. 'Don't worry. People don't go missing in Heaven's Cove. It's not that kind of place.'

Teenagers went missing in every kind of place, thought Caitlin, as she made her way carefully down the hill towards the centre of the village. And even if abduction was extremely unlikely, there was the sea Maisie could drown in, or the cliffs she could fall from...

Caitlin snuggled her chin into her soft scarf and tried not to worry – which was impossible because being responsible for a teenager was nerve racking, even when the teenager wasn't yours. Caitlin blinked as an icy wind slapped against her cheeks. Maisie felt like hers, even though the stroppy teenager would never believe it, or like it, for that matter. She still hankered after her real mother in Canada, who didn't appear to give two hoots about her. And now her father had let her down too, and Caitlin didn't have the heart to tell her. It was better that she hated Caitlin rather than her father, for a little longer at least.

Caitlin walked on through the narrow lanes until she reached the old church, and the village green, which today was an expanse of white. She stopped for a moment and caught her breath. It was more sheltered here, farther back from the sea, and utterly beautiful. St Augustine's was sitting at the centre of a winter churchyard, its gravestones topped with snow. There was a pillow of snow, too, on The Mourning Stone, which marked an ancient, local tragedy. And nearby stood a snowman, with a carrot for its nose, a tie around its neck and a straw hat on its head.

Caitlin began to walk around the green and only noticed a section local children were using as a slide at the exact same moment she felt her feet slip from beneath her.

She tried to keep her balance but it was impossible. Isla's boots couldn't gain traction, and she fell, landing with a bump on her backside and bashing her arm on the floor.

'Great!' she uttered, sitting dazed for a moment. The hem of her jacket was darkening as snow soaked into it, and she felt sick with the pain radiating from her elbow. Suddenly she felt hands beneath her armpits and she was hauled to her feet.

'Thank you,' said Caitlin, turning round. 'Oh.'

Sean was standing there, with a younger lad behind him who was eyeing her curiously.

'I saw you come a cropper,' said Sean, his fair hair hidden under a black woolly hat. 'We were coming out of the shop.' He nodded towards the Mini Mart that kept villagers and tourists supplied with everyday essentials.

'Well, like I said, thanks very much,' said Caitlin, wiping snow from her coat while her cheeks burned with embarrassment. Sean stepping in to help her again was mega-humiliating.

'I thought it was Isla who'd come a cropper, because of the boots,' said Sean, watching her. 'Then, I realised it was you, falling on your arse.'

His voice was deadpan but Caitlin caught a familiar twinkle in his bright blue eyes. She recognised it from fifteen years ago, whenever he'd looked at her. Only, back then, he'd thought she was wonderful. Now, he must think she was an anxiety-ridden mess who couldn't even stay upright.

'Did you hurt yourself?' he asked, shoving a small paper bag and its contents into his jacket pocket.

'Only my pride,' said Caitlin, ignoring the burning pain in her elbow.

'You were lucky, then.' He paused. 'Are you out for a walk?'

'Yes, well... no. I'm looking for someone, actually.'

'Have you lost Isla?'

'No.' Caitlin hesitated. 'Actually, I'm looking for my daughter, Maisie.'

Sean caught her eye and held her gaze. 'I didn't know you had children.'

'I don't. Not really. Maisie's my stepdaughter. She's fifteen.'

'And she's gone missing, has she?'

'Kind of. She went out walking in the snow a couple of hours ago and she hasn't come back.' Sean narrowed his eyes, obviously thinking she was being over-anxious – and perhaps she was. But he didn't understand the background. He didn't know what was going on right now. 'It's just, she's quite vulnerable sometimes and—'

When Caitlin paused again, Sean jumped in. 'All right.' He turned to the young lad with him. 'Charlie, get yourself back to the garage and let Jen and Lee know that I'll be out for a while.'

Charlie nodded and, with a final curious glance at Caitlin, scuttled off, his big boots sending up puffs of snow crystals.

'What are you doing?' Caitlin asked Sean, feeling panicky.

'Helping you to look for Maisie.'

'You don't have to do that.' Caitlin didn't want to spend time in this man's company. This man who resented her for some long-ago slight.

'I'm well aware of that. But I'll give you a hand anyway.'

'Aren't you needed at work?'

'They can cope without me for a while. All we seem to be doing anyway is pulling cars and tractors out of ditches. The roads are treacherous today.' He rubbed his hands together to keep them warm. 'So, where have you looked already?'

'I've walked around the village and there's no sign of her.' Caitlin breathed deeply to calm the anxiety she could feel rising inside her. 'Isla's on the look-out for her too.'

'Have you checked local caffs in case she's sitting drinking hot chocolate somewhere?'

'Most are closed because of the weather but I looked in the couple that were open and there's no sign of her.'

'Have you tried ringing her mobile?'

'Of course I have, but she forgot to take it with her.'

Caitlin felt her muscles tense. It was kind of Sean to give her a hand – though she wished he wasn't. But did he think she was a total idiot? *If he doesn't now, he will when he finds out what your husband has been up to.*

Sean tilted his head, as if he could almost hear Caitlin's thoughts. 'Have you got a photo of Maisie on your phone, so I know what she looks like?' he asked.

'Yes, I'm sure I have a few.'

Caitlin quickly scrolled through her pictures and showed Sean the first one she came to that included her stepdaughter. She was standing beside Caitlin and Stuart, during a trip to the theatre two months ago. Maisie looked bored, as usual, and Caitlin and Stuart were standing together, with Stuart's arm around her shoulder. He wasn't one for public displays of affection and had only given her a cuddle after being told to 'get closer' by the friend taking their picture. They looked like such a happy family, at first glance.

'Is that your husband?' asked Sean, peering at the screen.

'Yes, that's Stuart.'

'And that's Maisie, I suppose.'

'That's right.'

He looked as if he was about to ask another question, but then said: 'OK. Let's see if we can find her.'

The two of them walked side by side through the village, hardly speaking. But Maisie was nowhere to be seen and Caitlin's concern began to grow. Where would a stroppy fifteen-year-old go on such a cold day? What if she'd walked out of the village and got lost and now had hypothermia?

'Are you sure Maisie hasn't already gone back to Rose Cottage?' Sean asked as they hurried towards the ruins of the castle. 'Maybe we should try back there.'

Caitlin shook her head. 'Isla said she'd leave a very large note on the front door telling her to call me the minute she got back and...' She pulled out her mobile to double-check. 'Nope. There's no missed call. God, I hope she's all right.'

Sean stopped walking and leaned against the ruined wall of
the castle keep. 'You care a great deal about her, don't you?'

'Yes, I do, though she'd never believe it. I'm the archetypal
wicked stepmother in her eyes and she doesn't let me
forget it.'

Sean grimaced. 'Fifteen-year-olds can be brutal, and they
always kick against their parents. I certainly did at that age, and
you weren't much older when you snuck out of your gran's and
joined me on the harbour wall for a sneaky cigarette. Do you
still smoke?'

'No, I gave up ages ago,' said Caitlin, her mind drifting back
to their teenage days. Everything had seemed much simpler
then, before she'd begun to panic about being trapped in Heaven's Cove for years as a carer. Just as Isla had been.

Caitlin took a deep breath to stop guilt from overwhelming
her. 'What about you?' she asked. 'Are you still cadging cigarettes from people?'

'Nope. I never much liked smoking and only did it to seem
more grown up than I was. I was trying to impress you.'

'Were you?' Caitlin tried to smile but her frozen cheeks
hardly moved. 'You didn't need to. I was impressed already.'

She shouldn't have said that. It was best to steer away from
the past. Caitlin leaned against the ruined wall too, ignoring the
cold that immediately began to seep through her jeans, and
started flexing her numb toes in Isla's wellies.

'Do you want half a sausage roll?' Sean suddenly asked,
pulling out the paper bag that he'd stuffed into his pocket after
her fall.

'Shouldn't we keep looking?'

'We will, but you look like you need some food first. You're
very pale.'

'Um...' Caitlin was aware of her stomach rumbling. She'd
been so busy worrying about Maisie, she'd forgotten to have
breakfast. And when Sean opened the grease-stained bag, she

caught an enticing aroma of pastry and spices. 'Go on, then! That would be great, if you don't mind. I am quite hungry.'

Sean broke the sausage roll in half and passed it over. It was only luke-warm but still tasted delicious.

'One of Stan's specials?' asked Caitlin. Stan had run the village Mini Mart for ever, and his snacks were legendary in the village.

'That's right, though Stan's not well these days so it's mostly his family running the shop.'

'I didn't realise. That's a real shame.'

Caitlin hardly remembered Stan but the thought of him being ill and the shop changing made her sad. She'd once known Heaven's Cove like the back of her hand but a lot had changed while she'd been away. The cottages were as quaint and the air was still laced with the fishy smell of the sea, but the people were different. They'd moved on while she'd been gone.

'It can't be easy, being a stepmum,' said Sean, who'd polished off his food in two bites. 'Where's Maisie's real... I mean, her biological mother?'

Caitlin licked pastry flakes from her lips and glanced at Sean. He never used to be so forward but he'd changed too in the years since they'd last met. He seemed more confident, more self-assured... simply more grown up, she supposed, than the adolescent young man she'd once known so well.

'Her mother and Stuart split up a couple of years before I came on the scene. Maisie stayed with her dad because her life was in London and her mum was moving to Canada, for work. She's got a new family now.'

'That can't have been easy for Maisie.'

'It wasn't. She doesn't have a very close relationship with her mum.'

'At least she's got you.'

Caitlin gave a mirthless laugh. 'Yeah, poor girl. What about you?' she asked, to change the subject. 'Have you got kids?'

'Me?' Sean shook his head. 'Nope. No kids. No wife.'

Caitlin, who'd just taken a bite of sausage roll, stopped chewing and gulped it down. 'But Jen called you her hubby when I brought my car into the garage, and you were in the pub with her.'

Sean gave a wry grin. 'I can see that might be confusing. Jen *was* my wife, for a while. We got married when we were both very young but it didn't last long. We're still good friends, though. Which is what we should have been all along, really – rather than rushing off and getting hitched. She's married to Lee, now, the lead engineer at the garage. They were both out of work when I took over the garage and taxi company, so I hired them.'

'That was very magnanimous of you. Do you all get along well together?'

'Remarkably well, in the circumstances. Jen sometimes calls me Hubby Number One and Lee's a good friend. They're great together, and I'm godfather to their younger son.'

'That all sounds terribly civilised.'

'I suppose it is, but there's no point in being weird about all of this stuff, is there. Life slaps you in the face and you either adapt or you don't.'

When he shot Caitlin a loaded look, she glanced away, towards the sea that glistened in the sun peeping through cloud. She certainly wasn't adapting well to Stuart's latest bombshell that they would have to leave their beautiful home.

'So how long are you staying in Heaven's Cove, once you've found Maisie?' Sean asked, stamping his feet on the snow to warm them.

'I don't know. Not long. I'm hoping that Isla might agree to sell Rose Cottage, but I think Paul's going to move out of his flat and move in with her instead.'

'That doesn't surprise me.' Sean's jaw tightened.

'Don't you approve?'

'It's not for me to approve or not. It's just I don't...' He grimaced. 'Like I said, it's not for me to comment on other people's plans.'

'Don't you like Paul?' Caitlin asked gently.

'I don't really know him. But on the occasions we've met, I don't know... I just found him... hard to read.'

'I know what you mean. I'm not sure he's right for Isla. But I don't think I have the right to interfere.'

'Probably not, in the circumstances.'

When he gazed out to sea, Caitlin took the chance to really look at him. The years appeared to have treated Sean well. He'd filled out and the angular youth she'd once known had disappeared. His fair hair was shorter and he looked older, but the lines that now feathered around his eyes gave him a gravitas he'd once lacked. The snow piled on the castle's fallen stones meant the ruins were like the backdrop to a Disney film, or a Christmas romcom – and Sean looked like the handsome lead.

Caitlin pulled her eyes away from him and stood up straight. Why was her mind straying towards romantic feelings? She'd had her chance with Sean years ago but had thrown it all away.

Such a lot had changed since then. Sean had managed brilliantly without her, becoming the owner of a successful business and negotiating a civilised divorce with dignity. Whereas she was married to a man whom she was no longer sure she wanted to be with, but could not in all conscience leave because of his problems. And to top it all, she'd lost his daughter.

'I have to keep searching for Maisie,' said Caitlin, flutters of panic rising into her throat. 'Thank you for helping me to look for her, Sean, but you should get back to work now.'

'I don't mind helping you look for a bit longer.'

'And I really appreciate that. But she's my daughter, not yours.'

That didn't come out how Caitlin had intended and she

winced. Sean pushed his hands deep into his pockets and shrugged. 'You're right, Cait. She's not mine,' he said gruffly.

'I'll walk back with you into the centre of the village, and if I still can't find her, I think I need to call the police.'

'That's probably for the best.'

Sean set off walking, back along the sea wall, and Caitlin followed. The atmosphere between them had cooled and they trudged in silence through drifting snow.

18

MAISIE

'Go away! I don't want any food.'

Maisie sighed and wrapped her arms around her waist to keep out the cold. The old lady was being very insistent, and Maisie didn't understand why Freya and Ryan didn't read the room and leave her to it. Instead, they kept on shouting encouragements through her letterbox.

'Connie Carmichael keeps herself to herself and doesn't much like people,' said Beth, totally unnecessarily in Maisie's opinion. It was pretty obvious that the old woman wanted them off her land, like, right now.

Maisie looked around her. Connie's home – an old farmhouse, sad with neglect – was in the middle of nowhere, on the slopes of moorland that were coated in thick snow. The village was just visible in the distance, but Maisie shivered. It must get very lonely out here, and spooky at night.

'Why did you call her Creepy Connie in the truck when we arrived?' Maisie asked warily.

Beth winced, looking faintly embarrassed. 'I shouldn't have 'cos it's not very nice but it's what some of the local kids call her.

Connie's lived here for ever and is the last one of her family left. I heard her family were shunned in the village, like, loads of years ago, which also isn't very nice, because of their outrageous behaviour.'

'What sort of outrageous behaviour?' asked Maisie, perking up at the thought of some interesting gossip.

'I dunno,' said Beth. When Maisie frowned with disappointment, she added: 'Stealing and stuff, I think. My gran used to go to school with some of them and said they were always in dirty clothes. No one wanted to sit by them.'

'That's a shame.' Maisie, well used to being the girl no one at school wanted to sit by, felt a sudden companionship with the children brought up in this bleak, isolated place.

Ryan, who'd been crouched over the letterbox for the last five minutes, stood up straight with a groan. 'I don't think Connie's going to answer the door.'

You think? Maisie rolled her eyes, worried that she seemed to be losing all feeling in her frozen toes.

'One last chance,' said Freya, bending to shout into the letterbox again. 'Come on, Connie. You might not need provisions, but what about your cats? They'll find it harder to forage in this weather, and we've got a box full of cat food out here. There's no charge. It's free, if you want it.'

The prospect of free stuff did the trick. There was the sound of a bolt being dragged back and the door opened a crack. A woman with wild, long white hair poked her head around it and narrowed her eyes. 'Did you say cat food?'

'That's right.' Freya took a step back as the door was pulled wide open. 'Can we bring it in? And we can make you a cup of tea, if you'd like.'

'Perfectly capable of making my own tea,' the woman muttered in a broad Devon accent. But she stood to one side and let Ryan carry a box of cat food and vegetables into her hallway. Freya followed and, after a moment's hesitation, so did Beth and Maisie.

As the rest of the rescue party filed into what looked like the kitchen, Maisie stayed standing in the hallway. It was gloomy in here, with bare stone walls and a flagstone floor that dipped in places from the many feet that had walked across it over the centuries. Uncarpeted stairs led to the next floor and to Maisie's left was an open door.

With a quick glance towards the kitchen, Maisie stepped through the door, and tried to stop breathing in. This was a sitting room, with a stained, striped settee against one wall and a stone fireplace opposite it – and the whole room stank of cats.

One wiry black cat was stretched out on the settee, and another cat – this one larger and ginger – was lying on a tattered rug in the middle of the floor. It opened one eye and watched Maisie warily as she walked to the window, shoved her hands into the pockets of her jeans and looked outside.

This room faced away from the village, out across the moorland which rose into the distance. A large bird was flying across the landscape, making wide, lazy circles in the snow-heavy sky. It was a bird of prey, Maisie realised, searching for its next meal.

She began to take shallow breaths in and out, gradually acclimatising to the feline stench.

'What the hell are you doing in 'ere?'

Maisie swung round, pulling her hands from her pockets, and swallowed. Connie was standing in the doorway with her hands on her hips and a scowl on her face. 'I said, why are you in here? Are you snooping?' Maisie shook her head, feeling every muscle in her body tighten. 'You're gathering information on me, aren't you.' Maisie shook her head more vigorously. 'You're poking your nose in so you can get me out of this place.'

Maisie opened her mouth but only a squeak came out.

She was deliberating pushing past Connie and making a

run for it when the old lady's bright eyes focused on Maisie's feet. She pointed a gnarled finger at the floor. 'What's that?'

For a woman who, according to Beth, was in her nineties, Connie was surprisingly agile. Before Maisie had a chance to move, she'd walked forward and picked up the carved angel that had fallen from Maisie's pocket.

'Where did you steal this?' hissed Connie, grabbing hold of Maisie's arm. She was incredibly old – Maisie had never seen wrinkles like it – but she had the grip of a man half her age.

'It was a present,' gulped Maisie, finding her voice at last.

'Who from?' Connie's hair, frizzed out around her face, made her look both eccentric and terrifying.

'From Jessie.'

'What Jessie?'

'Jessie in Heaven's Cove. R... Rose Cottage,' Maisie stuttered. 'My... um, my great-grandmother.'

Connie's grip lessened slightly. 'Jessie's your great-grandmother, is she? And you say she gave you this?'

'Uh-huh. She did. That's right. Yeah.' Maisie nodded and swallowed again. She could hear people putting food away in the kitchen and banging cupboards, but no one was coming to rescue her. 'She left it to me in her will.'

Connie's hand fell from Maisie's arm and the old lady stepped back. 'She's dead, is she? That's a shame. She was always good to me – not like some of the others. You'd best have it back then.' Connie thrust the angel at Maisie. 'I'm surprised she still had it, mind. That's nice. Unexpected, really.' A flicker of sadness crossed the old lady's face, making her look less scary.

'How do you know about the angel?' Maisie asked, finding some courage.

'I made it, a long time ago.'

'*You* made it?' Maisie studied the angel, carefully crafted out of driftwood: its wings unfurled and ready for flight, its face serene and loving.

'Yeah, me. You sound surprised.' Connie's laugh sounded more like a cackle. 'I was a teenager and your great-grandmother was a little kid – a good few years younger than me, admittedly – but I made it for her as a thank you for being kind. She was one of the only locals who'd smile at me in the village and say hello. My family weren't much liked in Heaven's Cove back then.' She nodded at the angel resting in Maisie's hand. 'So, she kept it all these years.'

'She said it was her protector.'

'That's nice. I hope it did a good job.' Connie's pale, beady eyes narrowed. 'And she left it to you, then? She must have thought a lot of you.'

Maisie shifted uncomfortably. 'I don't know about that.'

'Actions speak louder than words.' Connie sank down on the sofa, next to the black cat, who stirred and stretched. 'All right, Dolly?' When she ran her hand across the cat's belly, Maisie noticed that the old lady's dress – a grey, nightie-like garment that added to the whole freaky vibe – was scattered with dark hairs.

'Do you live out here on your own?' Maisie asked, glancing out of the window at the swathes of white-cloaked countryside in every direction. Her curiosity about this unusual old lady was growing as her alarm at her manner and appearance faded.

'Yeah, it's just me. I like it out here on my own, with no one to bother me. I've lived here all my life and I'll leave here in a box.' The black cat got to its feet and padded across the sofa to reach Connie's lap, where it curled itself into a ball, purring contentedly.

'Dolly, here, keeps me company, don't you, girl? And now you've brought food for Dolly and Petra over there, we'll be right as ninepence 'til the snow goes.'

Her vowels were long and her consonants soft and Maisie decided she liked the Devonian burr which, contrary to Connie's wild appearance, made her sound warm and comforting. Jessie's accent, though noticeable, hadn't been so pronounced.

'Are you living in Heaven's Cove?' Connie squinted at Maisie, her eyes bright in her creviced face. 'I don't remember seeing you around.'

'Me? No, I'm just staying for a little while. I'll be going back to London soon.'

'That's a shame. I've been to London twice in my life, and hated it twice. Couldn't wait to get back to the sea and plenty of peace and quiet. Here with your mother, are you?'

'No.'

It's none of your business. She's thousands of miles away in Canada and I rarely see her, except on stupid FaceTime.

When Connie stared at her, without blinking, the back of Maisie's neck began to prickle. Could the old lady read her mind?

'I'm staying with my aunt. Well, she's not really my aunt. She's Jessie's granddaughter, like my stepmum. But we're definitely going home soon, when they stop stressing over a stupid old letter to some dead relative called Edith. It won't be long.'

Maisie was babbling. She stopped talking and snapped her mouth shut. Connie was still staring, and Maisie could swear that she still hadn't blinked.

'Edith Anstey? My mother knew her,' she said as the cat in her lap stretched and yawned. It seemed that Connie, in spite of living out in the wilds, knew a fair bit about people in Heaven's Cove. Maybe she even knew the answer to that stupid riddle Caitlin and Isla were obsessed with.

There was a noise outside and Maisie glanced through the window. Freya, Ryan and Beth had walked around the back of the house and were unloading more tins from the truck. Beyond them, the land stretched towards the sea, which was a blur of grey on the horizon, below the bleached sky. In the far distance, almost farther than Maisie could see, a faint ribbon of smoke rose into the air from a farmhouse chimney.

She turned back to Connie. 'Don't you find it too quiet here?'

'No but then it's not always quiet. Sometimes the wind wraps round the house and moans, like banshees rising from the grave.' She gave a gap-toothed grin at Maisie's horrified expression. 'But I've got Dolly and Petra for company, and no ghosts are going to bother with me. I'll be joining 'em soon enough, don't you think?'

'Um.' Maisie paused, wondering how to respond to Connie's question. 'No' was blatantly a lie. And *Yeah, 'cos you're ancient*, probably wouldn't go down too well. Why were old people so tricky? Maisie wondered. Not that she knew many old people. Only Jessie, really. And now she was gone.

Connie was peering at her so hard, Maisie wondered if her vision was impaired. A pair of glasses stood on the stone mantelpiece, though the lenses were so smeared, Connie could probably see better without them.

'I expect you'll go on for a bit yet,' Maisie said eventually.

Connie threw back her head and laughed. 'I like you,' she said, 'even though you're right nosy. I can see me in you.'

Maisie tried not to let her horror show on her face. She was nothing like this strange old woman who looked as if she hadn't had a bath in weeks. And, she promised herself, she would never end up living on her own in the back of beyond with only cats for company.

'Anyway.' Connie gently moved the cat off her lap and pushed herself to her feet. 'You're kind for coming and I dare say your parents are proud of you. Far more proud than my parents were of me. But then I don't s'pose you've got up to half the things that I have.'

Maisie sniffed. She'd been called lots of things in her life –

loud, difficult, complicated – but she couldn't remember ever being called kind. And her parents weren't proud. She rarely met up with her mother, who FaceTimed a couple of times per week – long, awkward calls that Maisie kind of dreaded. And her father was always out and far too busy to spend time with her, especially now he knew that she knew his secret.

There was Caitlin, of course, who was always around and had done her best, but she wasn't a proper parent.

Maisie suddenly remembered Caitlin coming along to parents' evenings at school, even though that involved being told how disappointingly Maisie was doing. And she'd been the one in the Head's office, asking them to reconsider Maisie's suspension after that stupid practical joke. Caitlin's pleas hadn't worked but that wasn't her fault. At least she'd tried.

An awkward cough signalled the arrival of Beth, who poked her head into the room. 'There you are, Maisie. We're about to leave and Ryan and Freya are bricking it, thinking you've wandered off and are freezing to death somewhere.' She glanced nervously at Connie. 'Is everything all right in here?'

'Fine, thanks,' said Maisie, moving past the old lady to stand with Beth in the doorway.

'We've left the cat food and some other stuff in the kitchen for you,' Beth told Connie, still sounding nervous.

'Good of you. Is there any soup?'

'Um, I don't think so.'

When Connie scowled, Beth muttered 'Sorry' and beat a hasty retreat along the hallway. Maisie followed her but stopped and retraced her steps. Connie was still standing in the middle of the room, staring at the door.

'Bye,' said Maisie. 'It was nice to meet you.'

Connie raised a hand in acknowledgement but said nothing.

Maisie looked back as the truck slid away from the house.

Connie was standing at the window, watching them go. She cut a lonely figure and Maisie felt a shiver run down her back.

Beth chattered on while they made their way back to the village. She seemed nice enough and Maisie felt less of a Billy-No-Mates now she at least knew someone of her own age in Heaven's Cove. Beth even wrote her phone number on the back of an old receipt and handed it over 'in case you fancy hanging out some time'. Maisie didn't think she'd be in Heaven's Cove for long enough to 'hang out', but she was touched by the gesture and thrust it into her pocket.

'Thanks so much for your help this morning, Maisie,' said Freya, as the truck moved slowly along the snowy lane that led to the quay. 'We love having younger members of the residents' association. People like Beth, and there's Ryan's daughter Chloe, too, who's in bed with a cold at the moment. If you move down here permanently, you'll have to join us.'

'Yeah, maybe,' murmured Maisie, quite sure that she wouldn't be moving to Heaven's Cove anytime soon, even if she wanted to. Which she didn't – even though the village looked stunning in the snow, and it might be quite nice living by the sea in the summer.

She suddenly caught sight of Caitlin, who was sliding along the lane with some random bloke.

'That's my stepmum,' said Maisie, wishing she hadn't after spotting that Caitlin was wearing the most hideous pair of wellington boots she had ever seen.

'She looks nice,' said Beth. 'Does she know Sean?'

Maisie didn't reply because she had no idea who Sean was, though presumably he was the tall guy wearing a black puffa jacket who had just given Caitlin a wave and walked off.

Caitlin watched him go before pulling her phone from her pocket and stepping back from the traffic trying to negotiate the narrow street. Her eyes met Maisie's and her jaw dropped as the truck drove past and pulled into a parking spot a little further down the road.

Maisie puffed out her cheeks. What was the betting she was about to get a lecture on stranger-danger and getting into people's vehicles? Pretty high, she reckoned, as Caitlin hurried along the street towards them, slipping and sliding in her appalling footwear.

19

ISLA

There was definitely something wrong with Caitlin, thought Isla, holding out her arms for balance as she negotiated a patch of ice. It wasn't just the loss of Jessie, or being away from London and her husband. She'd hardly mentioned Stuart since she'd arrived, and he hardly ever seemed to phone her. Plus, she seemed even more money-minded than usual. She was certainly still very off with Isla for not wanting to sell Rose Cottage.

Isla sighed and wiped a fat flake of snow from her nose. Whatever was going on, Caitlin didn't seem keen to tell her the truth, which was upsetting. Once they'd been so close and reliant on each other. Whereas now, they never spoke about anything personal. It was sad, thought Isla, trudging on through a deep drift. She missed the wonderful sister she'd once had.

Isla pulled the scarf tighter that her grandmother had made for her. Jessie had knitted it last winter, when she was starting to fade, and there were dropped stitches and small holes, here and there. But it was a riot of colour and Isla knew she would wear it for ever – it felt like being hugged by her grandmother, who would have loved this unexpected snowfall.

What would her gran have made of the latest revelations

about Edith's death? Isla wondered. Or was she aware that the aunt who'd died before she was born had been killed by exposure on wild Dartmoor? Perhaps that was information they were meant to find: a clue towards solving the riddle. *Don't get in a spin, girls, though mistakes can cost you dear. This one brings good fortune and, I hope, will make you cheer.*

It still meant nothing to Isla, who felt sure she was missing something obvious and letting her grandmother down.

She gulped back tears and walked on towards the beach, keeping her eyes peeled for a grumpy, cold teenager. To be honest, it was unlikely that Maisie would have taken herself off to the cove on such a freezing day. But Isla knew someone who might be there, thanks to her conversation on the phone with Rosie.

The resting snow was surprisingly deep in places as she walked along the lane that led out of the village towards the beach. The wind had moulded mini-drifts that piled knee-high against the hedgerow and a robin, its breast a splash of red, hopped along beside her for a while.

She walked past Liam's farm, its yard littered with footprints, human and animal. And on towards the beach whose sand was coated in white until you got close to the sea.

Isla spotted Ben immediately. He was standing with his back to her, gazing at the water that was eddying close to his feet. His head was down and his shoulders slumped.

Isla took a deep breath, pulling Jessie's scarf even closer to her goose-bumped skin, and walked towards him.

'Hi, there.'

He looked over his shoulder. 'Oh, it's you. I didn't expect to see you again.' Ben sounded thoroughly fed up and she couldn't blame him.

'I know. I thought we'd said our goodbyes yesterday.' Isla scuffed her foot into the damp sand.

Ben turned around. 'It's quite a coincidence, meeting up again here.'

'Not really because I was looking for you. Rosie said you'd gone out for a walk, and I bumped into a couple of people who'd seen you heading this way.'

'This village is full of spies,' said Ben drily. 'I thought I might as well spend some time by the ocean, seeing as there's little else I can do. Why were you looking for me?'

'I wanted to see you to apologise that you're trapped in the village and might not make your flight home.'

Ben grimaced. 'I definitely won't make my flight early tomorrow unless this snow dump disappears in the next couple of hours, which seems unlikely.'

'I'm afraid so, and...' Isla glanced at the heavy sky above them. 'It looks as if we might get a bit more.' She watched a few fat flakes drift down and melt into the water. 'We don't often get a lot of snow, being so close to the sea, but on this occasion...' She sighed. 'Anyway, I'm sorry.'

'You're apologising for what exactly?' Ben raised an eyebrow. 'For making it snow?'

'I'm just very aware that if you'd left Heaven's Cove yesterday, as you'd planned, rather than staying on an extra day to take my tour of the village, you wouldn't be stuck here now.'

Ben pushed his hands under his armpits in an attempt to warm them up. 'It's true I wouldn't be about to miss my flight if I'd left yesterday as planned. However, you weren't to know that a blast of cold air from the Arctic was going to drop a ton of snow on us overnight. I have to say, the weather forecasting round here isn't terribly impressive.'

'It's usually much better but this cold snap has taken everyone by surprise. I am sorry, though.'

Ben stared at her for a moment, but then he smiled – a proper smile which chased away every trace of sternness. 'Don't worry. I'm not holding you personally responsible for the weather.'

Isla smiled back, feeling relieved. 'What about you getting home?'

'I can re-book my flight, but there's no point in even trying until I know for sure how long I'm going to be stuck here.' His eyes widened in alarm. 'This snow won't last until Christmas, will it?'

'No, it'll definitely be gone long before then.'

'Just as well. Mom will kill me if I'm not home for the holidays, especially with Dad not being around.'

'Of course. Special times of the year are hard when the people we love aren't here. It would have been Gran's birthday tomorrow.'

Isla wished she hadn't mentioned her grandmother because now she wanted to cry.

'That's going to be tough,' said Ben, his voice full of sympathy. 'Can you maybe do something to mark the day?'

'That's what we're planning,' murmured Isla, desperate to change the subject before she dissolved into tears. 'Anyway, the snow definitely won't last over three weeks until Christmas. They're saying on the news it's likely to start thawing tomorrow, though that's not guaranteed. But,' she added brightly, trying to sound upbeat, 'if you're going to be stuck anywhere, at least you've got great views from Driftwood House. Heaven's Cove must look like a winter wonderland from up there.'

Ben nodded. 'I must admit the village does look kind of stunning in the snow. I need to take some photos for Mom, who'll lap this kinda thing up.'

'She'll have to pay us a visit one day. You can give her a tour and show her where William once trod.'

'Yeah. Maybe.'

Ben would never come back to Heaven's Cove, thought Isla, snuggling her chin into Gran's scarf. He would cross the ocean to America, just as Edith had planned to do. Until she'd changed her mind for some reason. Had she bottled out at the last minute?

Isla glanced down at Ben's feet. He was wearing his grey jacket and jeans, and large green wellies.

'Do you usually travel with wellies?'

'With what?'

Isla glanced at his feet and he followed her gaze. 'Do you mean my rain boots? These belong to Rosie's husband. He took one look at my footwear and took pity on me.'

'There's a lot of boot sharing going on today,' murmured Isla, trying not to shiver. An icy wind was blowing in off the grey sea and swirling around them.

'You look like you're freezing. Do you want my thicker scarf?' Ben asked. He gave a wry smile. 'Which is also borrowed from Rosie's husband.'

Isla shook her head. 'No, thank you, but thanks for offering. That's very gallant of you.'

'That's me. Gallant to a fault.' Snowflakes were falling more heavily now and beginning to settle on the long lashes that framed Ben's grey eyes. 'Look, shall we get out of this weather? Is there somewhere nearby where we could get a hot drink to warm up?'

'I know just the place,' said Isla, after a moment's thought. 'Follow me. And keep your eyes peeled for my niece, a stroppy teenager called Maisie, who's vanished.'

'Properly vanished?'

'No, she's gone for a walk and Caitlin's having kittens because she's been out for a couple of hours. She's fifteen so I'm sure she's OK.'

As Isla said it, she felt a stirring of concern. Maisie *was* all right, wasn't she? Caitlin wasn't the type of person to panic about nothing, and she hadn't rung to say that Maisie had been found.

'Your sister sounds like my mom when I spent time in the Amazonian rainforest. She was convinced I'd be eaten by a crocodile.'

'I didn't know you'd been to the Amazon as well. Was the rainforest amazing?'

'It was awe-inspiring, and I did see caimans, who are related to alligators, but I managed to avoid becoming lunch.'

'Tell me more about it,' said Isla, as they walked on, their boots squeaking in the virgin snow.

Ben obliged and Isla felt herself carried far away from Heaven's Cove, to a tropical forest alive with iridescent hummingbirds.

'So, is the Amazon on your bucket list as well now?' he asked, when the tale of his Amazonian adventure came to an end.

'Definitely. It sounds wonderful.'

He glanced at her, his nose red from the cold. 'Why don't you tell me about your favourite places abroad?'

'Me? I've been far too busy here in Heaven's Cove to go away very much.'

'I get that, with you looking after your grandmother. But I guess that you and Paul will have more of a chance to travel now.'

'Mmm, maybe,' murmured Isla. 'Though why do we need to travel when we live in such a beautiful place?'

She was parroting Paul's words, and the moment they were out of her mouth, she wished she hadn't said them.

Ben frowned. 'Because there are lots of other beautiful places out there, waiting to be discovered.' He stepped to one side as a white truck drove slowly past them. 'Awesome, magnificent places that I'm sure you'd love.'

'And I'd love to see them. I really would, only—'

Isla stopped talking.

'Only, what?' prompted Ben as the shops of Heaven's Cove came into view.

'Only I don't have much time to go gadding about and I'm perfectly fine here.'

Surprise flickered across Ben's face, but how could Isla tell this intrepid American how nervous she felt about straying too far from Heaven's Cove these days? Paul believed that the world out there was dangerous and she'd begun to believe it too. Her world had shrunk to this village and the people in it who were familiar and unthreatening.

Had Edith felt the same way? she wondered. Had she also been a coward who was too afraid to leave her little corner of Devon?

20

MAISIE

'You did what?' Caitlin glared at her stepdaughter but only for a second. She grabbed hold of Maisie's arm, obviously finding it hard to maintain eye contact and her dignity when her feet were sliding on the icy street.

Maisie, faintly irritated by her stepmother's lack of balance, repeated what she'd just told her, only this time at half speed and carefully enunciating each word. 'As I said, I helped Freya and Ryan to distribute food to the elderly.'

'Yes, I heard that but I don't understand why?'

'Because you're always saying I should think of others, rather than myself. Anyway, I wasn't murdered or abducted or anything.'

Maisie stepped sideways so her feet landed in a patch of thick, virgin snow.

'Well, obviously, but that's not the point. You didn't take your phone, and I didn't know where you were.'

'So?' Maisie huffed, thoroughly fed up with this stranger-danger lecture already.

'So, I was worried about you.'

'Why?'

'Why?' Caitlin sounded exasperated now. 'Because you're my stepdaughter, Maisie, and I'm responsible for you. Plus,' she added more quietly, 'I care about you.'

Did she? Maisie glanced sideways at her stepmother, a strange feeling fizzing in her chest. Did Caitlin really give a damn about her? Or did she feel obliged to care about her – to go through the motions, at least – because Maisie came with her dad, as a package?

'You don't need to get stressy because Ryan and Freya are members of the Heaven's Cove Residents' Association, which sounds dead boring. There was another girl about my age with them, too. Someone called Beth.'

'Was she nice?'

Maisie remembered Beth being kind, if rather talkative and inquisitive. 'She was all right, I s'pose.'

Caitlin raised an eyebrow. 'That's high praise from you seeing as you usually find most new people tedious. So what did you all do exactly?'

'We dished out food to various people living in isolated places outside the village.'

'Which people?'

'I dunno. I wasn't keeping a list. We went to six places. The last call was to a really strange old woman called Connie.'

'Not Connie... oh, what was her name?' Caitlin walked a few more paces. 'Connie Carmichael? That was it. She lives a way outside the village, on the edge of the moorland.'

'Yeah, in a spooky old house. Why?'

Caitlin frowned. 'She had a reputation when I was living in the village.'

'A reputation for what?'

'I can't remember, really. She was a bit of a recluse? Came from a dodgy family? Something like that.'

'Well, I liked her.'

Caitlin stopped dead in the street. 'You *liked* her?'

'Yep.'

'Wow. OK.'

That shut her up. And Maisie wasn't lying. There was something about Connie that had resonated with her. Some awkwardness with life. Some grumpiness about how... messed up it all seemed to be.

Maisie shook her head, faintly disgusted with herself for being introspective. What was the point? Any more of that and she'd end up like her aunt Isla, with a bossy boyfriend and a life going nowhere.

Almost as if Caitlin could hear her thoughts, which was a horrible prospect, her stepmother said: 'I must text Isla and tell her that you've been found.'

'I wasn't really lost,' moaned Maisie, but Caitlin was too busy jabbing at her phone to take any notice.

Message sent, they walked on through the streets which were beginning to look Christmassy, with fairy lights in gift shop windows casting pink, blue and gold across the snow.

Caitlin definitely wasn't taking the shortest way home and, just past Gilly's Bake Shop, she stopped outside what was the grandest building in Heaven's Cove – not that there was much competition. Most buildings in the village were small, many of them thatched, with a slight tumbledown air about them. This one was larger with a non-flammable roof, pillars flanking its double doors, and a large sign outside proclaiming: HEAVEN'S COVE VILLAGE HALL AND CULTURAL CENTRE.

'I didn't think the cultural centre would be open today but it looks like it might be,' declared Caitlin. 'It was worth making a detour to check. Have you ever been inside?'

Maisie laughed. Of course she hadn't been inside. Why on earth would she want to?

'Come on,' said Caitlin, swerving towards the front doors, which were ajar. 'Isla suggested visiting the cultural centre to see what life was like in the village when Edith was around.

Plus, I've never been inside either and it's about time I did. Follow me.'

The trouble with Caitlin, Maisie decided, was that, one, she appeared to be obsessed with a dead woman and, two, she could be very bossy at times, rather like Paul. But it was cold out here and it had started snowing again... With a sigh, Maisie followed Caitlin inside.

They were in a small corridor with a large hall leading off to one side. A poster tacked to the wall said in large letters:

Forties Forces Night –
Lindy Hop to the fabulous sounds of Glenn Miller.

'Sounds like fun,' said Caitlin, gesturing at the poster.

Was she being sarcastic? Maisie wondered. She didn't look as if she was taking the mick but it was sometimes hard to tell.

'S'pose,' she muttered.

'Do you even know what Lindy Hopping is?'

'Nope, but it sounds disgusting.'

Caitlin grinned and walked on towards a room at the back of the corridor that had Cultural Centre above it in enormous letters. When she disappeared inside, Maisie stopped, not keen on following her. But a cold draught was snaking through the front doors and, a few seconds later, she trudged after her stepmother.

It wasn't so much a centre as a large room, thought Maisie, glancing around. There were framed photographs everywhere, and several glass-covered cabinets hugging the walls. A woman with striking red hair was sitting cross-legged on the floor, emptying the contents of a large cardboard box. She got to her feet when she spotted visitors and smiled.

'Come on in.'

'Is that all right?' asked Caitlin. 'I wasn't sure anyone would be here, bearing in mind the weather, but the front door was open.'

'We're not officially open today. I was actually taking the opportunity to unpack a recent collection of memorabilia we've been left, hence the mess.' She laughed and waved a hand at the rubbish littering the floor. 'But you're welcome to come in and have a look around. I'm Lettie and I run the centre. Are you staying in the area?'

'Yes, at Rose Cottage. I'm Caitlin, Jessie's granddaughter.'

The woman's mouth turned down. 'I didn't realise. You must be Isla's sister, then. I'm so sorry about Jessie. Everyone is very upset about her death. She was such a wonderful woman.'

When pain ricocheted across Caitlin's face, Maisie took a step forward, her stepmother's vulnerability stirring unfamiliar feelings of protectiveness.

Caitlin glanced at her. 'And this is my stepdaughter, Maisie.' The pain had gone and her stepmother's neutral expression was back.

'Hi, Maisie.' Lettie grinned while Maisie tried to work out if the vivid colour of her hair was natural. Maisie knew a lot about hair dye, having tried out several colours herself – which had also got her into trouble at school.

'I like your hair,' she mumbled.

'Thank you,' said Lettie, touching her fringe self-consciously. 'It didn't always go down too well at school, believe me, but I'm very happy now to embrace being a redhead.'

Definitely natural, thought Maisie, deciding that Lettie seemed all right.

'We'll have a quick look round then, if you're sure that's OK,' said Caitlin. 'I'm trying to find out more about my gran's aunt, Edith Anstey, and wondered if you might have heard of her?'

Lettie frowned. 'The name rings a bell, but I can't think

why... no, I'm probably getting her confused with someone else. Sorry.'

'That's fine. It was a long shot but worth a try. Actually, now we're here, I'm interested to know more about Heaven's Cove in the early twentieth century, and it might do Maisie good to learn a bit more about the village.'

Do her good in what way? Maisie wasn't sure but she started following Caitlin around nonetheless.

Ten minutes later, Maisie had seen much of what was on display, and she had to admit it was less pants than she'd anticipated. The old photos of Heaven's Cove were intriguing: the buildings were much the same, with the village changing very little in centuries. But the people looked odd, in their old-fashioned clothes.

There was also a gorgeous brooch that was obviously the pride of the exhibition. Set in an alarmed case, it glittered as the lights above caught the ruby at its centre and the emeralds, diamonds and a fringe of tiny pearls surrounding it.

'That must be worth a fortune,' said Maisie, reading the card beneath it. The brooch was eighteenth century and had been found recently in the village.

'What do you think?' asked Caitlin, coming up behind her.

'Yeah, nice.'

'Not the brooch, though it is lovely. I mean the cultural centre.'

'Yeah, I knew what you meant,' said Maisie, even though she hadn't. 'There's a lot of history here.'

'There is.' Caitlin looked wistful. 'It's strange to think of my ancestors living around Heaven's Cove for centuries. It makes me feel more rooted to the place.' She cleared her throat, then asked, 'Do you feel rooted in our house in London, Maisie?'

That was a bit left field. Maisie sniffed. 'What do you mean?'

'I mean...' Caitlin's cheeks were turning pink. 'I don't know what I mean, really.' She sounded flustered. 'I suppose I just wondered if you love our house or if it's not that important to you.'

'It's all right,' said Maisie, wondering what on earth Caitlin was going on about. Of course their house in London was important to her. Though, to be honest, she spent most of her time there in her bedroom, scrolling through social media and getting upset at her classmates' snarky comments. School would be a nightmare when she went back after her suspension and had to face everyone. Would Madison and her friends push her to do something else unforgivable?

'Only it doesn't really matter where you live, does it, as long as you're with people who care about you? That's the important thing.'

Maisie stared at her stepmother, who was still going on about their house and not making much sense. The cold must have messed with her brain.

'Anyway,' said Caitlin briskly, 'I guess we'd better get back to Rose Cottage and sort out some lunch. There's nothing here to help us.'

Caitlin was heading for the exit, with Maisie following, when she stopped dead and squinted at a black and white photo on the wall. She walked closer to the picture, which, as far as Maisie could see, was a group of men and women in uniform.

'What's this?' Caitlin asked Lettie, who glanced up from unpacking her cardboard box. She got to her feet and wandered over.

'That's a lovely photo, isn't it? I put this and a few other old photos up a few days ago, to tie in with the Forties dance that's happening in the hall over Christmas. This one is actually from the First World War but it's such a lovely picture, I thought I'd include it. It's local men who were fighting at the front, and a couple of local women who were nurses.'

'Did you see this?'

When Caitlin pointed at the bottom of the photo, Lettie grinned. 'Aha! Well spotted.'

Maisie wanted to know what they were going on about but didn't want to give them the satisfaction of having to ask, so she remained silent. Caitlin took out her phone and began to tap and scroll.

'What are you *doing?*' asked Maisie after a while, unable to stay quiet any longer.

'I need to check something out,' said Caitlin, still scrolling. 'Yes! I thought as much.'

She was being so infuriatingly opaque, Maisie decided not to ask *any* further questions at all, even when she took a picture of the photo on the wall.

'I'd like to go home now. *Please!*' said Maisie, feeling her shoulders slump. There was only so much culture a bored teenager could take.

'Of course.' Caitlin's voice held a hint of excitement. 'Just wait until Isla hears about this!'

21

ISLA

'What exactly *is* this place?' Ben looked around at the faux-leather banquettes and grubby floor.

'A greasy spoon,' said Isla, lifting her fingers off the table top which hadn't been wiped in a while. 'Do you know the term? A greasy spoon is what we call this kind of... authentic place, where locals go to grab a coffee and a bite to eat.'

Not that many locals braved the interior of Bert's Bistro. Set back from the seafront, and hidden away down a side street that led out of the village, Isla was surprised that Bert's business was still trading. It had a reputation for serving weak coffee and, if rumours were to be believed, the occasional bout of food poisoning. But it still attracted a smattering of tourists who presumably craved the sausage butties, fried egg sandwiches, and all-day breakfasts that were highlighted in laminated photos stuck to the window.

Today, the place was empty of tourists, but at least it was open, and Bert was doing a roaring trade with council workmen who'd been gritting roads and helping people pull cars from ditches.

'It seems *very* authentic,' said Ben, wrinkling his nose at the coffee that had been set in front of him by a waitress in a ketchup-splattered apron. 'Only, that café we went to yesterday was nice. And the pub seemed great. They might be open, too, maybe?'

'True, but I thought you might like to see more of the village, as it really is.'

Isla stopped talking and bit her lip. Bert's Bistro wasn't representative of Heaven's Cove at all. It was a dump. But it *was* off the beaten track so she was very unlikely to be spotted here by Paul, or anyone who knew him.

'OK.' Ben took a sip of his coffee and tried to hide his grimace before placing it back down on the table. 'Are you all right? You seem distracted.'

'I'm OK, just wondering where Maisie wandered off to.'

'Your sister texted and said she was safe.'

'Yeah, but she didn't say where she'd been and—' She was interrupted by her ringing phone. 'Talk of the devil, it's Caitlin. Do you mind if I take this?'

'Of course not.'

Ben leaned back against the sticky banquette as she answered the call.

'Hey, you'll never guess what I've found,' her sister blurted out before Isla could say a word. 'You'll definitely never guess so I'm going to send you proof. Your idea to go to the cultural centre was spot on. Hello, are you there?'

'Yes, I'm here but you didn't give me a chance to sp—'

'I didn't expect to find anything,' Caitlin cut in. 'Not really. But there it was.'

She burbled on and Isla, giving up on a two-way conversation, listened intently, her eyes opening wide as Caitlin outlined her discovery.

After the call was done, Isla leaned across the table. 'Ben, the photo from your mum showed that William served in

France during the First World War. Do you know if he was wounded while he was there?'

'Whoa! Where did that come from?'

'It's something that Caitlin said. Do you know?'

Ben frowned. 'Afraid not. All Mom's managed to find out is that he died from an asthma attack after the war had ended.'

When Isla's phone pinged, she opened the photo that Caitlin had sent her, and her heart leaped.

'Look at this!' She pushed her phone in front of Ben's face. 'This picture was taken during the First World War and shows local men who were in the army and a couple of women who were—' She squinted to read the tiny lettering at the bottom of the photo. '"War effort nurses", it says here, who were about to be deployed to France. Their names are listed and they include Edith Anstey.'

'Wow.' Ben squinted at the monochrome photo. 'That woman there? Edith looks like you.'

'Caitlin said the same. That's why the photo caught her attention in the first place.'

Ben looked at the photo again and back at Isla. 'You two are so similar. Edith has the same delicate features and pretty eyes.' He cleared his throat. 'So, do you and your sister think Edith met William when she was nursing during the war?'

'Possibly. Caitlin did a quick Google search and read that nurses worked in France, dealing with injuries caused by the shelling. It sounds like dangerous work. Hang on.' Isla started googling herself. 'It says here female nursing staff served in field hospitals often near the front lines.' She looked up from her phone. 'Mustard gas was used as a weapon, wasn't it, and your mum said William's lungs were damaged? What if they were damaged when he was gassed, and he needed medical care?'

'That would make sense. He was taken for treatment, William's and Edith's eyes met across a hospital tent, and that was it. She captured his heart.'

'Maybe. And if that's the case, if Edith was in France…' Isla sucked her bottom lip between her teeth, deep in thought.

'If Edith was in France…? What?'

'It means the reason she didn't marry William can't have been because she lacked the confidence to leave Heaven's Cove and go to New York. How could she be scared of that when she'd volunteered to be a nurse on the front line?'

'It doesn't sound likely that she lost her nerve,' Ben agreed.

'So we might look similar but we're not really similar at all,' Isla murmured under her breath.

She cursed quietly when Ben asked, 'Are *you* too scared to leave Heaven's Cove?' Unfortunately, she hadn't realised he possessed super-human hearing.

'Of course not,' she said, feeling her cheeks begin to burn. 'Like I said, I don't have a lot of time for holidays and I'm happy here.'

'Are you, though?'

'Absolutely. Paul's very happy here and I am too.'

Isla bent her head, stirred her coffee and watched white flecks of milk swirl and coalesce. Why had she mentioned Paul when he hadn't been brought up in the conversation?

'OK,' said Ben, glancing at the door as a group of people burst into the bistro. They laughed, stamping their snowy boots on the tiles, and made their way to the counter. 'Sorry. I didn't mean to pry.'

'It's fine,' said Isla, stirring her coffee with more force. Ben must think she was a total wimp. He'd spent the last few weeks travelling on his own, with nothing but a backpack and a train ticket. She'd dreamed of doing that once upon a time. Before she got settled in Heaven's Cove. Before Caitlin had left. 'It's just that I'm settled here, that's all.'

'You and Paul.'

'That's right.'

'How did you two first get together?'

'We met when Paul was doing some teaching at an evening class I went to.'

'Is that even ethical?'

Isla shrugged. 'We were adults. He runs his own logistics business now but he has qualifications in accountancy and I was studying bookkeeping.'

When a faint smile played on Ben's lips, Isla asked: 'What's so funny?'

'I just can't see you as a bookkeeper.'

'Neither can I, to be honest. I gave up before the end of the course. I know it's all very important, but it wasn't...' Isla searched for the right word to convey a feeling she'd never fully articulated.

'Exciting?' Ben suggested.

'It definitely wasn't exciting. But that wasn't it, really. It was all a bit too regimented for me.'

'Perhaps there's a wild streak in you, that's desperate to get out?'

Isla laughed. 'I doubt it.' She relaxed, glad the conversation had moved on from comparing her with Edith, and enjoying being in Ben's company. 'So, will you be OK rearranging your flight? You should be able to get back to London tomorrow or the day after, now that forecasters are predicting a thaw.'

'Would those be the same forecasters who didn't anticipate half a ton of snow being dumped on our heads?'

Isla grinned. 'The very same. But you should be able to leave soon.'

'I expect you'll be glad to see the back of me,' said Ben, glancing over at a group of people making noise in the corner.

'Definitely not.'

'What makes me think that you're simply displaying admirable British politeness.'

'No, really. It's been good to meet you.'

And it had, thought Isla. There was something exotic about

Ben, even though he looked the same as any other young man, in his jeans and sweatshirts. Perhaps it was his accent, and his tan, and the knowledge that he lived thousands of miles away, across the ocean, in a country that Isla had once longed to visit.

'Actually, much as I hate to ruin the whole grumpy vibe I've got going on—' He raised an eyebrow. 'I'm not that upset any more about missing my flight. My mom's fascinated by the whole Edith-William story and it's starting to become more interesting than I'd anticipated.'

'Aha! You're being sucked into the mystery. Before you know it, you'll be coming up with a solution to Gran's final riddle.'

'Your grandmother's what?'

Isla screwed up her forehead. Damn. She hadn't mentioned the riddle so far, not wanting to bombard Ben with too much information. Not when he'd seemed so uninterested in the letter, and would probably think the whole thing was crazy.

She took a deep breath. 'Gran left a riddle for me and Caitlin, after her death.'

Ben shifted on his red plastic seat, looking puzzled. 'I can imagine your grandmother leaving you her jewellery or even her cat, but not a riddle. What do you mean?'

'Gran always loved crosswords and quizzes and riddles, and she wrote one for me and Caitlin to solve after she was gone. It's tied to the letter somehow and it says: Don't get in a spin, girls, though mistakes can cost you dear. This one brings good fortune and, I hope, will make you cheer.'

Ben ran a hand across the faint stubble peppering his chin. 'I'm beginning to think I've never met anyone quite like you, Isla, or your family. I mean, why would your grandmother leave you something like that?'

'Maybe she wanted to keep me busy, to take my mind off my grief.'

Realisation dawned in Ben's grey eyes. 'OK, it's all starting to make sense. You think the answer to the riddle is in the letter and that's why you're so keen to find out what happened to Edith and William.'

Isla shook her head. 'That might have been true at first but the more I learn about your ancestor and mine, the more I want to know what happened to them and why. If finding that out solves the riddle, that's great. And if it doesn't, that's still fine because I think it's really important that their story isn't lost. Does that sound bonkers?'

'A little.' Ben's mouth twitched in amusement. 'Look, I have no idea what your grandmother was alluding to in her riddle but I'm beginning to think if anyone can solve it, you can.'

'With your help?'

'Hmm.' Ben folded his arms. 'I would quite like to help you, even though I wasn't too keen on the whole Edith-William thing to begin with.'

'You surprise me,' said Isla drily.

Ben threw back his head and laughed. 'Ah, British sarcasm. I love it.'

Isla grinned, delighted that she'd made her American visitor laugh but experiencing mixed emotions. It might be fun having someone like Ben around for a little longer, someone to regale her with tales of his adventures. But it sparked a longing in her – a longing to rekindle her adventurousness that made her feel both restless and sad.

'Anyway,' said Ben. 'I might as well stay another few days now because I won't get a flight out until at least Wednesday. I did a quick check when I saw the snow this morning and everything's very booked up. Time of year, I guess. So I'd better get back to Driftwood House and ask Rosie if I can stay longer.'

He picked up his coffee to take a sip, gave it a sniff and put it back down again. And in that moment, as he watched the condensation running down Bert's plate-glass window, Isla saw an echo of William – in the tilt of Ben's chin, the line of his nose and shape of his mouth.

Isla dragged her eyes away, wondering if William had been a vibrant, interesting man, just like Ben, when he was sent to the front to face horrors beyond imagination. He'd suffered so much in his short life, so what had prompted Edith to cause him even more pain?

Half an hour later, Ben pushed open the front door of Driftwood House and held it for Isla to step inside first. She'd walked up the cliff with him, enjoying the crunch of snow under her boots, and revelling in his tales of life in New York. Ben's world sounded hectic and loud and unpredictable – everything her life here in Heaven's Cove was not.

Rosie came out of the kitchen, bringing a blast of warm air with her. Her cheeks were glowing and today she was wearing a tight top that showed the faintest curve of her pregnancy bump.

'I see you found each other.' She wiped a strand of dark hair from her forehead. 'What have you two been up to?'

'Isla took me to a quaint place called Bert's Bistro,' said Ben, sitting on the bottom stair to pull off his borrowed wellies.

'Bert's? Really? I'm not sure "quaint" is the right word for that place.'

Rosie shot Isla a questioning glance and Isla felt her cheeks begin to burn again.

'I thought Ben should see all sides of Heaven's Cove before he heads back to America.'

'Talking of which,' said Ben, getting to his feet. 'I was wondering, Rosie, if it'd be OK for me to extend my stay here a couple more nights?'

Rosie frowned. 'I'd love to have you here for longer but I'm afraid your room has already been booked by another guest from tomorrow. There's going to be a thaw overnight, apparently, and he's rung to say he'll definitely make it, and my other rooms are also taken.'

Ben's face fell. 'That's a shame. I was planning on being here a little longer.'

'You could maybe try in the village, but I know the B&B by the pub is fully booked, and the guesthouse near the quay closes down for the winter. I'm in a WhatsApp group with other business owners and we've been talking about how busy we seem to be at the moment.' She bit her lower lip. 'If you're really stuck, I could maybe squeeze you into the box room but I don't normally let that one out because it's tiny.'

Ben shook his head. 'Don't worry. Maybe it's better that I head back to London anyway.' He glanced at Isla. 'You can always keep in touch with Mom and let her know how your search is going.'

'Mmm.' Isla's mind was whirring. 'Or you could always stay with us for a couple of days. We have room.'

Ben looked taken aback. 'I couldn't impose on you, Isla, while you're dealing with the death of your grandmother. There's a lot going on in your life right now.'

'It wouldn't be an imposition. You'd be welcome to stay.'

'What about your sister and her daughter?'

Isla shrugged. 'They won't mind.'

Ben caught her eye. 'What about Paul?'

What about Paul, indeed?

'He'll be fine with it,' said Isla breezily, 'and he doesn't live at Rose Cottage anyway.'

She looked away before he could spot any anxiety on her face. It had been a spur-of-the-moment decision to offer Ben a bed and she didn't regret it – not really. It seemed churlish not to offer him somewhere to stay when he was only in Heaven's Cove because of her.

And, though she hardly dared admit it to herself, she was

sad at the thought of him disappearing back to America. She was enjoying their chats about the big wide world out there.

But she'd have to square it with Caitlin and Maisie – and Paul definitely would not be happy. She usually did what he wanted. To be honest, she usually didn't mind, and it avoided him sinking into a sulk. He was a champion sulker. But this time she would put her foot down.

There was something about spending time with this big, confident American which made her feel braver.

22

CAITLIN

'Thanks again for the hot chocolate,' said Maisie, stepping aside so Caitlin could fit her key into the front door at Rose Cottage.

Caitlin blinked. Her stepdaughter had been out helping people that morning and had admitted she quite liked the girl she'd been with. And now, she was repeating her thanks, unprompted, for the drink that Caitlin had just bought her.

'You're welcome,' she replied, trying to avoid flurries of snow being blown from the roof.

'That Heavenly Tea Shop place isn't bad, though the name is shocking.' Maisie shook her head, appalled by the twee business names littering the village.

Caitlin smiled. 'I'm just glad it was open on a day like today, and I really enjoyed spending some time with you.'

Which was true, even though she'd only taken Maisie out again for hot chocolate to stop her grumbling incessantly about being bored. Once in the café though, with melted marshmallow around her mouth, her stepdaughter had seemed softer and less combative. They'd had a proper conversation about the work of the local residents' association, which Maisie hadn't immediately dissed. And Caitlin had been tempted to tell her the truth about what her dad had done, but she'd wimped out. It was so nice to be having a decent, grown-up conversation with Maisie, she hadn't wanted to spoil it – though she would have to tell her soon.

'Is the key stuck?' asked Maisie behind her. 'Or are you getting so old, you can't manage to unlock a door?'

And the teenager she knew so well was back! Caitlin gave a wry grin and shoulder-barged the door, which did appear to be stuck. It swung open and Maisie pushed past her into the hall.

Was Isla back now? Caitlin wondered, closing the front door behind them. It was ridiculous how excited she felt about spotting Edith's photo at the cultural centre, as if she'd done something right for once. And she'd been disappointed that her sister wasn't at home when she and Maisie had got back an hour earlier. It was only an old photograph but realising its potential significance had made her feel like a detective: a history detective, piecing together clues from the past.

'You all right?' Maisie asked, kicking off Jessie's borrowed boots. They skidded across the hall, leaving a trail of melting snow in their wake.

'I'm fine, but could you please pick up your boots and put them by the door. I don't—'

Caitlin stopped talking at the sound of raised voices coming from the sitting room.

'What's goin' on?' asked Maisie, picking up her boots and dropping them in a heap on the doormat.

'I'm not sure. It sounds like Isla and Paul.'

It was definitely Paul. A deep male voice was going on and on, not shouting exactly, but speaking much more loudly than usual. Every now and again there was the murmur of a woman's voice.

'If they're having a bust-up, I'm outta here,' said Maisie, heading for the stairs. 'Good luck.'

She pulled earbuds from the pocket of her jacket as she

bounded up the steps, ready to listen to her music in the relative peace of her bedroom.

Caitlin was also tempted to escape upstairs, but she couldn't help feeling protective towards Isla, who didn't sound to be getting much of a word in.

Creeping to the closed sitting room door, she listened for a few seconds and then knocked. The male voice inside went silent and the door was wrenched open.

'Yes?' barked Paul.

'Um, I heard you both in here and...' She tailed off, not sure what else to say.

Paul glared at Caitlin for a second but then his expression softened. 'I'm so sorry. Where are my manners? Did you want to come in?'

He took a step back and opened the door fully. Isla was standing by the fireplace, biting her lip.

'I wanted to have a word with Isla but I can come back another time.'

'Don't be ridiculous. You can come in now, and perhaps you can talk some sense into your little sister.'

Caitlin gave Paul a tight smile and stepped into the room, which was gloomy and cold. Outside, through the bay window, a lone seagull was pecking at snow in the garden.

'Are you all right, Isla?' Caitlin asked.

'Yeah, fine,' Isla replied, though she didn't look it. Her face was strained and she appeared thoroughly miserable. Caitlin resisted an urge to rush over and pull her into a hug.

'What do you think, Cait, about Isla wasting her time with this bloke from the States?' asked Paul.

Caitlin felt her lips purse as she bristled at Paul shortening her name.

'I just don't think it's... seemly,' he went on, sounding as pompous as Caitlin had feared he was.

'Seemly?' Isla puffed air through her cheeks. 'We were

drinking coffee when you saw us yesterday. Not making out in a corner of the café.'

'Yet now you've invited him to stay here, at Rose Cottage.'

Had she? Caitlin gave Isla a questioning look but Isla ignored her.

'I've already explained to you that his flight isn't until Wednesday at the earliest and he can't stay on at Driftwood House. There's no room.'

'So you offered him your bed.'

'I offered him *a* bed, Paul. There's a difference. And you'll no doubt be staying here overnight when he is, anyway.'

'Why doesn't he just leave when the snow buggers off and go to London? I'm sure there's plenty he could be doing there while he's waiting for his flight.'

'I'm sure there is, but he's got more interested in Edith and William's story and, who knows, he might be able to help us solve Gran's riddle.'

Paul sighed very loudly. 'Isla, I know you miss Jessie, and you're not quite yourself at the moment. But I promise you that's a complete and utter waste of time. The letter is one hundred years old. The person who wrote it and the person who received it are long dead, and your gran's riddle is meaningless. She was just messing with you.'

'Why would she do that?' asked Isla, glancing at Caitlin.

Caitlin recognised that glance. She'd seen it often enough when they were younger. It meant 'please help me'.

'Isla's right, Paul. Our grandmother wouldn't have left us the letter and riddle for no good reason.'

'So you're going along with "solving" it too, are you?' When Paul put 'solving' into imaginary air quotes, Caitlin had a sudden urge to slap him.

'Yes, I am, actually.'

'And you think that this Ben bloke from America can help you?'

Caitlin shrugged. 'Who knows? Maybe. William was a part of his family, after all.'

Paul stood still for a moment, then he shook his head. 'Right. Well, you know my views, Isla. I'll be very disappointed if you waste more of your time with that American. I thought you were keen on organising something to mark your grand-mother's birthday? You won't have time for that if you're chasing after shadows. But, of course, it's up to you.' He glanced at his watch and sniffed. 'I need to go but I'll definitely be back later.'

With that, he strode out of the sitting room and, after a few moments, Caitlin heard the front door bang. When she glanced out of the window, he was marching along the garden path – though marching in thick snow was tricky and he slipped a couple of times.

'Sorry about that.' Isla pushed her hair from her face and sank onto the sofa, with one leg curled beneath her.

'Do you two argue a lot?'

'No, hardly ever.'

Probably because Isla usually did what Paul wanted, thought Caitlin, suddenly overwhelmed with concern for her sister. She'd been gone too long when she should have been here, looking out for her.

'What's Paul got against Ben?' she asked.

'I don't know. He's not great with outsiders.'

'Outsiders? He does realise, doesn't he, that this is the twenty-first century, even in Devon? There's a big wide world out there.'

'Mmm. Not as far as he's concerned.' Isla drummed her fingers on the arm of the sofa. 'So, you said you found Maisie. Is she OK?'

'Yeah, I think so. She'd gone out delivering food to far-flung houses with members of the Heaven's Cove Residents' Asso-ciation.'

'Really? That was kind of her.'

'Yeah.' Caitlin frowned, still taken aback by Maisie's sudden benevolence. 'Though she should have told me before getting into a truck with people she didn't know. Guess who she met, though, and had a chat with?'

'I have no idea,' said Isla, obviously not in the mood for guessing games.

But her face lit up with interest when Caitlin told her, 'Connie Carmichael.'

'Old Connie out on the moor? That must have been an interesting meeting. Connie isn't the easiest of people to get along with.'

'Then she and Maisie have a lot in common.' Caitlin grinned. 'Two stroppy people together.'

'Well, I didn't like to say as much.' Isla's smile quickly faded and she began twisting the silver ring on her middle finger round and round. 'Cait, do you think Paul's right and I – we – should stop trying to work out Gran's riddle? Is it all a total waste of time?'

Caitlin walked to the sofa and, after gesturing for Isla to move up, she sat down beside her.

'Being honest, I thought it was all a bit daft at first and a waste of time and effort. But the more I've found out about Edith and William, the more I'm interested in knowing the truth about what happened to them.'

'Me too. It seems important, somehow. As if Gran was trying to tell us something that we *should* know.'

Caitlin raised an eyebrow. 'So important, Gran thought she'd tell us in riddle format rather than just telling us outright?'

'There must be a reason for that too. Perhaps she simply wanted us to work together on it and, you know, talk... about stuff.'

'Stuff like the photo I saw at the cultural centre,' said Caitlin, deliberately misunderstanding what Isla was getting at.

She still wasn't ready to talk about how the life she'd left Isla for had so spectacularly imploded. Not when Maisie didn't even know yet.

'Yeah, that kind of stuff, I guess,' said Isla, disappointment in her voice. 'Anyway, what were you doing in the cultural centre?'

'You mentioned it might be worth a visit so I dragged Maisie there on our way home earlier. She was delighted, as you can imagine.'

'I bet. Where in the centre did you find the photo?'

'It was on the wall, near the main door. A really nice woman called Lettie was there who told me she'd put it up to tie in with the Forties Night in the hall.'

'It's definitely Edith.' Isla pulled up the photo on her phone, enlarged it and peered at their great-great-aunt's face. 'She looks so young and unaware of what was to come.'

'Just as well, don't you think? It's probably better that we don't know what's waiting for us around the corner.'

Would she still have married Stuart had she known what would happen a few years later? wondered Caitlin. Would Edith have stayed in Heaven's Cove and turned down the chance of going to New York?

Isla clicked off the photo. 'I think Edith and William must have met in France, while she was nursing and he was fighting in the trenches.'

'That makes sense. Did Ben say that William was injured?'

'He's not sure, but he knows that William had bad lungs and died of an asthma attack, which made me wonder if—'

'He'd been gassed and needed treatment—'

'And that's how he met Edith.'

Caitlin and Isla smiled at each other. They hadn't finished each other's sentences in a very long time.

'Perhaps you and Ben can find out some more about their time in France,' said Caitlin.

Isla grimaced. 'I'm not supposed to be wasting my time on the mystery of Edith and William, or on Ben. I have been told that very firmly.'

'When did you ever do what you were told?'

When Caitlin grinned, Isla grinned back and Caitlin recognised the girl her sister used to be: feisty, determined and brave. Before she started going out with Paul. Before she got stuck in Heaven's Cove, looking after their grandmother.

'So,' said Isla, 'are you really going to help me to unravel Edith and William's doomed romance, and solve Gran's riddle?'

Caitlin hesitated. She needed to get out of Heaven's Cove, before memories of the past became overwhelming, but she owed it to Isla to stay and help her. Bizarrely, she felt as if she owed it to Edith and William too – a young couple whose doomed love affair had ended long before she was even born. Plus, sticking around would annoy the hell out of Paul, which had to be a bonus.

'Yeah, sure, why not? Let's see what happened to Edith and William and solve the strange puzzle that Gran left us. Thanks, Gran.' Caitlin glanced down at the phone in her hand, which had just beeped with a message. It was from Stuart. 'Um, I need to read this. I'll see you later.'

'Sure.'

Caitlin glanced back when she reached the door. Isla cut a lonely figure, sitting with her shoulders slumped.

'Do you know what, Isla? We should definitely do something to mark Gran's birthday. It would have been her ninetieth, after all. What do you reckon?'

Isla turned, a sad smile on her face. 'Ben suggested something similar and I think that would be lovely. To show that though she's gone she's not forgotten.'

'What do you think Gran would have liked?'

'Every year, we'd line her birthday cards up on the mantelpiece, dress up in our finest, and have a takeaway in front of the

fire to celebrate. That was all she ever wanted, apart from—'
She shrugged. 'It doesn't matter.'

Apart from her family around her, thought Caitlin, who
always sent a card and huge bouquet of flowers but was never
around on the day itself. Being here for this birthday would be
too little too late for Jessie, but perhaps marking the occasion
would bring some comfort to Isla.

'Right then,' she said. 'Tomorrow night we'll have a dinner
party in front of the fire to remember Gran and mark her
birthday.'

'With a takeaway?'

'Obviously.' Caitlin laughed. 'A takeaway dinner party for
four.'

Isla wrinkled her nose. 'Five. You and Maisie, me and Paul,
and Ben will probably be here.'

'Which could be awkward. We don't have to invite him to
the meal.'

'We can't exclude him.' Isla's shoulders slumped again. 'But
you're right, it could be awkward. Maybe we should give the
whole thing a miss?'

Because Paul wouldn't like it? Caitlin said nothing as Isla
twisted her hands together. It was her decision. Her boyfriend.

'No,' she said suddenly. 'I'm sure Paul will be fine with it,
seeing as it's a special occasion. And anyway, it'll give him and
Ben a chance to get to know each other properly.'

'If you're sure.'

'Absolutely.'

'Then it's a date. We can sort out the arrangements later.'

Caitlin walked into the hall and pulled the sitting room
door closed behind her before opening the message she'd
received from Stuart. It was very brief and simply said: *Estate
agent called. We have a buyer for the house. Sorry x*

We, as if selling the house was the result of a joint decision.
Caitlin breathed out slowly to steady herself. She would have to

tell Maisie the truth this evening about what was going on. She deserved to know, and the situation had become so serious, so real, there was no hiding it any longer.

'Poor Maisie,' she murmured underneath her breath.

Poor you, echoed in her brain, but she pushed the treacherous thought away. She'd made her bed and now she'd have to lie in it.

23

MAISIE

Caitlin was being annoying again. Maisie watched as she walked to the window and back to the fireplace. Her step-mother had been criss-crossing the room for the last five minutes, and it was driving her mad.

'What's the matter with you?' she blurted out, when she couldn't stand the constant back and forth any longer.

'Nothing,' said Caitlin, which was obviously a lie. *You need to act more like a grown-up* – that's what Caitlin said to her often enough. Yet she continued to treat her like a child all the time. It was totally hypocritical.

'When are we going home?' Maisie asked, partly because she wondered when they'd be leaving Heaven's Cove, and partly for the effect this question seemed to have on Caitlin these days. As Maisie had anticipated, Caitlin's cheeks began to flush.

'I'm not sure when we'll be going back to London,' she said, going an unflattering shade of fuchsia. She bit her lip and came to sit beside Maisie, who shifted along the sofa, wishing she'd never asked the question. Not if Caitlin was going to get all heavy.

'The thing is...' Caitlin took hold of Maisie's hand.

Maisie stared at her stepmother's fingers, which were gripping her tightly. Caitlin knew. That was the only explanation for her acting all emotional and peculiar. Maisie had kept her dad's secret but Caitlin knew anyway.

'You and Dad are having problems, aren't you?' she gulped. 'I'm not stupid. I know what's going on with him and Chiara.'

'I'm sorry, Maisie. I should have told you earlier but I was trying to protect you. Yes, your dad and I are having problems but—' Caitlin stopped and narrowed her eyes. 'Hang on a minute. What do you mean, you know what's going on with him and Chiara?'

'I didn't say anything because Dad asked me not to and I didn't want to cause even more trouble. But it's been so hard knowing...' She bit her lip, worried that she might cry, partly with relief that she no longer had to keep this huge secret that was burning a hole in her brain.

'Knowing what?' Caitlin urged gently.

'Knowing that they're... you know...'

Was Caitlin really going to make her say it? Her stepmother stared at her for a moment and then her eyes widened.

'Oh. Do you mean...? Your dad and Chiara from his office are...?' She let go of Maisie's hand and leaned back against the sofa. 'Stupid! Stupid!' she muttered.

At first, Maisie thought Caitlin was talking to her. Until she realised that she was talking to herself.

'Stupid!' she muttered again, brushing away tears that were making her hazel eyes glisten.

'You didn't know, did you?' whispered Maisie, horrified that she'd been the one to tell her. 'I might be wrong. I am wrong. Definitely. I am definitely, definitely wrong.'

Caitlin closed her eyes briefly and took a deep breath. Then she brushed the back of Maisie's hand with her fingers. 'What exactly do you think you're wrong about, Maisie?'

Maisie considered lying, but one look at Caitlin's shocked face told her she couldn't do it. That, and the fact that she was a dreadful liar who would be instantly found out.

'I saw them together, Dad and Chiara, that weekend when Dad said he was golfing with his friends. But perhaps Chiara likes golfing too?' She tailed off.

'Where did you spot them?' Caitlin asked quietly.

'Waterloo Bridge.'

'There's not much golfing available in central London,' said Caitlin. 'What were they doing?'

'Nothing. Just standing there, looking at the view and getting in everybody's way.'

'Standing close together?'

'Yeah, I think so.' Maisie sighed. Her dad's arm had been around Chiara's shoulder, and Chiara had had her arm around his waist. It was absolutely disgusting because her dad was well old, and Chiara was only in her mid-twenties. But there was no need for Caitlin to know all of the details. Her stepmother could be annoying but, right now, Maisie felt sorry for her. 'I never did like Chiara. She always laughed too loud at Dad's stupid jokes.'

'Yes, she did.' Caitlin's lips pulled into a tight line. 'Did you tell your dad what you'd seen?'

Maisie shook her head. 'No. I tried to pretend to myself that I hadn't seen anything. I shouldn't even have been there. I was catching a train at Waterloo but it was delayed and I was bored, so I went for a wander to pass the time.'

'But you said that your dad asked you to keep quiet about it.'

'Yeah. Chiara must have spotted me and blabbed 'cos he came into my room a couple of days later and said I'd got it wrong and I shouldn't say anything to you about it. But if I'd got it wrong, why did I need to stay quiet?'

'Indeed.'

Caitlin was sitting very still and Maisie resisted the urge to push her arm through her stepmother's in a show of solidarity against the patriarchy.

'Is that why you've been so rude to him lately?' asked Caitlin, still not moving. Her cheeks had paled and she looked... old, thought Maisie. Old and sad.

'I s'pose. I didn't think it was fair of him.'

'It wasn't fair at all to ask you to keep a secret like that.'

'I didn't want to keep it. I didn't like what he was doing, even though you can be dead annoying sometimes.'

Caitlin gave a slight smile. 'So can you, Maisie.'

Maisie twisted her mouth. She knew it was true, but it was hard to be smiley and polite when, inside, all she felt was this unending rage and confusion and sadness. She loved her dad but she hated him for cheating on Caitlin. She'd grown more fond of Caitlin than she'd ever admit, but her stepmother would disappear soon enough – especially now her dad was playing away.

'If you didn't know about Chiara, why were you and Dad having problems?' she asked in a small voice.

Caitlin took hold of Maisie's hand again. 'I have something to tell you that's going to be hard for you to hear. I've had trouble getting my head around it.'

Maisie was finding it hard to breathe. What on earth was coming? What could be worse than your husband, the man you trusted, cheating on you? *Please don't tell me*, she thought, focusing on the branches of the tree in Jessie's garden that were swaying in the wind. They looked black against the snow still nestling on the roof of the cottage opposite.

'Your dad loves you very much, Maisie. You know that. But the truth is, he has a problem, with gambling.'

Was that all? Maisie began to relax because Caitlin was just being stressy. 'Sure, he likes betting on the horses and football. So what? It's not a crime.'

'He likes betting on anything and everything,' said Caitlin, sounding sadder than Maisie had ever heard her. 'And he's lost a lot of money recently. In fact, he's lost so much money, I'm afraid we need to lose our house to help pay off his debts. It's on the market now and is going to be sold.'

'Sold?' Maisie felt her mouth fall open and couldn't summon up the energy to close it. They had to sell their home. She pictured her bedroom and it suddenly didn't matter that the walls were a different shade of purple from Madison's regularly Instagrammed bedroom. It was her sanctuary – but it would soon belong to someone else.

'Dad contacted me today to say that a buyer's been found for it already. I'm so sorry, sweetheart.'

'So where's Dad now? Is he really working away?'

'Yes, he's in Gran Canaria at a work conference. He really is – I've seen it advertised online. And when he gets back, I expect he'll stay either with his parents or with Uncle Ray for a while.'

'Is Chiara at the conference too?'

Caitlin's face clouded over. 'Yes, she is. I hadn't thought anything of it, but now…'

'So I guess you two really are breaking up.' Maisie bit down harder on her bottom lip, determined not to cry.

Caitlin was crying, Maisie noticed. A fat tear slid off her chin and plopped onto her jumper, leaving a dark stain on the fabric. 'I think so. I'm sorry, Maisie.'

'Are you breaking up because I told you about him and Chiara?' Maisie tried to keep the desperation out of her voice. Was she responsible for ending her dad's marriage?

Caitlin shook her head. 'Your dad and I haven't been getting on brilliantly for a while, and his gambling was the final straw.'

'But isn't it an illness?'

'I think so, and I want him to get better. I've tried to get him help but he hasn't wanted to go down that route so far. I'm hoping your dad will have a good chat to Uncle Ray and that will persuade him.'

'If he does that, will the house still have to be sold?'

'I'm afraid so.'

'But where will we live?'

'I'm trying to work that out. I'm afraid we're not going to be very well off.'

'That explains it!' Maisie could see it all now. 'That's why you're so mad with Isla for not wanting to sell this house. You need the money.'

'The money from this place would be very helpful, that's true. But you don't need to worry. Whatever happens with me and your dad and with the house, I won't let anything bad happen to you.'

Maisie wanted to believe Caitlin. She wanted to believe her so badly. But it was hard to believe adults when they so often let you down. Her dad had just gambled away their house, for goodness' sake, and he *had* to take care of Maisie. He was her biological father. Whereas Caitlin had no biological ties at all. She probably didn't even like Maisie that much and would be glad to be shot of her.

'I'm going to my room,' mumbled Maisie, getting up from the sofa and running for the door. She rushed into the hall, up the stairs and flung herself onto the bed, which creaked and groaned. Then she put on headphones and played her music so loud it made her ears ring – anything to drown out real life and her fears of being abandoned.

24

CAITLIN

Caitlin sat in silence after the door had banged shut and Maisie's heavy tread up the stairs had died away. Stuart, who'd just hit forty-four, and Chiara, the nubile young researcher in his office. Honestly, he was such a midlife-crisis cliché. And such a liar. He'd always sworn that he was faithful through and through. Though he'd told Caitlin so many lies about money recently, what were a few more about the woman he must have been seeing for months?

But how could he have asked his own daughter to keep such a toxic secret? No wonder she'd been all over the place lately.

Caitlin sat, staring into the fire that Isla had lit earlier that afternoon, as shadows lengthened. She should put the lamp on – the glow from the flames didn't reach the corners of the room. But darkness suited her right now. It swallowed the fury, betrayal and pain that were consuming her. But as the fire died down and began to fade, Caitlin recognised something else flickering in her heart – a tiny spark of relief, because at least she knew the way forward. Calmness settled on her as she reached for her phone.

'Caitlin? Is everything all right?'

Stuart's voice was almost drowned out by a buzz of conversation and music in the background.

'Where are you?'

'At the end-of-conference party.' He added quickly, 'More of a networking event, really. You know what these things are like. Dead boring but I need to attend.' His voice became muffled. 'Thanks, Chiara. Put my drink down there, will you?'

Caitlin pulled in a deep breath and held it for a few seconds before exhaling. She was drowning in worry and heartache while her husband was drinking at a party in the Canaries. With his mistress.

'You still there?' he asked. 'You haven't rung up to yell at me again, have you?'

'I haven't yelled, not once, throughout all of this.' Caitlin was surprised by how level her voice sounded. 'I think I've been incredibly restrained, in the circumstances. I've tried to be understanding about how you got into this situation.'

'I know and I appreciate it, Cait. I'm gutted about everything, I really am. I mean, when you look at it, I'm as much a victim in all of this as you are. I'm losing my home too.'

Caitlin could feel her calm beginning to slip. 'What about your daughter, Stuart? Are you as big a victim in all of this as she is? You know she's having a difficult time at school and now her life has been turned upside down.'

Stuart paused. 'You've told her, then. How did she take it?'

'Not well.'

'Did you tell her, though, that she doesn't need to worry 'cos I've got plenty more irons in the fire? We'll be back on our feet again in no time.'

Caitlin stared into the dying flames without answering. Stuart was in denial about everything – the extent of his gambling problem, the loss of their home, the effect his actions were having on his wife and daughter.

'Cait, are you still there? Not now, obviously, but we'll need to sort out some stuff when I'm back from this conference. When are you going to be back in London?'

'I'm not sure I am coming back to London,' said Caitlin, feeling strangely disconnected from her words.

Stuart gave a snort of disbelief. 'Of course you are. You can't wait to be out of that sleepy village and back in town. I know things are difficult, and I'm sorry about that. You know how sorry I am, but once we get the blokes we owe money to off our backs, we can find somewhere else to live.'

'The blokes *we* owe money to?'

'All right. There's no need to rub it in. I know I'm the one who's messed up big time, but we can always move in with my parents or Ray for a while.'

'Your parents won't want the upheaval and your brother lives in a one-bedroom flat miles from Maisie's school.'

'I know it's not ideal, but it'll do until we get ourselves sorted out. Ray's is the best bet and he's on board with the plan.'

'I'm not going to live at Ray's.'

'We won't be *living* at Ray's. We'll only be stopping there for a while until everything's back on track.'

'I've already told you. I'm not coming back, because you lied to me.'

'Hang on a minute. Let me find somewhere quiet.' The background buzz began to fade as Stuart moved away from the party. 'Look, I know I told a few fibs, and I've apologised again and again. But gambling's an addiction. I couldn't help it.'

'Have you rung that number I gave you, to try and get some support?'

He sniffed. 'Not yet, but I will, I promise, when I'm not so busy. I just want things to go back to the way they were. We don't need a posh house to be happy together.'

'No, we don't. But we do need trust.' Caitlin's calm had vanished. 'I'm so angry with you for losing the house. I'm furious that you were so reckless with Maisie's happiness and future. But I reckon I could get over that. It would take a while but it's only bricks and mortar at the end of the day.'

'Exactly.'

Caitlin tensed, trying to stop her body from shaking. She was about to blow up her life. Once she said the words there was no going back. But who was she kidding? Her life was in pieces anyway. She screwed her eyes shut and pressed the red button.

'What I can't get over is Chiara. I know about the two of you. For goodness' sake, she must be young enough to be your daughter. Are you sharing a room in Gran Canaria? Holding hands under the conference table and kissing on the beach?' When a silence stretched down the line, Caitlin's head began to swim.

'Did Maisie tell you?' said Stuart at last.

Caitlin opened her eyes, feeling sick with disappointment. A part of her had wanted her husband to deny it, to say that Maisie had made a huge mistake, to make her believe that he hadn't betrayed her. But Maisie had been right all along, as Caitlin had known in her heart that she was.

'Is that how you found out?' demanded Stuart.

'Don't blame Maisie. She thought I knew already, and it wasn't fair to ask her to keep such a big secret.'

'I only got Maisie involved because I was scared of losing you. You have to believe me.'

Caitlin shook her head. 'The trouble is, I don't believe you, Stuart. Not any more. First, you lied about money, all the time, and now I find out that you're having an affair.'

'Affair is a big word,' muttered Stuart as if he didn't want to be overheard. 'It's not like that.'

'You're with Chiara in Gran Canaria right now, so are you telling me there's nothing going on while you're both away together?'

'You're reading this all wrong,' said Stuart, but the slight hesitation before he spoke, and the trace of guilt in his voice told Caitlin everything she needed to know. Her marriage was over.

'Let me know when you're back at Ray's so Maisie can come and join you,' she said, her voice flat as the realisation hit her that the life she'd wanted so much had turned out to be a sham. 'I'll look into how she can get to school. Maybe if she takes a couple of buses, or the Tube and a bus, it might work. I don't know.'

'Don't send her back on her own, Cait. Can't she stay with you for the time being, until you've had time to calm down? Only I'll be at work and Ray won't want a teenager moping around the flat on her own.'

It was obvious to Caitlin that now she was out of the picture, it was Stuart who didn't want a teenager moping around and cramping his style with Chiara. Poor Maisie. Caitlin could have cried for her stepdaughter. She could have cried for herself. But the flash of anger had gone, leaving her hollowed out and numb.

'We'll talk about Maisie another time,' she said, needing to bring the call to a close. 'I have to go.'

'Cait, you are going to change your mind, aren't you?'

Caitlin stared at the shadows dancing around her grand-mother's sitting room.

'I'm afraid not. My mind's made up.'

So, that was that. Caitlin ended the call and dropped her phone onto the sofa as if it was red hot. She knew about Stuart's affair and her marriage was done. She'd had her life all mapped out but now the way ahead was uncertain and scary.

'Gran, I wish you were here to talk to,' she whispered into the dark room. But Jessie was gone for good, Isla resented her, and Maisie was distraught. What a mess.

Caitlin got up, chose a log from the pile on the hearth, and placed it on top of the dying fire. There was a crackle of sparks, and orange flames curled around the wood as she sat back on her heels, her mind on her stepdaughter.

When Maisie had asked if spilling the beans about Chiara made any difference, Caitlin had said no. But she'd lied to make Maisie feel better because the truth was it had changed everything.

Before Caitlin knew about Stuart's mistress, she was determined to stay with her husband. He'd recklessly gambled with their money and destroyed her trust, but how could she leave a man whose life was on the slide, even if he didn't accept the reality of the situation? She'd abandoned too many people in her life to do that again.

But his clandestine relationship with Chiara was the final straw. That deception wasn't born out of addiction. It was born out of his selfishness and lust and lack of regard for his family. It was the ultimate betrayal and indicative of the state of their relationship. Her marriage was over and she could leave Stuart without the crushing guilt that had shackled her to him.

But what about Maisie? Caitlin stared into the fire and made a vow to herself. She'd walked away from Isla when her sister was not much older than her stepdaughter, and she would never make the same mistake again. She would never abandon Maisie, even though the stroppy teenager clearly disliked her intensely and would probably insist on staying with her father anyway. In which case, Caitlin would be truly alone.

Tears fell into her lap as she wished with all her heart that she'd made different choices all those years ago, when she'd had the chance.

25

ISLA

Isla shivered as she crossed the hall to turn up the thermostat on the wall. The snow was thawing this morning. Every now and then, there was a thud as parcels of snow slid from the roof and landed in the garden. But it was still cold and the paths outside were treacherous.

A sudden knock on the front door made her jump and she lowered her hand, the thermostat temperature still unchanged. A dark shape was visible through the stained glass.

Isla swallowed. She'd thought he might cry off but here he was, on today of all days. She ran her hands down her pink sweatshirt before walking to the door and opening it.

'Hi, there. Are you quite sure this is OK?' Ben was standing on the doorstep, a rucksack over his shoulder. 'I can try to find somewhere else for tonight. Or I can squeeze into the box room at Driftwood House if it's not convenient.'

'No, it's fine. Come on in.'

Isla ushered him inside, out of the melting snow, and they stood awkwardly in the hall. It was a shock, seeing the American in her home, even though she was the one who'd invited him. He brought a different energy to Rose Cottage, a sense of new life and adventure.

'You have a lovely home,' said Ben, sweeping his arm around the square, bright hallway. 'I love these old houses. How old is this place?'

'Early nineteenth century. My family were living in Heaven's Brook, which is a hamlet nearby, but they moved into the village when this house was built.'

'Interesting.'

Ben nodded, without catching her eye. He seemed nervous and Isla wondered again if inviting him to stay had been a horrible mistake. But it was too late to change things now.

She waited for him to untie his boots and slip them off. Then she said, 'Come with me and I'll show you to your room,' leading the way up the stairs and onto the landing. When they reached the doorway to Jessie's room, Isla stopped, her hand on the doorknob and aware of Ben standing closely behind her. Would Jessie mind this man having her room?

How can she possibly mind? She's gone.

Isla closed her eyes and felt Ben's hand on her arm. 'Are you sure this is OK?'

Isla opened her eyes. 'Of course,' she said brightly, stepping into the room and gesturing for Ben to follow her. 'I hope you'll be comfortable in here.'

'I'm sure I will be.'

He put his rucksack on the bed, on top of the sheets that Isla had changed earlier that morning. The old bedsheets, that still smelled of Jessie's lavender perfume and talcum powder, were in the washing basket. Isla didn't have the heart to bundle them into the washing machine and wash away her gran's perfume for ever. Not yet.

'There are towels over there, on the dressing table, and the bathroom is just along the landing, past the bookcase. Anyway, I'll leave you to unpack.'

She glanced at Ben's rucksack. Unpacking would only take a matter of minutes, but Paul had a habit of calling in unexpectedly and she didn't want him to find her and Ben in the bedroom together. It wasn't worth the look of disappointment on his face.

'Just give me a shout if you need anything else,' she said, heading for the door. 'Anything at all.' Did that sound over the top? Paul would think so. 'I mean...' She stopped talking and smiled instead. If she started second-guessing what Paul would think about everything, Ben's stay with them would be hard going. 'See you later.'

She'd reached the foot of the stairs when the front door opened and Caitlin stepped inside after her trip to the Mini Mart for provisions. Although the snow was gradually disappearing, getting out of the village would still be more trouble than it was worth.

'Is he here?' Caitlin asked, glancing at the large boots in the corner. Her face was pale this morning, apart from the dark circles under her eyes. She looked as if she'd hardly slept.

'Yes, he's upstairs in Gran's room, unpacking.' Isla swallowed. 'Are you sure that Gran wouldn't mind? It just feels wrong, especially with it being her birthday today.'

To Isla's surprise, Caitlin put down the bulging carrier bag she was carrying, walked over and put her arm around her shoulders. 'I don't think Gran would mind at all. She wouldn't want her room kept as some sort of shrine. I'm sure she'd much rather it was being used.' Caitlin raised an eyebrow. 'Especially by a handsome young American.'

'Is he handsome?' Isla grinned. 'I hadn't noticed.'

'Don't let Paul hear you saying that.'

Isla's smile faded. 'He's not here, is he?'

When she looked around, she felt Caitlin's arm tighten across her shoulders. Being so close to her sister felt unfamiliar after years apart, but it felt nice. It felt safe.

The sound of Maisie's music began to drift through the air and Caitlin dropped her arm. 'Sorry about the racket. I'll ask her to turn it down.'

'It's all right. I've got quite used to having her music in the house. It'll cheer the place up, especially today. I can't believe Gran would have been ninety. What a milestone! I wish she'd lasted just a few more weeks...'

Suffocating grief settled on Isla like a blanket.

'I know,' said Caitlin, her face drawn. 'Me too. But we'll mark the occasion tonight and drink to her memory. Happy birthday, Gran.'

'Yeah, happy birthday,' said Isla, feeling her throat tighten.

'I'm not sure Maisie will be keen on the whole idea of a dinner party, mind.'

'Not keen on what?' asked Maisie, who'd just appeared at the top of the stairs, still in her pyjamas. She pushed a hand through her hair which looked as if it hadn't seen a brush in days.

'Hi, Maisie. Are you all right?' asked Caitlin. 'I put my head around your door earlier but you were fast asleep. I thought you might want to talk?'

Isla glanced between the two of them. Talk about what? There was something going on between Caitlin and her step-daughter that she didn't know about. Maisie looked tired, too, as if she'd been up half the night.

But Maisie shook her head. 'What won't I be keen about?'

'We're holding a dinner party this evening, to celebrate Gran's birthday,' Caitlin explained.

Maisie scratched her backside distractedly. 'But she's not here.'

'No, but she'll be here in spirit and Isla and I want to celebrate her life.'

'Bit ironic when her life's over,' muttered Maisie, before being silenced with a glare from Caitlin.

'So, do you want to come, or not?' she asked her step-daughter.

'Not really. It's not my kind of thing.'

'We're having a takeaway.'

Maisie's eyes lit up. 'Can we have a curry?'

'I expect so. Does that sound all right, Isla?'

When Isla nodded, Maisie grinned. 'In that case, count me in. I'd kill for a decent chicken bhuna with onion bhajis.'

'Let's say seven o'clock then, in the front room,' said Caitlin. 'I'll sort everything out – all you two need to do is turn up in your finest.'

'Our finest?' spluttered Maisie.

'Yes, evening dress, to celebrate the life of Jessica Gillard née Anstey. Though as neither you nor I have an evening dress here, we'll have to do the best we can.'

'Can I wear my jeans?'

Caitlin sighed. 'Yes, I suppose so, if it gets you there.'

'I'll come as long as you don't both spend all night talking about that stupid letter and riddle.'

Isla smiled. 'I promise that any talk about them will be brief and targeted. There's not much to say anyway, because we still know very little about William or Edith so the riddle is far from being solved.'

'That old woman knew Jessie. Maybe she knows something,' said Maisie, shifting from foot to foot at the top of the stairs.

'Which old woman?' asked Isla, thrown by the conversation going off at a tangent.

'Connie, who lives out in the wilds. She made the angel that Jessie left me.'

Isla's jaw dropped. She'd never known where the carved angel had come from. She'd assumed that Jessie had bought it years ago in one of Heaven's Cove's many gift shops.

'Did she know Gran well?' she asked.

Maisie shrugged her shoulders. 'No idea. She grabbed the angel when she saw it and accused me of stealing it. As if I'd steal a bit of old driftwood. Then she said she'd made it for Jessie 'cos she was kind to her. She said she'd known Edith too. Or her mum did. Connie's old but I don't think she's *that* ancient.'

Breath caught in Isla's throat. 'She knew Edith?'

'Why didn't you tell me?' asked Caitlin.

Maisie sniffed. 'You didn't ask me, and I've told you now, haven't I? She didn't tell me anything about her anyway.'

'Do you think she'd speak to me about Edith?' Isla asked.

'Doubt it. She doesn't like strangers.'

'But it sounds as if you and her got on well.'

'I wouldn't put it as strongly as that. She couldn't wait for me to leave.'

'OK, but she does know you – kind of – so why don't we take a trip out there later?'

'What, in your Mini?' Maisie scowled at Isla's car through the hall window. 'We'll end up in a ditch.'

Isla glanced at Caitlin's posh car, parked on the road, next to her beloved Mini. But there was no way her sister would risk pranging the car that would take her back to London.

'Tomorrow, then? It's supposed to thaw a lot overnight.'

Maisie sucked air through her teeth. 'Connie won't be happy if we just rock up on her doorstep.'

'But it's worth a try?'

Maisie sighed. 'I s'pose so if it stops you all going on about that letter and stupid riddle. But you've been warned.' She headed back towards her bedroom. 'You'd better bring cat food,' she called over her shoulder.

'Cat food?'

'I have no idea,' said Caitlin, pulling up the zip on her jacket. She looked at her watch and frowned.

'Are you going somewhere?'

'Yeah, I thought I might go out again for a walk.'

'Would you like me to come with you?'

'No,' said Caitlin quickly. 'No need. I just want some fresh air and I won't be long. See you later, yeah?'

'Yeah, see you later,' said Isla, but Caitlin had disappeared through the front door before she'd finished speaking.

There was definitely something going on, thought Isla, finally getting round to turning up the thermostat. Caitlin was concerned about Maisie for some reason, and now she was off on some mystery mission that was making her nervous. Isla had known her sister long enough to recognise when she was flustered.

But it was none of her business, Isla decided, going into the kitchen to make Ben a cup of strong coffee. There were enough old secrets about Edith and William to unravel, without trying to uncover Caitlin's present-day ones too.

26

CAITLIN

Caitlin checked her watch for the third time in as many minutes. She'd hurried to get here on time, but Sean was late and there had been no text or call to explain why. Surely he wouldn't have arranged a meeting to then leave her standing here, on a snowy cliff high above Heaven's Cove, as some sort of twisted revenge? Caitlin shook her head, ashamed that the thought had even crossed her mind. Sean had been kind and decent as a teenager and she had no reason to suspect that he'd changed.

He'd helped her look for Maisie yesterday, for goodness' sake. Which, in a roundabout way, was why this meeting was happening at all. When Caitlin had texted to let him know that her stepdaughter was safe, he'd replied with a request that they get together for a chat.

Caitlin's first inclination had been to gently decline. Why did Sean want to meet up again? What good would it do? But on second thoughts, it had seemed churlish to say no – though she had insisted on the location of their rendezvous.

He'd suggested meeting at The Smugglers Haunt, but Caitlin had changed it first thing this morning for the cliff that rose above the village. She didn't want locals gossiping about the two of them, and she did desperately need fresh air. Ever since finding out about Stuart's betrayal last night, she'd felt as if she was suffocating. And she had no idea how Maisie was coping with the news. The teenager had clammed up as usual.

Caitlin glanced around, wondering if Rosie might spot her out here. But Driftwood House was quiet behind her, with no one to be seen. The snow around it was thawing and patches of grass were emerging across the clifftop. But the road down to the village was still slippery and she noticed that Ben had walked to Rose Cottage rather than chance taking his hire car.

She turned back to the swelling tide that was booming into the foot of the cliff. Seagulls were circling overhead and a boat, a splash of red in the water, was chugging towards the quay. It was so peaceful up here, and beautiful with the sun lighting a golden path across the waves.

Heaven's Cove lay far below her, hugging the curve of the land where it began to rise away from the sea. Smoke curled from chimneys, and the village Christmas tree – erected but not yet garlanded with lights – was a smudge of snowy-green near the church tower. This wasn't such a bad place to be when you needed a break from the cut and thrust of London, from the pain and heartache of a broken marriage.

'Hey!' Sean had just appeared, hurrying up the path. 'Sorry I'm late,' he called. 'My stupid watch stopped. It needs a new battery.' He reached Caitlin, his cheeks red. 'And I'm not getting any younger. I used to jog up this cliff and now walking up it almost kills me.' His smile faded. 'Are you OK? You look cold.'

'Yeah, it's freezing up here. Shall we walk to warm up?'

'Sure.'

The two of them wandered along the clifftop, away from Heaven's Cove, their feet leaving prints in the snow. They'd walked across the cliff dozens of times before but, this time,

Caitlin didn't know what to say. Impacted snow squeaked under their feet as they walked on.

After a while, Sean cleared his throat. 'Thanks for letting me know that you'd found Maisie. You said she'd been out helping the residents' association?'

'That's right. She should have told me first but... Anyway, she's safe and that's all that matters.'

'Are you sure you're all right?' Sean glanced at her. 'You sound... I don't know. Different.'

'Sorry. I didn't sleep well last night and there's a lot going on.'

They walked on further, making small talk about her car and the upcoming Forties Night dance, and villagers whom Caitlin remembered from her adolescence. So many people seemed to arrive in Heaven's Cove, put down roots and stay for ever. People like Isla, who was determined to stay put.

'I wasn't sure you'd agree to meet me,' said Sean, coming to a halt. Driftwood House was a way behind them now and Caitlin could just see the chimneys of Heaven's Brook in the distance.

'You helped me look for Maisie. I was happy to meet up for a chat.'

'Even if you didn't fancy a get-together in the pub?'

'I didn't want to feed the Heaven's Cove rumour mill. Is it still as bad as it used to be?'

'Oh, yeah.' Sean whistled through his teeth. 'The new gossip queen of Heaven's Cove is a woman called Belinda. She's nice enough, but nosy as hell. Do you know her?'

Caitlin shook her head. 'I don't think so.'

'Probably best to keep it that way unless you want all of your deepest, darkest secrets up for grabs.' He nodded at a wooden bench they were walking past. 'Look, shall we sit down for a minute?'

He swept snow from the seat and sank onto it. Caitlin

followed, ignoring the cold that immediately began to seep through her jeans. Sean cleared his throat. 'Anyway, the reason I wanted to see you before you go back to London is because I have something to ask you.'

'OK.'

He shifted round towards her and took a deep breath. 'Why did you drop me like a hot potato the minute you left Heaven's Cove?'

'What do you mean? I didn't,' she protested, feeling adrenaline prickle through her.

'You didn't?' He gave an incredulous laugh. 'Come on, Cait. I've been waiting fifteen years for an answer and all you can do is deny what you know very well happened. But if you need reminding, before you left we sat here on the cliffs and you cried. You must remember that, surely. You promised you'd be back soon and we talked about me coming up to the city to visit you. We vowed to stay together. But the minute you got up to London, everything changed.'

Caitlin opened her mouth to protest but closed it again. What could she say?

'I mean, I get that we were young and people change but the way you did it...' Sean shook his head. 'Basically, you ghosted me, Cait. Your calls became increasingly sporadic and before long I could never get hold of you. You stopped texting and you stopped coming home.'

'I did come back to Heaven's Cove sometimes,' said Caitlin weakly.

'Very occasionally for fleeting visits, and you never had time for me, did you? I only found out about your visits after you'd gone back to London.'

Caitlin opened her mouth again, to argue that she hadn't behaved quite so badly. But she couldn't do it. Every word of what Sean had said was true.

She breathed out slowly, feeling like a balloon deflating.

Deep down, she'd known this was coming, from the moment she'd seen Sean at the garage when she'd brought her car in for repair. She'd known that she deserved it.

'Well?' he urged. 'Are you going to run away again without giving me any answers?'

Caitlin slowly shook her head, wishing she'd never got out of bed that morning. 'You're right. I behaved appallingly and, though you probably won't believe me, I'm very sorry about it.'

'Was I really that awful, that you couldn't wait to drop me? Did our relationship mean so little to you?'

Sean ran a hand through his hair in a gesture of frustration that Caitlin remembered so well. She sniffed, close to tears.

'No, it was the opposite of that. Our relationship meant everything to me.'

'So, why did you drop me like that?' Sean's face was a picture of confusion. 'I just don't get it, Cait. What did I do wrong?'

'Absolutely nothing. You did absolutely nothing wrong.' Caitlin was shivering with emotion.

'So what's the truth? I think you owe me that much.'

He was right, and she knew it. 'OK. The truth is it wasn't you, it was me.'

'Great!' Sean jumped to his feet. 'I put my dignity on the line to ask you for an answer and all you can do is feed me a cliché?'

'Please don't go.' Caitlin grabbed hold of Sean's arm and pulled him back onto the bench. 'I promise it's not a cliché. Well, it is sometimes, but in this instance it's not because it's the truth.' She blinked, her eyes swimming with tears. 'I did care about you, Sean. I really cared. A lot. And that was the problem.'

Sean shook his head. 'I still don't get it.'

'I was desperate to get away from Heaven's Cove but I hadn't factored you into my escape plan. I hadn't factored in...'

She swallowed, almost unable to admit it to herself. 'I hadn't factored in falling in love.'

Sean was staring at her, saying nothing.

'I wanted to stay in touch but I knew that if we did, or if I saw you, then I might want to come back to Heaven's Cove for good. And I couldn't. I needed to get away from this suffocating place and make something of myself.' She was finding it hard to catch her breath. 'I should have told you but I was a coward and pretty mixed up. That's not an excuse but I hope it's an explanation. I know what I did was wrong and cruel, but I felt lost and I made bad choices. I protected myself at the expense of other people – I hurt you and I hurt Isla and my grandmother. And I can't take any of that back. It's too late. But I can say sorry.' Her chest was so tight, she could hardly breathe. 'And I am sorry. Truly sorry.'

Tears were trickling down her cheeks. Tears for what might have been and tears for the marriage she'd just lost. She felt them run across her jaw and plop onto her collarbones.

Sean reached into the pocket of his jeans and pulled out a clean tissue, which he handed to her. 'Here. You'd better have this.'

'Thanks,' gulped Caitlin, dabbing at her cheeks. She looked at him as he gazed out to sea, his face in profile. 'I'm so sorry, Sean. I missed you so much,' she whispered, her words caught in the breeze and carried out across the waves.

If he heard, he didn't show it. He continued staring at the blue horizon.

'Was it worth it?' he asked after a while. 'Was it worth leaving everything and everyone here behind?'

'I threw myself into studying and work and I did well. I got promotions and I made friends and I met Stuart, my husband, and I gained Maisie as my daughter.'

Sean turned to face her. 'So are you saying that it *was* worth it?'

'I thought so at first but now...' Caitlin blinked frantically and swallowed but it was no good. She began to sob like she hadn't sobbed for years. Her head bent towards her knees under the weight of emotion pressing down on her.

'Sorry,' she managed between sobs. 'So s-sorry.'

She was sorry to dissolve into a snivelling, snotting mess in front of Sean, but mostly she was sorry for the hurt and upset she'd caused over the years. And she could now see, in startling clarity, the extent of the loss she'd inflicted on herself and those around her in the name of escape – a loss of friendship, close-ness, love. And when it came to Jessie, there would never be the slightest chance of redemption.

Caitlin suddenly felt strong arms around her and she was pulled in tight against Sean's chest. She sobbed against the prickly wool of his jumper, feeling again like a young teenager who had just lost her mother. She hadn't allowed herself to cry like this back then. She'd had to be strong for Isla. But now Isla didn't want her protection.

Caitlin wiped the tissue roughly across her nose and managed to stop sobbing. But when she pulled away from Sean, exhausted, he gave her such a compassionate smile it almost set her off again.

'Blimey, Cait, you don't half look a sight.'

Caitlin imagined she did, with her hair on end and mascara down her cheeks. She started to scrub at her cheeks with the tissue but gave up. What was the point in trying to keep up appearances?

'Sorry,' she murmured, feeling worn out.

'You've said that already,' said Sean, fishing another tissue from his pocket and handing it over. 'Many, many times.'

Caitlin sniffed. 'I've messed up big time with everything, Sean. I behaved so badly back then and have got so much wrong since.'

'You always seemed a bit... I don't know... out of control,

when we were younger. But you should cut yourself some slack. You'd lost your mum and had been responsible for Isla from such a young age. I can see why you wanted to break free.'

There was the kindness she'd always seen in Sean coming out. She was the one at fault, the one who'd screwed up. Yet he still found it in his heart to make excuses for her when the truth was she hadn't deserved him all those years ago.

When she said nothing, too emotional to speak, he added: 'Anyway, what's so wrong about your amazing life in London? It can't be that bad.'

Caitlin hesitated, but she was so tired of putting on a brave face. So tired of pretending.

'My marriage is over,' she said quietly. 'It turns out that Stuart, apart from having a gambling problem, has been having an affair under my nose. And he owes so much money to so many people, we're having to sell our house to pay off his debts, which means I'm about to be homeless, along with Maisie, who can't stand me. Isla is so disappointed with my behaviour, she can hardly bear to look at me. And I never got to say goodbye to my grandmother who sacrificed a great deal to take me and Isla in, because I've been selfish and stupid and have stayed away.'

She stopped talking and the silence was broken only by the rush of the wind swirling eddies of snowflakes around them.

'You're right, it *is* that bad,' said Sean. 'Your life's a total mess.'

'Wow, thanks,' said Caitlin, remembering that one of the things she'd always loved so much about Sean was his inability to fudge and obfuscate. Unlike Stuart, he didn't lie or take risks with people's feelings.

'So where's this Stuart now then?'

'He's in Gran Canaria.'

'How can he afford that if he's as broke as you said?'

'He's there for a work conference, with his girlfriend, who happens to work in his office.'

'Let me guess, she's much younger than him?'

'Yep.'

'Classic.' Sean shook his head. 'So what are you going to do?'

'I don't know. I'm applying for jobs and I was hoping that Gran's house could be sold so I'd have enough for me and Maisie to rent somewhere in London for a while. But Isla wants to stay there. And so does Paul.' A shudder of distaste crossed Sean's face. 'What is it?'

'Nothing, really. It's just... like I said, I'm not that keen on Paul.'

'Me neither.'

'I've seen him and Isla out together around the village. He can be very dismissive of her.'

'And controlling. I'm worried about her but she won't let me in.'

'Have you told her what's really going on in your life?' He frowned when Caitlin shook her head. 'That'll be why, then. She thinks you're still living the perfect life in London that you left her for.'

'Whereas, in reality, my life has imploded, which means that not only was I a total cow to her, I abandoned her for absolutely nothing.'

'You moved away, yes, but you didn't abandon her.'

'As good as. There's no point in sugar-coating any of it. I've behaved appallingly and I've got my just deserts: no family, no husband and no home.'

It sounded so stark laid out like that, but it was the truth. And there was no one to blame but herself.

Caitlin sighed. 'I'd be grateful if...'

'You'd be grateful if what?'

'I was going to say I'd be grateful if you didn't tell anyone else what I've just told you, but I realised that I don't need to ask.'

'I always was boringly trustworthy.'

'Wonderfully trustworthy,' corrected Caitlin, 'and a very decent man. Thank you for letting me cry on your shoulder. Literally.'

Sean stared into her eyes for a moment and then leaned forward and briefly kissed her cheek. His lips felt as if they burned her skin.

'Thank you for telling me the truth, at last. And I'm sorry for the troubles you're having. I really think you should tell Isla.'

Caitlin nodded. 'I know you're right, and I will. It's just hard to find the words.'

'Just tell her what you told me.' He did up another button on his jacket. 'I'm sorry, Cait, but I really need to go. One of our best customers rang earlier and asked if he could drop his car in to the garage today, in about twenty minutes. Do you want to walk down with me?'

Caitlin shook her head. 'No, thanks. I'll sit here for a while and enjoy the view.'

'You're not going to do anything daft, are you?' He glanced nervously at the cliff edge. Loose stones, dislodged by the wind, were tumbling down the cliff face and into the churning sea hundreds of feet below.

'No, I think I've done quite enough daft things already.' She smiled up at him. 'But thank you for caring.'

He shrugged. 'Don't leave it too long before you go back to Rose Cottage and get warm. I'll see you around, Cait.'

He started making his way down the path and Caitlin watched him go. His walk was the same – long strides with a swing in his shoulders – but he was no longer the teenaged boy she'd fallen in love with fifteen years ago. He was a man now and, as she touched her cheek where his lips had brushed her skin, she realised that she still had feelings for him.

27

ISLA

Isla wasn't the best of cooks, as Paul often jokingly remarked, but there was something about baking a cake that she found profoundly soothing. Perhaps it was the rhythmic beating of the eggs, or the memories it invoked of Gran, who had the sweetest tooth of anyone Isla knew. Jessie loved cake – any sort of cake – and could often be found in this kitchen, following a new recipe, with flour dusting her clothes. She always wore an apron but still managed to make a mess.

Isla folded flour into the Victoria sandwich she was making, so engrossed in her memories that she only realised Ben had come into the kitchen when he cleared his throat behind her.

'Hi.' Isla swung around, the spoon in her hand dripping cake mixture onto the floor. 'How are you doing? Are you all unpacked?'

Ben gave a grin. 'It didn't take long because I travel light. Apologies for disturbing you but I wondered if there's anything I can do to help, seeing as you're very kindly having me stay in your home?'

'I don't think so, but thank you. I guess you'd have been flying about now, if you hadn't missed your flight.'

'I'd have been somewhere over the Atlantic. But it doesn't matter. I've managed to book another flight from Heathrow, first thing Thursday morning. I don't have anything much to do in London – I've visited the city before – so I thought I'd stick around in Heaven's Cove until Wednesday and maybe explore the area more. What do you think?'

'I think there's a lot to see, especially if the weather improves.' Isla bent over, deliberately hiding her face as she cleaned the splattered floor tiles. There were pros and cons to Ben's longer stay: on the one hand, more opportunities to hear about his travels; on the other, more time for Paul to get arsey about having another house guest. She straightened up, all trace of mixed emotions gone and her expression re-set to pleasant. 'Help yourself to some lunch if you like. There's a loaf in the bread bin over there and ham and tomatoes in the fridge.'

'Maybe in a minute? I'm still full of Rosie's amazing cooked breakfast. You should try it some day. It's unbelievable.'

'So I've heard from other people.'

'What are you making?'

'I'm making a cake for Gran, which sounds kind of crazy, but today wouldn't only have been her birthday, it would have been her ninetieth so it's extra-special.'

Isla blinked when tears began to prickle. What a day of celebration they could have had, with Jessie opening cards and presents. Perhaps Caitlin would even have made it to Heaven's Cove, rather than wishing Gran a happy birthday over the phone.

'I'm sorry. You must miss her even more.' Ben pulled out a chair and sat at the kitchen table. 'You miss them all the time but special birthdays, anniversaries, Thanksgiving, Christmas – they're the worst. So what are you going to do with the birthday cake?'

'We're going to have it for dessert this evening after our

birthday meal in honour of Gran.' Isla twisted her mouth. 'Does that sound really odd, or even ghoulish?'

'Not at all. It sounds like a touching way to remember someone you loved.'

Isla poured the mixture into two baking tins, smoothed them with a knife and opened the oven. A blast of heat hit her as she pushed the tins inside and slammed the door shut.

'Right. That's done.' She pushed hair from her hot forehead with the back of her hand and sat at the table, opposite Ben. 'You're invited to the meal tonight, if you'd like to come. It's only a takeaway because that was what Gran always wanted. She loved spicy food.'

'Thank you for the invitation but I couldn't possibly intrude. It's a family occasion. What would Caitlin say?'

'She's not always been terribly family orientated. She won't mind.'

'Are you sure? I get the impression she can be a little fierce.'

'Ah, you've realised that, have you?' Isla grinned. 'Her bark is worse than her bite, once you get to know her, I promise. She kind of had to be fierce growing up because she was looking after our mum, who died when I was eleven, and then she was looking after me, with Gran's help, obviously.'

'Your sister sounds like a formidable woman.'

'She is,' said Isla, remembering how Caitlin had spent years looking out for her, until it all became too much. 'Anyway, she definitely won't mind, and Paul's going to be there, so it's not just family.'

'Won't Paul mind, having an interloper at the special meal?'

He wouldn't be overjoyed, thought Isla, but they could hardly leave Ben sitting alone in his bedroom while they tucked into curry and cake downstairs.

'Paul won't mind at all,' she assured him, crossing her fingers behind her back.

28

CAITLIN

The room looked amazing, even if Caitlin said so herself. She stood with her arms folded and looked around her. A table had been set up in front of the hearth – with grudging help from Maisie – and firelight was twinkling on the crystal glasses and silver cutlery that Caitlin had found at the back of a kitchen cupboard: a stash of elegant tableware that Jessie, always down-to-earth, had rarely used.

A lamp by the door was exuding a golden glow that puddled shadows in the corners of the room. And propped on the mantelpiece were photos of Jessie, as a young woman, as middle age had beckoned, and as old age had arrived. Among them were pictures of Jessie with teenaged Caitlin and Isla, photos that had brought a lump to Caitlin's throat.

'Happy birthday, Gran,' she said quietly, smiling at the photographic array. 'Thank you so much for everything.'

'Are you talking to yourself?' asked Isla, who had slipped into the room while Caitlin's back was turned.

'I was talking to Gran.'

'I do that all the time,' said Isla as Caitlin turned round. 'It makes me feel better.'

'Wow!' Caitlin did a double-take as she took in her sister.

It wasn't that Isla was wearing the silk dress she remembered on Mum, or the fact that her hair – usually up in a ponytail – was hanging loose over her shoulders. What caught Caitlin's eye and held her gaze was the glow radiating from Isla's face. When had her little sister grown up and become so beautiful? she wondered, feeling a deep frisson of regret. She'd missed so much over the last few years. She and Isla had still met occasionally, but there had been an accompanying undercurrent of resentment and guilt that had made both sisters reticent and glum.

When Caitlin left Heaven's Cove, Isla was an awkward sixteen-year-old, with braces on her teeth and an arsey attitude. She still sported the attitude at times but, in the intervening years, she had turned into a stunning, wonderful woman.

Isla smiled, the candles on the dining table flickering light across her face. 'What do you think? Wearing Mum's special dress seemed appropriate for this gathering, seeing as I like to think that Mum and Gran are together again, mother and daughter having a good catch-up in heaven. Do you think Gran would approve of this get-together?'

There was the hint of tears in her eyes and Caitlin stepped closer to her sister. 'I'm sure she'd love it – the fact that we're remembering her and honouring her birthday. Even if we can't, for the life of us, work out that damned riddle she left us.'

Isla laughed. 'I think Gran would be chuckling at our ineptitude. She always claimed she was better at quizzes and puzzles than me.'

'And she had to prove it one last time.'

Isla twisted her mouth. 'Probably.' She nodded at Caitlin's dress. 'You look nice. Really nice.'

'So do you. Lovely, in fact.'

'Really?' Isla's cheeks flushed pink and she ran a hand down the blue silk that brought out the colour of her eyes, just as it had done with Mum. 'This dress makes me feel closer to her, you know.'

'I do know.'

Caitlin grasped her hand and gave it a squeeze – two sisters united in shared memories of the woman they'd lost so long ago.

She released Isla's hand when Paul walked into the room. 'Sorry. I didn't mean to interrupt a family moment.' He gazed around him and his jaw dropped. 'Good grief, it looks very different in here. You've been busy.'

'Caitlin has, with Maisie's help.'

'Then, well done, Caitlin and Maisie. It's quite the effort.'

Paul had certainly made an effort. He was wearing a charcoal suit, with a crisp white shirt and a black tie. He looked smart and suave, as if he was going to a wedding – or working as an undertaker, on the quiet.

He walked over to Isla and kissed her on the cheek, then drew back to look at her, his hands on her shoulders. 'You decided on that dress, then?' It was said with a smile but Caitlin caught an edge to his tone.

Isla flushed pinker and bent her head. 'It felt right to wear it for Gran's birthday meal, seeing as it was once worn by her daughter.'

'And it suits Isla beautifully, don't you think?' interjected Caitlin, giving her sister's arm a pat in solidarity.

'Absolutely.' Paul let go of Isla and began to fiddle with his gold cufflink that was sparking candlelight across the room. 'It's just a little low-cut, don't you think?'

Isla folded her arms self-consciously across her chest as Caitlin studied the neckline of the beautiful dress. It was square, showing off Isla's long neck and delicate collarbones, but it only grazed the tops of her breasts. The dress was perfectly proper.

'If you think that's low-cut, you should see some of Maisie's T-shirts,' Caitlin shot back, annoyed with Paul for denting Isla's confidence. She seemed to have shrunk in stature since his comment. 'I think the dress is totally fine. Mum always loved it, and I'm sure that Jessie would have approved.'

Isla shot her a grateful smile and went to sit by the fire.

'Is Maisie joining us?' asked Paul frostily, glancing at the table, which was set for four.

Caitlin shook her head. 'No. She was going to but had a last-minute change of heart and decided she'd rather eat in her bedroom. She's been in touch with a local girl called Beth who's coming over for a while, which is great. Maisie could do with some company because she's coping with a lot at the moment.'

A lot that she refused to discuss. Caitlin had tried a few times during the day to engage her stepdaughter in conversation, to check that she was doing all right. But Maisie had insisted that she was 'totally fine' and had urged Caitlin not to be so 'stressy' about everything.

'So, who's the fourth guest?' asked Paul, obviously not the slightest bit concerned about Maisie's welfare. 'Ah.' His lips pulled into a pout. 'Our American guest. Of course.'

Caitlin bristled. Ben wasn't '*our* American guest' at all because Paul didn't live here – though she supposed it was only a matter of time now Jessie was gone.

Paul smiled, all peevishness gone from his face as if he'd flicked a switch. 'May I say, Caitlin, that you're looking particularly lovely this evening.'

'Thanks.' Caitlin caught sight of herself in the mirror above the fireplace. She was wearing the only dress she'd brought for what was supposed to be a short stay in Heaven's Cove. But the pale green of the jersey fabric suited her.

The doorbell rang and there was a sudden thundering of feet, down the stairs and through the hall.

'That'll be Maisie,' said Caitlin with a grin. 'She's hungry.'

A minute later, Maisie came into the room in her pyjamas, carrying two large carrier bags, which she plonked onto the table. The smell of Indian food began to drift around the room, making Caitlin's stomach grumble. She was hungry too.

Isla began to pull out plastic tubs and place them along the middle of the table. 'Maisie, do you think you could get the plates which are warming in the oven?'

When Maisie came back with the plates, she ladled an obscene amount of curry and rice onto hers. At least the stress of losing her home didn't appear to be affecting her appetite.

'Leave some for the rest of us.' Isla laughed and, rummaging in the paper bag nearest to her, pulled out a poppadum and waved it at her niece. 'Don't forget one of these – oh, and don't forget that we're going to see Connie tomorrow, if the snow's on the way out.'

'You're wasting your time trying to talk to her. And mine,' muttered Maisie. But she said a nice thank you for the food before grabbing the poppadum and disappearing up to her bedroom.

'Who's Connie?' asked Paul, taking off his jacket and hanging it over the back of his chair. He ran his hand along the lapels, smoothing out imaginary creases.

'Connie Carmichael, who lives up on the edge of the moors.'

'Really?' Paul sniffed. 'Why on earth are you going to see her?'

'Maisie thinks Connie's mum knew Edith, or knew something about her, at least. It's worth a quick trip to see what Connie might have heard.'

Paul shook his head. 'I might have guessed it would be about that odd letter that you're all obsessed with.'

'Hardly obsessed,' murmured Caitlin, but Paul had already sat down and was grabbing his share of onion bhajis.

Caitlin and Isla spooned out their rice and had begun ladling curry onto their plates when the door opened and Ben walked in. 'I smelled the food. Sorry I'm late.' He stopped talking and looked around the room. 'Wow, when you invited me to join you for takeout food, I didn't realise it was going to be such an occasion.' He glanced at Paul in his crisp white shirt and looked down at his jeans. 'You didn't mention there was a dress code.'

'I don't suppose you have a dinner suit stuffed in your rucksack,' said Caitlin with a grin. 'And you look perfectly fine, so take a seat. It was a tradition that Jessie would dress up on her birthday and enjoy her favourite takeaway food. And even though she's gone...'

Caitlin stopped talking and swallowed hard as Ben slipped into his seat.

'I'm all for traditions being upheld,' he said, giving her a sympathetic smile. 'I think it's wonderful to honour your grandmother's memory in this way. And you all look amazing.'

He smiled at Caitlin and Paul and then his eyes fell on Isla, across the table. 'Hey, look at you. Now I'm feeling *very* underdressed.'

'Don't worry about it. We're all friends here,' said Paul with unexpected bonhomie. 'Can I suggest you have some food before it all goes. We Devon folk have good appetites. Here, let me help you,' he urged, getting to his feet and leaning across the table.

But when he pushed a container full of rice towards Ben, his elbow caught the side of a chicken korma and Caitlin watched, horrified, as it slid off the table and into Isla's lap.

'Oh my God, I'm so sorry,' said Paul, grabbing a handful of paper serviettes and thrusting them towards Isla, who had yelped and jumped up. Great clumps of curry were sliding down her dress, leaving streaks of yellow grease across the delicate blue silk.

Ben and Caitlin were also on their feet, but there was nothing to be done. Isla, her face twisted in despair, scooped up the bottom of her dress, to stop curry from falling onto the carpet, and ran from the room, towards the kitchen.

'I'd better go and help her. Just eat,' said Paul, following his girlfriend.

There was silence after the door had banged shut behind him.

'What a terrible shame,' said Ben, sitting down slowly. 'That was a beautiful dress.'

'It belonged to our mother,' said Caitlin, feeling close to tears. No dry cleaner would be able to remove those stains from silk. 'It meant a lot to Isla, a lot to both of us.'

She began to spoon rice onto her plate. Her appetite had disappeared but she didn't know what else to do.

'Paul must feel awful about it,' said Ben, glancing out of the window into the darkness beyond.

'Yeah,' said Caitlin, spooning out more rice.

He would feel awful. Who wouldn't? She placed the spoon carefully back on the table. Yet Paul was not an accident-prone man. He'd made that very clear when he'd berated Isla for leaving the hob on and doing 'daft' things.

A horrible thought wormed its way into Caitlin's brain. Had Paul deliberately ruined their mother's dress? He wasn't happy about Isla wearing it, and Caitlin had seen the shadow that crossed his face when Ben looked at her sister.

But no, she was being ridiculous. Paul loved Isla and would never do something to hurt her like that. She pushed the container of rice, very carefully, towards Ben. 'Help yourself. I'm sure they'll be back soon.'

The two of them ate almost in silence, save for a few pleasantries, until a few minutes later, Paul and Isla came back into the room and took their seats. Isla was back in her usual 'uniform' of jeans and sweatshirt, and she'd scraped her hair into a ponytail. Her face was pale and there was a smudge of mascara on her cheek.

'I'm so sorry about that,' said Paul, lifting Isla's hand to his lips and kissing her palm.

Isla tried to smile. 'Don't worry. It wasn't your fault. It was an accident.'

'I know, but I can't believe how clumsy I was. That's not like me at all. I'll have the dress dry-cleaned tomorrow.'

'I'm not sure there's much point,' said Isla. She grabbed hold of her wine glass and raised it, her hand trembling. 'But please don't let this spoil Jessie's birthday celebration.' She held her glass aloft. 'Happy birthday, Gran. We love you and we miss you.'

'To your gran, who sounds like a wonderful woman,' said Ben, before taking a sip of wine.

'Yeah. To Jessie,' said Paul, his mouth turned down at the corners. He drank his glass of wine in three long gulps.

What had her grandmother made of Paul? Caitlin wondered. And what would her verdict be on Ben, who was staring at Isla and Paul with a thoughtful look on his face?

'More food, Ben?' Paul asked, sounding very jolly all of a sudden. 'I promise not to throw it over anyone's lap this time. We can enjoy our meal to mark poor Jessie's passing, and I'll even allow talk of William and Edith and that damn letter without yawning.'

When he laughed, Ben and Caitlin smiled politely but Isla hardly raised her eyes from her food while they ate.

29

ISLA

The house wasn't quiet. It was never truly quiet, even at almost three in the morning, thought Isla, as she crept down the stairs. Every step creaked under her bare feet, and she could hear the grumble of the ancient boiler, doing its best to keep the worst of the cold at bay.

The big thaw was happening. There was a steady drip-drip from outside, where the snow on the roof was melting. But Isla's pink towelling dressing gown wasn't thick enough to keep out the chill, and, padding across the hall tiles, she cursed her bare feet.

The kitchen tiles weren't any better. So, after grabbing orange juice and leftover sponge from last night's birthday meal, she sat on the kitchen table, her legs swinging back and forth. Moonlight dappled across her lap as she bit into the cake and savoured its comforting sweetness.

It was silly to be so upset about her mum's dress, she told herself. Many happy memories were attached to the dress, but owning it and wearing it wasn't the same as having her mum around. And her distress at the dress's demise only made things worse for Paul, who was upset about the accident. He was snoring upstairs right now, but he'd apologised again before falling asleep.

'So, Isla, you need to accept it's happened and move on,' she told herself firmly, taking another bite of the sponge. She glanced up and a scream caught in her throat when a shape appeared in the doorway.

'I'm sorry. I didn't realise... I didn't mean to scare you.' Ben rubbed his eyes with the heels of his hands. 'I'll go back to bed.'

'No, it's OK,' managed Isla, her heart pounding with adrenaline. She swallowed her mouthful in one gulp. 'Did you want something?'

Ben ran a hand across his chin. 'Just a glass of water, if that's all right. I crept down trying not to wake anyone. I didn't know you were in here.'

'Not surprising, seeing as it's the middle of the night.'

Isla carefully wiped her mouth, wishing she'd run her fingers through her hair before venturing downstairs. It must be sticking up all over the place. And there were cake crumbs all down her dressing gown.

'What's this, a midnight feast?'

Ben nodded at the half-eaten sponge while she tried not to look at his legs. He'd thrown a sweatshirt on but obviously slept in his boxer shorts. And although the light was dim, she could see that his legs sported the same golden tan as his face and arms.

'Something like that,' she managed. 'I don't normally get up at three to raid the kitchen, I promise. But I couldn't sleep.'

'Did you have bad dreams?' asked Ben, taking a clean glass from the dishwasher and filling it with water from the tap. Around them, Rose Cottage creaked and groaned as it settled, and an owl screeched its lonely cry from the garden.

'No, not dreams. I was kept awake by memories. Actually, I was thinking about my mum. The dress I was wearing tonight belonged to her.' She smiled. 'I can remember her wearing it, before she got sick. I thought she was the most elegant creature alive.'

Ben set his drink down on the marble worktop. 'You looked pretty elegant yourself. It's a beautiful dress.'

'It was,' said Isla sadly. She sniffed. 'But it was an accident and Paul's really upset about it so...'

'So you need to accept it's happened and move on?'

Isla grimaced. 'Ah. You heard me talking to myself, I take it?'

'Uh-huh.' Ben nodded.

'Which, again, is not something that I normally do. Though I have been talking to my gran recently, even though she's dead. Maybe I'm just losing my mind.'

'Me too, then, 'cos I talk to my dad *all* the time.' He frowned. 'Not that I've ever admitted that to anyone before.'

'Don't worry. I won't tell a soul, and I reckon it's only if they start answering us back that we need to worry.'

Ben grinned and sat down on the table beside her. 'I am sorry about your dress. And while I agree that accepting things and moving on is a very sensible course of action, it's not always the easiest thing to do.'

Isla glanced at him, aware that his bare thighs were only inches from hers. Though, fortunately, her thighs were currently encased in thick towelling. 'It sounds as if you're speaking from experience.'

'Kind of. It's nothing like losing a parent, but—' He cleared his throat. 'I had a bad break-up with a girlfriend a couple of years ago and it took me a while to accept that it was over.'

'I'm sorry. Is that why you first went travelling, to get away from things?'

'Initially, yes. But I realised how much I loved seeing new places and experiencing a bigger life than the one I'd been living. And I got kinda hooked.'

'You're going to miss it when you go back to work.'

Ben nodded. 'Not for long, though. Being in Heaven's Cove over the last couple of days, without lots to do, has given me time to think, and I've decided that I'm going to give up my job straightaway and travel across Asia for a few months. Then, I'll head to Australia and New Zealand before going back to the States. Or I might just keep on travelling.'

'Wow. A real adventure! What does your mum think of that?'

Ben winced. 'I haven't told her yet. I've only just decided to do it. But she's got my sister and grandchildren living nearby so I'm sure she'll come around to the idea, especially if she can unearth ancestors on every continent for me to chase.' He nudged his shoulder against Isla's. 'I bet she'll be pleased for me that I'm seeing the world.'

'I envy you,' said Isla, acutely aware of Ben's body close to hers. He was so full of life – a life filled with adventure and possibilities.

'You talk as if you're stuck here, shackled for ever to Heaven's Cove, just like Edith,' said Ben, his eyes finding hers.

'Sometimes it feels like it. Caitlin got away and is living an interesting life.'

'And you'd like one too?'

'Sometimes, though I have this house and Paul and I had my gran.'

She blinked to stop tears from falling. It was strange but in the dead of night was when she missed Jessie the most. When she knew that her grandmother's bed was empty – although now it was taken by a young American who had appeared in their lives, out of the blue. All thanks to Jessie's riddle and the mystery surrounding Edith and William's ill-fated romance.

Ben reached out his hand, as if he wanted to comfort her, but then pulled it back.

'Do you know what?' he said briskly, hopping off the table, 'I think we'd better return to our beds or we'll both freeze.'

'Right,' said Isla, thrown by Ben's abrupt manner.

She went to slide off the table but her dressing gown caught on a corner and pulled her off balance. Ben reached out his hand again and she grasped hold of it to steady herself as her bare feet hit the tiles.

His fingers wrapped tightly around hers, and he didn't let go. They both looked at their hands entwined and neither of them moved. The sitting room clock struck three, its chimes echoing through the house. And when Ben bent his head towards her, Isla found she could hardly breathe. Was he going to kiss her? Did she want him to?

There was a sudden crash upstairs as a door hit a wall and Ben and Isla sprang apart.

'What the hell was that?' he muttered, running a hand through his hair. The hand that had just held Isla's.

'That's Maisie going to the loo. She's like a herd of elephants in the middle of the night.'

'She sure is noisy. Anyway' – Ben shrugged – 'we'd better go, don't you think?'

'Yeah, sure, you head off. Though I'll wait for a minute before I come up. I don't want Maisie leaping to any wrong conclusions.'

She smiled to show she was joking, but Ben had already murmured 'goodnight' and disappeared into the gloom of the hall. His glass of water sat forgotten on the worktop.

A few minutes later, once Maisie was safely back in her bedroom, Isla moved up the stairs like a ghost and slid into her warm bed.

'All right?' grunted Paul, turning his back to her.

'Fine,' said Isla quietly, pulling the duvet up to her chin.

She lay on her side and looked at her ruined dress, hanging on the wardrobe door. A shaft of moonlight had crept through a chink in the curtains and the wide smears of grease staining the dress fabric looked almost translucent. Isla rolled onto her back and stared for a while at the ceiling, sleep still eluding her. Her mind was whirling with memories of the past – and memories more recent. She could almost feel the warmth of Ben's skin against hers.

Isla must have slept eventually because it was gone eight o'clock when she opened her eyes. Paul was clattering around the bedroom, getting dressed. He'd half-pulled the curtains and, in the pale light of dawn, the curry stains on her mum's dress looked even worse.

Isla groaned and turned over. Then she remembered her early hours meeting with Ben in the kitchen and groaned again. He'd held onto her hand and had bent his head towards her, as if... Isla pushed herself up onto her pillows. She was too imaginative for her own good. Ben had simply grabbed her hand to stop her from falling, and had probably bent his head to see if she was ever going to let his hand go. What had happened in the kitchen in the early hours felt like a dream, and dreams faded, just as her dreams of travelling had melted away.

'Paul,' she said, brushing hair from her face. 'Can I ask you something?'

Paul, who was sitting on the bed, put his sock on before answering. 'Yes. As long as it's nothing daft, sweetheart.'

Isla wasn't sure what would constitute 'daft' in Paul's eyes, so she ploughed on. 'Just a thought, but when things are settled with the house, and Caitlin and Maisie are back in London, why don't we go away somewhere?'

'Away?' Paul frowned as he pushed a foot into his second sock.

'Just for a week or two. We could both do with a break and it would be great to find some sunshine.'

'And how far would we have to go to find that at this time of year?'

'Not too far. The Canary Islands, maybe – Tenerife or Lanzarote?'

'Isla.' Paul shuffled along the bed, closer to her. 'It'll be sunny here, soon enough. And you know that I can't tolerate heat, plus I dislike Spanish food. All that tapas. I don't want small plates of snacks. I want a decent meal.'

'It doesn't have to be Spain. We could maybe go to Florida or even Dubai for a break. People fly there all the time for holidays.'

Paul shook his head. 'I don't think so.'

'Don't you want an adventure? To see new sights and meet new people?'

'There's quite enough to see around here and I'm meeting new people all the time at work.'

'Are you phobic about flying?'

Paul got to his feet. 'I'm perfectly fine with flying. I've flown in the past but I didn't enjoy it. All that hanging around at the airport and being herded around like sheep. And for what? Sunburn, dreadful food, and stomach upsets.'

'OK.' Isla took a deep breath. 'I get that you don't like travelling so maybe I could go away for a week on my own, sometime.' Paul had begun to scowl. 'Or maybe I could go with Caitlin.'

'Caitlin who ignored you for years?'

Isla winced. 'She did. You're right. But we do seem to be getting on better these days, on and off.'

'That's only because she's trying to persuade you to sell this house.'

'That's a little harsh.'

'Harsh, but true. And if you want to spend time away from me you only have to say and I'll leave.'

'That's not what I'm saying at all,' said Isla with a sigh.

'Well, that's what it sounds like.' Paul's face softened and he sat back down on the bed. 'Look, sweetheart. I love you and I want you to be happy and you're happiest when you're with me. That's the truth of it. And there's no way I'm going to Tenerife or Lanzarote.' He leaned over and kissed the tip of her nose.

'Honestly, the sooner that man stops putting ideas in your head and goes back to America, the sooner we can get on with our lives in Heaven's Cove. I'll see you later, yeah?'

Isla nodded and, suddenly feeling overwhelmingly weary, closed her eyes again.

30

CAITLIN

'I wish you'd woken me!' Caitlin glanced up as Isla hurried into the sitting room in her dressing gown, her long hair streaming behind her. 'Have you seen the time?'

'Yes,' said Caitlin calmly, closing the newspaper she'd bought from the Mini Mart half an hour earlier. 'It's ten o'clock.'

'Exactly! I only closed my eyes for a minute and I fell asleep again. You should have knocked on my bedroom door.'

'Why? Having a lie-in isn't a crime. Have you noticed the hours that Maisie keeps?'

'Yes, but the difference is she's fifteen and I'm thirty-one, with lots to do today.'

'Like what?'

'Like packing up Gran's clothes and trying to find out more about Edith and William, so we can solve the riddle.'

'And get our hands on the fortune that Gran alludes to? Well, that would be nice.' Caitlin put the newspaper down in her lap. 'Look, Isla, I didn't wake you because you obviously needed the sleep. You were pretty upset after what happened last night.'

'What do you mean?' demanded Isla, pushing her hands through her hair.

'I mean Mum's dress being ruined, obviously.' Caitlin narrowed her eyes because something was off with Isla who seemed unusually agitated. 'Why? What else happened last night?'

'Nothing. Why? What do you think happened?'

'Nothing, except for half a ton of curry landing in your lap.'

'Right.' Isla flopped onto the sofa and folded her arms.

'Has Paul gone to work?' asked Caitlin, although she knew he had. She'd seen him striding down the garden path before breakfast. She'd been sitting here, thinking about him, and wondering whether it was wise to broach her suspicions with Isla. It might not be, when her relationship with her sister was already on shaky ground.

'Paul left ages ago.' Isla inspected her nails and began to pull at a loose cuticle. 'Where's Ben? Have you seen him this morning?'

'Briefly, but he's gone.'

Isla stopped fiddling with her nails and looked up. 'What do you mean he's gone?'

'He came down early, all packed up, and said he didn't want to impose on us any longer.'

'Has he gone back to London?' asked Isla, a hint of something in her tone that Caitlin couldn't quite place. Then she realised that it was forced indifference. If you didn't know Isla well, you'd think she was simply being casual and unconcerned. But Caitlin knew her well enough to catch the edge in her voice.

'I don't think he's going to London today. The roads around Devon are rammed, apparently, now the snow's melting and motorists are being advised to stay at home. But he's decided it's fairer on us if he moves back to Driftwood House. Rosie messaged him first thing to say that her guest was a no-show last night, if staying here was a problem, seeing as we've just lost Gran.'

'OK.' Isla nibbled at a hangnail.

'Is something going on?' asked Caitlin gently.

'Of course not.'

'Only you can talk to me, about anything.'

Isla tilted her head and gave her a straight stare. 'Yeah, right. Like you talk to me about everything that's going on in your life.'

'I don't know what you mean.'

The newspaper fell from Caitlin's lap but she left it on the floor. Her sister had got out on the wrong side of the bed this morning and seemed up for a fight.

'I mean that there's all sorts of things going on with you but you don't tell me about any of them. I know we're not close any more, but...'

When Isla opened her arms and shrugged, Caitlin felt her heart break. How could she have grown so far apart from this young woman whom she'd once loved so fiercely.

'I'd like us to be close again,' she said quietly.

'Then talk to me, Cait.' Isla shook her head. 'You shut me and Gran out of your life for years.'

'I still saw you,' protested Caitlin.

'Very occasionally, and you never spoke to us about anything important. It was all inconsequential stuff, about your big house and your friends who I never met and your perfect life. You kept us at a distance.'

'That's because I felt guilty about... everything,' she blurted out.

'OK, I'm not surprised. But I'm also not stupid. I know there's other stuff going on at the moment that you're not telling me.'

Isla wasn't going to let her off the hook and Caitlin didn't blame her. She'd screwed up big time.

She sighed and clasped her hands in her lap because they

appeared to be shaking. 'The truth is, I haven't told you what's going on because my perfect life has turned out not to be so perfect after all.'

When Isla said nothing, Caitlin continued: 'Stuart has a gambling problem and owes so much money that we need to sell the house immediately to pay off his debts.' Isla's mouth had fallen open. 'And I've just learned that he's been cheating on me for at least the last few months.' She swallowed, her mouth as dry as a bone. 'Anyway, the cheating thing is good, really, because it means I can leave him with a clear conscience. Having abandoned you and Gran, which was unforgivable, I didn't feel able to do the same to him, even though we haven't been getting on for a while. But his infidelity solves the problem. So, like I say, that's good. Really good. And I'm fine with it.'

She stood up quickly and walked to the window. She could hear her heart hammering in her chest and a rushing noise in her head.

'I'm sorry,' said Isla, getting to her feet and taking a step towards her. Was she going to come over and hug her? Caitlin would fall apart. She folded her arms defensively and Isla stepped back. 'Is that why you sent Maisie to us at Easter? Because you and Stuart weren't getting on?' When Caitlin nodded, she frowned. 'I wish you'd told me.'

'Well, I've told you now.'

'Does Maisie know about everything that's going on?'

'Yes, but she only found out very recently so I'd rather you didn't say anything to her.'

'Of course not.' Isla thought for a moment. 'Is that why you're so keen for me to sell Rose Cottage? To pay off Stuart's debts?'

Caitlin shook her head, feeling close to tears. 'The money wouldn't be for Stuart. Maisie and I will be going it alone – if she wants to stay with me, which she probably won't, actually.'

Caitlin pulled in a deep breath. 'So, the money would be useful, that's all.'

'I can't believe that Stuart would be such a... such a...' Isla's face was flushing pink with indignation. 'How dare he betray you like that! Did you know about the gambling?'

'I gradually realised that he had a problem but he refused to do anything about it and I didn't realise how bad it had got. But then he lost the house. He owes money to some pretty unsavoury characters, by the sound of it, so the house will have to go.'

'Are you and Maisie in any danger from these people?'

'God, no. I don't think so.' Caitlin felt a shiver run through her. 'I hadn't really thought about it. Stuart seems sure that the money from the house will get them off his back.'

'And as if that wasn't bad enough, you've stood by him and then he goes and cheats on you.' Isla was going pinker still. 'Who with?'

'With a young woman in his office, which isn't terribly imaginative of him.'

'You sound so calm about it all, Cait.'

'I am now. But I wasn't.'

'No, I bet.'

Isla pulled the belt of her dressing gown tighter. 'I get it now, why you were so keen on me selling up, but...' She sighed. 'I'm sorry, Cait. I should be more supportive but I really can't face losing this house. It's been in our family for over a hundred years. William's letter to Edith arrived here, Mum was born upstairs, and there are so many memories of Gran everywhere.'

'I know, and I get it now, too. You shouldn't have to sell Rose Cottage because my husband has made a mess of everything. Maisie and I will manage. I'll get another job and we can rent somewhere cheap. Or' – Caitlin gave a wry smile – 'we can solve Gran's riddle instead, and find the vast fortune that she's promised us. Though why she couldn't just leave the money to us in her will like normal people do, I don't know.'

Isla grinned and looked up at Caitlin from beneath her eyelashes, just like she used to when she was a child. 'I don't think Gran mentioned a *vast* fortune and, to be honest, it's been nice working on solving it with you. Mostly.' Her grin disappeared. 'Look, I'm glad you've told me what's going on, and I am sorry. I just wish you'd told me before.'

'What, and admit that my perfect life was a sham and I'd abandoned you and given up everything here...' An image of Sean swam into Caitlin's mind and she batted it away, desperate to get the words out. '...for nothing, in the end? That's not really my style, is it?'

She gave what she hoped was an insouciant shrug, but the pity on Isla's face showed that her sister could see right through her bravado.

'You have Maisie.'

Caitlin nodded. 'I do, and I'm so fond of her. She reminds me of myself – always wanting what she can't have. Striving. Discontented. Not realising the value of what she has. Or in my case, had.' She smiled. 'But that's kids for you.'

Isla smiled back. 'Kids, huh?' She turned towards the door, aware of heavy footsteps in the hall. 'Talking of which...'

Maisie pushed open the door and stood with her hands on her hips. 'There you both are. Why aren't you dressed, Isla? I thought you wanted to go and speak to that weird old woman.'

'Yes, I do.'

'Then you need to get dressed now 'cos I got up specially and it's not, like, even half past ten.'

'Yes, sir.' Isla gave a mock salute and followed Maisie from the room but stopped in the doorway and looked back. 'Do you want to come with us, Cait?'

'No, you're all right, if you don't mind going, just the two of you?' said Caitlin. She felt wrung out and couldn't face dealing with Connie Carmichael right now. The woman had a reputation for being irascible.

'No, that's OK. Maisie and I can have some quality bonding time.' Isla twisted her mouth. 'Are you sure you're all right?'

'Yes, you know me,' said Caitlin brightly. 'I'm always fine, in the end.'

And though that was a lie because she felt far from fine, Caitlin did feel lighter somehow and hopeful – hopeful that it might not be too late to repair her relationship with her beloved sister.

31

ISLA

Maisie was grumbling about something as Isla drove out of Heaven's Cove, towards Connie's isolated house, but Isla was only half listening. Her mind was still on the conversation she'd just had with Caitlin and the problems that her sister was facing.

It was the first time in years that she and Caitlin had really talked, and she was glad that her sister had finally trusted her with the truth.

As the grumbles to her left continued, she swerved to avoid a patch of gleaming ice that she hadn't seen until the last minute. She was too busy thinking about Caitlin's revelations, and then there was the news that Ben had fled back to Driftwood House. Memories of their night-time kitchen meet-up kept nudging into her brain. Memories of what he'd said and what she'd said. How he'd sat beside her on the table and told her of his plans to travel the world. The way he'd caught her when she stumbled and they'd clasped hands. The fact that she hadn't wanted him to let go. What kind of girlfriend to Paul did that make her?

'Isla!' said Maisie forcefully.

'What?' Isla pulled her attention back to the narrow lane that was still edged with snow.

'I said you need to turn left just past that big tree.'

'I know,' said Isla, slowing down carefully to avoid sliding as she turned off the road. She would have missed the turning without Maisie's warning but she wasn't about to admit it.

The car climbed higher, surrounded by fields still coated in white, and Maisie began to shift about in the passenger seat.

'How did it go with Beth last night?' asked Isla.

What she really wanted to know was how the teenager was coping with the bombshell news about her dad's gambling and the marriage separation. But Caitlin's plea not to stray into that territory was still ringing in her ears.

'Yeah, she's all right. I thought she was a bit... you know, at first. But now we've met up again, I can see she's quite... you know.'

Isla didn't know, but that seemed to be all the answer she was going to get from Maisie, who was now leaning forward and peering out of the windscreen.

'I'm not sure this is a good idea,' she said, when Connie's isolated cottage came into view. 'She wasn't very welcoming when I turned up the other day and she's a bit...' She stopped talking and crossed her arms.

'A bit what?' asked Isla, frustrated with truncated sentences going nowhere. She stopped the car and turned off the engine.

Maisie shrugged in the silence. 'I dunno. A bit weird and scary. The kind of person who might have a shotgun in the cellar.' She paused. 'Do you think she's got a shotgun in the cellar?'

'No, of course she hasn't.' Isla forced herself to laugh, hoping she sounded more confident than she felt. The Carmichaels' reputation for being troublesome and hell-raising lived on in Heaven's Cove, even though the only member of the family left was ancient Connie.

Isla swallowed. 'Well, we're here now. I'll go and knock on the door and you stay in the car until I've had a word with her.'

'Do I have to?'

'Yes,' said Isla sternly before sliding out of the car, slamming her door shut and walking to the front door. The blue paint was peeling and any metal letterbox was long gone. A piece of plywood covered up the rectangular hole left behind.

Isla hesitated and then knocked loudly on the door. 'Hello, Miss Carmichael. I'm Isla, Maisie's aunt. You met Maisie the other day when she brought you some food.'

She knocked again, more loudly this time, and, when nothing happened, turned to the car and raised her palms to the sky. Maybe Connie was out, though that was unlikely.

She turned back to the door and knocked again but inside the house everything was silent.

The car door slammed and Maisie appeared at her elbow. 'Here, let me have a go.' She leaned over to what was once the letterbox, lifted the plywood flap and shouted: 'Connie, it's Maisie and I have food for Dolly and Petra, and soup.'

'Dolly and Petra?'

Maisie stood up when a door inside banged and there was a distant shout: 'Wait!'

'My job is done,' she declared, with a smug smile. A carrier bag Isla hadn't noticed before was banging against the teenager's shins.

'Is that cat food and soup, by any chance?'

'Yep. I went to that supermarket by the church before you hauled yourself out of bed this morning. Though it's so small, it's a travesty to call it a supermarket. It's smaller than the corner shop down our road in London.'

The front door was suddenly wrenched open and Isla couldn't help taking a step back. Connie, in all her glory, was impressively scary. Her sparse white hair was standing on end and huge crevices lined her face. In their midst was a pair of beady brown eyes and a thin mouth pulled into a tight line.

'You can come in,' she declared, nodding at Maisie. She fixed her gaze on Isla. 'You can't.'

'She's all right,' said Maisie. 'Isla's my aunt, Jessie's grand-daughter, and she only wants to ask you a couple of questions.'

'I don't answer questions. I get too many nosy folk poking their noses in from social services.'

'She's not social services. She's a librarian.' She glanced at Isla. 'Are you a librarian? I've never properly asked.'

'That's close enough.'

Connie sniffed at this latest piece of information and stepped back to allow the two of them into her home.

Maisie went straight in but Isla stood on the doorstep. This had seemed like a good idea at the time – speak to Connie and see if she could shed any light on Edith and her decision not to go to New York with William. But now she was here, the isolation of this place and Connie's appearance and belligerence were giving her the heebie-jeebies. Perhaps she did have a shotgun in the cellar.

'Are you coming in or not?' huffed Connie. 'Makes no difference to me.'

Isla swallowed, stepped into the dark, narrow hall and followed Maisie into a large, old-fashioned kitchen. Connie came in behind them and pointed at a table covered in chipped Formica.

'You can put the cat food and soup over there. What sort of soup have you got?'

'I got a selection,' said Maisie, pulling tins from the bag. 'Cream of tomato, chicken broth, leek and potato, and beef and veg.'

'Leeks are revolting.'

'You can just eat the rest, then.'

Connie sniffed before shuffling away. After a moment, Isla

followed her along the hall into a large sitting room, which reeked of cats. The old lady made her way to a shabby armchair that had been placed right next to the window and sank into it. She glared at Isla.

'Following me now, are you? Who are you again?'

'I'm Isla, granddaughter of Jessie in Heaven's Cove who died recently. I think you knew her.'

'She died, did she?' Connie looked out of the streaked glass, at the fields still covered in snow, down to the sea beyond. 'I fancy someone told me that the other day but I'd forgot 'til now. That's a shame.'

'Maisie told me that you gave Gran – Jessie – the carved angel that she always carried with her.'

'That's right. She was kinder than the rest of them in the village.'

'Shall I get you a cup of tea, Connie?' asked Maisie, poking her head around the door.

'That would be kind of you, child.'

'Uh, Isla, did you want a drink, too?'

Isla tried not to let the surprise show on her face. Maisie had never offered her a drink before. She thought about Connie's kitchen with its grimy wooden countertops and chipped mugs piled up in the sink.

'No, I'm fine.' She smiled. 'But thanks for offering.'

'Yeah. Whatever.' Maisie disappeared into the kitchen and began clattering about.

'She's a good girl,' said Connie. 'You've brought her up well.'

'That's nothing to do with me. It's my sister who's Maisie's stepmum.'

'What happened to her real mum?'

'I'm not one hundred per cent sure. She went to live in Canada a few years ago.'

'Without her daughter?' Isla nodded. 'So Maisie's living with you in Heaven's Cove now, then.'

'Just for a while, until she and my sister have sorted out their… issues.' Isla changed the subject because Connie didn't need to know the ins and outs of their family history. 'How are you getting on, living out here on your own?' She glanced at the Zimmer frame in the corner and the dust piling up on top of the bookcase.

'Perfectly fine,' retorted Connie. 'You're not a do-gooder, are you? Here to try and encourage me to leave?'

Isla shook her head. 'Definitely not.'

'Good. I'm content up here on my own and will never join' – she shuddered – 'a retirement community. If I'd wanted to be part of a *community*, I'd have moved into the village long ago. I like it up here where I can hear the bird song and the wind in the eaves, and no one bothers me… Usually,' she added pointedly.

'It is very peaceful up here, and I hear that the village residents' association gives you a helping hand sometimes.'

'They help me get my groceries delivered and they came out in the snow to check on me, which was unnecessary. That was when I first met Maisie.'

'Do you like her?'

Connie tilted her chin, her eyes boring into Isla's. 'She reminds me of me and how I used to be.'

The door suddenly whammed into the wall and Maisie came into the room, carrying a mug in one hand and a chipped plate bearing two digestive biscuits in the other.

'Here you go,' she said gruffly, manoeuvring a side table towards Connie with her foot. 'I thought you might be hungry 'cos it's almost lunchtime.' She handed the mug to the old lady and put the plate on the table, within her reach.

Connie lifted the mug to her lips with shaky hands and took a sip. 'I've been talking to your aunt.'

'Yeah?' Maisie shot Isla a nervous glance. 'Talking about what?'

'This and that,' said Connie, taking another sip of her tea, which looked awash with milk.

'Actually,' said Isla, as Maisie perched on the arm of a faded sofa. 'If you don't mind, I was hoping to ask you about an ancestor of mine. Maisie said you remembered her.'

'Who's that then?'

'A lady called Edith, Edith Anstey. She was Jessie's aunt, so my great-great-aunt.'

Connie regarded her coolly. 'What's so interesting about her after all these years?'

'It's a bit complicated, but Jessie loved crosswords and riddles, and she left me and my sister a riddle to work out after her death.'

'What does the riddle say?' asked Connie, taking a big slurp of her drink.

'It says: Don't get in a spin, girls, though mistakes can cost you dear. This one brings good fortune and, I hope, will make you cheer.'

'That makes no sense whatsoever.'

'Not yet, but we're hoping we can solve it with the help of an old letter she left us too. It was written to Edith in 1919. That's why I'd like to find out more about her.'

Connie put her mug down on the table and sat, without moving, staring across the room. Isla followed her gaze but there was nothing there. After a while, she glanced at Maisie, who mouthed 'let's go'.

'Edith was nice, by all accounts,' said Connie suddenly, making both Isla and Maisie jump. 'That's what my mother told me when I was a child, and she didn't like many people. Edith was one of the only people in the village to speak to her – kind and not judgemental, like her niece, Jessie. I know my mother was upset when she died. She told me.'

'Edith died in 1922, which must have been before you were

born. Do you know why your mum was still mentioning her years later?'

'Because of the way she died, of course. Frozen to death on the moors. My mother told me about her as a warning so I wouldn't wander off too far. I always was a headstrong child and my mother was terrified I'd come to harm. It's funny, really – I can't remember what happened yesterday and yet the past feels as if it's still happening around me.'

Isla felt a shiver run down her back in this house full of Connie's ghosts.

'Do you know how Edith came to die of exposure on Dartmoor? Did your mother ever tell you that?'

'All she said was poor Edith Anstey was too sad for this world. Mourning the loss of a lover and waiting for a letter that never came. A letter that never came,' she repeated in a sing-song voice, sounding like a child, as a black cat jumped into her lap.

'Was the letter from a man called William?'

'The only William I know is the old fisherman who lives by the lifeboat station. Keeps ferrets, and a mistress in Exeter.'

Out of the corner of her eye, Isla saw Maisie frown at this random information.

'William is the man who wrote the letter to Edith in 1919 that I mentioned a minute ago. He wanted to marry Edith and take her back with him to America.'

'America?' Connie sucked air through the gaps in her teeth. 'That's even farther than London. I wouldn't like that.' She thought for a moment, her fingers raking through the cat's fur. 'Did you say 1919? That's when the Spanish flu hit Heaven's Cove. It was the flu that did for my older sister. I never met her, of course. Wasn't born yet.'

'That's terrible,' piped up Maisie. 'We learned about the Spanish flu at school. It killed, like, millions of people.'

'Several of 'em around here, sadly. And TB got my older

brother when I was only small. My mother was never the same after that.'

Maisie leaned forward, her elbows on her knees. 'So your sister *and* your brother both died when they were kids? That's literally so sad.'

'You youngsters don't know how good you've got it. Life was harsh back then.'

'Do you think the flu epidemic might have been the reason why Edith didn't go with William to America?' asked Isla, her mind full of what-ifs and maybes.

'How am I supposed to know? I've told you everything I can remember from those days.'

When Connie blinked, lost in the past, Isla shivered. It was cold in here. The grate lay blackened and empty, with only a small pile of logs next to it.

'Aren't you chilly in here?' she asked gently.

'No,' said Connie, sticking out her chin. 'If I get cold I can make a fire.'

'You'll need more logs than you've got in the hearth.'

'There's plenty in the outhouse that need chopping.'

'Do *you* chop them?' asked Isla with alarm. Connie, for all her bluster and belligerent attitude, looked as if a strong wind might blow her over.

'I manage. Why? Are you going to report *that* to social services?'

'Absolutely not,' Isla assured her, noticing Maisie slip out of the room.

'They're looking for any excuse to make me leave. And I won't go. I couldn't take Dolly and Petra with me. What would happen to them?' Connie's bottom lip wobbled and she stroked the cat on her lap so vigorously, it stirred in its sleep.

'I'm sure your cats would be well cared for, but I'm honestly not here to report you or to try and persuade you to do anything you don't want to do.'

'If you say so.'

'Have you always lived here?'

'I was born here and I'll die here.'

'Have you travelled? You know,' Isla added, when Connie peered at her blankly, 'gone on holiday or spent time anywhere else?'

'Never. My family didn't have the money for jaunts and where would we have gone anyway when we've got all of this?'

Connie went back to staring out of the window and Isla sat quietly with her for a while, imagining what it must have been like, growing up in this isolated spot. This house and the land surrounding it was Connie's whole life and it struck Isla as appropriate that she would see out her days here. But it was also sad. There was a whole wide world out there that Connie had never seen and never would. Just like Paul.

Both women looked up when Maisie barged back into the room, her arms filled with logs, and cobwebs sticking to her hair.

'I went through the logs outside and found these,' she declared, dropping them with a clatter onto the stone hearth. 'Save you from bringing them in. The rest are too big to put on the fire but I couldn't find an axe.'

Isla's eyes widened. She'd never seen Maisie being so consistently helpful before.

Connie nodded. 'That's good of you, girl.'

'I could always come up and have a go at chopping the wood if you want. If you give me the axe,' said Maisie, scuffing her feet against the threadbare rug and biting the inside of her cheek. 'While I'm here, that is. I expect we'll be going back to London soon.'

'Poor you,' said Connie.

'Yeah, poor me,' murmured Maisie so quietly that Isla almost didn't catch it.

'That was kind of you offering to chop firewood for Connie,' said Isla as their car made its way slowly along the lanes that led into Heaven's Cove.

Maisie continued scrolling on her phone as she spoke. 'Yeah, well. Don't want her accidentally chopping off her leg with an axe or she will end up in care and then the cats will die.'

'I don't think that would happen to the cats. Someone would take them in.'

'Yeah, but they'd still die. Of a broken heart.'

Isla took her eyes off the road to glance at the teenager sitting beside her. Maisie was prickly and combative and a right royal pain in the backside. But dig a little deeper and she was just a confused kid with a well-hidden heart.

'You didn't seem too happy at the thought of going back to London,' said Isla, driving by the quayside.

Maisie stopped scrolling. 'Has Caitlin told you my dad has lost our house?' she asked, watching the grey sea that stretched to the horizon.

'Yes, she told me this morning. How do you feel about that?'

'How do you think I feel?' Maisie shot back, then her shoulders slumped. 'Sorry, but school's been... difficult, and now I don't know where I'm going to live. My dad's a mess who's never been around much, and don't even mention my mum.' She shot Isla a warning scowl.

'OK, I won't.' Isla pulled into the steep hill that led up to Rose Cottage. 'But there's always your stepmum.'

'Caitlin won't want me.'

'I think you're wrong about that.'

'No, I'm not,' said Maisie fiercely. 'But I don't want to talk about it. And don't tell her about me chopping Connie's logs or she'll go all stressy about it not being safe.'

'OK,' Isla promised, although the thought of Maisie swinging a sharp axe around was not a comforting one. 'What's the matter with school, though? Can I ask about that at least?'

Maisie sat quietly for a moment, as the car climbed higher. Then she began to speak, the words tumbling out.

'The thing is I played a stupid joke on a teacher so I've been suspended for a while and the staff hate me. And some girls in my class think I'm a troublemaker now, so they keep their distance. And the other girls, who encouraged me to do the joke in the first place, keep making comments about me in our WhatsApp group.'

'Bitchy comments?'

'A bit,' said Maisie, gnawing at the inside of her cheek.

'Do your dad and Caitlin know what's going on?'

'No, I can handle it. The girls will say I'm a crybaby if I go whining to them, and Dad and Caitlin are already upset about the practical joke thing.'

'Can't you just leave the WhatsApp group?'

'That wouldn't stop them posting stuff about me and I kind of need to know what they're saying. If I don't know, I just imagine worse.'

It was a circle of torment that Maisie didn't appear able to break away from. Isla sighed. 'They sound like a bad influence.'

'And you sound just like Caitlin.'

'Like I say, she cares about you.'

'Yeah, whatever,' said Maisie briskly. 'Anyway, I expect the joke will all be forgotten by the time I go back to school.' She went back to scrolling.

Isla had almost reached Rose Cottage when Maisie gave a strangled squeal.

'Are you all right?' Isla glanced at her passenger, who'd slumped in her seat. 'What's the matter?'

'Nothing.'

'Are those girls saying things again? I wish you'd quit that WhatsApp group and—'

'It's nothing. Just drive!' ordered Maisie. Her face crumpled into a scowl and the second the car came to a halt outside Rose Cottage, she leaped out and ran up to her bedroom.

'How did it go?' asked Caitlin, coming out of the kitchen with a flapjack in her hand. She glanced curiously up the stairs, at Maisie's retreating figure. 'Is Maisie all right? Is she upset about her dad and me?'

'Probably, but we didn't talk much about that. I think she's having some issues with friends at school.'

'Poor Maisie. Being a teenager is hard anyway, without all the extra angst her dad and I are throwing at her. Is this friends issue something I need to worry about?'

Caitlin seemed smaller, somehow, when she looked at Isla, her eyes filled with concern. She was losing weight – that was clear enough from the way her trousers were slipping down from the waist. But it wasn't simply a physical diminishing. Her whole persona seemed to have shrunk as she dealt with life's blows. And for once, Isla felt like the older sister, trying to protect her sibling from harm.

'You've got quite enough to worry about right now so leave it with me. I'll have a word with her,' said Isla firmly.

'If she'll talk to you. She won't speak to me. I wish she would. I really care about her, you know.'

'I know you do.'

Before she could think better of it, Isla pulled Caitlin towards her into a hug and patted her awkwardly on the back. Her sister softened in her arms and the years fell away to a time when the girls had been a united force against a scary world.

The sound of Maisie's bedroom door slamming vibrated through the house and Caitlin pulled away.

'Thanks,' she said gruffly. 'Anyway, you'd better tell me how the visit to Connie went.'

'Right.' Isla gathered her thoughts. 'It went well, I think. Maisie played a blinder by bringing cat food and soup that persuaded Connie to let us in, and she made her a cup of tea.'

'Maisie made Connie a cup of tea? Without being asked?'

When Isla nodded, Caitlin puffed air through her lips. 'Just when I think my life can't get any more surreal, Maisie starts being helpful. Whatever next?'

Whatever next, indeed? wondered Isla. The last few weeks had been crazy: bereavement, an estranged sister confessing that her glittering life was tarnished, a precious ruined dress, a stranger from America who'd grabbed her hands in the middle of the night.

'Did Connie tell you anything we don't know about Edith?' Caitlin continued. 'Though that wouldn't be hard, seeing as we know so little about her.'

'She did know a bit more. Apparently, her mum frightened her with tales of "poor Edith" freezing to death on Dartmoor, so Connie wouldn't wander off as a child.'

'Effective, but probably not what you'd find in a parenting manual: scare your child into submission.'

'Her mum had lost two children already, one to TB and the other to the Spanish flu epidemic that swept through the village in 1919, so she was probably scared herself.'

'Yeah, that makes sense. Poor woman.' Caitlin frowned. 'Did you say the flu hit Heaven's Cove in 1919? Could that be a reason why Edith felt she had to stay? Did she or her family get ill?'

'Perhaps. It gives us another avenue to explore at least.'

'The sister detectives, back on the case.' Caitlin gave a wry smile. 'We can get cracking on that tomorrow, maybe.'

'Yeah, sure.'

Tomorrow, thought Isla, which would be a day closer to Ben leaving for America and she would never see him again.

'Oh, by the way,' said Caitlin, walking to the hall table. She moved her newspaper and pulled out a mustard-coloured beanie hat that was lying beneath it. 'Look what I spotted on the floor under the coat stand. Is it Paul's?'

Isla felt her heart skip a beat. 'Paul won't wear anything on the yellow spectrum.'

He reckoned it didn't suit his complexion but Isla decided not to add that fact. She got the feeling Caitlin already thought her boyfriend was high maintenance.

'It'll be Ben's then.' Caitlin wrinkled her nose. 'I would return it to him but I can't face that climb up the cliff. Perhaps you could nip it up to him before he leaves? You were always more athletic than me.'

Isla hesitated. The thought of seeing Ben again made her feel instantly more cheerful, yet nervous, too. He must have had a good reason for leaving without saying goodbye after their early hours meeting in the kitchen. He must have been embarrassed by Isla gazing into his eyes. He must think her rather pathetic and horribly boring – the poor, bereaved librarian who rarely set foot outside Devon.

'What do you reckon?' asked Caitlin, tilting her head and raising an eyebrow. 'Will you drop Ben's hat back to him before he goes home to America?'

Isla pushed down her misgivings and held out her hand for the hat. 'I suppose I could. The walk will do me good.'

32

MAISIE

It was stupid watching it over and over again, painful even, but Maisie didn't seem able to stop.

She clicked on the video for the eighth time and watched as viscous yellow liquid poured from the top of the doorframe where it had been balanced in a plastic tub. It arced through the air as Miss Welby stepped into the classroom.

If only she'd been moving a little faster it wouldn't have made contact. But Miss Welby was a slow mover and the liquid – a gloopy mixture of food dye, flour and water – landed squarely on her head.

Maisie disliked Miss Welby intensely and the feeling was mutual. The fact that Maisie found algebra and statistics bewildering was incomprehensible to the middle-aged maths teacher who took every opportunity to accuse her of being lazy and not trying hard enough. The irony was that her accusations merely fuelled Maisie's panic when faced with numbers and equations and dissuaded her from trying at all. What was the point when she'd get it wrong anyway and Miss Welby would humiliate her in front of the class? The teacher deserved to be humiliated herself – that's what Madison had said.

But as Maisie clicked on the video again and watched the teacher's expression change from shock and upset to hurt disappointment, she wished for the hundredth time that she'd never done such a cruel thing.

'It'll teach her a lesson.' That's what the girls in Madison's group had told her. They'd encouraged her to carry out the joke but had denied all knowledge of it afterwards, when Maisie was suspended. And now, just when she was hoping the fuss had all died down and she could go back to school without it hanging over her, one of them had posted this video on TikTok. And whichever girl it was – the TikTok account was new and anonymous – had tagged her so she couldn't miss it.

There was a gentle tap on her bedroom door.

'Maisie? Can I come in?'

Maisie ignored Isla, hoping she would go away, but her door opened and her aunt poked her head around it.

'Sorry to disturb you but I wanted to check that you're all right. Caitlin's worried about you and I am too.'

'Did you tell her about the girls at school?' demanded Maisie, placing her phone face down on the bed.

'No, not exactly. But is there anything that Caitlin or I can do to help? We're both good listeners if you'd like to get anything off your chest. We were your age, too, a long time ago.' Isla grinned.

She was only trying to be nice. But Maisie couldn't tell her about this latest humiliation. Not only was her bad behaviour all over the internet, the video must have been posted by one of the girls she'd tried so hard to make like her.

It was plain to see that they didn't like her at all and never would. They would have a field day when it came out about her dad's gambling and Maisie losing her home. What if her dad turned up at a school event, unlikely though that was, with stupid Chiara in tow?

Maisie shuddered because if she thought school was difficult now, it was about to become unbearable.

'Honestly, Maisie. We're happy to help if we can,' repeated Isla.

But Maisie shook her head. Caitlin had enough to cope with, and if she found out that Maisie's bad behaviour had now been seen *everywhere*, there was no way she'd stick around once the divorce was underway. Why would she when Maisie was such a huge disappointment? And Isla would only tell Caitlin what was going on. They were sisters after all, even if they didn't always seem to like each other very much.

'No, thanks. I'm good,' said Maisie, leaning back against her pillows, closing her eyes and hoping that Isla would take a hint.

It worked because she heard the bedroom door click softly shut and, when she opened her eyes, Isla had gone.

Maisie went to pick up her phone but stopped, her hand hovering above it. Her aunt was right. She could leave the bitchy WhatsApp group and delete her TikTok app. But who was she kidding? Ignoring it wouldn't mean it wasn't happening – and maybe she deserved it anyway?

Maisie turned her phone over and watched yellow gloop slide down Miss Welby's shocked face for the tenth time.

33

CAITLIN

This was not the way to the bakery. Gilly's Bake Shop, which locals boasted sold the best Devon apple cake this side of Exeter, sat in a side street close to the ice cream parlour. All she had to do was head straight down the hill, turn left at the bottom and follow the sea wall. She could buy the loaf of bread that Isla had requested and be home in fifteen minutes, tops. Simple.

But instead, Caitlin had turned off halfway down the hill and was now walking along Smugglers Lane, which led directly past Sean's garage.

'This isn't a good idea,' she told herself, swinging the canvas bag she'd brought with her. 'This is a terrible idea.' But her feet kept on walking and she pulled her shoulders back, feeling lighter now her sister knew the truth about her life. 'You need to tell Isla,' Sean had told her, and he'd been right.

Thinking of Isla made Caitlin's thoughts turn to Ben. Would she return his left-behind hat? she wondered, not sure why it felt important that she did. Perhaps Caitlin was hoping that spending time with the personable American would remind Isla that there were other men out there. Men who would treat her better than Paul.

She sighed and glanced to her right as she reached the garage. Its doors were wide open, in spite of a chill wind, and two cars were up on hydraulic lifts. But Sean was nowhere to be seen. *Just as well*, she thought, ignoring a swell of disappointment. *Just as well when I'm leaving Heaven's Cove.*

'Oops, watch out!'

Caitlin was so busy staring into the garage – while trying to look as if she was doing nothing of the sort – that she hadn't seen Jen coming in the opposite direction. 'Sorry.' She did a quick side-step to avoid a collision with Sean's ex-wife.

Jen laughed. 'Don't worry. No harm done.' She waved the sheaf of papers in her hand. 'I'm on my way to the garage with the latest orders. Are you looking for Sean?'

'Sean? Me? No,' said Caitlin swiftly, remembering that the last time Jen had seen her she'd been having a panic attack in the pub. 'I was just passing by, taking a short cut, on my way to the bakery. Gilly's Bake Shop. Fantastic Devon apple cake, I'm told, though I'm not going there for cake. Bread. We need bread. A loaf.'

She stopped talking, wishing the ground would open up and swallow her. She was burbling like an idiot.

'Right,' said Jen, a smile playing on her lips. She must know that Smugglers Lane was in no way a short cut from Rose Cottage to the bakery 'When are you going back to London?'

'Soon. Maisie, that's my stepdaughter, will need to get back to school. She's having a bit of a break at the moment.'

'When she goes back, she won't have long to wait until the Christmas holidays.'

'That's right, not long at all and she's very much looking forward to them.'

'I bet,' said Jen, twirling a strand of black hair around her finger.

A silence stretched between them and Caitlin began to fidget. She was usually at ease talking to anyone but this pleasant, pretty woman, who had once been loved by Sean, made her flustered. Caitlin couldn't help wondering if Jen secretly hated her for callously breaking her ex-husband's heart. Or maybe Caitlin was vastly exaggerating her own significance in Sean's life and Jen knew nothing about her history.

'Anyway,' said Jen, hugging the papers close to her chest. 'I'd better get on.'

'Yep, me too. Lots to do,' said Caitlin, though she had absolutely nothing to do other than buy a loaf of brown bread, with no seeds or Maisie would moan about them getting caught in her teeth. 'It was good to see you again.'

'You too. Take care, Caitlin.'

With an awkward half-wave, Caitlin walked off but she hadn't gone far when Jen called after her, 'I'll tell Sean I saw you, though you might see him yourself, of course, if you're going to the Christmas market that's being held by the church. He's manning a stall there, the fundraising one for Max, and probably will be for the next hour or so. If you just happen to be in the area.'

Caitlin smiled to herself, embarrassed that Jen had seen through her lie about the short cut, but glad that Sean's ex-wife definitely didn't hate her. She turned and raised a hand to the young woman, who smiled in return and gave a brief nod.

Around two dozen stalls were clustered together, draped in fairy lights, and festive music was blaring out across the village green. The huge fir tree, paid for by the residents' association, was now covered with Christmas decorations, and a smell of caramelised sugar and cinnamon wafted under Caitlin's nose.

It was such an evocative scene that reminded her of markets

long gone. She and Isla would browse the stalls, spending what little money they had on enamel jewellery, hot chocolates and gingerbread men.

Pulling out her phone, Caitlin sent a quick text to Maisie: *Xmas fair on village green near church. You should come down. It's fun.*

A reply shot back immediately: *Is it though? Sounds sad to me.*

Her words were followed by a vomit emoji.

At least she'd tried. Caitlin decided not to think about Maisie and bought three gingerbread men instead, which she dropped into her canvas bag, alongside the loaf from Gilly's Bake Shop.

She began to wander around the fair, enjoying the sounds and smells but also on the look-out for a mop of fair hair. And when she eventually spotted Sean in the distance, she felt an unfamiliar rush of happiness. He was selling cakes on a stall beneath a large banner that read: HEAVEN'S COVE FUNDRAISING FOR MIGHTY MAX.

Caitlin watched him for a moment while he chatted and laughed with customers and dropped fairy cakes into paper bags. It was ridiculous but she had the same feelings of butter-flies in her stomach that she'd had fifteen years ago.

'Hi, there.' Sean glanced round and gave her a beaming smile. 'What are you doing here?'

'I'm soaking up some festive spirit, though it seems a little early when we're only just into December.'

'Are you one of these people who doesn't put the tree up until a week before the big day?'

'Not until Christmas Eve, actually,' she joked.

'Perfect. You're a woman after my own heart.' He winced slightly and gave a sheepish grin. 'Probably not the best choice of words in the circumstances.'

'Probably not,' Caitlin agreed with a smile. 'Anyway, if

you're such a scrooge on the quiet, why are you here at a Christmas fair?'

'It's for a good cause. Gavin at the garage has a young son with disabilities, who's called Max, and he's trying to raise enough money to set up an inclusive playground, here on the green. Kids in wheelchairs miss out when they can't go on swings and roundabouts, but there's specially adapted equipment available that they can use. All kids should be able to play and have fun.'

'I quite agree. How much do you need to raise?'

'A lot. We've raised a fair bit already, with sponsored walks and swims, but I'll need to sell a shedload of cakes to reach the target.'

'Did you make the cakes?'

'Good grief, no,' Sean snorted. 'I wouldn't inflict my cooking on anyone, except for my curry. I make a mean chicken balti.'

'I remember.'

'My repertoire hasn't expanded much in the last fifteen years so Gavin's friends and family made these. Would you like some?'

'Sure. Give me three of those lurid Santa cupcakes.' Sean pushed three cakes covered in bright red icing into a bag and Caitlin handed over a five-pound note. 'Keep the change.'

'Are you sure?'

'Of course. I wish I could donate more but you know how things are with me at the moment. Speaking of which' – she cleared her throat – 'thanks for being so understanding yesterday, when we talked.'

'You're welcome. What are friends for?'

'You're far more forgiving than I expected.'

He shrugged. 'It was a long time ago, Cait, and now we've cleared the air it's water under the bridge.'

'Thanks. I told Isla, by the way.'

'Yeah? And how did that go?'

Caitlin grinned. 'It was good, actually. I feel lighter for telling her and facing up to the truth. I feel better being here, in Heaven's Cove.'

'Perhaps you should stay, then,' said Sean, smoothing out creases in his pile of paper bags.

'I sometimes wish I could,' said Caitlin, realising that it was partly true. There was something about this village, some magic that was starting to ease the knots in her muscles and the emotional tangles in her brain.

'So why don't you?' Sean caught her eye and time seemed to stand still in spite of the festive hubbub all around them.

'I just can't,' said Caitlin, and time moved on once more. A small girl ran past, squealing and leaving a trail of pink candy floss. 'I might be able to help you, though,' she added, an idea coming to her. 'If you need any support with applying to charities and other organisations for grants? One of my jobs was in a fundraising department so I'm up to speed with making fundraising applications.'

'I know Gavin's applied for a few grants but we're muddling through, so if you could help, that would be great.'

'It's the least I can do. Let me have any paperwork and I can start looking into it before I, um...'

'Before you leave?'

When Caitlin nodded, Sean selected a cake from the array in front of him.

'Here, have a Rudolph cupcake on the house, as thanks in advance for your fundraising expertise.'

He pushed the reindeer cake into a bag and handed it over. His hand brushing hers felt like sparks of electricity against her skin.

'Payment in sugar is always appreciated,' joked Caitlin, feeling flustered. 'Anyway, I'd better get back to Rose Cottage or Isla will be sending out a search party.'

'I'll get Gavin to drop in the paperwork,' said Sean, turning to serve a customer who was pointing at the cakes she wanted. 'Maybe I'll see you around before you leave, Cait.'

'Yeah, maybe,' said Caitlin jauntily, keeping it light while feeling anything but.

She walked off without looking back because that was the only way to safeguard her heart.

34

ISLA

Isla shifted from foot to foot outside Driftwood House, psyching herself up to knock on the door. She hadn't slept well last night, after visiting Connie had led to dreams of scary women with wild, white hair striding across Dartmoor. And her swift walk up the cliff this morning had puffed her out.

She leaned over to catch her breath. Ben's hire car was parked at the top of the potholed road, which meant he was still here. But what if he'd rather not see her after that awkward encounter in the kitchen? He'd not been in touch at all and perhaps it *was* best if he disappeared from her life without any further contact.

She straightened up, paralysed with indecision. Knock on the door or not? Say goodbye, even though things had got awkward between them, or send him an impersonal 'thanks for your help' email once he was back in America?

'Are you looking for me?' said a deep voice behind her. A deep voice with an American accent.

She swung round, feeling flustered. Ben was standing there in his jacket and hiking boots, his dark-brown hair tousled by the breeze.

'How did you know I was here?'

'I was watching out the window and saw you walking up the cliff. So I took my coffee cup into the kitchen and came out through the back door. I didn't mean to startle you.'

'No, you didn't. Not really. I mean, you made me jump but not much,' Isla gabbled, feeling ridiculously wrong-footed.

'So, *are* you looking for me?'

'I am.' Isla brushed hair from her face, which was burning, in spite of the chill breeze.

'Look, I'm sorry I left without saying a proper goodbye,' said Ben quickly. 'You weren't around yesterday morning when Rosie messaged saying a room was free, and I thought I'd get out of your hair. Caitlin said she'd tell you, and I was going to message you from London.'

'Of course. It's fine but I'm not here about that.' Isla reached into the pocket of her jacket. 'You left this.'

'Oh.' Ben took the hat Isla was holding out and gave a sheepish grin. 'I did wonder where it had gone.'

'Under the coat stand in our hall.'

'Well, thank you for bringing it back.'

'I didn't want you leaving without it. When are you going?'

'Tomorrow morning, now. I've booked a hotel near Heathrow for tomorrow night and I fly early the next day.'

'Fabaroo.' Isla tried to keep her expression neutral. She'd never said fabaroo in her entire life. Ben would think she was an idiot.

If he did, his face didn't show it. 'Shall we walk a while?' he asked. 'I'm going to be in a car for hours soon and some exercise would be great.' *Paul wouldn't like it.* That's the thought that ran through Isla's mind as Ben waited for her answer. 'Of course, if you're busy and—'

'No. I have time to walk.'

'Great.'

He led the way out of Rosie's wind-blown garden and onto

the clifftop where scattered patches of melting snow glinted in the sunlight. They walked together out to where the land fell away into the churning sea and stood watching seagulls swoop above them.

'It's such a beautiful day.' Isla tried to keep her voice level but the thought of Ben disappearing off to his life, far across the Atlantic, was making her feel... She didn't quite know how she was feeling. Envious. Sad. Shackled.

The sea far below her was a moving sheet of aquamarine. The clouds were puffs of white and Heaven's Cove hugged the coast, as it had done for hundreds of years. People, tiny in the distance, walked cobbled streets strung with Christmas decorations, and boats clustered around the ancient stone quay.

How could she feel shackled to such a beautiful village? She was fortunate to live in such a picturesque place and in such a comfortable home. She was fortunate to have a loyal man like Paul by her side, even if sometimes his intensity made her feel claustrophobic.

'It's funny,' said Ben, his words almost whipped away by the wind.

'What is?' asked Isla, tucking the end of her ponytail into the collar of her jacket.

'It's funny that I didn't want to come to Heaven's Cove at all. I was annoyed with Mom for insisting on it.'

'I'd never have guessed.'

He grinned. 'I know, I know. I was very transparent.'

'Completely see-through.'

'Fair comment, but I thought the whole thing was a waste of time. An old letter. A five-hour drive from London. But I've got caught up in what happened to William and Edith and, though I only came here to be kind to my mother' – his eyes met hers – 'I now find I don't want to leave. Strange, huh?'

'I didn't realise you'd grown so fond of the village,' said Isla, holding his gaze.

'Not the village, so much. More the people in it.' Ben looked away. He seemed flustered. 'Look, I'm sorry about what happened in your kitchen the other night.'

'Is that why you left without saying goodbye?' When Ben nodded, Isla's heart sank. 'I'm so sorry. I didn't mean to embarrass you.'

'Embarrass me?' Ben's mouth fell open. 'Is that what you think, that I was embarrassed?' He shook his head. 'The truth is that I was ashamed with myself for almost stepping over a line.'

Isla opened her mouth to speak but no words came out. She'd thought she'd maybe imagined the frisson between them but it had been real.

'I shouldn't have put you in that situation... I know there's Paul although he—' Ben shook his head.

'I'll miss you,' said Isla before she could think better of it. She shouldn't say it, but it was true. She would miss this vibrant American who had breezed into Heaven's Cove and reignited her dreams with tales of his travels.

'Me, too.' Ben turned suddenly and caught hold of her arms. 'I was thinking... it's crazy, I know... We've only just met... but you should come, too. Come and see amazing places and meet wonderful people. With me.'

'What?'

When Isla stepped back, Ben let go of her arms and winced.

'I didn't mean to come out with that so bluntly. I wasn't sure I was going to say anything at all, but...' He stopped and rubbed a hand across his face. 'You're stifled here, Isla. Heaven's Cove is a wonderful place, but it'll still be here after you've seen the world.'

'I can't.'

Isla turned and began to walk down the cliff path, but Ben moved past her and blocked the way.

'Please, wait. You don't have to travel with me, if you don't want to. We hardly know each other. But please, go on your great adventure, Isla. There's so much of the world out there, just waiting for you. Rainforests in New Guinea, the deserts of Namibia, the pyramids, great white sharks off the Gold Coast of Australia. It's all amazing… and so are you.'

He stopped again, his face flushed. 'You're an inquisitive, quirky, amazing person, Isla, and you don't deserve to be stuck in Heaven's Cove your whole life. So come with me, or don't come with me, but do yourself a favour and go somewhere, just for a while.'

'What about Paul? He'd never come with me.'

Ben sighed. 'Paul is a decent guy…' He stopped, the muscles in his jaw tightening. 'Actually, I don't think Paul is a decent guy at all. He wants to control you.'

'That's not true.'

'Yes it is. He comes across as controlling and jealous, and he restricts your life.'

'That's not fair,' declared Isla. How dare Ben stand there and criticise the man she loved. 'You don't know him. You've only just met him.'

'That's true. But I've known men like him. Men who abuse women.'

'He doesn't abuse me,' said Isla, aghast. 'He's never laid a finger on me.'

'He might not be physically violent but I bet he tries to control you in other ways.'

'Of course he doesn't,' said Isla, feeling so angry she was almost crying. Not that she would, in front of this brash American who thought he could psychoanalyse her life after a few days' acquaintance.

'Are you sure about that?' asked Ben, sorrow etched across his face. 'Men like that are sly and cunning, Isla. They seem charming and loving but it's all on their own terms. They love you as long as you do exactly what they want. They're the masters of gaslighting.'

'No, you're wrong.' Isla's breath was coming in gasps. She couldn't get past Ben or she would run. She didn't want to hear this.

'He ruined your mom's dress because I dared to look at you across the table at your grandmother's birthday meal.'

'No, that's definitely not true.'

'I saw his face, Isla, before he knocked the food into your lap. He knew exactly what he was doing.'

'Please stop telling me these lies!'

Isla pushed past Ben so roughly he stumbled, and she started running towards the village, her feet skidding on loose stones.

'I'm sorry, Isla.' Ben's call drifted past her. 'I'll be on the quayside at ten tomorrow morning if you change your mind.'

Isla stumbled on, tears blinding her. Ben didn't know Paul at all. He didn't know how loving he could be. It was good that Ben was leaving Heaven's Cove tomorrow. Isla would never have to see him again and she could go back to her perfectly lovely life in this perfectly lovely corner of Devon.

'Everything's lovely!' she yelled, and a flock of startled seagulls rose as one into the air and flew across the sea, towards the distant horizon.

35

CAITLIN

Caitlin couldn't find Isla anywhere. She'd come in after taking Ben's hat back and rushed straight upstairs but now she seemed to have disappeared.

'Isla!' called Caitlin, wandering along the landing. 'Where are you? I have chocolate digestives.' That always did the trick when they were kids, but not today. Caitlin glanced into Isla's bedroom again, in case she'd magically appeared in the last two minutes.

'Why are you yelling?' demanded Maisie through the open door of her room. 'She hasn't been murdered or anything, so why are you so desperate to find her? Have you ever considered that she might be trying to get away from you for a while?'

Caitlin ignored Maisie's remark – she was trying to be understanding while the teenager was processing her father's news. For the sake of peace, she also didn't insist that Maisie should take off her shoes while lying on the bedspread that Jessie had crocheted.

'Why do you need to see Isla anyway?' asked Maisie sulkily.

'I have some news, and I'd just like to see her.'

'What sort of news?'

'News about Edith.'

Maisie's face collapsed into a grimace. 'Ugh, *so* boring.'

'Actually, it's not,' replied Caitlin, but Maisie was busy phone scrolling so she left her to it.

It was hard to explain to a stroppy teenager but Caitlin had a sixth sense that Isla was in trouble. The same back-of-the-neck prickle she'd get twenty years ago, when Isla was so dependent on her for comfort and security. Back when she was important in Isla's life.

Caitlin ran a hand across her forehead that was beginning to ache and stood still on the landing. Maisie was right – Isla would turn up when she felt like it. Her coat was still hanging in the hall but perhaps she'd gone out in her car without it.

Caitlin had reached the stairs, planning to check on the whereabouts of Isla's Mini, when she heard a noise above her head. A scraping of wood on floorboards. She turned back and went to the end of the landing where the door to the attic was hidden by the airing cupboard.

No one ever went up to the attic but Caitlin opened the door and climbed the narrow stairs, dipping her head to avoid a cobweb hanging from the ceiling.

'Isla?' she said tentatively on reaching the top step. It was gloomy up here but, as her eyes adjusted to the low light, she spotted a figure sitting next to the small window set into the roof.

'Isla, there you are! Are you all right, sitting up here on your own? I was worried about you.'

'Sorry.' Isla turned her head. 'I needed some breathing space, that's all.'

'Would you like me to go?'

'No. Come on in, if you don't mind braving the spiders. I think there might be a few mice, too. There are some droppings scattered around.'

Caitlin, a fan of neither spiders nor mice, gulped but picked her way across the dusty room that was littered with boxes and redundant furniture.

Isla was sitting on an old dining chair, looking out of the window, which provided a bird's eye view of roofs cascading down the hill to the sea. Her hands were in her lap and a shaft of light through the glass was catching her hair and making it shine. She looked like the serene subject of an Old Masters portrait.

'What's going on?' Caitlin perched on a dusty crate and fidgeted when a corner of the box dug into the back of her thigh. 'You usually go for a walk if you need space to think.'

'So many people in Heaven's Cove know me, I get stopped all the time.' Isla raised an eyebrow. 'It's difficult to be incognito when you're as famous as I am.'

'Infamous, more like.' Caitlin grinned and reached into the pocket of her long cardigan. 'Do you fancy a chocolate biscuit? I found a few in the kitchen that Maisie hadn't polished off.'

Isla gave a faint smile and took a biscuit from the packet. 'Thanks. Chocolate digestives are my favourite.'

'I know. I remember. How did you get on at Driftwood House? Did you see Ben and return his hat?'

'I did.'

'When's he leaving for London?'

'Tomorrow morning.' Isla dropped the biscuit into her lap and went back to staring out of the window.

'I've found out some more about Edith's family – our family,' said Caitlin, trying to pique her sister's interest. 'While you were out, I found some census records online and trawled through them. There was a census in 1911 and 1921, with nothing in between, unfortunately. But Edith is living here at Rose Cottage in both.'

Isla turned from the window. 'Who else is listed?'

'In 1911, when Edith was thirteen, she was living here with

her mum and dad. Ten years later, her mum, Emily, is gone and her dad, Archibald, is listed as a widower.'

'That's sad.'

'The saddest thing is that Emily also left behind two younger children, a boy and a girl who were twelve and thirteen in 1921.'

'Were Archibald, Edith and her younger siblings all living together in 1921 at Rose Cottage?'

'They were, so I looked up to see when Emily died and guess when it was.'

Isla sighed, her expression unreadable. 'I don't know, Caitlin. Just tell me.'

'She died on the fourteenth of April 1919, of influenza.'

That got Isla's full attention. 'April the fourteenth? That was a few days before William arrived.'

'Exactly, and poor Edith had just lost her mum. How could she leave for America when her younger brother and sister were grieving and motherless?'

'So do you think she stayed put to look after them? Like you looked after me when Mum died?'

'Probably, and from what Ben and Nell have told us, William was responsible for his grandmother so he couldn't have stayed here. He would have had to go back to the States without Edith.'

'I bet she was hoping to join him later, once her brother and sister were a little older or other arrangements had been made to help support them.'

Edith must have been torn between the responsibility she felt towards her siblings, thought Caitlin, and her desire to build a new life. She shivered because that push and pull, that tug between being selfish and selfless, was very familiar. 'Whatever they were planning to do, William died in New York not long afterwards, swiftly followed by his gran.'

'That's incredibly sad. Would Edith have known what happened? Who would have told her?'

'Of course!' Caitlin ran a hand across her face, bringing to mind what Connie had remembered. 'Connie's mother said Edith was too sad for this world, waiting for a letter that never came – a letter from William. She must have thought he'd given up on her but in fact—'

'He was dead,' said Isla dully. 'That's awful. No wonder poor Edith was broken-hearted. She must have believed she'd been abandoned by the man she loved, and then, not that long afterwards, she died a lonely death on Dartmoor. I wonder why she was out there on her own, in such a windswept and deserted landscape. It doesn't make sense.'

All at once, the pieces of the puzzle slotted into place for Caitlin.

'You said yourself that Edith's grave was hard to find because she was buried by the wall in the graveyard, away from her relatives. What if she was so broken-hearted, she couldn't bear to go on? So she took herself off to Dartmoor, on a freezing cold St Valentine's Day.'

Isla's mouth fell open. 'Are you saying that her death was suicide?'

Caitlin ran a hand through her hair. 'We'll never know, but that would fit. People who died by suicide were treated appallingly in the past so perhaps she was consigned to a corner of the graveyard.'

'That's even more sad,' said Isla, wiping away a tear that was trickling down her cheek.

'Poor Edith, who never got away from Heaven's Cove.'

Caitlin traced her finger through a film of dust and thought about their great-great-aunt and her fiancé, whose lives had been so tragically cut short.

'Do you think Gran wanted us to know all of this?' asked

Isla. She picked up her biscuit, to take a bite, before changing her mind and placing it back in her lap.

'Maybe, but I don't see how knowing what happened helps us to solve Gran's riddle.'

'Me neither.' Isla sighed. 'All I do know is that Gran really wanted us to work this one out together, but it's beaten us.' She fidgeted on her chair and rolled her shoulders as if her neck was hurting. Her gaze turned again to the cliff that was visible through the window, and Driftwood House perched on top.

'How was Ben when you saw him this morning?' asked Caitlin.

'OK. Getting ready to leave for London.'

Caitlin looked closely at Isla, who was clasping and unclasping her hands in her lap. She seemed thoroughly miserable. 'I expect you'll miss him,' she said quietly.

'Why?' Isla looked up. 'Why do you say that?'

'I don't know. The two of you seemed to get on well, once he'd got over his irritation at being in Heaven's Cove in the first place.'

'He was hard work at first, but we did get on well in the end. We do.' Isla stopped and bit the inside of her cheek. It made her look so young, just as she'd looked after their mother had died.

Caitlin reached forward and put a hand on Isla's pale wrist. 'It's OK to miss people. We both miss Mum, and we miss Gran – especially you.'

'Do you know...' Isla stared at the dusty floor. 'He asked me to go with him.'

'Ben did?' When Isla nodded, Caitlin's eyes opened wide. 'He asked you to go to America with him?'

'No, to go travelling with him. He's leaving his job to go travelling around Asia and Australia and he thought I might like to go.'

'Has something happened between you two?'

'No. Not really. There was something that happened in the kitchen. That's all.'

'Something?' Caitlin moved her hand. 'What kind of something?'

Isla lowered her voice, even though no one could possibly overhear them up here, at the top of the house. 'He held my hand and we had a moment.'

'What sort of a moment?'

Isla waved her arm around, looking pained. 'Shush! It shouldn't have happened, Caitlin.'

'*What* shouldn't have happened? Did he kiss you?'

'No, nothing like that.'

'Then, what's the problem?'

Isla swallowed. 'The problem is I felt disappointed that he didn't kiss me, and I've been torn up with guilt ever since, because I'm in love with Paul.'

'Are you, though?'

Isla sat up straight. 'What do you mean? Of course I am. Paul and I have been together for months and he's very special to me.'

'I'm sure he is but...'

'But what?' Isla leaned forwards. 'Tell me, Caitlin. I know there's something you're dying to say.'

Caitlin hesitated. She didn't want to wreck the fragile relationship that she and Isla were rebuilding, but how could she stay quiet when her misgivings about Isla's boyfriend were growing?

She grabbed hold of Isla's hand. 'I'm not sure that Paul is the best person for you.'

'Oh, really?' Isla pulled her hand away. 'And you're such an expert on my life, are you, when you haven't been a part of it for years?'

'I'm so sorry about that. I really am. I've behaved very badly and let you down, but I honestly never stopped caring about you.'

'You had a funny way of showing it.'

Caitlin deserved that. She swallowed. 'I know. I got many things wrong. But you're an amazing person, Isla – kind, funny and gentle – and I don't want you to make mistakes too. I just think that Paul might not be the best person for you.'

'Why would you say that?'

'Because he can be quite forceful and he's not always kind to you.'

'We argue sometimes and I'm sure I'm not always kind to him.'

'He comes across as quite controlling and jealous.' When anger flashed across her sister's face, Caitlin knew she'd gone too far but it was too late now. 'He seems to suck the joy out of you,' she told her. 'He keeps you small.'

'That's a horrible thing to say. Are you jealous because your relationship has disintegrated? You've always had more than me – you made sure of that. And now I've got a relationship and you haven't, you're trying to wreck it.'

'That's not true,' spluttered Caitlin.

But Isla was on her feet, her cheeks bright red. 'I get what this is. You're hoping I'll break up with Paul and go travelling with Ben, so you can sell this house and get your hands on the money. That's what you've wanted all along.'

Caitlin felt so winded by Isla's accusations, she leaned forward to catch her breath. Isla watched her, the flush in her cheeks starting to fade.

'If you want to go travelling,' said Caitlin, keeping her voice as level as possible, 'I'll back you because I think you should get to see the world and have the adventure that I had. If you want to stay here with Paul, I'll back you too because all I want is for you to be happy. Do you really believe I'd be willing to wreck your happiness, for money? Do you think so little of me?'

Isla ran a hand across her face. 'I don't know. I don't know you any more, Caitlin. I thought we were getting closer, getting back to how we used to be, but now you throw this at me. Paul loves me and I love him and he'd never do anything to hurt me, so you're wrong.'

She pushed her way past the detritus in the attic and had reached the stairs when Caitlin called after her, 'He ruined Mum's dress on purpose.'

Isla stopped and turned around, her expression blank. 'What are you talking about?'

'You looked amazing in that dress and when Paul saw Ben looking at you, he couldn't stand it, so he deliberately pushed the curry into your lap.'

An emotion flickered across Isla's face. Caitlin was expecting fury, surprise, contempt, but it was none of those. It seemed more like resignation. But then Isla snapped: 'That's ridiculous.'

'Are you sure? Paul said it himself, he's not a clumsy man, and I saw the jealousy on his face just before the accident happened. He did it deliberately, even though he knew that spoiling Mum's special dress would break your heart.'

Isla shook her head. 'I can't believe how low you'd stoop to get your hands on this house, Caitlin. It's pathetic and I really hate you.'

'But I don't want to sell this house,' Caitlin blurted out, realising for the first time that it was true. 'I've changed my mind and feel like I belong here.'

But Isla was clomping furiously down the stairs and didn't hear.

Caitlin sat quietly for a moment, not sure what to do next. Not only had her relationship with Isla sunk to new depths, she'd also admitted to herself what she'd been trying to ignore – that she'd been putting off returning to London because she liked being at Rose Cottage and wouldn't mind staying in Heaven's Cove for longer.

A crashing of feet on the stairs broke into her thoughts. Was Isla coming back? Caitlin wiped tears from her cheeks and tried to hide her disappointment when Maisie appeared.

'What's going on?' she demanded. 'And where the hell am I? Ugh, this place is totally gross. What are those pellet things on the floor?'

'Mouse droppings,' said Caitlin wearily.

'What the...? That is disgusting. This place should be condemned.' Her nose wrinkled in distaste as she edged forwards. 'So why are you up here and why did Isla just run past my room? Have you two been fighting?'

When Caitlin nodded miserably, Maisie frowned and began to fidget. 'Well,' she said after a while, 'you should come down. Right now.'

Caitlin began to cry. She hadn't meant to dissolve into tears, especially not in front of Maisie, who was coping with enough. But after the last few weeks she'd had, the row with Isla was the final straw.

As fat tears rolled down her face, Maisie stared at her in horror.

'Stop!' she insisted.

But Caitlin couldn't. She scrabbled in her pocket for a tissue and dabbed at her nose. 'Sorry,' she managed between gulps. 'Go downstairs.' But Maisie didn't move. 'Please,' she begged, desperate to bring her emotions under control.

Maisie watched her, wide-eyed, and then walked across the attic, through the mouse droppings, and put an arm around Caitlin's shoulder. 'All right?' she asked, awkwardly patting her arm.

Caitlin leaned against her stepdaughter for a moment before pulling herself together with a herculean effort and wiping her eyes. The weight of Maisie's arm across her shoulders was comforting.

'Yeah, I'm OK now. Sorry about that.'

'Was it a bad argument with Isla?'

'Mmm.' Caitlin nodded, frightened to say any more in case she broke down again.

'She'll be OK with you again soon,' predicted Maisie, moving her arm from Caitlin's shoulders. 'I mean, look at us. We argue all the time but that doesn't mean we don't get on later.' She sniffed. 'Right, I'll get back to my music and you'd better come downstairs. And don't start crying again 'cos it makes you look terrible. Your nose is bright red and you've rubbed all your make-up off.'

When Caitlin laughed, Maisie frowned at her in surprise before clomping back down the stairs.

Caitlin moved to the chair Isla had just left and looked through the streaked glass at sunlight bouncing off the silver sea. It was so sad, she thought, if Edith had been forced to choose between the man she adored and caring for the family she loved. It would also be sad if her great-great-niece chose to stay with a rubbish boyfriend rather than take a chance on her American and travel to the corners of the globe.

Caitlin desperately wanted her sister to have a big adventure, even if it did mean that Rose Cottage might have to be sold if Isla needed money to fund her travels.

How the tables had turned, she thought, giving her eyes a final wipe. Isla was now the one who needed to fly the nest, and she was the one who found herself becoming increasingly fond of this peaceful place. Caitlin sighed. She could almost imagine staying in Heaven's Cove and putting down roots here, but it was too late. Fifteen years too late.

36

ISLA

Isla was aware of Fizz, Paul's new assistant, giving her a once-over when she walked into the business space he rented on the outskirts of Heaven's Cove. Fizz was sitting behind a desk that almost filled the tiny reception area, tapping away on a computer keyboard.

'Can I help you?' she asked, fingers poised above the keys, her nails long and purple. She was acting as if she didn't know who Isla was, even though they'd met twice since she'd been taken on three months earlier.

'I'm here to see Paul,' said Isla, feeling scruffy in her jeans and sweatshirt.

'Do you have an appointment?' Fizz asked, smoothing a hand down her cream silk blouse.

Was she being dense or deliberately obtuse? Isla wondered. What kind of name was Fizz anyway?

'I don't need an appointment because I'm Paul's girlfriend.'

'Oh.' Fizz's hand flew to her mouth. 'Of course you are. I'm so sorry. I didn't recognise you.'

'No problem.' Isla smiled, even though her appearance hadn't changed in the last twelve weeks. 'Is Paul free?'

Fizz took a moment to consult her large desk diary before announcing that Isla would be allowed to take up a few minutes of Paul's precious time. But definitely no more than five because he had an important call to make to a valued client.

She was like a snooty, well-dressed rottweiler, thought Isla, knocking on Paul's door.

Isla knocked again, wondering if she was doing the right thing. She could ignore it all. Forget Caitlin's wild claims about her ruined dress, and the mean things Ben had said about Paul – and she'd been tempted to do just that, but an email had arrived from the American twenty minutes ago which simply said:

> We parted on bad terms but it was good to meet you, Isla. Climb that mountain and swim in warm seas. You deserve the best. Ben x

You deserve the best. Isla knocked once more and when there was still no reply she opened the door and went in.

Paul's office was double the size of the reception area, with a leather-topped desk, a black filing cabinet, and a window overlooking the headland that stretched into the sea. He was sitting with his back to her and his feet up on the windowsill but he spun round when he heard his door close.

'Hey, Fizz, I was just... oh, Isla. What are you doing here?'

'I wanted to see you, if that's all right?'

Paul looked puzzled. 'Yes, of course. What have you been up to today? You said you were going to be in but when I rang the house earlier no one answered. I tried your mobile but it went to voicemail. Didn't you get my messages?'

'I saw you'd left me several messages but I was busy.'

'Too busy to talk to the man who loves and looks after you? Charming.' He scowled before his features relaxed into a smile that didn't reach his eyes. 'So what *were* you busy doing?'

'This and that,' said Isla, glancing round the office, which was incredibly tidy with everything in its place – from the pen pot on the desk to the books neatly lined up on top of the filing cabinet.

'What does this and that mean?'

Isla turned her palms up to the ceiling. 'Nothing you'd find very exciting.'

'Only…' Paul frowned and closed the lid of his laptop. He peered at Isla over the top of his computer glasses. 'As I said in my messages, if you'd taken the time to listen to them, you were seen walking up to Driftwood House.'

Good grief, did Paul have spies everywhere?

Isla sank into the chair that faced Paul's desk. 'Ben left his hat at Rose Cottage so I returned it.'

'Couldn't Caitlin have done that?'

'Possibly. Probably, but I thought I would instead.'

'Without telling me?'

'I was returning his hat, Paul, and saying goodbye. I don't have to tell you everything.'

Paul's dark eyes shone glittery and hard. Then, his face softened and he leaned back in his chair. 'Of course you don't, sweetheart, but I worry about you and need to know that you're all right at all times.'

Isla ran a finger inside the collar of her sweatshirt, which felt as if it was strangling her.

'So when is our American visitor going back to the States?' Paul asked.

'Thursday morning. He's leaving Heaven's Cove tomorrow.'

'That's good, and not before time.'

'You really don't like him, do you? You took against him from the start.'

Paul scowled. 'What's to like about a brash American?'

'He's not brash, Paul. He's confident, that's all. And though he was a bit grumpy at first, he's a nice man – as you'd know if you'd taken the time to speak to him properly.'

'I spoke to him quite enough to make up my mind, thank you.'

'You weren't particularly welcoming.'

Paul huffed and drew his eyebrows together. 'I'm perfectly welcoming. I haven't made a fuss about Caitlin and that child being in our house, have I?'

'Caitlin is my sister and *that child* is her stepdaughter,' said Isla quietly. 'It's Caitlin's house as much as mine.'

She was trying to stay calm but her heart was hammering. It felt wrong to be challenging Paul in this way. In any way. Caitlin had been right when she'd described his personality as forceful. He rarely shouted or made a scene but, when she thought about it, that was probably because he usually got his own way.

'But when are they planning to go back to London?' Paul moaned. 'It was awkward enough having your grandmother around all the time, let alone a stroppy fifteen-year-old banging doors and playing Godawful music.'

Isla blinked, feeling the prickle of tears. How could Paul be so unkind about her grandmother? She'd do anything to have her around for longer.

'Have they said when they're going?' he repeated.

Isla remembered her argument with Caitlin less than an hour earlier. 'I don't think they'll be staying much longer.'

'Thank goodness for that.'

Isla shivered, feeling very alone. Her grandmother was gone for good, Caitlin and Maisie would soon return to London and have little to do with her, and Ben was about to fly thousands of miles across the Atlantic – and they weren't parting on the best of terms.

Everything was going to hell, but at least she had Paul. Isla studied him across the desk. He'd opened his laptop again and gone back to work.

'I was thinking,' she said quietly.

'Uh-oh, it's never a good sign when a woman says that.' Paul looked up from his computer screen.

'I've been thinking about what you said about not wanting to go on holiday.'

Paul gave a theatrical sigh. 'Not this again, Isla.'

'I know we've already discussed it but I really need a break and I think it would do our relationship good if we spent some time together.'

'Which we can do very easily in Devon.'

'Or in Paris or Berlin or... I don't know... Krakow. Just for a few days.'

Paul ran his tongue across his bottom lip. 'I have no urge to visit any of those places and I'm far too busy to go on holiday anyway, Isla. That's the end of it. I don't want to hear any more on the subject.'

He went back to his computer but looked up again when Isla didn't move. Closing the lid of his laptop, he came out from behind his desk and knelt at her feet.

'Look, sweetheart, I don't mean to be harsh but sometimes you go off on flights of fancy and you need me to rein you in. We're fine here, just the two of us. You don't need to go abroad.'

Isla took a deep breath. 'Ben suggested I should go to Peru and trek the Inca Trail to Machu Picchu.'

Paul rocked back on his heels and got to his feet. 'Did he? Well, that's ridiculous, obviously.'

'Why "obviously"?'

Paul laughed, as if the answer was patently clear. 'Because you're far too timid to go so far, especially without me. Face it, Isla. You're glad your sister never came back for you all those years ago because you feel safer in Heaven's Cove. It's a big, dangerous world out there and you'd never cope with it.'

Isla glared at Paul, unfamiliar rebellion stirring in her soul. 'How do you know I wouldn't cope?'

'I just do.'

'I've coped with a lot in my life – Mum dying, Caitlin leaving and now losing Gran.'

'I know, sweetie,' said Paul, his voice soft and cloying, 'and look at you. You're a mess and you'd fall apart without me by your side.' He leaned forward and kissed her on the forehead. 'So let's have no more talk about going to Peru.' He walked back behind his desk and sat down. 'Now, if you don't mind, Isla, I have work to finish but we can talk later. I'll come round at seven thirty and we'll go to The Smugglers Haunt for a meal.'

'I don't feel like going out tonight.'

'Of course you do. I'll collect you at seven thirty and we'll have a lovely time.'

It was a fait accompli as far as he was concerned. Isla shifted in her seat. It was like she was seeing Paul properly for the first time, and there was something she had to know.

'When we had Gran's birthday meal on Sunday and you knocked curry into my lap—'

'Why on earth are you bringing that up now?' demanded Paul. 'I've already apologised profusely.'

'Did you do it on purpose?'

Isla felt as if all the air was being sucked from the room when Paul stared at her, his eyes cold. Then he smiled.

'Of course I didn't do it on purpose. That's a very strange idea. What have Ben and Caitlin been saying?'

'Nothing,' lied Isla, determined not to involve them. 'But I've been thinking about what happened and it seems to me that you might have knocked the food container on purpose with your elbow.'

Paul gave a harsh laugh and glared at her. 'I can't believe you're being so stupid. Why would I do that?'

'You tell me,' said Isla, holding his gaze even
fibre in her body was screaming at her not to.

Paul was the first to blink and look away. He
through his teeth and slumped back in his chair. 'All ri
fair cop. You've got me. But it was for your own good,
heart. You should thank me, really.'

Outside in Reception, a phone had started ringing b
sounded to Isla as if it was underwater. There was a rushing
her ears and a lump in her throat.

'Why should I thank you for deliberately knocking curry all
over me?'

'It was the only way to protect you.'

'Protect me from what?'

'From making a fool of yourself in that unsuitable dress
when we were entertaining guests.'

'Did you think I was making a fool of myself when I wore it
to the residents' association dance last Christmas?'

'Why are you harking back a whole year?'

'Because it's important.'

Paul sighed. 'OK. Yes, if you really want to do this, I
thought it was totally inappropriate.'

'Why?'

'Because you're my girlfriend, Isla, and I won't have men
ogling you.'

'Ben wasn't ogling me the other night, Paul. He was simply
looking at me from across a table. And it wouldn't matter even if
he was "ogling", as you put it, because I might be your girlfriend
but I'm not your property. I can wear whatever I want.'

Paul's composure was beginning to slip. He banged his
hands down on the desk. 'Don't give me all that empowerment
rubbish, Isla. Of course I don't own you, but I do know what's
best for you. I don't feel proud of what I did that night but I'd do
it again in a heartbeat, for your own good.'

'You ruined my mother's dress,' whispered Isla, her head reeling.

'I'll get you another dress.'

'But I don't want another dress. I want that one. That's the dress my mum wore the night she met my dad, and I remember her wearing it on special occasions when I was growing up.'

'And I'm sure it suited your mum. But it didn't suit you.' He pulled his mouth into a pout. 'I just lost my head, Isla, and I will admit that perhaps I over-reacted.'

'You think?' said Isla, a sick feeling in the pit of her stomach.

'OK. I'll hold my hands up to that. But I only did it because I care about you so much, and I know that you believe me.' He stood up, walked around the desk to Isla and kissed the top of her head. 'You're fragile, sweetheart, and particularly vulnerable right now, following Jessie's death, especially with your sister turning up. But you don't need to worry about anything because you've got me to look after you. And the sooner everyone leaves and it's just you and me, the better. I know you feel the same way.'

Isla got slowly to her feet, her heart heavy.

'The thing is, I don't feel the same way as you do about Caitlin and Maisie leaving. I don't feel the same way about my mum's dress, or about going to Machu Picchu. I'm not the same as you and I won't be controlled.'

'Controlled?' Paul's cheeks were reddening. 'Where have you got all this guff from? Your sister, no doubt.'

'Yes, my sister, in part. But she's opened my eyes to what's really been going on here. We've been together for a while and it's been fun at times, but I don't think we're right for each other. Actually, I don't think you're right for me, and I deserve the best.'

Paul's mouth had fallen open. He snapped it shut, his nostrils flaring. 'You're not feeling yourself, Isla. That's all this is. You're having a bad day and need a bit of time to yourself. You love me.'

Isla walked to the door and looked back. 'Do you know, I'm not sure that I do. Not enough, anyway, to get over the flaws in our relationship. I'm not the right woman for you – I'm not right, full stop. That's what you imply a lot of the time, isn't it? And I can see now that you're definitely not the right man for me.'

'Let me get this straight. Are *you* breaking up with *me?*' spluttered Paul, specks of spittle flecking his beard.

'Yes,' said Isla sadly. 'I do believe that I am. Goodbye, Paul.'

She stepped into Reception, closed the office door behind her and stood still for a moment. What had she just done? Her heart was aching and yet she felt stronger, as if she'd glimpsed the old Isla – how she used to be, when her gran was alive and Caitlin was her ally at home in Rose Cottage.

'I've had to apologise to a client that Paul wasn't available to take his scheduled call at three o'clock,' said Fizz snippily. Isla glanced at her watch. It was only two minutes past the hour. 'It's really not appropriate to call in unannounced and take up Paul's time when he's such a busy man.'

Isla breathed out slowly and approached Fizz's desk. She leaned against it, her thighs hard against the wood.

'Do you know, Fizz? I think you might benefit from some interpersonal training, some guidance on how you should speak to people who come into the office. If you talk to Paul, I'm sure he'll fund it.'

Isla pushed herself away from the desk and walked through the door without a backwards glance.

37

MAISIE

It was unbearable that she was expected to live in this atmosphere, some might say tantamount to child abuse.

Maisie glanced between Isla and Caitlin, who were sitting with trays of food on their laps, though neither of them were eating their evening meal. Both of them were pushing food around their plates and glaring at each other. Isla's eyes were red-rimmed and Caitlin looked drawn and unwell.

No wonder she felt so upset all the time, having to live with a couple of emotional wrecks, thought Maisie, spearing a sausage and lifting it to her mouth. Though, to be honest, she wasn't very hungry either. The charged atmosphere in the room was draining her will to live.

'I broke up with Paul,' said Isla suddenly.

Caitlin put down the knife she wasn't using. 'O-K,' she said slowly.

'OK? Is that all you have to say on the matter?'

Maisie glanced nervously between the sisters. It was all going to kick off, she could feel it, and she wasn't sure she could cope with much more today.

The last time she'd checked, the stupid TikTok video had

thousands of views and comments ranged from people posting laughing emojis to others accusing her of being vile, and worse. Her heart fluttered as the more vitriolic comments, forever seared into her brain, began to spool across her mind.

Caitlin pushed her tray away, making everything clatter. 'I don't know what you want me to say, Isla?'

'You could say that you're happy that Paul and I have split up. Happy that you were right and he did knock the curry over me on purpose.'

Whoa! Maisie put her unbitten sausage back on her plate. This was a piece of information that she'd so far been unaware of, and it was wild. Pompous Paul was even more horrible than she'd suspected.

'I can't say that I'm unhappy about it,' said Caitlin slowly, carefully choosing her words. 'You deserve better than Paul, but I'm sure you feel sad about the whole thing.'

'Sad?' Isla laughed. 'Yeah, I do feel sad about it, even though it turns out that he's a controlling arse. Looks like I couldn't manage my life without you after all, hey, sis?'

Caitlin frowned, her face caught in the glow from the fire that was blazing in the grate. 'I think you've managed fine and I get why you're mad at me. But I think, in this instance, that it's Paul you're really angry with?'

'Are you my psychoanalyst now, Cait? You've come back to Heaven's Cove to sort out my life and stop me from making a terrible mistake?'

'There's no need to be so mean,' countered Caitlin, a flush rising across her face.

Maisie sighed because Caitlin was right and, although Isla had every right to be annoyed with her, this anger was fuelled by her break-up with Paul. Maisie had done it often enough – taken out her frustration and upset on her dad and stepmum when things at school were going badly.

'How dare you accuse me of being mean?' Isla shot back. 'I've welcomed you into my home and—'

'It's my home, too.'

'Not according to Gran, who left it to me, basically, for as long as I want it.'

'You like to keep rubbing that in my face, don't you?'

'Only because you can't wait for me to go off travelling so you can sell this place.'

'I've told you that I don't want to sell Rose Cottage. All I want is for you to do what makes you happy.'

'Maybe I was happy before you turned up.'

Maisie watched them, two adults bickering like children. Her head was aching with everything going on in her life – her dad had more or less disappeared, her home was being sold, Caitlin would be off soon, and school would be a nightmare now the video had been posted on TikTok. At least it must have been taken down by now.

She'd finally sent a message to the WhatsApp group – not blaming anyone or being too stressy, but begging them to delete it – and Madison had promised, while not saying who'd posted it, that it would be taken down at once. That was kind of her, wasn't it? They probably hadn't meant to cause Maisie so much angst.

Maisie half-turned her attention back to the warring sisters in front of her as she grabbed her phone and went to TikTok. Caitlin and Isla were now arguing about the stupid letter that they were obsessed with these days.

'Gran specifically left this and the riddle for us but you never took it seriously, not really,' said Isla, grabbing the letter from its envelope on the top of the bureau and waving it at her sister. 'You only stuck around to try and get me to sell up.'

'How many times do I have to tell you that I don't want you to sell this place? And what do you mean I never took the letter seriously? Of course I did. Who was it who got hold of Edith's death certificate *and* found out vital information at the cultural centre? I've done loads and it's not my fault that Gran's riddle makes no sense.'

'It does make sense but we just can't see it,' said Isla through gritted teeth. 'There must be a reason she wrote it – "don't get in a spin, girls, though mistakes can cost you dear. This one brings good fortune and, I hope, will make you cheer."'

'Please stop repeating the riddle! What good fortune is she talking about? If Gran had a stash of money somewhere, we'd have found it by now. We've been through her bank accounts and there's no pot of gold hidden under her mattress.'

Had they even checked under Jessie's mattress? wondered Maisie, feeling increasingly hot and uncomfortable as the argument continued to escalate. It reminded her of school, when the WhatsApp girls ramped up their bitchy remarks.

Her eyes went back to her phone and she felt the blood drain from her face because the video was still on TikTok and she'd been tagged into another one. The second video had obviously been shot by someone else in the classroom, from a different angle, and Maisie's face was in close-up as the gloop covered Miss Welby – at first Maisie was laughing, and then her expression morphed through concern and horror into fear.

'The answer *must* be in this letter,' said Isla, her loud voice breaking into Maisie's thoughts.

'No, it isn't,' Caitlin shouted back. 'We have to stop kidding ourselves. I know why it's so important to you to solve what Gran—'

'Oh, you know why, do you, Caitlin? You know nothing about me after fifteen years away. I can't believe you—'

'Stop it!' yelled Maisie, jumping up and grabbing the letter from Isla's hand.

Her tray and its contents tumbled to the floor but she didn't care. Her life was falling apart.

'Give me the letter,' said Caitlin, taking a step towards her. 'Give it back now.'

'No!' Maisie turned and threw the piece of paper towards the fire.

Time seemed to stand still as it floated through the air and, like a magnet, was pulled into the flames. The letter curled and crackled as it caught alight.

'Grab it quick!' said Isla, rushing to the fireplace and kneeling down.

But it was too late, Maisie realised as the flames flared higher and the paper blackened, turning to ash. It was all far, far too late. She ran from the room, grabbed her coat from the coat stand and fled into the night.

38

MAISIE

She had to be in. The good thing about visiting an ancient recluse was that they were never out. Maisie hammered again on the front door and yelled 'Connie!' at the top of her lungs. It was scary being out here on her own in the dark, with the wind whistling round the corners of Connie's isolated farmhouse.

Upset and anger had carried her along after she'd stormed out of Rose Cottage and marched through dark lanes that led towards the moors.

But as the lights of the village had disappeared into the distance and spits of sleety rain hit her face, Maisie's anger had begun to fade. Now all that was left was upset – and fear. What on earth was she doing out here, all alone?

When the front door was suddenly wrenched open, Maisie let out a scream and jumped back. Connie, in a long white nightdress in the barely lit gloom of the hall, looked like a ghost of Carmichaels past.

'Well, that's nice,' the old lady grumbled. 'You frighten me half to death, hammering on my door in the dead of night, and then you scream when I open the door.'

'Sorry,' Maisie managed. 'I didn't think you'd be in bed.'

'Not much to stay up for round here, and I'm always up with the dawn.' Connie narrowed her eyes. 'What are you doing here in the dark?'

'Um...' Maisie looked at her feet. She didn't know why she was here. Not really. She'd had nowhere to go after storming out of the house and the only place she could think of – her only refuge – was here, with a ninety-seven-year-old woman who hated everyone. Including her.

Connie let out a long sigh that echoed the wind wrapping around the eaves. 'I would leave you outside to freeze but I s'pose that'd cause a stir with the authorities, and I'm trying to keep my head down right now. So you'd best come in.'

She pulled the door wide open and, once Maisie had stepped inside, banged it shut behind her. Maisie felt prickles of fear run down her spine. What if the rumours about the Carmichael family were true and Connie was a serial killer on the quiet? At least Maisie would have the benefit of youth if it came to hand-to-hand combat.

'Come on,' said Connie, leading her into a room Maisie hadn't been in before. She switched on a bare lightbulb that hung from the nicotine-stained ceiling. 'Go on, sit down.' She grinned her gap-toothed smile. 'Don't worry. I'm not going to murder you.' Picking up a grey cardigan from the back of a chair, she pushed her arms into it. 'So what brings you to my door at such an ungodly hour?'

'It's only half past eight,' protested Maisie.

But she was silenced by a wave of Connie's hand. 'Cut to the chase. Some of us have less time left to waste than others.'

'I've run away,' Maisie declared, trying to stop the wobble in her voice. 'I did something bad and I can't go back so I need to find somewhere else to live.'

'Did you think you might move in with me?' Connie's cackle of laughter echoed around the room. 'I can imagine what people might say about that.'

'No, of course I don't want to move in. I—' Maisie stopped.

'Just say it, girl.'

'I just need somewhere to keep my head down while I figure out my next move.'

'Your next move? How old are you?'

'Fifteen,' said Maisie, squaring her shoulders in a useless attempt to feel braver.

Connie sat down heavily in an old armchair near the stone fireplace. 'Fifteen! I'd left school by then.'

'Lucky you,' murmured Maisie, surveying the room. There was a faded splendour to this space. Stained covers in ruby-red silk on the sofa and two armchairs, a fringed standard lamp standing in one corner, and a large Persian rug, now faded, that covered most of the flagstones.

Connie saw her looking round the room and grinned. 'Bit posher than you were expecting, is it? We did have a bit of money once upon a time, not that you'd like to know how we got it. My dad and brothers were light-fingered and kept us afloat.'

Connie sniffed and stared at her bare feet. Maisie stared at them too, in horrified fascination. Her toenails were yellow and so thick, you'd need garden shears to cut them.

'Anyway, what's the bad thing that you've done? Did you kill someone?'

'What? No, of course not.' Maisie glanced at Connie's expression, trying to work out if she was joking. 'I threw a letter on the fire.'

Connie leaned forward and, when she realised that was all Maisie had to say, sat back again with a frown. 'Is that it, you threw a letter on the fire? Why did you do that?'

'I don't know. I was just so angry about... all kinds of stuff and the letter was there and Caitlin and Isla were going on about it again and it was doing my head in so I grabbed it and threw it away and it fell into the fire and now everyone hates me and I mean *everyone* in my whole life.'

Maisie stopped burbling, out of breath and close to tears. Connie was watching her thoughtfully.

'I'm guessing this is the letter your aunt was talking to me about when she came round, at a far more sensible hour, I'd like to add.'

Maisie nodded. 'They think there's some mystery attached to it, when all it is is an old letter from some random bloke to a woman who didn't want to marry him, and I don't blame her.'

'You don't fancy getting married then?' said Connie, pushing herself to her feet.

'Eeuw! No way.' Maisie grimaced in distaste. 'Not everyone does. You didn't.' A shadow of something raw, some distant pain, crossed Connie's face and was gone. 'Marriages never last, especially when...' She stopped. 'My dad gambles,' she blurted out, before she had the chance to stop the thought reaching her lips.

Connie's eyes narrowed. 'Does he now? How do you know that?'

'He's gambled away our house. Caitlin told me. So we're technically homeless. Good, huh?'

Connie whistled through her sparse teeth and sat back down. A puff of dust circled around her when her backside hit the cushion.

'So where's your dad now?'

Maisie shrugged, feeling an ache in her heart. 'I dunno. At some work conference abroad and I bet he's taken Chiara with him.'

'Who the hell's Chiara?'

'She works in his office. They're... well, you know... they're...'

She couldn't say it. It was too humiliating, but Connie didn't need the situation spelled out.

'Like that, is it?'

Maisie nodded miserably. 'Yep.'

'So your stepmother, what's she like?'

'Caitlin's not too bad, I s'pose.'

'Does she treat you all right?'

Maisie had a sudden flashback to Caitlin bending over her in the dead of night while lightning flashed and thunder shook her London bedroom. Maisie had been frightened of the storm. Her dad had slept through it but Caitlin had got out of bed and come to comfort her.

'Yeah.' Maisie nodded. 'But I'm not her real daughter and now she's not with Dad any more she doesn't have to look after me. We've not been getting on that well. They sent me to a school that's horrible and I'm a big disappointment to both of them. She'll be off as soon as she can dump me on someone else – my grandparents, probably, who won't want me either.'

Maisie felt tears prickle her eyes and she bit down hard on her lip. Connie watched from the gloom of her armchair as the silence was broken by the screech of an animal outside.

'Life's tough,' said Connie, glancing at the window when rain began to hit against the glass. The frayed curtains were open and outside everything was black. Someone could be looking in right now and they'd never know. Maisie shivered and sank further back into the sofa. She yawned, feeling exhausted.

'You need to get some sleep.' Connie pushed herself up from the chair with a groan. 'Tomorrow you need to go back to your stepmother, but you can't go out in this weather so you can sleep down here. I'll get you some blankets. And you need to let people know where you are so they don't think I've abducted you. Have you got a phone? I don't have a landline.'

When Maisie nodded, she went out of the room and returned a few minutes later with a pile of blankets.

'There you go. I'm off back to bed and you'd best make yourself comfy.'

Once she'd gone, Maisie gave the blankets a sniff. They

were old and threadbare but they smelled fairly clean. She took out her mobile. Should she tell Caitlin and Isla where she was? She could text them, maybe. But when she looked at her phone, she had no coverage. Decision made, then. She stuffed the mobile back into her pocket and tried to settle down on the sofa.

But the darkness outside, the creaks and groans of the old house, and the memory of what she'd done made sleep impossible. She remembered snatching the letter and throwing it towards the flames.

Why had she done that? She hadn't really wanted to destroy the letter. It meant a lot to Isla in particular, and Isla had been kind to her. But she'd felt so furious about everything – about her dad's betrayal and losing her home, about dreading going back to school, about nobody really loving her.

Being ninety-seven must be the pits. What was there to look forward to other than death? But being fifteen was no walk in the park either. Maisie stifled a sob and rolled over in her scratchy blankets.

~

Maisie was dreaming of school, a fevered nightmare of trying to stop the yellow goop from falling onto the teacher's head. Only the goop had turned into acid and the door was banging back and forth with the deadly mixture balanced above it. She had to stop it from falling, but someone was distracting her by waving a letter in her face. Edith was waving it and shouting. She'd come back from the grave to punish her.

Maisie stirred in her sleep, as the banging grew louder, and gradually came to, sneezing when the blankets tickled her nose. She was lying in Connie's dark house and a loud banging was echoing through the building. What the hell?

She pulled the blankets higher around her chin. Her heart

was hammering so hard, she felt sick. But then the banging stopped and an eerie silence settled on the house.

The curtainless windows were blank and dark, and Maisie let out a scream when a white face loomed up against the glass. She should never have come to this place that was full of ghosts. Maisie wished with all her heart that she was tucked up in bed at Rose Cottage, with Caitlin and Isla nearby. Safe in Heaven's Cove.

The ghost at the window began to knock on the glass and call her name.

'Maisie! Maisie! Is that you? Thank goodness! Stop being such a complete prat and open the door.'

Surely, the spirit of Edith Anstey would never call her a prat. Maisie peered closely at the face pressed up against the glass. It was Caitlin, and she did not look happy.

Maisie stumbled out from under her blankets and fumbled her way into the hall where she found the light switch on the wall. Blinking in the light, she pulled the front door open.

'Maisie!' Caitlin almost fell over the threshold and pulled her into a tight bear hug. 'Why did you run off like that? You scared the life out of us.'

'Us?' mumbled Maisie.

She looked over Caitlin's shoulder at her aunt's car, which was parked outside. Her aunt was leaning against it and gave her a half-hearted wave.

'How did you know I was here?' Maisie asked, extricating herself from the hug.

'We didn't at first and were about to call in the police—'

'Police?' interrupted Maisie, her knees wobbly. She hadn't realised that running off might cause so much trouble.

'Yes, police, because we were so worried. But Isla thought of this place. Honestly, I can't believe you walked all this way in the dark.'

'It wasn't so bad,' muttered Maisie.

'It was foolish and dangerous.' Caitlin shook her head, seemingly close to tears. 'But that doesn't matter right now. All that matters is that you're safe and sound and we can get you home.' She glanced up the stairs and gasped. 'What the hell?'

Maisie followed her gaze. Connie was standing on the landing, still giving off major ghostly vibes in her long nightdress.

'Sorry, Connie,' said Maisie as the old woman walked slowly down the stairs.

Caitlin swallowed and held out her hand. 'You must be Miss Carmichael. I'm so sorry for all of this fuss.'

Connie ignored Caitlin's hand and spoke to Maisie. 'The stepmother, I presume?'

Maisie nodded. 'And Isla's outside. I need to go home with them now.'

'Good idea,' said Connie, her white hair catching the light. 'Then I might be able to get some sleep.'

'I really am sorry, Miss Carmichael, for all the trouble you've had, and I appreciate you taking Maisie in and keeping her safe.'

Connie scowled. 'Couldn't leave her standing out in the cold, could I? She needs people looking after her. People who give a damn.'

She tilted her head at Maisie and watched while she and Caitlin walked to the car where Isla was waiting.

'I'm so sorry about the letter,' said Maisie, hanging her head.

But Isla pulled her into a hug and whispered into her ear, 'It doesn't matter. All that matters is that you're OK. Let's get you home.'

Isla slid into the driving seat and Caitlin got in next to her.

'Come on, Maisie,' said Isla. 'It's really late.'

Maisie turned back towards Connie. She looked so alone and vulnerable, framed in the doorway in her nightdress. She didn't have family who would come out in the middle of the night to make sure she was safe. All she had were her cats and her ghosts.

'Shall I call round to see you sometime, before I go back to London?' she called out to her.

Connie gave her a straight stare and then a small shrug. 'If you like,' she said, before slamming the door shut.

39

MAISIE

Maisie was sitting in the conservatory at Rose Cottage, gazing disconsolately at the back garden. Last night's drama seemed like a dream now – a nightmare when Caitlin's face had loomed out of the dark. But she felt bad and embarrassed about her behaviour, and wondered if Connie, like her, had a headache after her broken sleep.

A robin was scratching at the soil in Jessie's garden – its breast a cheerful splash of red against the dark earth. It must be nice being a robin, Maisie thought, watching its beak bob up and down: no family dramas to deal with, no scary school, nothing on your mind except finding the next juicy worm.

She sighed loudly, aware of the ridiculousness of wanting to be a bird, and pulled her feet up under her in the high-backed armchair. It was so quiet in this house. The wind had dropped overnight and all she could hear was the faint hum of the old boiler in the kitchen.

One thing that she'd come to appreciate here in Heaven's Cove was peace, and that really surprised her. There was little peace in London – it was all busy hustle and bustle and noise everywhere. Even at three in the morning, the wails of emergency vehicles and the shouts of people walking home punctured the night. Maisie had thought she liked it, but she'd never really known anything else. And she had to admit that the peace in Heaven's Cove – the silence at night, broken only by the sound of wind and waves – was calming.

But Caitlin must be desperate to be back in the city, and Maisie would soon be dumped with her grandparents. She sighed at the thought.

Her paternal grandparents' interest in her had waned as she'd changed from a pliable child into a stroppy teenager with a stud in her nose. But no doubt they'd step up and take her in. They'd probably feel obliged to do so, seeing as it was their son's gambling that had made her homeless.

Maisie dug her nails into the palms of her hands until the pain blocked out the black despair that was swirling through her body. Honestly, life was hard enough without all the adults around you making you feel unwanted.

Maisie pushed her nails in harder and had curled, foetus-like, in the chair when she heard footsteps approaching. She'd snuck down into the conservatory precisely so she wouldn't have to face Caitlin or Isla and endure the lecture on behaving more responsibly that was surely heading her way. But the footsteps were getting louder.

'I can't, Sean,' said a voice that Maisie recognised as Caitlin's. Fortunately, she couldn't see Maisie because the back of her chair stood between them.

'Why can't you?' Sean's voice was laced with the Devonian burr that, to Maisie's ears, made everyone sound half asleep. 'I think, deep down, that you want to.'

'You sound like Paul, telling me what I really want.'

Caitlin sounded weary and slightly irritated, which was fair enough, thought Maisie. Mansplaining was the pits.

Sean sighed. 'Sorry. I don't mean to be like him. He's a nasty piece of work.'

Yes! Maisie wanted to shout that she completely agreed but she couldn't let them know she was here. She should have shown herself immediately but it was too late now. It would look as if she'd been eavesdropping.

'You should stay,' Sean continued. 'Not for me, but for you. This place does you good, Cait. Admit it. You look much better than when you first arrived. Even a short time by the sea has made you seem more—'

When he stopped speaking, Caitlin urged: 'Seem more what?'

'More yourself.' Maisie frowned because that was pretty cheesy. 'What I mean is, more how you were when I first knew you.'

'Have I found myself again amongst Heaven's Cove's community?' Caitlin groaned. 'Sorry. I'm doing what I always do. I'm being sarcastic to avoid facing up to the truth.'

'Which is?' urged Sean gently.

'Which is that a part of me – a big part, actually – would like to stay in Heaven's Cove. That's ironic, seeing as I couldn't wait to get away. But I'd forgotten over the years what it's like being here, where people care about you and accept you for who you are.'

'So what's making you go back to London? Is it Stuart?'

'No, my marriage is over. It's been on the rocks for a while, before he started gambling big time. Who knows, maybe being unhappy with me helped to fuel his addiction? Or perhaps I'm just making excuses for him.'

Maisie knew that her dad's marriage to Caitlin was over, but hearing it set out in such blunt terms still made her heart lurch.

'So why go back to London?' asked Sean again. 'What can possibly be dragging you back to a place where you've been unhappy?'

'Maisie,' said Caitlin quietly.

Maisie's eyes opened wide at that.

'Maisie's life and school are in London, and she's suffered enough recently, with finding out that her dad's behaviour has cost her our home. Being fifteen is awful, Sean, don't you remember? All those hormones and emotions. I can't add to the disruption in her life.'

'Doesn't she have other people who can look after her in London? What about her dad?'

'He's all over the place and isn't reliable enough to be her sole carer. There are grandparents – Stuart's parents – who would probably have her, but Maisie would hate it there.'

'You've told me that Maisie hates you,' said Sean gently.

'I think she does, sometimes. I'm the evil stepmother, and I've not always handled things well. I'd parented Isla for so long and I wasn't sure I was up to doing it again. Maisie and I were landed with each other six years ago. She was stroppy, I was scared, and I didn't really know what I was doing.'

That was true enough, thought Maisie. But the next thing Caitlin said made the breath catch in her throat.

'To be honest, I love her, Sean. I've grown to love her like a mum and I desperately want to be a good mum to her. She deserves that and her happiness is more important to me than anything else. So that's why I need to go back to London with her.'

Maisie blinked furiously as tears spilled from her eyes and ran down her cheeks. Her nose was running too but she couldn't rummage in her pocket for her tissue. She couldn't move or she would be discovered.

There was silence, broken only by the boiler's hum, until Sean said: 'You're so annoying, Cait. When you left, I was heartbroken, and I'll be sad when you leave again. But you're going for the right reasons. I can see that.'

Caitlin gave a peculiar gulp. 'You're a good man.'

'And you're a much better woman than you think you are. I

reckon we could have been good together, Cait, but I have to say our timing is absolutely terrible.'

Caitlin's laugh ended in a sob and, when they went quiet, Maisie plucked up the courage to peep over the top of her chair.

They were kissing! It was gross and kind of upsetting because it wasn't her dad – but he'd had his chance and he'd blown it. They looked good together: Sean with his arms tight around Caitlin, and Caitlin with her eyes closed and her lips pressed against his.

Maisie sat down again very quietly. Caitlin was willing to give up a chance of new happiness, because of her. She squeezed her eyes tightly shut and tried very hard not to sob.

40

CAITLIN

If she'd known that Sean was about to kiss her on the lips – which she hadn't – she would have expected it to feel very familiar. After all, they'd kissed plenty of times fifteen years ago.

But when it happened, when Sean slid his arms around her waist and pulled her closely into him, his kiss didn't feel familiar at all. It was more experienced, more grown up – and much more sexy than she had ever remembered.

She leaned into it, wrapping her arms around Sean's neck and, when they eventually pulled apart, she could hear her heart beating.

'Sorry,' he said, taking a step back. 'I shouldn't have done that.'

'No, it's fine,' Caitlin assured him.

'No, it's not because what's the point? You're still going back to London, aren't you.'

'I have to, Sean, for Maisie's sake. She's been let down by everyone around her and I can't let her down too. Do you understand?'

'Of course I do.' He gave a sad smile. 'But I don't have to like it.'

'I'll be back in Heaven's Cove more often now. Much more often.'

'I know, but long-distance relationships are tricky. You need to be in London and I need to be here, in Heaven's Cove. I've built up a good business and the lads at the garage rely on me for their livelihoods.'

They were pulled in two different directions, just like Edith and William, thought Caitlin. Two people who cared about each other but couldn't be together because of their responsibilities.

'But when I do come to visit, at least we can be friends again,' she said, her voice breaking with emotion.

'Yeah, friends again,' said Sean gruffly. 'We missed our chance, Cait.'

When Maisie gets older, maybe I can move back to Heaven's Cove. That's what Caitlin wanted to say, but Sean had waited for her once, and she had no right to ask him to do so again.

She nodded sadly. 'Yes, I think we did.'

Sean scuffed his heavy boots across the floor tiles. 'I have to get back to the garage. There's always lots to sort out first thing and I never normally nip out. Will I see you before you go?'

'Of course. We can have a drink in The Smugglers Haunt – damn the gossips! – and pretend to be teenagers again. It'll be just like old times.'

It wouldn't be like old times at all. It would be a painful parting that, this time, neither of them wanted. But there was no other way.

Caitlin watched Sean leave and was about to find Isla when her attention was caught by a noise behind her. It sounded like an animal snuffling. She looked around, expecting to see next door's cat which had a habit of coming into Rose Cottage, searching for treats.

The room was empty but there was that sound again. Caitlin went to the huge windows that faced the back garden but there was nothing out there except a bright robin, pecking at the ground.

She turned and that was when she spotted Maisie.

Her stepdaughter was curled up in the wingback chair, with a tissue pressed hard against her nose and her face screwed up tight.

'Maisie, what's the matter?'

Caitlin knelt at Maisie's feet and had begun stroking her leg before she realised exactly what the matter was. Maisie must have heard everything that had just gone on, including her kissing a man who wasn't Stuart. 'I expect you heard everything that...' She swallowed hard. 'We didn't know you were here, obviously, or we'd never... Look, I can understand why you're so upset. I'm so sorry, Maisie. My relationship with your dad has broken down but nothing has happened with Sean... well, apart from what just happened. But that won't be repeated.'

Maisie gulped and scrubbed her face with her tissue.

'Honestly, Maisie, I'm telling you the truth. Sean was an old boyfriend who I treated very badly years ago. We've grown closer again since I've been here but it won't change anything. We'll still go back to London and make a good life for ourselves up there.'

'I don't want to go back to London.'

Maisie said it so quietly, Caitlin wasn't sure if she'd heard correctly.

But Maisie repeated it more loudly: 'I don't want to go back to London.'

'Why? Because we've lost the house? We can get something else. It'll be rented but I'll make sure it's decent. And you honestly don't have to go and live with your grandparents when we go back to the city.' Caitlin shrugged. 'Unless you'd like to, that is.'

Maisie shook her head. 'They don't want me. I thought you

didn't want me either, but then you said you'd go back to London because of me.'

'I would. If that's best for you, that's what we'll do. We'll go to London and get you back to school.'

'I can't go back to school.'

'Yes, you can. I know you've been in trouble but I'll help you to fit back in.'

'No, you don't understand. I cannot go back to school.' Maisie was almost howling. 'I hate that place and now there's the video of me playing the joke on Miss Welby and they said they'd take it down but they lied to me and put up another one. And thousands of people have seen it so all the teachers will hate me even more and anyone I want to be friends with will hate me too.'

Caitlin rocked back on her heels, not sure what to do. She'd never seen her stepdaughter like this, with her carefully cultivated blasé attitude stripped back to the bone.

'I… I don't know anything about a video,' she ventured.

'It's on TikTok.' Maisie was gasping, hardly able to get her words out. 'Two videos now. Madison and her friends posted it.'

Caitlin knew who Madison was, having been introduced to her at a school event. The girl had looked at her in such a smug, almost impertinent, way, she was hard to forget.

'Then I'll get the videos taken down,' said Caitlin, anger bubbling at the thought of her child being tormented by Madison and her pals. 'I'll contact Madison's parents today and insist that the videos are deleted.'

'Will that work?'

When Maisie turned up her hopeful, tear-stained face, Caitlin's heart almost broke.

'I'll make sure it works. I promise,' she whispered. 'I didn't realise that you hated school so much. You never said. Even after the practical joke and your suspension, you told us you were happy there.'

'Because I thought that's what you and Dad wanted me to say. I wanted you to be proud of me.'

Caitlin's shoulders slumped as she realised that Maisie had been keeping more secrets than her father's infidelity. She gestured for the teenager to budge up and squashed into the chair beside her.

'Listen to me,' she said, running her fingers through Maisie's hair. 'We are very proud of you and want you to tell us the truth, always. Your happiness is far more important to your dad and me than you realise, and you don't have to go back to that school. There are plenty of others in London and I'll find somewhere to rent near a school that you like.'

'We won't have enough money to rent anywhere.'

'Yes, we will, and that's my problem to sort out, not yours.'

Maisie sniffed. 'Or I could go to school down here.'

'You hate it down here. I know you heard what I just said, but you don't have to stay in Heaven's Cove because of me.'

'It wouldn't be because of you, not all of it anyway. The school that Beth goes to sounds pretty decent and no one there would know what I've done.' Her face clouded over. 'As long as they're not on TikTok.'

'Even if they are, that doesn't mean they've seen the videos that we are going to get taken down today.'

Maisie grinned and Caitlin grinned back. The chance of a whole new life in Heaven's Cove had just opened up in front of her. But she mustn't leap ahead too quickly.

'Emotions are riding high after you running away last night and me ki—' Caitlin stopped. Had she really just kissed Sean? Tingles of happiness shot through her body. 'Anyway, let's have a good chat once we're both feeling less emotional and we can decide what's best.'

'For both of us?' asked Maisie, uncurling herself from the chair and standing up, the damp tissue still balled in her fist.

'Yes, for both of us.'

'Can I go and listen to my music for a while? I'm tired.'

'Of course you can. Try to get some sleep.' Caitlin pulled herself fully into the chair that was still warm from Maisie's body. 'I think I'll sit here for a while and calm down.'

Maisie sloped out of the conservatory but quickly doubled back. 'I love you too, Caitlin,' she said. Then, she was gone.

41

ISLA

The snow had melted away. Jessie's garden had reappeared from beneath its white blanket and tiny green shoots were peeping from the earth, beneath the bay window. Were they early snowdrops? Isla wondered, peering through the glass. Her gran had always loved them for brightening up winter and heralding a new beginning.

So much had changed in the few weeks since her grandmother had died. There were so many new beginnings and endings for Isla to navigate as this difficult year drew to a close and a new one beckoned.

She and Paul were no longer together, which was for the best but still hurt like hell. Her relationship with Caitlin had become even more complicated, with her sister's confession about her troublesome life, swiftly followed by their bitter argument. And then there was Ben with the smiling eyes and the adventurous soul who had invited her to leave Heaven's Cove with him. If only she were brave enough.

She turned from the window when Caitlin came into the room and flopped onto the sofa.

'Is everything all right?' she asked. 'There's been a lot happening this morning.'

First, Sean had called in unexpectedly and disappeared with Caitlin, and then there had been what sounded like wailing from Maisie. Isla had thought it best to keep out of the way, whatever was going on.

'Maisie just told me that she loved me,' said Caitlin, astonishment lighting up her face.

Isla's resolve to be distant with her sister, after last night's shouting match, disappeared in an instant as she took in Caitlin's shining eyes.

'Of course she does, you idiot. That's been obvious to everyone, except you and her. Is Maisie OK? She sounded upset.'

'There's been some trouble with a girl putting videos on TikTok but I've got her mother's phone number from a mutual friend. She's not picking up at the moment but I'll be trying again later and getting her to sort out her daughter.'

'Caitlin to the rescue?'

Her sister shrugged. 'You stand up for the people you love. Talking of which, I'm sorry about yesterday and what I said about Paul. I shouldn't have interfered in your life when I've not been a proper part of it for so long.'

'Maybe not, but, like I said, you were right about Paul spilling curry down Mum's dress on purpose.'

'How do you know?'

'He admitted it when I confronted him. According to him, the dress was too revealing so he did it for my own good.'

'What an absolute—' Caitlin pressed her lips together and began to massage her brow with the heels of her hands. 'Sorry. I know he meant a lot to you, Isla, but that is unforgivable.'

'I know. I can hardly believe it myself.' Isla paused, frightened to ask her next question but needing an answer before she could move on to whatever her new beginning might be. 'Do you think I'm a screw-up who can't cope with life, Cait? Paul told me that I'm fragile.'

Caitlin got up from the sofa, crossed the room and held tightly onto Isla's hands.

'It suited him to say that, to make you more dependent on him,' she told her sister, their faces close. 'But of course you're not fragile, Isla. You're tough and resilient. You survived Dad leaving when you were small, and Mum's death, and moving to a whole new life in Heaven's Cove and—' Caitlin's voice broke. '—and you survived being abandoned by your sister. You looked after Gran, and I know how hard it is to be a carer. The truth is you're one of the strongest people I know, little sis. You're stronger than me, and if you want to see a screw-up...' She let go of Isla's hands and pointed at herself. '...here you go.'

'You're no screw-up and you are way stronger than me. You made a whole new life for yourself away from here.'

'Yeah, and look how that's turned out.'

'It's just a blip. You'll go back to London and make a brilliant new life for you and Maisie.'

'Yeah, about that...' Caitlin bit her lip. 'I've got something to run by you. A kind of new beginning for all of us. How would you feel about me and Maisie perhaps staying on in Heaven's Cove for a while? Maisie hates her school so could start a new one here and I could look for a local job and somewhere to rent so we wouldn't invade your peace for too long and—'

Isla didn't give Caitlin a chance to finish. She threw her arms around her sister and hugged her tightly. 'You can both stay at Rose Cottage for as long as you like.' She glanced over Caitlin's shoulder at the clock on the mantelpiece, her sister's words about her strength and resilience still ringing in her ears. 'But my new beginning might be very different from yours.'

42

ISLA

He was standing at the quayside, with his back to her, and his rucksack, bulging at the seams, was lying at his feet. It was one minute to ten and she'd run all the way.

Isla walked up behind him as quietly as she could – not easy when she was panting – and stood for a second, watching him unobserved. He was shifting gently from foot to foot in his tan boots, as if he couldn't stand still. The collar of his thick jacket was turned up and he was wearing the mustard beanie hat to protect him against the cold. Beyond him, the grey sea churned, mirrored by a cloudy sky.

'Ben,' said Isla.

He swung around, a huge grin on his face. 'You came!' His grin faded when he glanced at Isla's hands and realised she had no luggage with her. 'Ah.' Disappointment crossed his face. 'You came to say goodbye.'

'That's right.'

Ben pulled the hat from his head and ran a hand through his chestnut hair. 'I thought... well, I hoped you might come with me... but I was being ridiculous. You have a boyfriend here, and a life, and I'm just a stranger who turned up a few days ago.'

When he looked down at the ground, Isla felt a rush of emotion. He really cared that she wasn't going with him.

'I didn't finish what I was saying,' she said gently. 'I came to say goodbye because I can't simply up and leave Heaven's Cove today.'

'No, I get that. Like I said… boyfriend, life, stranger. I totally get it.'

'But maybe I can soon, after Christmas.'

Ben looked up, confusion in his eyes. 'What do you mean?'

Isla smiled. 'I can't just drop everything and go with you to America and start travelling around the world. There are things I need to wind up and sort out first. But I think I'm overdue for an adventure so how about I book a flight to New York for early January? I can come and visit you, if that's what you'd like. And if things work out, we can start planning our travels.'

'What about your boyfriend? He won't like it.'

'He'll absolutely hate it. But he isn't my boyfriend any more.'

Ben frowned. 'I'm sorry, Isla. I've caused chaos. You shouldn't have broken up with Paul.'

'Do you really believe that?'

'No, he was horrible to you. But what if you come to America and you miss home too much? You'll have thrown everything away.'

'No I won't because it'll still be waiting here for me – not Paul, obviously, though I think that's for the best.' Isla felt a shudder of sadness but ignored it. 'And if America and travelling turn out to be dreadful, at least I'll have seen the world out there.' She looked into Ben's eyes. 'But I don't think it will be dreadful. Do you?'

When Ben shook his head, Isla reached out and brushed dark curls from his forehead. He caught hold of her hand and, turning it, kissed the sensitive skin on the inside of her wrist.

'I think it could be amazing. I realise you might want to

book your own place to stay in New York but I have a spare couch if you'd prefer.'

He looked up and his eyes met hers. There was heat in his gaze and Isla shivered. 'That's really kind of you. I guess it would be a shame to miss out on an authentic stay with a native New Yorker.'

'A terrible shame.' Ben glanced at his watch and swung the rucksack onto his back as if it weighed nothing. 'I think you'll like New York, Isla.'

'Just as Edith would have, too.'

'William and Edith brought us together and now you're getting to make the trip that she never managed.' He frowned. 'I know this has all happened fast. To be honest, nothing like this —' He stumbled over his words. '—like you, has ever happened to me before. But it feels absolutely right. You won't change your mind once I've gone, will you?'

'I'm sure I won't.' Isla had never been more sure of anything in her life. 'Anyway, Caitlin won't let me. She's determined that I head off and have an adventure.'

'Oh, I'll definitely give you that,' said Ben, leaning closer.

His lips gently brushed hers and then his arms were around her waist and he was kissing her as if he couldn't bear to let her go: a long kiss that held the promise of so much more.

He stepped back and swallowed. 'I have to go and catch that flight or Mom will kill me, but I look forward to seeing you in New York after Christmas, Isla.' He looked around him, at the sea and the sky and the cliff soaring high above them. 'I never thought I'd say it when I first arrived here, but I'm going to miss Heaven's Cove and its unusual inhabitants. This village has become special to me.' He shrugged. 'Along with you.'

He grabbed hold of Isla's hand and looked so vulnerable all of a sudden, Isla squeezed tight, enjoying the feeling of his fingers wrapping around hers.

'I have to go,' he whispered. 'I'll call you.'

'You better had,' said Isla with a smile, even though her heart was aching at the thought of Ben leaving. But she would see him again soon, and who knew where their travels would lead them?

With one last longing look at her, he turned and walked briskly away.

Isla dabbed a tear that was trickling down her cheek, and sat down on the cold stone wall of the quay.

She would miss this amazing village, which had welcomed her into its heart when she'd first arrived as a grief-stricken child. The beauty and community of Heaven's Cove had nurtured her over the years, and it would do the same now for Caitlin, whose heart needed mending – Sean would help with that as well.

Being a part of the village would do Maisie good, too. It would smooth off some of her rough edges and make her feel that she belonged amongst good people who cared about her.

Isla would miss Caitlin and Maisie so much, but she knew it was time to leave, at last. Time to go off and have her long-overdue adventure. Maybe she'd come back to Heaven's Cove for good one day. She thought of Ben and smiled. Or maybe not.

43

CAITLIN

Three Weeks Later

'Another message from Ben?' asked Caitlin, although she already knew the answer. Isla's soppy smile was a dead giveaway.

'Yeah, he's clearing clutter out of his apartment, ready for my arrival. Look, you can see the view from his window in this pic. Don't you think it looks amazing?'

She thrust her phone into Caitlin's face so she could agree that, yes, it looked fabulous. Which it did. Caitlin peered at the elegant brownstone buildings in the tree-lined street. Isla was going to have a wonderful time, and she deserved it.

Her sister had booked her flight, given notice at her job and started working out what she was going to pack. She'd spent very little time with the man who would be meeting her at John F. Kennedy International Airport on the 17th of January, but she and Ben were getting to know one another better, thanks to a stream of phone calls and messages – and Caitlin trusted her sister's instincts when it came to this new man in her life.

She'd also begun to wonder, though she'd never admit it to

Isla, if their gran was watching over them somehow and pushing them along the right path. The letter and riddle she'd left had sparked so much – new beginnings for all of them.

Isla was off travelling with a man who made her eyes light up, Maisie would be starting her new school in January, and Caitlin felt at peace in this old house. She had a couple of job interviews lined up, and Stuart had promised to pay his daughter a Christmas visit in a few days' time.

Seeing him would be tough, Caitlin knew, but she would encourage him to get the help he needed to stop gambling, and try not to say anything too cutting about Chiara. She wouldn't mention Sean, who was spending more and more time here, but if Maisie did, so be it. He was an old friend who was fast becoming a lot more.

She glanced at Maisie, who was huddled in the corner with Beth. The girls were relaxing after spending the afternoon doing chores for Connie, and were laughing at something on YouTube. Maisie was still giving TikTok a wide berth, even though Madison's mother had made her daughter take down both videos immediately and had, apparently, grounded her for a fortnight. And she seemed happier already: accepting of their change in circumstances and willing to try out a different kind of life.

Surely that amounted to the 'good fortune' alluded to in her grandmother's riddle? Caitlin smiled to herself because she was being daft, thinking that Jessie was guiding them somehow. But it was comforting, nonetheless.

'What are you smiling about?' asked Isla, pushing her phone into the pocket of her jeans. She was sitting next to the Christmas tree whose fairy lights were giving her hair an angelic glow.

'I was thinking about Gran and the riddle that we never solved.'

'I still think about it too and worry that we've let Gran down because it's beaten us. Paul reckoned the riddle was nonsense, but he spoke about Gran as if she was unwell and confused when, in reality, she was sharp right up to the end.'

'She was,' Caitlin agreed, automatically scowling at the mention of Paul's name. He'd been a pain at first, messaging Isla constantly, wanting to know where she was all the time, and sending her flowers. Then he'd turned nasty when she'd told him she was off travelling. But his mean texts had dried up over the last few days and Sean had spotted him arm in arm with a woman who, Isla said, sounded very much like Fizz from his office. Romancing your younger assistant seemed to be de rigueur for some men, thought Caitlin.

'At least we found out what happened to Edith and William.'

Isla reached into her handbag and pulled out the envelope – all that was left of William's letter. She ran a finger across the handwritten address before placing it on the table next to her.

'I'm almost out of drink,' Maisie announced, getting up from the floor in one fluid movement. 'Do you want another one, Beth?'

When Beth said she would, Maisie squeezed past the gap between the Christmas tree and Isla's chair. She spotted the envelope and muttered: 'Sorry.'

'You've apologised already, many, many times, so just let it drop now. We all do things we're not proud of. Even me.' Caitlin grinned. 'I'm afraid that's part of being human.'

'S'pose', said Maisie, waving her not quite empty can of fizzy orange around.

'Could you put the envelope into the bureau please, Maisie,' said Isla, obviously imagining a flood of soft drink swamping the only remaining piece of evidence they had that William and Edith had ever been in love.

'Yeah, sure,' Maisie grunted. She picked up the envelope

and studied it as she walked to the bureau. 'Shame he couldn't even stick the stamp on the right way round.'

'What?' Caitlin looked up from the book on her lap.

'Nothing.' Maisie peered more closely at the envelope. 'Nah, it is the right way round. It just looked odd.'

'Show me, please,' said Isla. Maisie walked back and pushed the envelope at Isla, who studied the stamp and frowned. 'Take a look at this, Cait.'

Caitlin went to stand behind her sister and peered over her shoulder. She'd hardly looked at the envelope before. She and Isla had been too busy focusing on William's words in the letter. The stamp had red edging with 'US Postage' written at the top in white and, at its centre, a simple drawing of an old-fashioned bi-plane – only, Maisie was right, the plane was depicted upside down.

'Maybe it's upside down to represent aerial acrobatics, or it marks a tragic accident in the air?' said Caitlin. She leaned further over Isla's shoulder, inhaling comforting notes of vanilla and rose from her sister's perfume.

'That's well out of order,' said Maisie, wrinkling her nose. 'Drawing the plane upside down after an accident's disrespecting the people who probably died.'

'I agree. It wouldn't be in very good taste. What do you think, Isla?'

Her sister turned the envelope this way and that. 'Maybe the plane isn't meant to be upside down. Perhaps there was a printing error.'

'Oh-oh!' Maisie was bouncing up and down on the spot as if her feet were on fire. 'It might be worth something.'

'I doubt it,' said Isla, still turning the envelope around as if the plane might shift.

'No, it might be valuable. I heard that some first editions of *Harry Potter* with a misprint in them sold for loads of money. I read through my copy twice to check but I couldn't find any.'

'That's a bit different,' said Isla, passing the envelope to Caitlin.

'Uh-huh?' Maisie wasn't properly listening. She'd put down her drink and was stabbing into her mobile phone that seemed permanently welded to her hand. She stabbed and scrolled, her brow creased in concentration. 'No way,' she said quietly. Then her face broke into a wide smile. 'Look at that.'

'Look at what?' asked Caitlin.

'The stamp!' Maisie thrust her phone at Caitlin, who started to read the article on the screen.

'Good grief! It can't be the same stamp, surely.'

'It is,' declared Maisie, grabbing the envelope and almost shoving it up Caitlin's nose. 'It looks exactly the same, see. It's upside down.'

'What are you two going on about? I—'

Before Isla could say any more, Maisie had snatched the phone back from Caitlin and begun to scroll and read snippets of information from the screen.

'"The Inverted Jenny is a rare stamp printed in error by the US Postal Service in 1918. Um... one hundred stamps were printed, all featuring a plane which mistakenly appears upside down. It says here the stamp is of great interest to collectors, with some changing hands for large sums. And some of the stamps are either missing, damaged, or believed destroyed."'

'It can't be the same,' said Caitlin, peering at the stamp until she was almost cross-eyed. 'Though it certainly looks the same. And it's obviously old because William sent the letter one hundred years ago.' She looked at Isla and grinned. 'Do you think this is what Jessie's riddle was all about? The stamp, rather than the letter?'

'Did you say, Maisie, that the stamp was called the Inverted Jenny?' Isla pulled Jessie's handwritten riddle from her handbag and read it aloud: '"Don't get in a spin, girls, though mistakes can cost you dear. This one brings good fortune and, I hope, will make you cheer." That's it!' she breathed. 'That's the answer to the riddle. It was staring us in the face all the time.'

'What are you going on about?' asked Maisie, still bouncing up and down. Beth was staring at them all from the corner, with her mouth open.

'Have you done the Industrial Revolution in history at school?' Isla asked.

Maisie frowned. 'Possibly. I might not have been listening.'

'Give me your phone, will you?' Maisie handed over her mobile and Isla began typing into it. 'Yes!' she exclaimed after a moment. 'I was right, it was the spinning jenny.'

'The spinning what?' Caitlin's memory of history lessons at school was hazy to say the least.

'The spinning jenny,' repeated Isla. 'It says here that a new type of spinning wheel was invented in the 1700s which revolutionised the textile industry, and it was called the spinning jenny.'

'Oh, my goodness.' Suddenly it all made sense to Caitlin, too. '"Don't get in a spin, girls" is referring to the spinning jenny, with "jenny" being the clue to point us in the right direction. Then Gran's riddle says, "though mistakes can cost you dear. This one brings good fortune..."' She stopped, feeling breathless. 'Gran must mean the stamp because it's known as the Inverted Jenny, it was printed by mistake, and that mistake is worth money.'

'I'm so glad I didn't throw the envelope on the fire,' said Maisie, going chalk white and almost collapsing back down onto the floor. Beth was still staring at them all, her mouth agape.

'So what do we do with it?' asked Isla, taking the envelope from Maisie and gingerly placing it back on the table as if it might explode.

'I have no idea, and if Gran knew about the stamp, why

didn't she tell us about it or sell it?' Caitlin thought for a moment. 'I'll ring Gran's solicitor in the morning to see if she ever mentioned anything about it to her. But what about the letter itself – Edith and William's story?'

Isla shrugged. 'I bet it was a red herring. Gran always was keen on red herrings, throwing people off the scent, and she certainly managed it big time with this one. It turns out that the letter wasn't important at all.'

'Actually...' Caitlin smiled. 'The letter was crucial. Piecing together Edith and William's story brought us closer together and has led indirectly to me and Maisie moving to Heaven's Cove permanently. It also brought Ben into your life and got you to come to your senses and ditch Paul, no offence.'

'None taken.'

'And it's led to you planning a fantastic adventure that will take you all over the world. The good fortune mentioned in the riddle meant the stamp, I guess, but it's the letter that's brought us the best fortune of all.' Caitlin blew a kiss to their grandmother, who was smiling down at them from her photograph on the mantelpiece. 'Gran's final riddle proved to be an amazing legacy.'

'She'd be delighted,' said Isla.

'And very happy to know that you're off travelling.'

'She would be, wouldn't she?'

'And if it turns out that the stamp *is* worth a bit of money, it'll help to fund your time away, and tide me and Maisie over while we're getting settled here.'

Isla smiled contentedly. 'I'm looking forward to travelling with Ben so much. I want to see... everything that's out there.'

'Everything?' Caitlin laughed.

'Well, everything I can. It's going to be great but—'

'But what?'

Isla swallowed. 'I'm a bit scared, Cait. Scared of leaving all of this behind.'

'Of course you are. That's normal.' Caitlin pulled her sister towards her, into a hug. 'But I know you're going to have a wonderful time.' She rested her cheek against Isla's soft hair. 'And when you're ready to come back to Heaven's Cove, whenever that might be, for however brief a time, I'll be here, little sister, waiting for you.'

EPILOGUE

My darling girls,

Frances, my solicitor, is under strict instructions to give you this letter eight weeks after my will is read, or sooner if you go to her seeking answers. I hope you've solved the riddle I've set you but, most of all, I hope that trying to solve it has given you a shared purpose. You are so good together, and it pains me that circumstance has pushed you apart.

My feisty, brave Cait, you bore the burden of responsibility from such a young age and I completely understand your need to strike out on your own. I'm so proud of the woman you've become. And my kind, clever Isla, who has inherited my love of crosswords. I am so grateful for your care that has enabled me to stay at Rose Cottage until the end. I hope you will be free now to find your own path, wherever that may lead.

You might have realised, by the time you read this, that the actual letter I'm leaving you, while a poignant piece of family history, is not necessary to solve the riddle. However, I do hope the letter has played its part in bringing the two of you closer again as you piece together the story behind it. You always worked so well as a team when you were teenagers: looking out for one another, even finishing each other's sentences. The distance between you has loosened the ties but I feel sure they're still there, waiting to be tightened by spending time together.

As for the letter, I came across it recently in an old trunk of my mother's belongings in the attic. I never knew my aunt Edith and her name was rarely mentioned in the family, which makes me suspect there must be some tragedy or disgrace in her story. Poor Edith. I hope you uncover what happened to her and William – I'm a great believer in people's life stories needing to be told, or those people disappear into history. I hope you will be talking about me, and how much I loved you both, for years to come.

If you spotted the errant stamp immediately, well done, but I hope you will both pursue the contents of the letter, anyway.

Now to the stamp – I'm sure you can get some money for it, and perhaps it's worth a fair bit. I would make enquiries but I'd rather leave it for you girls to find out for yourselves. Think of it as my legacy to you both, along with my enduring love.

Be well, my darling girls, be happy together, and thank you for bringing joy into my life.

Your devoted grandmother, Jessie

xx

A LETTER FROM LIZ

Hello,

Thank you so much for reading my book. I hope that The Sisters at the Last House Before the Sea has given you a few hours of enjoyment, along with a brief escape from day-to-day life, if you needed one.

You can keep up to date with all my latest releases by signing up at the following link. Your email address will never be shared and you can unsubscribe at any time:

www.bookouture.com/liz-eeles

I had great fun writing this story (once I got past my usual first draft angst) and particularly loved imagining Heaven's Cove with Christmas drawing near. I'm a sucker for snow and fairy lights! Did Jessie's riddle keep you guessing? The Inverted Jenny stamp really exists – you can google it, if you're interested, and you'll see that, although I may have employed a little artistic licence here and there, the basic information is correct. The Spinning Jenny is also real and, surprisingly, I *do* remember learning about it at school, even though that was a long time ago.

If you did enjoy Isla and Caitlin's story of family love and redemption, I'd be grateful if you could take the time to write a review. Even the shortest of reviews can encourage other readers to make a visit to Heaven's Cove themselves, so thank you in advance.

Do stop by on social media and say hello, if you'd like to. There are links below to where you can find me.

Until next time,

Liz x

www.lizeeles.com

facebook.com/lizeelesauthor

twitter.com/lizeelesauthor

instagram.com/lizeelesauthor

ACKNOWLEDGEMENTS

Thank you so much to a whole host of people without whom this novel would never have seen the light of (publication) day. They include my marvellous editor Ellen Gleeson who 'gets' my books, understands my writing process, and helps me to make every book the best it can be. My grateful thanks also to Lauren Finger and Jenny Page for their insightful edits, and everyone behind the scenes at Bookouture.

My family and friends deserve a grateful shout-out for the love and encouragement they provide. In particular, my wonderfully supportive husband, Tim, whose eagle eye when reading this book during edits caught a few anomalies and typos that I was able to put right – if you find any others, please blame him. Also, my fabulous friends, Sue Becker and Rachel Brown: Sue, for the suggestion that the riddle in this book might centre on a stamp (an inspired idea), and Rachel, for being a brilliant cheerleader for my novels. She keeps buying them for her family and friends – I can only hope that they like them...

Printed in Great Britain
by Amazon